THE
DEVIL'S
ELIXIR

ALSO BY RAYMOND KHOURY

The Last Templar

The Sanctuary

The Sign

The Templar Salvation

THE DEVIL'S ELIXIR

RAYMOND KHOURY

First published in Great Britain in 2011 by Orion Books,
an imprint of The Orion Publishing Group Ltd
Orion House, 5 Upper Saint Martin's Lane
London WC2H 9EA

An Hachette UK Company

1 3 5 7 9 10 8 6 4 2

A CIP catalogue record for this book is
available from the British Library.

ISBN (Hardback) 978 1 4091 1405 5
ISBN (Export Trade Paperback) 978 1 4091 1406 2

Printed and bound by CPI Group (UK) Ltd,
Croydon, CR0 4YY

The Orion Publishing Group's policy is to use papers
that are natural, renewable and recyclable products and
made from wood grown in sustainable forests. The logging
and manufacturing processes are expected to conform to
the environmental regulations of the country of origin.

www.orionbooks.co.uk

For my loving mom,
because I know it'll put a smile on her face every time she sees it.

THE
DEVIL'S
ELIXIR

There is a lurking fear that some things are not meant to be known, that some inquiries are too dangerous for human beings to make.

—Carl Sagan

Either he is making a colossal mistake, or he will be known as the Galileo of the 20th century.

—Dr. Harold Lief, discussing the work of Dr. Ian Stevenson in
the *Journal of Nervous and Mental Disease*

I

Durango, Viceroyalty of New Spain
(Present-Day Mexico)

1741

Álvaro de Padilla was overcome by dread as his visions dissipated and focus returned to his tired eyes.

The Jesuit priest wondered what world he was emerging into, the uncertainty of it both terrifying and, oddly, exhilarating. He could hear his throat straining against his ragged breaths and feel his strained heart pounding in his temples, and he tried to calm himself. Then his surroundings slowly took shape again and placated his spirits. He could feel the straw of the mat under his fingers, confirming to him that he was back from his journey.

He felt something odd on his cheeks and reached up to touch them, only to realize they were moist with tears. Then he realized his back was also wet, as if he'd been lying not on a dry bed, but in a puddle of water. He wondered why that was. He thought perhaps he had drenched the back of his cassock with sweat, but then he realized his thighs and his legs were also soaked, and he wasn't sure it was sweat anymore.

He couldn't make sense of what had just happened to him.

He tried to sit up, but felt all the strength had been drained out of his body. His head was barely off the mat when it turned to lead, and he had to recline, dropping back onto the straw bedding.

"Stay rested," Eusebio de Salvatierra told him. "Your mind and your body need time to recover."

Álvaro shut his eyes, but he couldn't shut away the shock that was coursing through him.

He wouldn't have believed it if he hadn't experienced it himself. But he just had, and it was unnerving, terrifying, and . . . astounding. Part of him was scared to even think about it, while another was desperate to relive it, now, immediately, to venture back into the impossible. But the harsh, disciplined part of him was quick to stomp out that insane notion and set him back on the righteous path to which he had dedicated his life.

He looked at Eusebio. His fellow priest was smiling at him, his face an edifice of tranquility.

"I'll come back in an hour or two, when you've regained some strength." He gave him a slight bob of encouragement. "You did very well for a first time, old friend. Very well indeed."

Álvaro felt the fear seep back into him. "What have you done to me?"

Eusebio studied him through beatific eyes, then his forehead wrinkled with thought. "I'm afraid I may have opened a door that you'll never be able to close."

It had been well over a decade since they'd traveled here, to Nueva España—the New Spain—together, ordained priests of the Society of Jesus, sent by their elders in Castile to continue what was by now a long tradition of establishing missions in uncharted territories in order to save the wretched, indigenous souls from their dark idolatry and their wicked, pagan ways.

Their task was challenging, but not unprecedented. Following on the heels of the Conquistadors, Franciscan, Dominican, and Jesuit missionaries had been venturing into the New World for more than two hundred years, and after many wars and uprisings, many indigenous tribes had been subdued by their colonizers and assimilated into the Spanish and mixed-blood *mestizo* cultures. But there was still a lot of work to do, and many tribes to convert.

With the help of early converts, Álvaro and Eusebio built their mission in a lush, forested valley deep in the folds of the Sierra Madre Occidental, in the heartland of the Wixáritari people. With time, the mission grew. More and more small communities that had been living in isolation throughout the wild mountains and canyons joined them in their *congregación*. The priests formed a strong bond with their people, and together Álvaro and Eusebio had baptized thousands of natives. Unlike Franciscan reductions, where the Indians were expected to adopt European lifestyles and values, the two priests followed the Jesuit tradition of letting the Indians retain many of their precolonial cultural practices. They also taught them how to use the plow and the axe and introduced them to irrigation, new crops, and domesticated animals, all of which dramatically improved their subsistence farming lifestyle and earned their gratitude and respect.

It also helped that, unlike the more rigid and exemplary Álvaro, Eusebio was a warm, gregarious man. His naked feet and humble attire had inspired the natives to refer to him as Motoliana, which meant "the poor man," and, against Álvaro's advice, he'd embraced the name. His humility, his exemplary life, and his thoughtful conversation, all of which were illustrative of the principles he preached, greatly inspired the natives. He also soon developed a reputation as a miracle worker.

It began when, during a drought that threatened to annihilate the natives' approaching harvests, he recommended that they form a solemn procession to the mission's church, complete with prayers and vigorous flagellations. Copious rains soon relieved the locals of their fears and turned the season uncommonly fruitful. The miracle was repeated a couple of years later, when the region was suffering from excessive rains. By a similar remedy, that blight was checked, and Eusebio's reputation grew. And with it, doors gradually opened.

Doors that might have been better kept shut.

As the initially guarded natives started opening up to him, Eusebio found himself drawn into their worlds more deeply. What had begun as a mission to convert turned into an open-minded journey of discovery. He began to take trips deep into the forests and canyons of the forbidding mountains, venturing where no European had gone before, meeting tribes that usually welcomed strangers with the tip of an arrow or the edge of a spear.

He never returned from his last trip.

Almost a year after he'd disappeared, Álvaro, fearing the worst, set off with a small contingent of tribesmen to find his lost friend.

Which is why they were here now, sitting around a small fire outside the tribe's thatched *xirixi*—the ancestral house of God—discussing the impossible.

"It seems to me that you've rather turned into their high priest, or am I mistaken?"

Álvaro was still shaken by his experience, and although the food had restored some strength to his limbs and the fire had warmed him up and dried his cassock, he was still highly agitated.

"They've shown me more than I can possibly show them," Eusebio replied.

Álvaro's eyes widened with shock. "But—my God, you're embracing their methods, their blasphemous ideas." He looked scared, and he leaned in, his brow crowding his eyes. "Listen to me, Eusebio. You must end this madness now. You must leave this place and come back to the mission with me."

Eusebio looked at his friend and felt his spirits sink. Yes, he was happy to see his old friend, and he was delighted to have shared his discovery with him. But he found himself wondering if he hadn't made a huge mistake.

"I'm sorry, but I can't," Eusebio told him, calmly. "Not yet."

He couldn't tell his friend that he still had a lot to learn from these people. Things he hadn't dreamt possible. It had taken him by surprise to discover—slowly, gradually, and despite his preconceptions and deeply ingrained beliefs—how strong the natives' connections were to the land, to the living beings that shared it with them, and to the energies that seemed to emanate from it. He'd talked to them about the creation of the world, paradise, and the fall of man. He'd told them about the Incarnation and the Atonement. They'd shared their insights with him. And what he heard startled him. For his hosts, the mortal and the mystical realms were intertwined. What seemed normal to him, they deemed supernatural. And what they accepted as normal—as truth—seemed like magical thinking to him.

At first.

He now knew better.

The savages, he discovered, were noble.

"Taking their *medicina*, their sacred brews," he told Álvaro, "has opened up new worlds for me. What you just experienced is only the beginning. You can't expect me to turn my back on such a revelation."

"You must," Álvaro insisted. "You must come back with me. Now, before it's too late. And we must never speak of this again."

Eusebio flinched back with surprise. "Not speak of it? Think, Álvaro. This is all we must talk about. It's something we need to study and understand and master—in order for us to bring it home and share it with our people."

Álvaro's face flooded with shock. "Bring it back?" The words sputtered out of his mouth like poison. "You want to tell people about this, this—this blasphemy?"

"This blasphemy is an enlightenment. It is a higher truth they must experience."

Álvaro was outraged. "Eusebio, I warn you," he hissed. "The Devil has sunk his claws into you with this elixir of his. You are at risk of perdition, my brother, and I can't sit back and allow it—not for you, not for any fellow member of the faith. You need to be saved."

"I've passed the gates of heaven already, old friend," Eusebio replied, calmly. "And the view from here is magnificent."

———

It took Álvaro five months to send a message to the archbishop and to the prelate-viceroy in Mexico City, get their replies, and assemble his men, and it was winter by the time he ventured back into the mountains at the head of a small army.

To stop his friend.

To put an end to his sacrilegious ideas using whatever means necessary.

To thwart the Devil and his insidious temptations, and save his friend from eternal damnation.

Armed with bows, arrows, and muskets, the combined force of Spaniards and Indians ascended the first folds of the sierra on steep, rough paths that were covered by thick, matted bushes. Winter torrents had broken up the trails that snaked up the crumpled mountains into deep, stony channels, while straggling branches, flung horizontally across them, made the contingent's progress even more difficult. They'd been warned about the mountain lions, jaguars, and bears that inhabited the region, but the only living things they encountered were voracious *zopilote* vultures that hung overhead in anticipation of a bloody banquet and scorpions that haunted their fitful sleep.

As they rose higher, the cold became more intense. The Spaniards, used to a much warmer climate, fared badly. They spent the days fighting the wet, rocky inclines and the nights huddled around their bivouacs, kindling their fires until, mile by arduous mile, they finally neared the dense forest that enshrouded the settlement where Álvaro had left Eusebio.

To their surprise, they found the pathways that wormed through the trees strewn with huge pieces of timber that had clearly been felled by the natives. Fearing an ambush, the troops' commander ordered his men to slow their pace, prolonging their suffering and straining their nerves and their vision as they crept through the thick gloom of the funereal pines. After enduring toil and torment for three weeks, they finally reached the settlement.

There was no one there.

The tribesmen, and Eusebio, were gone.

Álvaro didn't give up. He prodded his men forward, the native scouts following the tribe's trail through the folds of the sierra until, on the fourth day, they reached a deep *barranca* at the bottom of which flowed a thunderous river. The ravine had been spanned by a rope and timber bridge.

The bridge had been cut down.

There was no other way across.

Álvaro stared at the ropes that hung over the edge of the cliff, consumed by anger and despair.

He never saw his friend again.

11

Mexico

Five Years Ago

"Pull the goddamn trigger and get your ass out here," Munro barked through my earpiece. "We've got to clear out NOW!"

Tell me something I don't know.

My eyes darted around, reacting to the three-bullet bursts and the longer, wild frenzies of gunfire that were echoing around me from all over the compound. Then some dull thuds and a searing grunt tore through my comms set, and I knew that another operative from our eight-man team had been cut down.

My body froze as opposing instincts dueled for control. I swung my gaze back to the man who was cowering next to me. His face was all sweaty, locked in anguish from the big, bloody gash in his thigh, his lips quivering, his eyes wide with fear, like he knew what was coming. My grip on the handgun tightened. I could feel my finger hovering over the trigger, tapping it indecisively, like it was red hot.

Munro was right.

We had to get out of there before it was too late. But—

More gunfire pummeled the walls around me.

"That's not what we're here for," I rasped into the mike, my eyes locked on my wounded prey. "I've got to try and—"

"—and what," Munro rasped, "carry him out? What, are you Superman now?" A long burst ripped through my comms set, like a jackhammer to my eardrums, then his manic voice came back. "Just cap the sonofabitch, Reilly. Do it. You heard what he's done. 'It'll make meth seem as boring as aspirin,' remember? That's the scumbag you're worried about wasting? You happy to let him loose, is that gonna be your contribution to making this world a better place? I don't think so. You don't want that on your conscience, and I don't either. We came here to do a job. We have our orders. We're at war, and he's the enemy. So stop with the righteous bullshit, pop the bastard, and get your ass out here. I ain't waiting any longer."

His words were still ricocheting inside my skull as another volley of bullets raked the back wall of the lab. I dove to the floor as wood splinters and glass shards rained down around me, and took cover behind one of the lab's cabinets. I flicked a quick glance across at the scientist. Munro was, again, right. There was no way we could take him with us. Not given his injury. Not given the small army of coke-fueled *banditos* bearing down on us.

Dammit, it wasn't supposed to go down this way.

It was meant to be a swift, surgical extraction. Under cover of darkness, me, Munro, and the six other combat-ready guys that rounded off our OCDETF strike team—that's the Organized Crime Drug Enforcement Task Force, a federal program that drew on the resources of eleven agencies, including my own FBI and Munro's DEA—were supposed to sneak into the compound, find McKinnon, and bring him out. Him and his research, that is. Straightforward enough, especially the sneaking in part. The thing is, the mission had been ordered up hastily, after McKinnon's unexpected call. We hadn't had much time to plan it, and the intel we were able to put together on the remote drug lab was sketchy, but I thought we still had decent odds. For one, we were well equipped—sound-suppressed submachine guns, night vision scopes, Kevlar. We had a surveillance drone hovering overhead. We also had the element of surprise. And we'd been pretty successful in raiding other labs since we'd first arrived in Mexico four months earlier.

Quick in and out, nice and clean.

Worked like a charm for the *in* part of the plan.

Then McKinnon sprang his eleventh-hour surprise on us, caused Munro to go apeshit, got hit in the thigh, and screwed up the *out* part.

I could now hear frantic shouts in Spanish. The *banditos* were closing in.

I had to make a move. Any longer and I'd be captured, and I didn't have any illusions about what the outcome of that would be. They'd torture the hell out of me. Partly for info, partly for fun. Then they'd bring out the chainsaw and prop my head in my lap for a photo op. And the worst part of it is, my noble death would all be for nothing. McKinnon's work would live on. In infamy, by all indications.

Munro's voice crackled back to life, blaring deep inside my skull. "All right, screw it. It's on your head, man. I'm outta here."

And right then, my mind tripped.

It was like a primeval determination bypassed all the resistance that was innate to me and brushed aside everything that was part and parcel of who I was as a human being and just took control. I watched, out-of-body-experience-like, as my hand came up, all smooth and robotic, lined up the shot right between McKinnon's terrified eyes, and squeezed the trigger.

The scientist's head snapped back as a dark mess splattered the cabinet behind him, then he just toppled to one side, a lifeless mound of flesh and bone.

There was no need for a confirmation tap.

I knew it was final.

My gaze lingered on the fallen man for a long second, then I rasped, "I'm coming out," into my mike. I took a deep breath, popped the strikers off two incendiary grenades and lobbed them at the *pistoleros* who were hunting me down, then sprang to my feet, laying down a wall of gunfire behind me as I bolted toward the exit. I stopped at the back door of the lab, took one last look at the place, then I burst out of there as the whole place went up in flames behind me.

III

LOS ANGELES, CALIFORNIA

SIX MONTHS AGO

In his corner office on the twentieth floor of the Edward R. Roybal Federal Building, Hank Corliss stared at his monitor and continued to grind over the latest morsel of background information he'd unearthed. Then he leaned back, swiveled his chair around so he could face the window, and frowned at his trembling fingers.

It's him.

Again.

Corliss clenched his fists, tight, and took in some long, deep breaths, trying to corral the fury that was galloping through him.

I have to do something.

I have to put an end to this.

I have to make him pay.

His knuckles were bone-white.

Corliss—the Special Agent in Charge of the LA field division of the DEA and the OCDE task force's executive director—turned and glanced at the plasma screen that sat on the shelves across from his desk. Four days later, coverage of the recent outrage was still all over the airwaves, although it had now degenerated from the endless, repetitive loops that cable news networks somehow managed to thrive on into even more mindless and less relevant peripheral pieces.

He blew out a weary sigh and adjusted his posture, feeling a familiar pain lighting up in his spine. He shut his eyes to try to push it back and mulled over what he'd just read.

The attack had taken place up the coast from Corliss's office, at the Schultes Ethnomedicine Institute. Overlooking the rolling surf thirty miles northwest of Santa Barbara, the institute was a state-of-the-art research center that was devoted to finding new cures for all kinds of diseases—or, to put it more accurately, to uncovering old cures that had eluded the modern world. Its researchers—physicians, pharmacologists, botanists, microbiologists, neurobiologists, linguists, anthropologists, and oceanographers, among others—roamed the globe, "bioprospectors" seeking out isolated indigenous tribes, spending time with them, and ingratiating themselves to their medicine men in the hope of prying from them the ancient treatments and cures they'd been handed down over generations. It was home to a world-class collection of MDs and PhDs who were great outdoorsmen and adventurers in addition to being outstanding scientists, real-life Indiana Joneses whose survival skills came in handy when it came to trekking deep into Amazonian rainforests or climbing up to oxygen-starved villages high in the Andes.

Their survival skills hadn't been too useful that fateful Monday.

At around ten A.M., two SUVs had driven up to the institute's entrance gate. The security guard manning it had been shot dead. The SUVs had carried on into the facility unchallenged and pulled up outside one of its main labs. A half-dozen armed men had coolly marched into the building, shot up the place with snub-nosed machine guns, grabbed two research scientists, and whisked them away. Another guard had, by sheer coincidence, stumbled upon them as they were coming out. In the gunfight that ensued, the guard, as well as a resident who got caught in the crossfire, had been killed. Three other bystanders had been injured, one badly.

The kidnappers, and their victims, were gone. There had been no ransom demands as yet.

Corliss didn't expect any.

Early speculation from the detectives on the scene was that drug dealers were behind the kidnappings and the bloodshed. Corliss didn't disagree. Scientists like the two men who were taken weren't plucked from their labs in a hail of bullets by Pfizer or Bristol-Myers. Especially not when they had skill sets that were highly prized in the wild frontiers of illegal narcotics.

Frontiers that were changing by the day, and not for the better.

Initially, it was mostly about getting people with the right technical expertise to help produce mass quantities of popular synthetic drugs, chemists who could create, say, methamphetamine from its precursor chemicals, ephedrine or pseudoephedrine, without blowing themselves up in the process. With tighter regulations complicating the sale of the base chemical ingredients—much to the chagrin of the big pharmaceutical companies' army of lobbyists—alternatives had to be found. Corliss remembered participating in the arrest of an American chemist in Guadalajara a few years back, in the days when Corliss was running the DEA field office in Mexico City. The man, an embittered out-of-work chemistry teacher, was working for the cartels and had earned himself a small fortune by figuring out how to use legal, off-the-shelf reagents to engineer meth precursors from scratch. The perks—the cash, the women, the booze, and, yes, the drugs—were an added bonus that sure as hell beat grading papers and dodging switchblades at his local high school.

Beyond the actual designing and manufacturing of the drugs, scientists were also proving invaluable in dreaming up original ways of smuggling them across borders. One of Corliss's strike teams had recently intercepted a shipment of Bolivian powdered mashed potatoes. It had taken the agency's scientists a couple of weeks to discover that two tons of cocaine had been chemically infused into it. A month later, a similar shipment of soya oil had yielded another mother lode.

Chemicals had mysterious, hidden qualities.

Unlocking them and putting them to work in original ways could make a world of difference—and billions in profits—for the cartels.

Hence the need for brainiacs with the technical chops to make it happen.

Hence the kidnappings.

So far, the investigators didn't have much to go on. No suspects had been nabbed, and CCTV footage and witnesses had pegged them as white and beefy, and that was about it, since the men had worn fabric face masks and caps. One witness, however, had gone further, referring to them as "biker-gang types." That wasn't a big break in and of itself, not in Southern California, where biker gangs were rampant and big into drug dealing—they'd actually started the whole meth craze—but it was significant in other ways.

The rules of the game had changed.

Over the last decade or so, the Mexican cartels had taken over drug trafficking across the United States, bringing a ferocious new level of violence with them. Not content with their long-established role as the nation's major supplier of marijuana, their growth exploded after the so-called War on Drugs of successive U.S. administrations that targeted Colombian traffickers severely curtailed the latter's activities through the Caribbean and into southern Florida. The Mexicans stepped in to fill the gap. They started by taking over the distribution of cocaine from the harried Colombians, then they broadened their horizons. They went from mules to principals and took over the supply chain. And they weren't content with just pumping coke and heroin into the United States. They forged ahead and embraced the drugs of the future—the ones you could make anywhere, the ones users could enjoy without too much hassle. It was the Mexican cartels that saw the real potential in methamphetamine and took it from being nothing more than a crude biker drug with limited use in the valleys of Northern California and turned it into the biggest and most widespread drug problem now facing America. Other synthetic drugs—easy-to-swallow pills that didn't need all the cumbersome paraphernalia—were soon following suit.

The Mexican cartels were now calling the shots from Washington to Maine, bringing in eighty percent of the illegal drugs that entered the country, with local bikers, prison gangs, and street gangs as their foot soldiers. At last count, the DEA had tracked the cartels' operations to more than two hundred and fifty cities across the country. Their reach was limitless, their ambition voracious, their impudence unbounded. They didn't seem to blink, even though they were basically at war with the U.S. government—an undeclared war that was affecting American lives far more than the wars being fought in the deserts thousands of miles to the east.

A war that had left deep scars on Corliss.

Scars he'd never forget.

Mementos of that savage night in Mexico, like the pain that was now throbbing across his spine, a reminder that always reared its malignant head when it was least welcome.

The speculation that a Mexican cartel was behind the violent kidnapping of the scientists was supported by the fact that the DEA and other law enforcement agencies had made significant inroads into shutting down hundreds of meth labs across the United States. This had driven production south of the border, where the narcos had set up superlabs far from the reach of the Mexican authorities and where the talents of the missing scientists were a more likely fit. Furthermore, this wasn't the first time something like this had happened. Other researchers had gone missing. In four earlier, separate incidents, chemists working for pharmaceutical corporations had been grabbed while doing fieldwork in Central and South America. No ransoms were ever demanded. The men were never seen again. Then things escalated. Two other incidents followed, this time on Corliss's side of the border. A university chemistry professor in El Paso, a little over a year ago. Then another, a few months later, just outside Phoenix, snatched along with his lab assistant in an early morning swoop.

And now this.

Bang in Corliss's jurisdiction.

A vicious, deadly shoot-out on an idyllic stretch of the Pacific coast.

A shoot-out that had snared Corliss's interest even more than it naturally merited, given that he was heading the local DEA field office.

He knew it wasn't just any narco.

He'd suspected it was Navarro the second he heard the news. Unlike his colleagues at the DEA, Corliss had never bought the story that Navarro had been killed by internal cartel bloodletting. He knew the monster was still alive, and when he'd dug deeper into the missing scientists' areas of expertise, as he'd done for the previous kidnappings, he'd been left in no doubt. It fit a pattern, a common thread that ran through all their work, one only he had picked up on, one he'd kept to himself.

For now.

Raoul Navarro—El Brujo, meaning the shaman, the black arts practitioner, the sorcerer—was still after it. Corliss was sure of it.

The burn in his spine intensified.

He's getting wilder, more bold, more reckless, he thought.

Which meant one of two things.

The bastard was getting desperate. Or he was getting close.

Either way, it was bad news.

Or, maybe . . . it was an opportunity.

An opportunity for retribution.

The retribution that Corliss had been hungering for since the day Raoul Navarro and his men came for him.

His hands shaking and sweaty, Corliss reached into his desk drawer and pulled out the small, innocuous plastic bottle. He glanced furtively at the door to his office as he fished out a couple of capsules, making sure no one was on his way in to see him, then flicked them into his mouth and swallowed them without water. He didn't need anything to chase them down with. Not anymore. Not after being on the pills for all these years.

He didn't have any proof that it was Navarro, of course. He wasn't about to voice his suspicions either. He'd been there, done that, years ago, and he knew what watercooler chatter was going on behind his back. He knew that his colleagues and his superiors had little time for what they viewed as his delusional obsession with the man who'd ruined his life, the man who'd taken away what he held dearest on this earth.

He didn't care what they thought.

He knew El Brujo was still out there. And, as it did for most of his waking life and a big part of his sleeping one, the mere thought of it whipped up a storm in the pit of his stomach.

He stared at the muted screen again, his numb eyes taking in yet another loop of the same footage, and thought about the part of the story that he was most sensitive to: the pain and destruction the armed raid will have left behind. The new widows and orphans. The partners, parents, and children who'd probably never know what happened to the disappeared. The innocent whose lives would be altered forever.

He reached for his phone and hit a speed dial key.

His star operative answered promptly.

"Where are you?" Corliss asked.

"The marina," the man informed him. "About to sit down with an informant."

"I've been reading up on the scientists that were grabbed up at that research center."

"Those *cabróns* are getting out of hand."

"I don't think it's just any old *cabrón*," Corliss specified.

The man paused for a second, clearly thrown by it, then said, "You think it's him?"

"I'm sure of it." Corliss visualized the Mexican kingpin—and triggered a deluge of painful imagery that would be hard to push back.

His fingers tightened around the handset, its casing creaking under the strain. "Come in when you're done," he finally said. "I've been doing some thinking. Maybe there's a way to nail his ass."

"Sounds good," Jesse Munro replied. "I'll be there in an hour."

SATURDAY

1

San Diego, California

Present Day

The doorbell chimed shortly after nine A.M. on a lazy, sunny Saturday morning.

Michelle Martinez was in her kitchen, emptying a dishwasher that had been stacked far beyond anything the laws of physics could explain while accompanying the rousing choral outro to the Red Hot Chili Peppers' "Under the Bridge" that was belting out from the radio. She looked up, used her forearm to sweep back the chestnut-brown bangs that kept playing games with her baby blues, and gave a gentle yell in the direction of the living room.

"Tom? Can you get that, *cariño*?"

"You got it, *alteza*," came a reply from the front of the house.

Michelle grinned, threw a glance over her shoulder at her four-year-old son, Alex, who was playing out in the backyard, and got back to emptying the cutlery tray. In the background, the lead Chili was lamenting the dark days he'd spent chasing speedballs in the bowels of LA. She loved that song, with its haunting guitar intro and its epic closing chorus, despite the emotions its lyrics stirred in her. Being a retired DEA agent, it was a world of pain and devastation that she knew well. But right now, what she loved far more was when Tom called her that—*your highness*. It was so *not* her, so wildly off the mark, and the sheer absurdity of it never failed to tickle her.

He usually said it when she asked him for something, which didn't happen that often, not even with her consciously reminding herself to do so every once in a while. The fact was, there wasn't much that Michelle Martinez couldn't, or wouldn't, do for herself. She was as self-sufficient as a military spouse, which is exactly what her mother had been, something that had probably been ingrained in her by watching her mom all those years while growing up on army bases in Puerto Rico and New Jersey. It was that self-sufficiency, combined with her iron will and her intolerance for bullshit, that had got her into all kinds of trouble—she'd been expelled from a handful of schools before dropping out of high school altogether—but it was also what had helped her straighten up, get herself a General Education Diploma, and parlay her wild streak, her sharp tongue, and a series of brushes with the law into a meteoric, if ultimately cut short, career as an undercover agent of the Drug Enforcement Administration.

The thing was, guys didn't appreciate feeling like you didn't need them. At least, that's what her girlfriends kept telling her. Apparently, it was some vestige from man's hunter-gatherer days, and, truth be told, they weren't all wrong. Tom seemed to enjoy the occasional request, whether it was for something as trivial as opening the front door or for something more, shall we say, intimate. And it had generated the *alteza* nickname that she'd grown to love, one she far preferred to the various macho nicknames her fellow agents had for her back when she was on the force. *Alteza* was much smoother on the ears and had an old-world, romantic ring to it. It was a word that triggered a little grin at the edge of her mouth every time she heard him say it.

The grin didn't last long.

As the chorus gave way to the song's closing solo guitar strums, the next sound she heard wasn't as pleasing.

It wasn't Tom's voice. It was something else.

Two sharp, metallic snaps, like someone had just fired a nail gun. Only Michelle knew it wasn't a nail gun at all. She'd been around enough sound-suppressed handguns in her life to know what the automatic slide action of a real gun sounded like.

The kind that fired bullets that killed people.

Tom.

She yelled out his name as she sprang to action, propelled by instinct and training, almost without thinking, as if the threat of death had triggered some kind of Pavlovian reflex that took over her body. Her eyes quickly picked out the large kitchen knife from the mess of cutlery, and it was already firmly in her grip as she rounded the counter and hurtled toward the kitchen door.

She reached it just as a figure emerged from it, a man in white coveralls, a black cap, a black pull-up mask covering his face from the nose down, and a silenced gun in his hand. The split-second glimpse she got of him shouted out some vague features—thickset, bad skin, what looked like a buzz cut—but most of all, she was struck by the unflinching commitment that emanated from his eyes. She took him by surprise as they almost collided and she leapt at him, pushing his gun hand away with her left hand while plunging the knife into the side of his neck with the other. His eyes saucered with shock, and the blade had pulled down his face mask, exposing his thick, black Fu Manchu mustache just as blood spewed out of his mouth. He dropped the gun and reached up for the knife with both hands and grappled with it, but Michelle had plunged it in deep and it was solidly embedded. She'd also clearly hit his carotid as blood was geysering out of the wound, spraying the doorjamb to his left.

She wasn't about to hang around and watch. Especially not when her gut was screaming at her that the man probably wasn't alone.

She threw a flat kick at the gurgling intruder's midsection, sending him crashing into the wall of the hallway, away from the fallen handgun, which was lying there, tantalizingly close. She bent down to grab it when another man appeared, at the other end of the hallway, similarly masked and armed. The man flinched with a stab of shock at the sight of his bloodied buddy, then his eyes locked on Michelle's and his gun sprang up in a solid, two-fisted grip. Michelle froze, caught in the crosshairs, staring death in the eye, right there, in the hallway outside her kitchen—but death never came. The shooter held his stance for a long second, long enough for her to dive at the handgun, spin around, and loose a couple of rounds at him. Wood and plaster splintered off the walls around him as he ducked out of sight, and she heard him yell out, "She's got a gun."

There were others.

She didn't know how many, nor did she know where they were. One thing she did know: Alex was out back. And it was time to hightail it out of there and get him to safety.

Her mind rocketed into hyperdrive, focused acutely on that single objective. She darted back and took cover behind the kitchen wall, tried to ignore the pounding in her ears, and listened to any sounds coming at her from the front of the house, then she made her move. She fired off three quick rounds down the hall to keep them guessing, then rushed across the kitchen and flew out the patio doors, running to the drumbeat of survival as fast as her legs would carry her.

Alex was there, on the grass, orchestrating yet another epic confrontation between his small army of Ben 10 figurines. Michelle didn't slow down. She just stormed over to him, tucking the gun under her waistband without breaking step, and scooped up his tiny, three-and-a-half-foot frame in her arms and kept going.

"Ben," the boy protested as a toy flew out of his tiny grasp.

"We gotta go, baby," she said, breathless, one arm clasped around his back, the other pressed down against the back of his head, holding him tight.

She sprinted across the lawn to the door that led to the garage, stopping to glance back only once she reached it, her heart jackhammering its way out of her rib cage. She saw one of them appear through the patio doors just as she flung the garage door open and ducked inside, fiddling with its key to lock it behind her.

"Mommy, what are you doing?"

His mouth was moving, but nothing was registering as her eyes surveyed in all directions, her mind totally channeled on one thought: escape. She told him, "We're just going for a ride, okay? Just a little ride."

She flung open the door of her Jeep, hustled Alex inside, and clambered into the driver's seat. The Wrangler was parked with its back to the garage's tilt-up door, which was shut.

"Down there, sweetie," she told Alex, herding him into the passenger's foot well with a careful mix of urgency and tenderness. "Stay there. We're gonna play hide and seek, okay?"

He gave her a hesitant, uncertain look, then smiled.

"Okay."

She dug deep and found him a smile as her fingers fired up the ignition. The V6 sprang to life with a throaty gurgle.

"Stay down, all right?" she told him as she threw the gear lever into reverse, floored the gas pedal, then turned to face back and yanked her foot off the clutch.

The Jeep bolted backward and burst through the garage door, careening onto the street in a storm of rubber and twisted sheet metal. She spotted a white van parked outside the house and slammed the brakes, and just as the Jeep screeched to a halt, she saw two men, also in white coveralls, rushing out from her front door. She slammed the car into gear and roared off, keeping a nervous eye in the mirror, expecting the white van to come charging after her, but to her surprise, it didn't. It just stayed in its spot and receded into the distance before she hung a right and turned off her street.

She snaked her way past slower cars and turned left, right, and left again at the next crossings, zigzagging away from the house, keeping one eye peeled on her rearview mirror, her mind ablaze with questions about Tom and what had happened to him. She didn't know what state he was in, didn't know whether he was even still alive, but she had to get help to him, fast. She reached into her back pocket, pulled out her phone, and punched in nine-one-one.

The dispatcher picked up almost instantly. "What's your emergency?"

"I'm calling to report a shooting. Some guys showed up at our house and—" She suddenly realized Alex was in the car with her, eyeing her curiously from the foot well of the passenger seat, and paused.

"Ma'am, where are you calling from?"

"We need help, okay? Send some squad cars. And an ambulance." She gave the dispatcher her address, then added, "You need to be quick, I think my boyfriend's been shot."

"What's your name, ma'am?"

Michelle thought about whether or not to answer as she glanced at Alex, who was still staring up at her, wide-eyed. She decided there was no point in adding any more information at this point.

"Just get them there as fast as you can, all right?"

Then she hung up.

Her heart was thundering away furiously in her chest as she checked her mirror again and flew past another slow-moving car. There was still no sign of the van. After about five minutes, she started to breathe easier and helped Alex up and into the front seat, where she belted him in. It took her another half an hour of just putting miles between her and her house before she felt she could pull over, and finally did so in the parking lot of a large mall out at Lemon Grove.

She didn't move for a while. She just sat there, in shock, picturing Tom—and started to cry. The tears smeared her cheeks, then she looked over and saw Alex staring at her, and she forced herself to stop and wiped them off.

"Come on, baby. Let's get you back into your seat."

She got out of the car and helped Alex into the back and onto his booster seat, belted him in, then got back in and sat there again, shivering, collecting her thoughts, trying to make sense of what had just happened.

Trying to figure out what to do next. Who to call. How to deal with the insanity of what had just happened.

She looked up into the mirror and glanced at Alex. He was just sitting there, looking tiny, staring at her with those big, vulnerable eyes of his, eyes that fear had now firmly in its grip, and as she stared at his face, one name broke through the daze and the confusion swirling around inside her head. And although it was someone she hadn't spoken to for years, right now, it seemed like the right move.

She scrolled her phone's contacts list, found his name, and, mumbling a silent prayer that his number hadn't changed, hit the Dial button.

Reilly picked up on the third ring.

2

MAMARONECK, NEW YORK

I was dumping some dry cleaning and a beer-heavy grocery bag on the passenger seat of my car when my BlackBerry warbled.

It was a typical July morning in the small coastal town, hot and still and humid, but I didn't mind it. Between the unrelenting heat wave that had turned Manhattan into a sweaty, oxygen-starved cauldron for the past couple of weeks and the heightened-alert July Fourth weekend I'd just spent there dealing with its associated onslaught of false alarms and hysteria, a quiet weekend by the ocean was definitely a heavenly proposition, regardless of the supernova looming overhead. As an added bonus, my Tess and her fourteen-year-old daughter, Kim, were out in Arizona, visiting Tess's mom and her aunt at the latter's ranch, and I had the house to myself. Don't get me wrong. I love Tess to death and I love being around them, and since Tess and I got back together, I've realized how much I hate—truly *hate*—sleeping alone. But we all need a few days alone, now and then, to take stock and ponder and recharge—euphemisms for, basically, vegging out and eating stuff we shouldn't be eating and being the lazy slobs we love to be when nobody's watching. So the weekend was shaping up pretty sweet—until the warble.

The name that flashed up on my screen made my heart trip.

Michelle Martinez.

Whoa.

I hadn't heard from her for—how long had it been? Four, maybe five years. Not since I'd walked away from what we had going during that ill-fated stint of mine down in Mexico. I hadn't thought of her for years either. The marvelous Tess Chaykin—I don't use the term lightly—had burst into my life not too long after I'd got back to New York. She'd snared my attention in the chaotic aftermath of that infamous horse-mounted raid at the Metropolitan Museum of Art and had quickly engulfed my world, infecting me with that earnest, addictive lust for life of hers and crowding out any musings I could have had about any past loves or long-gone lovers.

I stared at the screen for a long second, my mind running a meta-trawl through possible reasons for the call. I couldn't think of any, and just hit the green button.

"Meesh?"

"Where are you?"

"I'm—" I was about to make a joke, something lame about sipping a mojito poolside in the Hamptons, but the edge to her voice ripped the notion to shreds. "You okay?"

"No. Where are you?"

I felt the back of my neck stiffen. Her voice was as distinctively accented as ever, a vestige of her Dominican and Puerto Rican descent with an overlay from growing up in New Jersey, but it had none of the laid-back, playful sultriness I remembered.

"I'm out," I told her. "Just running some errands. What's going on?"

"You're in New York?"

"Yes. Meesh, what's up? Where are you?"

I heard a sigh—more of an angry grumble, really, as I knew full well that Michelle Martinez was not one to sigh—then she came back.

"I'm in San Diego and I'm—I'm in trouble. Something terrible has happened, Sean. Some guys came to the house and they shot my boyfriend," she said, the words bursting out and stumbling out of her. "I barely got away and—Christ, I don't know what the hell's going on, but I just didn't know who else to call. I'm sorry."

My pulse bolted. "No, no, you did the right thing, it's good you called. You okay? Are you hurt?"

"No, I'm all right." She took another deep breath, like she was calming herself. I'd never heard her like this. She'd always been clear-headed, steel-nerved, unshakeable. This was new territory. Then she said, "Hang on," and I heard some fumbling, like she was moving the phone away from her mouth and holding it against her clothing. I heard her say, "Sit tight, okay, baby? I'll be right outside," heard the car door click open and slam shut, then her voice came back, less frantic than before, but still intense.

"Some guys showed up. I was home—we were all home. There were four, five of them, I'm not sure. White van, coveralls, like painters or something. So they wouldn't raise eyebrows with the neighbors, I guess. They were pros, Sean. No question. Face masks, Glocks, suppressors. Zero hesitation."

My pulse hit a higher gear. "Jesus, Meesh."

Her voice broke, almost imperceptibly, but it was there. "Tom—my boyfriend—if he hadn't . . ." Her voice trailed off for a moment, then came back with a pained resolve. "Doorbell goes, he gets it. They cut him down the second he opened the door. I'm sure of it. I heard two silenced snaps and a big thump when he hit the ground, then they charged into the house and I just freaked. I got one of them in the neck and I just ran. I grabbed Alex and—the garage has a door that leads out into the backyard, and—I got the hell out of there." She let out a ragged sigh. "I just left him there, Sean. Maybe he was hurt, maybe I could've helped him, but I just ran. I just left him there and ran."

She was really hurting over that, and I had to move her away from that remorse. "Sounds to me like you didn't have a choice, Meesh. You did the right thing." My mind was struggling to process everything she'd said while stumbling over the canyon-size gaps in the overall picture. "Did you call the cops?"

"I called nine-one-one. Gave them the address, said there was a shooting, and hung up."

Then I remembered something she'd just said. "You said you grabbed Alex. Who's Alex?"

"My son. My four-year-old boy."

I heard her hesitate for a moment, I could picture her weighing her next words, then her voice came back and hit me with a three-thousand-mile knockout punch.

"Our boy, Sean. He's our son."

3

O*ur son?*
Two small words were all it took to turn the holes I was sidestepping into a huge, gaping chasm that just sucked me in.

I felt my mouth dry up, felt a torrent of blood surge into my skull, felt my chest coil up.

"Our son?"

"Yes."

Everything around me disappeared. The cars and strollers gliding past in the sweltering heat, the mundane bustle and din of a suburban shopping strip on a sunny Saturday morning—it all just died out, like some big cone of silence had dropped out of the sky and cut me off from the rest of the world.

"What are you talking about?"

"You, me. Down in Mexico. Things happened. What, you forgot already?"

"No, of course not, but . . . You're sure?"

Now I was the one in shock and fumbling around for words, my mouth buying time, waiting for my brain to catch up. It was a dumb thing to say, and I knew it. I didn't need to ask. I knew Michelle. Knew her well enough to know that if she was anything, she was solid. Reliable. She could joke and be a real goof when she wanted to, but when it came to the serious stuff, the stuff that mattered, she didn't mess around. If she was saying I was the father, it had to be true.

Scary how easily that just came out.

Something else I knew about her: She didn't take kindly to anyone doubting her word, least of all someone she'd been as close to as yours truly, and even less on something this important.

"I wasn't seeing anyone else on the side. You were it. I thought that was kind of obvious."

It had been.

"That's not what I meant," I backpedaled.

"It was. But that's okay. You're pissed off. And you have every right to be."

A maelstrom of conflicting emotions was coursing through me. Selfish, I know, given what she'd just been through, but it's not every day you get a call informing you you've got a four-year-old son.

"Well, yeah, I am," I replied. "I mean, Jesus, Meesh. How could you not tell me about this?"

"I—I'm sorry, Sean." Her voice went softer with contrition. "I really am. I wanted to. And this isn't how I ever imagined telling you about it, obviously, but . . . it wasn't easy. Keeping it from you. All this time. The amount of times I picked up the phone to call you and tell you . . . but every time, I just—something kept me back." She paused, then said, "I'm sorry. I shouldn't have told you, not now, not like this. I'm just not—I'm not thinking straight."

My mind was still tripping over itself, struggling to get to grips with the notion—but I had to vault that for now and change tack. The reasons and blame games could wait. Michelle had just gone through hell, and she needed my help. My more immediate concern had to be making sure they—making sure she and her son, *our* son— were out of harm's way.

"All right, don't worry, we can talk about it later." I took in a breath, fast-reviewing the sketchy information I had, then asked, "Where are you now?"

"I'm parked outside a mall. Plenty of people around. I'm safe for the time being. I think."

"Were you followed?"

"I don't think so."

I tried to form a mental picture of it all, but there were still too many unknowns. "You think this could have anything to do with your work? You back on the job?" I'd heard that she'd left the DEA, not long after I'd left Mexico City, but that information was ancient.

"I'm out, Sean. Those days are long gone. I teach at a high school now. Nothing dark or dangerous there. I'm a basketball coach, for God's sake."

"So you don't know who or why?"

"Not a clue. All I know is, they weren't there to kill me."

"Why do you say that?"

"One of the shooters, in the house. He had a clear shot. But he didn't take it. If they'd wanted me dead, I'd be dead, for sure."

"So they were there to grab you?"

"I guess. And it's got me real scared, Sean. I mean, dammit, what about Alex? What would have happened to him?"

I didn't have an answer to that, but I needed to move her away from that train of thought. "We need to get you somewhere safe. You still have friends at the agency?"

"Not really. Besides, I'm not sure I want to go there. Not right now."

"Why not?"

"This was a professional tag team," she said. "They were there for a reason. And that's got me racking my brain and second-guessing everything, 'cause I can't for the life of me think of what the hell anyone could want from me. I mean, ever since I left the agency, my life couldn't be any more ordinary. Which can only mean that it has something to do with my past life. And if it does, then I'm not sure who I can trust at the agency. I worked undercover. Not many people knew what I did. Which means that if someone's after me because of my days on the job, then they've got a feed from the inside. That's partly why I called you."

The other part was obvious. And anyway, I was glad she did.

"All right. What about San Diego PD?"

"I can't call them up. Not like this. If they found Tom dead in our front hall, how's it going to look? Spouses and girlfriends make great suspects, right? Hell, the gun I took off one of them's probably the one they shot him with, and now it's got my prints all over it."

"You not calling it in makes it look worse."

"I know. But if I do a walk-in, it's gonna get messy. You know how these things play out. They're gonna assume the worst and they're gonna want to hold me while they figure things out. And I don't want to do that and have Alex palmed off to some CPS deadbeat," referring to the state's Child Protection Services agencies. "He's four, Sean."

"Do you have family nearby?"

"No, but it doesn't matter. I don't want to be away from him, not for a second," she fired back forcefully. "Not while those *mamabichos* are out there."

"If they're after you, he might be safer away from you."

"No way. I'm not letting him out of my fucking sight," she shot back.

"Okay," I said as something warm stirred up inside me, a flash of memory of her indomitable force of will, sparked by the colorful expressions she liked to throw around. I checked my watch. It was a little after half past twelve. "I need you to lay low for a few hours, until I get there."

"Sean, I didn't—"

"I'm coming, Meesh," I cut in. I was already climbing into the car and firing it up. "I'll grab the first flight out. Should be with you in seven, eight hours tops."

She went quiet for a moment, then said, "Wow."

"What?"

"No, I . . . Thanks. I guess deep down I was hoping you'd say that."

"Just sit tight, okay?" I was already out of my parking spot and weaving past slower cars. "Where can you stay till then?"

"I'll find a hotel, near the airport. I'll wait for you there."

"Sounds good. You got cash?"

"There's an ATM here."

"Use it and put your cards away." I thought about what she'd said. A professional tag team. "Pull your phone's battery, too. And ditch the car. Take a cab or a bus."

"Okay," she replied. "I'll call you from the hotel to let you know where I am."

"All right, I'll probably be on the plane by then, so leave me a voicemail," I said, flying past a slow-moving car while trying to make sure I had all the bases covered. "Hang in there, Meesh. We'll sort this out."

"Sure," she replied, sounding far from convinced.

I hesitated, then said, "Hey, Meesh."

"What?"

"You should have told me."

I had to say it.

It's what I felt, and, dammit, she should have.

The line went silent for a long second, then she said, "Yeah," her tone pained and remorseful. "Well . . . better late than never, huh?"

My heart felt like it was in a vise. "Is he okay? Alex?"

"He's great. You'll see."

I felt a little tear inside. "Hit that ATM and pull your battery," I reminded her. "I'll see you in a little while."

I clicked off and hit the speed dial for Nick Aparo, my partner at the Bureau. I needed to let him know what was going on and get him to help me figure out how I was going to get to San Diego as fast as possible.

Staring ahead as the call connected, I felt drained, reeling from the bombshell Michelle had lobbed at me. Drained, and torn by conflicting emotions—I'd been desperate to have a kid, so desperate that it had almost split me and Tess up, but at the same time, I knew this news would hit Tess hard. Real hard.

4

❦

I had just enough time for a quick swoop on the house I shared
with Tess and Kim, where I threw a few things into a backpack and
holstered up before hopping on the I-95 and riding it all the way
down to Newark.

My fastest option, as per my call to my partner, was an early afternoon United flight that connected via Denver. I'd lose an hour on
the ground there, but there was no way around that. Not unless I was
prepared to try to bullshit my way into getting a Bureau jet to fly me
out there and, assuming that worked, end up facing an OPR investigation that would most likely get me fired. I'd been down that route
before. I'd narrowly avoided a run-in with the open-minded sweet-
hearts from the Bureau's Office of Professional Responsibility a few
years ago, after I'd followed Tess onto a flight to Istanbul without
clearing it with my boss first. Problem was, I couldn't be open about
why I needed a jet this time, not without spilling the beans on what
was going on with Michelle. Aparo and I had argued about the mer-
its of gaining an hour versus the extra risks Michelle could face if her
whereabouts were more widely known, and I had grudgingly agreed
with him that an hour's delay in getting to her was worth risking if it
meant she got to stay dark till I got there.

Traffic was sparse, and as I drove on, my mind was skittering all
over the place. Michelle's revelation was no less than a life-changer.
There would be a whole host of ripples I'd need to deal with. Of
those, none would be more delicate to navigate than the one that had

hogged my thoughts the whole way down—the same one, in fact, that was now rousing my BlackBerry as I took the off-ramp toward the terminal.

For a moment, I debated whether or not to pick up, but I knew I couldn't duck the call.

"Hey."

"Hey, handsome," Tess's voice boomed. "How's the bachelor weekend going? The Shermans haven't had to call the cops out, have they?"

Her voice was like a balm to my battered senses. "They threatened to, but we're cool."

"How'd you manage that?"

"I invited them over and offered them one of our bongs. The thing is, now I can't get rid of them. Those kids can party."

I heard her chuckle as she probably pictured the seventy-something-year-old couple next door in full frat-house mode—not an attractive sight, trust me—and I grabbed the moment.

"Hey, I can't talk right now. I'm about to jump on a plane."

"Oh, baby," she teased, "you can't wait till next weekend, huh?"

I managed a small chortle. "Not exactly."

Tess dropped the playful tone. "Yeah, I kind of figured. What's going on? Where are you flying?"

"San Diego." I hesitated, then added, "Something's come up. I need to be there."

"Anything I should be worried about?"

"No." I was hating the lie, even though it was more of a lie of omission—not that anyone ever bought that line, least of all me right now. But I couldn't tell her, not now, not over a car speakerphone.

"But it's enough to have you jumping on a plane at the drop of a hat?"

I hesitated again, feeling too uncomfortable with the lie. I just had to cut the call short. "It's nothing serious. Look, I'm at the airport, I've got to go. I'll call you from there, okay?"

She went silent for a moment, then said, "Sure. Okay. Just—Sean?"

She didn't have to say it. The worry was coming through loud and clear. She always said it, even after all the time we'd spent together and all the close shaves we'd been through.

"I know," I told her.

"Call me."

"I will."

I hung up, feeling awful about having her worry unnecessarily, and feeling a lot worse about not telling her the truth.

The fact was, I didn't know how I was going to break the news to her. No matter how I prefaced it or framed it or sugarcoated it, it was going to hurt.

We'd tried, and failed, to have a baby for a couple of years. Who really knows why that happens. The doctors will run all kinds of tests and explain why they think it's happening, but ultimately, I think it was just our bad luck. As far as the specialists were concerned, the likely cause lay with Tess's age and her being on the pill for so many years, but whatever it was, and despite trying the very best IVF treatments on offer, it just wouldn't happen for us. The grueling process had turned into a drawn-out ordeal, with each failed attempt causing more emotional trauma. Tess, in particular, had grown more and more depressed with feelings of inadequacy, something that seemed insane to me—she was the most capable and giving woman I'd ever met. But she knew how much I had wanted to be a dad myself, and not just a stepdad to Kim, and although I'd done my best to play down the disappointment I felt deep down and no matter what I said, I guess I just hadn't been able to hide it convincingly enough. She started finding it harder and harder to be around me and ended up flying off to Jordan, using the excuse that she needed to do some research for a Templar novel she was prepping. It was only recently, and by fluke—a near-death one, at that, after Tess had been kidnapped by some whackjob Iranian operative while she was in Petra—that we'd gotten back together again.

And now this.

It was definitely going to hurt.

It was also the kind of wedge that could drive a couple apart, and that was a prospect I was desperate to avoid. I mean, Tess was my life. But I knew that the sudden reemergence of an ex-girlfriend with my young child in tow would be, at best, a source of recurrent friction and, at worst, a complication that could wreck us. It wouldn't help that Michelle Martinez was smart, funny, seriously hot, and—the deal breaker—someone I'd never mentioned to Tess. I'd blanked out that whole episode of my life. And no matter how attractive Tess was herself—which she was, in spades, the word *luminous* springing to mind whenever I try to describe her—and despite the fact that I was nuts about her and that she knew it, I had a strong feeling she'd inevitably feel threatened by my blast from the past. Anyone would. I get that. Hell, I would, too, no question. And, again, I'd probably end up having a hard time convincing her that she had nothing to worry about. Which she didn't. Michelle had been a serious flame for me, but Tess, without a doubt, was the full bonfire.

Definitely not a conversation I was looking forward to, though it was already playing itself out in my mind. And as I drove into the parking lot worrying about Tess, far darker thoughts intruded and took center stage again, thoughts of Michelle and a little boy I'd never met and the dangers lurking around them.

I was starting to have a sinking feeling that maybe I should have grabbed a jet.

5

❧

A s the door swung open, my heart froze.

Not in a bad way. It froze in an oh-my-god, paralyzed-from-sensory-overload kind of way. The good kind of sensory overload.

She still had it. The smooth, honey-hued skin. The delicate dusting of freckles across her thin nose and sculpted cheeks. The dazzling blue eyes, windows into the cauldron of intelligence and mischief within. The body, curvy and taut, that could make Hugh Hefner's head spin. It was all just as I remembered it.

But that wasn't what froze my heart.

What did it was the four-year-old boy standing quietly by her side, holding onto her hand tightly and staring up at me.

The sight of him made me forget to breathe.

When Michelle had said that Alex was four, I hadn't quite realized just how tiny a four-year-old was. How tiny, and how fragile. I just hadn't been around many kids of that age. I didn't have any nieces or nephews, Kim was around ten when I first hooked up with Tess, and, aside from Aparo, I wasn't socially close to any of the people I worked with, some of whom had young kids. Hence the shock and awe rolling through me. And right there and then, standing in that bland and uninspiring hotel hallway, my heart soared as it never had before. I just knew that Alex was mine.

"You gonna just stand there like a *burro*, or you gonna give me a hug?" Michelle asked.

I dragged my eyes away from Alex and up to hers. Despite the apparent bravado, there was a smoldering fear in her eyes. It was subtle, barely there, and not everyone would have spotted it, but I did. I smiled, took her by the shoulders and pulled her closer, and gave her a kiss, a slightly awkward one that wasn't quite on the lips but wasn't on the cheeks either. Her arms slid up and she hugged me, tight, burying her head in the crook of my neck.

I'm not gonna lie to you, and don't hate me for saying it, but right there and then, it felt great. Awkward, yes—but great.

Then I felt the shivering and any notion of "great" vaporized.

We stood there for a long moment, breathing each other in, a riptide of confusing emotions tugging at us, an unfinished past colliding with a brutal present, standing there in silence, stretching out the enjoyable part of our encounter, knowing the real reason for us being there, together again, would soon take over. Then we pulled back, holding each other's eyes in a silent commemoration of what we'd once had until Michelle turned and, palms out, game show hostess–like, gestured at her son.

"So . . . this is Alex," she said, her face a mix of pride, unease, and pain.

I glanced back down at the boy, who was staring at me uncertainly, and something twisted inside me. Alex's eyes were wide with what I suddenly realized was more than just uncertainty. It was fear. I bent down to say hi to him, but as I did, Alex shrunk back and tucked himself in behind his mother's thigh, hugging it tightly while burying his head into it.

"No," he pleaded in a small voice.

Michelle swiveled her head around to him.

"Alex, what's wrong?"

The kid didn't say anything. He was still cowering behind her leg, not looking out.

I looked a question at Michelle. She turned and crouched down and pulled Alex out from behind her, but he resisted and screamed, "No," again.

"Alex, stop it." Her tone was even, but firm.

"No, Mommy, no," the boy whimpered.

"Meesh, it's okay," I offered.

Michelle ignored my plea. "Alex, stop," she insisted, firmer now, but still calm. "This is my friend, Sean. Now would you please stop being silly and say hi to him. He's here to help us."

The boy glanced up at me, then ducked back out of sight and tucked himself away even more. He was trembling visibly.

"It's all right," I told her, raising my hands in a calming motion. "He's been through a hell of a lot today."

Michelle studied Alex for a second, then hugged him against her and nodded. "I know, but . . . I don't know what's got into him. He's usually really friendly, and I thought that, at least, with you here . . ." She let the words drift off, clearly flustered and frustrated.

"Given what you've both been through today . . . Maybe it's not a bad thing for him to be wary of strangers."

"I guess," she said, shaking her head. "It's just that . . . He's been having nightmares and, well, it's . . . complicated." She looked up at me with real hurt in her eyes, and I suspected that, despite everything she'd been through today, she probably felt awful about my first get-together with Alex turning out this way. "God, I'm really sorry. It's nothing to do with you, you know that, right?"

"Don't worry about it."

I got down on one knee so my face was almost level with his, and extended a hand. "Hey, Alex. It's really great to meet you."

After a long second, the kid peeked nervously at me, then shut his eyes tight and shrank back behind his mother.

I glanced at Michelle. She was watching intently, and the heaviness in her heart was clear. She gave me a look of exasperation and apology. I gave her a soft nod. At least Alex and I had now met, even in these circumstances. It was only a minuscule step, but it was still a major one, for all three of us. There was still a long and, I'm sure, bumpy trail to travel, a lot of lost time to make up—and a lot of tough decisions to make.

"You'd better come on in," she told me.

I stepped in and saw her glance warily down both ends of the hall before locking the door behind me.

6

We talked out on the balcony, with Alex inside, watching TV. He was big on *Ben 10*, which was—I'd just learned—a hugely popular TV show. He had all the gear: the small figurines of Ben and a whole bunch of weird-looking aliens, the sneakers, even a big, cool-looking gizmo around his wrist that—I also just learned—was called the Omnitrix and that any true *Ben 10* fan just had to have. It was the device that gave Ben the ability to turn into any of ten alien characters, which he used to defeat his enemies. And right now, I was glad he had it. Given what he'd been through, Alex needed all the super-powers he could summon up.

It had taken a little while for Michelle to calm him down, but somehow she'd managed it while I stayed out of sight and took in the view. The room was on the third floor of the low-rise hotel, facing the marina and the ocean beyond. Across the street, people strolled and jogged along the water's edge, watching the sailboats slip in and out of the harbor's mouth while, overhead, planes were gliding in, low and slow, on final approach. The whole world seemed to be out and about, enjoying the end of a glorious day by the ocean, talking and laughing and basking in the setting sun's balmy em-brace, oblivious to the horrorfest that had crashed into Michelle's life that morning.

The sliding door was half open, but there wasn't much risk that Alex would overhear us, not with the TV on. Still, we kept our voices down. Four-year-olds, Michelle told me, had a way of surprising you with what they caught on the fly and brought up when you least expected it. Both guns—my Browning Hi-Power, and the silenced Glock 22 she'd grabbed off one of the guys who'd attacked them—were laid out on the flimsy white balcony table, along with a couple of Coke cans we'd liberated from the room's minibar.

I was having trouble making sense of what had happened, but at least, with Michelle there, I could start filling in the blanks. The ones in my mind as well as the ones plaguing her, starting with the one that, I knew, mattered the most.

"He's dead," I informed her. "The first cops on the scene found him by your front door. I'm sorry."

Michelle just shut her eyes and nodded as her eyes welled up and a couple of tears glided down her cheeks. I pulled her in and held her for a moment, feeling her tremble against me.

"You spoke to them?"

"I called our local field office. I got them to look into it."

She nodded again, still tucked in against me, but didn't say anything. She was still shaking.

I gave her a moment, then said, again, "I'm sorry."

"Yeah." She edged back and wiped her eyes, looking all lost in a daze, a painful one—then her eyes sharpened slightly. "The guy I took out—was he still there?"

"No. Just a lot of blood. They must have taken him away with them. How bad did you get him?"

"Well, unless he's some kind of circus freak who can swallow swords through the side of his neck, I'd say he was dead before they got him back to their van." She blew out a frustrated sigh. "I'm telling you. These guys knew what they were doing."

"I know." I watched her for a long second, then waded into the silence. "So . . . how close were you and Tom?" It felt a bit awkward to be asking her about him like that, and I felt bad about wondering how close he had been to Alex. But I needed to try to figure out what had happened, and why.

Michelle shrugged. "We've only been dating a couple of months."

She shook her head with regret and looked out at the ocean. "He was a great guy."

"Was he living with you?"

"No," Michelle said. "He has a place over in Mission Hills. But he stayed over most weekends, when his kids weren't staying with him. He was divorced. Fuck," she blew out a hard, ragged sigh. "The kids. Oh, God. Who's gonna tell them?" She looked up at me. "I need to talk to them."

"Not now, Meesh. Let's figure things out first."

"They're gonna be crushed," she said, her eyes misting up again. "Crushed."

I gave her a moment, then asked, "What line of work was he in?"

"He's an architect. Was an architect. He had a nice practice going. Loved his work, you know?"

I could see that talking about him, especially in the past tense like that, was tough on her, but I needed to be thorough. Michelle, though, was no stranger to the process, and she shook her head angrily, visibly trying to focus her thoughts. "Look, I know where you're going with this, but this isn't about him, Sean." The frustration rose in her voice before she visibly caught herself. "They shot him the second he opened the door. They came for me. And if it wasn't for me, if he hadn't slept over last night, he'd still be—"

"Come on, Meesh," I interjected. "You can't beat yourself up about that. It's just bad luck, that's all. Just horribly bad luck. And not to sound callous or selfish or anything, but if they were after you and he hadn't been there, they would have got you and we wouldn't be standing here." I paused, giving it a chance to sink in, then added, "What about peripheral stuff? Business partners, friends, family— how much did you know about the rest of his life?"

"It's not about him," she insisted. "He was a sweet, straightforward guy. Trust me, there was nothing about his life that would've led to this. Nothing. He just happened to be there."

I studied her for a moment, then said, "Okay," deciding to park it for the time being. I'd still get the local bureau to run a background check on him, although deep down, I trusted Michelle's instincts. "So if this is about you . . . what is it? You said your life was smooth sailing."

"Totally."

"So what then? Some kind of blowback from your days on the job?"

"Must be. I mean, I can't see what else it could be about, but . . . why now? I walked away from that life four, five years ago."

Her objection was valid. It didn't ring true that something from that long ago would resurface now.

"And you've been coaching hoops ever since?"

"Yeah. It's not like I had unlimited options, given my skill set. Besides, I like it. It gives me a chance to work with the kids and keep them on the straight and narrow, you know? And I like making a difference in their lives. They open up to me about stuff."

"What kind of stuff?"

"Teen stuff."

"Drugs?"

She nodded. "Of course. It's a big part of their lives, you know that. And I figure, maybe I can still make a difference, maybe I can help keep them healthy beyond making sure they get enough air in their lungs, and do it without having to wear a badge."

I wondered if there was anything there. "What are we talking about here? You been causing anyone some major grief? Enough to have some pissed-off dealer come after you?"

"No way," she replied. "It's all just small stuff. Local. Talking to the kids, sharing what I've seen with them. I'm not playing local sheriff or anything."

I reflected on that for a brief moment. Again, it was something to explore, although given the way she'd described the hit team, it didn't seem like the right fit.

"All right. What about your life pre-Tom. Who else were you seeing? Any ex-boyfriends this could be connected to?"

Her face crinkled as she thought about it for a moment, then she said, "Well, there was this one guy, this dickhead FBI agent who knocked me up and split." She looked at me, flatly, then gave me a half-smile of contrition. "Sorry. Totally uncalled for, I know. The thing is, after you . . . I had a newborn baby to look after. You think I was out hitting the clubs and living *la vida loca*?"

"No, but . . . it's been a few years. You must have seen some other guys before Tom?"

She waved it off. "Yeah, sure, there were a couple of guys. But nothing serious. And nothing even remotely shady about either of them. I didn't want to have anything to do with that life after I left the job. I had a baby to think of. I didn't want to deal with that kind of bullshit."

A slight grin creased my cheek. She caught it.

"What?"

"It's just hard to think of you in those terms," I told her. "Leading a quiet life."

She let out a small, nervous laugh. "It took some adjusting, believe me. But Alex was all the motivation I needed."

"And that's why you left the DEA."

"Pretty much. I didn't want to stay on the job and risk leaving an orphan behind. And I didn't want to stay in Mexico either. There was too much blood in the streets after Calderón decided to take on the cartels," she said, referring to the then newly elected president's decision to send out his army to try to wipe them out from his very first day in office, back in 2006—a war that, at last count, had claimed more than thirty thousand lives. The lucky ones had been gunned down, the rest either beheaded or burnt alive, their remains often buried in anonymous mass graves or dissolved in caustic soda.

An uncomfortable question clawed its way out of the tangle of questions clogging up my mind. I frowned and went silent, unsure about bringing it up now. But I couldn't resist. I needed to know.

"Tell me something," I asked. "When did you find out?"

"That I was pregnant?"

"Yes," I pressed, half-reluctantly. "Was it before or after I left?"

She looked at me for a moment, then said, "Before."

I felt a boil of anger bubble up inside my temples. It wasn't the answer I'd hoped for. I just shook my head and looked away.

"Hey, you were the one who took off, remember?"

I turned to face her. "That doesn't mean anything. I didn't know. You had my number. Why didn't you call and tell me? Did you think I wouldn't want to be part of it?"

"No. I just didn't want you to be part of it," she replied, holding my gaze, her tone firm and unrepentant. She paused, watching me, then added, "I didn't want you in our lives, Sean. Not the way you were back then. Come on, don't you remember? You were in a hell of a bad place. One big barrel of rage, all angry and bitter and consumed by guilt about what happened."

All, sadly, true.

"It was a bad time," I said, bitterly, as memories of that night, in that lab way out in the Mexican backcountry, came rushing back.

Memories of things I hadn't shared with her.

Michelle wasn't part of our task force—her deal was working the money trail undercover and taking away the drug barons' easy cash—and she didn't know the full story of why we went out there that night. I didn't either. It had come out of the blue, an urgent, sudden rescue-and-retrieve op that I'd been drafted into. And when we got back, I was so torn up and felt so bad about what we'd done that I couldn't face telling her about it. I couldn't face telling anyone about it, least of all her. During those few turbulent days, all I'd been capable of sharing with her was that it all went wrong and that innocent civilians, including the guy we'd been sent there to bring back, had died.

I didn't tell her I was the one who had executed him.

"I know it was," she said. "But you didn't have to bail like that. Maybe if you'd stuck around, I could have helped you work through it. And if you had, maybe we'd still be together now." Her voice broke with a hint of some lingering regret.

I was feeling it, too.

She was right, of course. I should have told her. Maybe she would have been able to help me through it. Maybe I wouldn't have had to carry it inside me all those years like I'd swallowed a nuclear detonator. But I could barely face myself back then, and I couldn't bring myself to let anyone else know about it.

"I'm sorry," I said, feeling lousy.

She waved it away. "You know, the thing I never got was, yeah, he was an American civilian and he was forced to do what he did. But he still came up with some really nasty superdrug, right? I mean, that's why you went out to spring him. And the fact that he died—sure, it was tragic. But maybe it was better this way. Who knows what kind of damage his drug would have done if it got out. No?"

I shook my head and let out a weary breath. "We never did see eye to eye on that, did we?"

"You know the damage he could have caused, the lives he would have wrecked, intentionally or not . . . maybe it was for the greater good."

I shrugged, not wanting to get into it anymore. "Maybe." Moving away from it, I said, "So, who else knew? About Alex being mine. What did you say when you told them you were leaving?"

"I didn't tell anyone. I just said I needed a break and I just left. No one knew." Then she remembered something and corrected herself. "Except Munro. The sleazoid saw me at the airport and just guessed. He even made a play for me. Knowing I was pregnant. At least I got to see the priceless look on that douche's face when I shot him down. It was brutal."

I nodded and looked away, and stared at the horizon, feeling the sun's reflection on the water burning my eyes, wishing it could burn away the cascade of images from that day that were tumbling through my mind's eye.

After a moment, I felt Michelle's hand settle on mine.

"You know what? I'm sorry, too," she offered. "Maybe it was a shitty thing to do."

I turned to face her and shrugged. It was unfair of me to blame her. "No. I was in a really bad place." I felt a need to move on, to get away from those memories. "Anyway, there's no point stewing over it. Not now."

Michelle just said, "Okay."

I pulled out my phone. "I told my guys to sort out a safe house for you. It should be ready by now. I'll give them a call to get the address and take you over there."

"What about homicide? They need to know the details about what happened."

"First things first," I said. "Let me get you and Alex tucked away somewhere safe. Then I'll go see them."

"I don't want Alex taken away from me, Sean. Not for a minute. Promise me you won't let that happen."

I looked at her and nodded. "It won't."

It wasn't something I could definitely guarantee, not without having cleared it higher up first. Had we been in New York, I would have felt more comfortable making that promise. But out here, I was at the mercy of the local field office's Special Agent in Charge, David Villaverde. I'd never met him, but he seemed to be a stand-up guy. So far, he'd been accommodating, but he hadn't yet heard the full story. Whether or not he'd still be as accommodating once he had remained to be seen.

I made the call and got the safe house's address. It was in a place called Mira Mesa, close to the Marine Corps' Miramar airbase, about ten miles north of where we were. The plan was for us to take a taxi to the airbase's entrance, where two agents would be waiting to escort us to the house.

When I hung up, she was looking at me like something was churning away inside her.

"What?" I asked.

"Are you with someone?"

"Yes."

She winced, then said, "I'm sorry. To have dragged you out here."

I gave her a little bob of my head to acknowledge her concern. "Don't worry about it."

We gathered by the door of the room, with Michelle holding onto Alex's hand. He was still keeping well away from me and eyeing me nervously.

"All set?" I asked, reaching under my jacket and clicking the safety off my handgun.

Michelle nodded. "We're good."

I dropped my gaze to Alex. The four-year-old edged farther back behind his mother, and my heart cracked a bit. I looked at Michelle. She gave me an *It'll be fine* nod. I acknowledged her with a slight nod back and opened the door.

I glanced up and down the hall. There was nothing to cause me alarm. The corridor was empty.

I led them to the elevators and hit the Down button. Moments later, a telltale whir and a high-pitched ping announced the car's arrival. I glanced at Michelle and turned to face the doors as they slid open.

There were people in there.

Men, specifically—three of them, three tough guys in Windbreakers and dark caps who were pulling up their face masks just as the doors opened, three pairs of bad-ass, cold stares that suddenly flared with surprise.

I understood instantly—I didn't need to see Michelle's jaw drop or hear her blurt out "It's them." I was already moving, lunging left to push her and Alex out of harm's way, my right hand diving for my gun, my eyes locked on the three thugs as they reached under their jackets, their handguns' grips coming into view—

—then the bullets started flying.

7

"Take Alex, I'll cover you," I yelled as I bolted away from the elevator doors.

Michelle was already doing it, scooping the four-year-old off his feet and holding him tight against her as she sprinted down the corridor.

I was right behind her, moving sideways, my gun arm extended and aimed down the hall, covering the elevator, eyes at DEFCON one, ready to lock onto any movement. I saw one of the men stick his head out from the cabin's opening, the silenced muzzle of a handgun appearing at the same time, and we both fired at the same time, me blasting away with several rounds, the goon recoiling back just as he squeezed off a few shots of his own that zinged around me and crunched violently into the walls of the corridor.

"Keep going," I shouted to Michelle over my shoulder while flicking a lightning-quick glance behind me to get my bearings. I saw that the corridor doglegged to the left, and Michelle was already disappearing into it. I cursed inwardly, angry at the fact that I hadn't had a choice other than to push her out of the way and not pull her toward me, thereby committing us to head down that side of the corridor and away from the room, which was now out of our reach, on the other side of the elevator. I wasn't sure what lay beyond the dogleg, but it wasn't like we had much of a choice.

I reached the bend in the corridor just as the shooter's head popped out again, this time down at carpet level, his gun out front and center, spitting out more rounds. Bullets blew past me as I fired back, my aim wild as I made the turn. I sucked in a quick breath, then poked an urgent eye around the edge of the corner. I only managed to get a jarred glimpse of another shooter diving out of the elevator and taking up a kneeling position alongside the corridor wall before a riot of gunfire erupted around me, one of the rounds splintering the wall inches from my face in a burst of wood and plaster. I felt something nick me in the cheek as I pulled back into cover, felt its heat and its sting but ignored it and spun my gaze behind me to see where Michelle was.

She was around fifty feet away, standing by an open doorway at the end of the corridor, waving me over frantically and hissing, "This way."

I took another deep breath with my back against the wall, then swung my gun out and unleashed a few blind rounds toward the elevator without risking a look before charging after Michelle.

We burst through the doorway and hustled down the stairs, Michelle leading, Alex still in her arms and tight against her, me staying several steps behind, trying to minimize the risk of either of them getting hit by a stray that was meant for me, flicking quick glances behind me to make sure I didn't miss a step while keeping the stairwell above us covered.

It didn't take long before I heard the shooters burst into it and stampede down the stairs after us. I glimpsed flickers of their movement higher up and traced it with my gunsight, resisting the urge to fire, not wanting to waste any bullets unless I had a clear shot. The bastards didn't give me much of one as they hugged the walls and kept out of sight, only peering over the balustrade once for a split second that goaded a couple of rounds out of me. We were all hurtling down six flights of stairs as fast as was humanly possible. Then Michelle, Alex, and I hit the ground floor and burst out of the stairwell and into the hotel's lobby.

I waived my gun in the air and shouted "Everybody down!" as we sprinted across the large open space and beelined for the exit. The lobby wasn't crowded, but the few people who were in there turned in startled confusion, some of them screaming out in panic and scurrying for cover while others simply froze. We were flying past the elevator just as its doors slid open and a lone shooter burst out of it, straight into our path. Michelle sidestepped him like a quarterback on a rush out of hell and kept going, leaving him for me. I rammed him, hard, my raised forearm connecting with the goon's jaw and channeling the full momentum of my run into it and sending him crashing down to the floor. I saw the man's gun clatter across the floor by my feet and managed to kick it out of the way without breaking step while staying on Michelle's tail.

We flew out of the lobby and skittered to a stop in the hotel's forecourt. It gave onto a medium-size lot where guests parked their own cars, as the hotel didn't offer a valet service. I knew we couldn't afford to stop for longer than a heartbeat. I swung my gaze across the lot, breathing hard, my heart kicking and screaming furiously against my rib cage, and to our left, I spotted what I'd expected—a white van, parked facing the hotel's entrance, one silhouette inside it, that of another shooter who flung its door open and climbed out the instant he saw us.

"That way," I blurted as I herded Michelle away from the van—then I saw a car drive into the lot and head for an empty parking spot.

"Over there," I told Michelle, pointing at the blue sedan. "That car. Go."

We raced toward it with me keeping our rear covered, and we were flying past a row of parked cars when a new volley of bullets erupted, crunching into body panels around us and taking out a windshield we'd just streaked past.

"Don't stop," I yelled to Michelle as I spun around and fired back at the two shooters rushing toward us.

We reached the Ford just as its driver, a paunchy, bald man in a suit, had pulled in and was getting out of his car.

"Give me your keys," I barked, shoving my gun in his face and leaving him no room for indecision. The poor guy held them out with two fingers. I snatched them from him and pulled him out of the car and pushed him away, ordering him, "Stay down."

The man hit the ground. I yelled out to Michelle, "Get in," flinging the rear door open for her before loosing a few more rounds at the shooters.

Michelle hustled Alex into the car and was flying in behind me when I saw one of the crew raise his head and put a bead on us. I lined him up, but just as I pulled the trigger, I saw the man fire and heard a sharp *unnnh* coming from my right.

A stab of dread ripped through me as I flicked my head sideways and caught sight of Michelle staggering into the rear seat after Alex.

I also spotted a small, dark patch at the base of her chest.

"Meesh?!"

She didn't reply and just disappeared into the car.

I cursed inwardly, knowing what had just happened, knowing it wasn't good, not in that spot, not where you've got lungs and a heart and all kinds of other soft, crucial bits all packed in tight next to each other, but I couldn't do anything about it right now, couldn't do anything other than get them the hell out of there. I jumped in, punched the ignition key in, and threw the car into reverse, twisting around to look over my shoulder as I blasted the car out of its parking spot.

I couldn't manage more than a quick glance at Michelle, but the sight of her sent an ice pick through my gut. Her eyes were wild with fear and anguish, and her face had burst into sweat.

"Jesus, Meesh," I rasped.

She glanced down at her wound, then looked up and just held my gaze, her face flooded with confusion. She tried to say something, and her mouth just couldn't form the words at first, then she said, "I'm—fuck, Sean, I'm hit."

Behind her, through the windshield, I could see the two shooters still coming at us. One of them, the bastard who'd shot her, was moving with more difficulty and I saw that he had a dark patch on his shoulder. I figured that was where my bullet went, though it had obviously got there a split second too late.

I wasn't about to give him a second chance.

"Hang on," I told Meesh, keeping my foot down, flooring the pedal, hard, like I was trying to ram it through the foot well, sending the Ford rocketing backward and straight into the shooters' path.

One of them managed to avoid it by taking a flying leap over the hood of a parked car, but the guy I really wanted wasn't as light-footed. I just plowed into him and pushed him along before crushing him against the side of another car, obliterating the lower half of his body in a sickening, wet crunch that sounded damn good to me. Then I threw the car back into gear and we flew out of the hotel's lot, hanging a squealing right before tearing down the seafront, my head snapping back and forth as my eyes searched for any kind of reassurance about Michelle and the bullet that had found her.

8

"**M**eesh, stay with me, okay? Just hang in there," I yelled, breathless, all kinds of expletives coming out thick and fast inside my head as I threw quick glances behind me to see how she was while I pulled out my phone.

As I hit the green button twice to redial the last called number, I caught a glimpse of her looking up at me, and it wasn't good. Her eyes were half-closed, her mouth was twisted with pain, and the sheen of sweat on her face had turned into a full-on drench. Her chest was now soaked in blood, and she had her right arm around Alex, squeezing him tight against her. Her eyes widened and hooked mine, and she started to say something, but it was cut short as she coughed and blood spurted out of her mouth.

My gorge shot up into my neck.

"Hang in there, baby," I repeated as Villaverde picked up the call.

"Reilly?"

"I'm with Michelle, she's been shot, we need help," I told him. "I'm in the car with her and her kid and—" I scanned the area around us, looking for markers to give him. "I'm on the seafront, heading west, away from the hotel."

"You being pursued?"

I glanced in the mirror, but couldn't see any sign of the goon squad.

"No. But I need to get her to a hospital, fast."

I heard Villaverde call out to one of his men, then he said, "Okay, you must be on Harbor Drive, which means the nearest hospital to you is . . ." He paused, thinking about it.

"Come on," I hollered, "she's bleeding out"—and just then, something caught my eye, in the sky, to my left. An airliner, coming in to land.

My pulse tripped. "Forget the hospital. I'm by the airport." My eyes scanned the road ahead and, sure enough, I spotted a big overhead sign for the airport, announcing an exit for Terminal Two. "Get them to send an ambulance to meet me outside Terminal Two. I'm in a blue Ford sedan."

"Hang on."

I heard him yell out the order to get onto the airport's EMS dispatcher, then Villaverde came back.

"What about the shooters?"

"I got one of them in the parking lot, some of him might still be there when your people get there, but the others'll be long gone."

"All right, I'll keep you posted. And good luck with her."

I chucked the phone onto the seat next to me and crunched the pedal. As we blew past some slower vehicles, I adjusted the mirror and locked it onto Michelle's face.

"Almost there, Meesh, you hear me?" I urged her, "We're almost there."

Her eyes were struggling to stay open.

Fear swamped my heart as I guided the Ford past a blur of cars before veering off the six-lane road and throwing the car onto the winding ramp that led to the terminal. Less than a minute later, we were pulling up to the curb by a startled traffic cop.

I leapt out of the car and threw a quick glance up and down the ramp, looking for the EMS van. There was no sign of it.

"There's an ambulance on its way," I shouted to the cop as I flung open the rear door to get to Michelle. "See if you can find out where it is. We've got an emergency here."

I leaned in, and the sight that greeted me froze me stiff. Michelle wasn't moving. Her breathing was shallow and when it did come, it wasn't much more than a feeble wheeze. There was a messy streak of blood and saliva running down from the side of her mouth, and the car seat was drenched.

Softly, I reached out and pulled up her shirt, looking for the wound. There was a dark crevasse just under her left breast, and thick blood was seeping out of it. I put my hand on it and applied some pressure, trying to stem the bleeding, anticipating the pain I'd be causing Michelle, and sure enough, she flinched hard as my hand pressed harder. I moved my other hand up to her face, giving her pale, clammy cheek a caress, unsure about whether or not she could even feel it. As I did, my eyes drifted off her face and down to find Alex, who was tucked in under her arm, his face down, his eyes shut tight. He was shivering wildly.

"Hey," I said, softly. I reached over, then hesitated and pulled my hand back before it settled on the boy's head. "It's gonna be okay," I told him in that annoying, desperate way that we sprout out these platitudes. "She's gonna be fine."

Alex didn't look up. Instead, he remained still for a moment, still coiled up tight and trembling, then he gave me a minuscule nod before going back to his shell-like seclusion.

I felt my heart stall as Michelle's warm blood kept seeping through my fingers—then I heard a faint siren growing in the distance.

"They're here, Meesh, you hear that? The ambulance is here."

Her eyelids flickered half open, allowing her eyes to connect with mine momentarily. Her face scrunched up as she tried to say something, but she couldn't manage it and just coughed up some more blood.

I leaned in closer. "Don't talk, sweetie. Just hang in there, we'll have you in the ambulance in no time."

She seemed insistent and tried again, but the words shriveled up in her throat.

"What is it, baby?" I asked as I heard the siren's shriek grow louder, almost with us now.

Her eyes widened briefly, like it was the result of some superhuman effort, and she met my gaze again, even though it seemed to be taking a huge toll on her. "Alex," she wheezed. "Keep . . . keep him . . . safe."

"Of course. Hey, I'm not going anywhere," I said, managing some feeble attempt at a reassuring smile, stroking her cheek while keeping my other hand pressed down on the entry wound. "We're both right here with you," I told her as I glimpsed the ambulance pulling up behind us.

Within seconds, the paramedics were in the car, checking her out. My gut twisted as I read the look on their faces when they first saw how pale and weak she was and when they saw the amount of blood that she'd lost. With more and more curious onlookers congregating around the car, I helped them lift her out of it and onto a stretcher, keeping Alex close and hanging onto his hand before doing my best to shield Michelle from his view as the paramedics tended to her on the curb.

The sound bites coming from them weren't reassuring.

"She's got massive internal bleeding," one of them finally told me while struggling to set up a second intravenous line into her arm. "I can't tell what's been hit, but we can't do anything about it here. She needs surgery."

Just then, some sensors started beeping wildly and the other paramedic blurted, "She's crashing." The first paramedic sprang to action and they both went frantic, hands and mouths moving at lightning speed as one of them started on the CPR while the other looked into her mouth to secure an airway for intubation. I stood back and watched in numb silence as they worked on her, feeling my whole body seize up every time she convulsed under the paramedic's compresses, holding Alex tight against me, making sure the kid couldn't see what was going on, hoping against hope that they'd be able to save her, but somehow knowing it wasn't going to work out, feeling impotent and helpless at not being able to step in and make things right and bring her back to her vibrant, mesmeric self, feeling a surge of fury converging in my temples and making them feel like they were going to erupt, then the beeping stopped and the flatline took over and the lead paramedic turned to me with a tenebrous look and a small shake of the head that reached deep into my very core and shredded everything in its path.

9

"How the hell did they find her?"

We were back at the ranch, the ranch in this case being the FBI's San Diego field office, a squat, glass-and-concrete three-story structure a couple of miles east of Montgomery Field. Villaverde and I were in his top-floor office. Besides everything that had happened, I'd spent ages briefing a couple of homicide detectives on what had gone down and describing the shooters as best as I could, and right now, I was tired and angry as hell, and my head felt all heavy and clogged up, like someone had pumped molasses into my skull.

"Maybe they followed her from the house," Villaverde speculated, leaning against the edge of his desk. He was tall and lean and with the clear olive skin and the combed-back onyx-black hair, a walking, talking ad for the bureau. I imagined the suits loved him, and to be fair, from what I'd seen so far, he was a straight-shooting, efficient guy.

"She said she wasn't followed," I fired back, more testily than I should have. "Michelle was good. She would have spotted a tail. Especially after what happened. She was looking out for one."

"What about her phone?"

"She killed the battery after calling me."

"Maybe she called someone else from the hotel?"

My head snapped left and right. "No way. Michelle was a pro. She wouldn't take that risk, not after what she'd been through."

Villaverde shrugged. "Well, we'll know soon enough. If she did call anyone, it'll show up on her room's phone records."

Another possibility was clawing away at me.

"How many hotels and motels do you think there are out there, by the airport?"

"I don't know. Not that many. Why? You think that's how they found her? Trawling them?"

"When she called me from the mall, Michelle said she'd find somewhere to hole up by the airport. If they hacked her phone and were in on that call . . . they'd be looking for a woman and a kid with no luggage and no credit card. Maybe they got lucky."

"Well if that's what happened, and depending on how they did it, there might a cloning trail on her phone." He picked up his desk phone and punched in a couple of buttons. "I'll get the lab to check it out."

I stood by the large window as Villaverde made his call and stared out in silence, seething with rage. The sun was long gone, and darkness was now firmly in control, gloomy and oppressive. The streetlamps in the almost empty parking lot were low and subdued, and there was no moon or stars in the sky that I could see, no beacon, no light at the end of the harrowing tunnel that this day had turned into. It was as if nature itself was conspiring to accentuate my sense of loss.

"I don't get it," I fumed. "She said they weren't after a kill. She said one of the shooters had her in his sights back at the house, but didn't take the shot."

"Maybe one of them screwed up," Villaverde offered as he hung up. "You said it yourself, bullets were flying all over the place." He hesitated, his expression uncertain, then added, "Maybe the one that got her was meant for you."

My stomach flooded with acid. It was something I'd been wondering about, along with second-guessing everything I'd done, every decision I'd made from the moment Michelle had called.

"Yeah, that's a great feeling right there," I grumbled. I tried to shake away the anger and the remorse and focus on what had to be done. "Okay, so what have we got to go on besides her phone? CCTV footage from the hotel, ballistics from the hotel and from the house . . . what else? Fingerprints? Blood from the shooters?"

Villaverde nodded. "We've got lots of DNA to work with, from the house and from the mess you left behind in the parking lot. I don't know what the score is on the camera footage, but forensics are running what they got through NCIC."

"What about neighbors?"

"Homicide's had people out there since her nine-one-one call, but I can't see much coming out of that. What are they going to get? The van's plates?"

I remembered seeing the shooters' van in the hotel's parking lot, but in the heat of the moment, my eyes hadn't registered its plate. It was irrelevant, anyway. Stolen, rented with a fake ID—either usually did the trick.

"I need you to go downtown and look at some faces," Villaverde said, referring to the monster database of mug shots on tap. Not something I was relishing.

I nodded grudgingly, wondering about who these guys were and going over what I'd seen, what their faces and their moves told me. They were tough and committed, and they moved well together, like they'd had a lot of practice doing it. It made me wonder what else we'd find out when we finally did track them down.

"They've got two guys down, either seriously hurt or more probably dead," I said.

"They're not about to roll them to any ER," Villaverde replied. "Best case, we'll find their bodies dumped somewhere sometime soon, but I'm not holding my breath. More likely they'll end up as worm food in one of the canyons or out in the desert."

Which is what I would have done, if I were them. The thing is, you've still got to cover all possible angles, in case the bastards who killed Michelle and whoever was calling the shots for them slipped up—which, luckily for us, they sometimes did.

"They lost two guys in one morning. You know of many crews that can take that kind of damage without blinking?" Before Villaverde could answer, I added, "We need to reach out to the DEA."

"Why?"

"Michelle couldn't figure out why anyone would want to come after her. The only thing she could think of was that maybe it was some kind of blowback from her years on the job. We need to ask them about that."

Villaverde's face contorted, like this was news to him. "I know the ASAC who runs their local office. I'll give him a call." He thought about it for a moment, then asked, "Was she based back east with you?"

I shook my head. "No. Mexico City."

"Mexico? Is that where you were posted, too?"

"No, I was Chicago."

"So how'd you guys hook up?"

"I was down there as part of a multi-agency task force. We were chasing down a new outfit that was cooking up some seriously pure crank that was hitting the street. I'd been backtracking the trail through some Latin Kings gangbangers they were supplying."

"Operation Sidewinder?" Villaverde asked.

"Right. Anyway, Meesh was already there, working out of the DEA's main digs at the embassy, hitting the kingpins where it hurt most—in their wallets. It didn't take long for our paths to cross."

"Okay. Who was the country attaché when she was down there? That's who we need to talk to."

I frowned in agreement. "Hank Corliss."

Villaverde winced. He clearly knew the name. "Corliss. Jesus."

I nodded. "Is he still DEA?"

He shrugged. "Hell, yeah. After what he went through, what else would he be doing, you know what I'm saying?" He paused, as if out of respect for the man, then said, "He's top dog in LA. Runs the So-Cal task force." The name had evidently conjured up some questions in his mind, and his brow knotted. "You think what happened to him could be tied to all this?"

The thought had bounced around in my mind, but it was hard to give it too much credence. It was close to five years later now—a long time for anyone to wait before unleashing a second wave of savagery.

"After all this time? With Michelle off the force for years? Doesn't sound right to me. Besides, she wasn't part of our task force; she was working a different caseload, undercover. But we do need to talk to him." I paused for a moment, then added, "Better the request come from you. Corliss and I—we're not exactly on each other's Christmas cards list." I was being generous.

Villaverde blew out a mild chortle. "Noted."

He went silent for a long second, like he was weighing what he was about to say.

"Look," he finally said, "this is all good, and maybe something'll pan out from talking to them, but . . . we can handle this, okay? You've got something else to think about right now."

I looked a question at him.

Villaverde turned and thumbed a finger in the direction of the glass wall that stood between his office and his secretary's desk. "The kid."

I looked through the partition. Alex had calmed down and was just sitting there quietly on a black leather couch, staring at the carpet. Two women were now seated next to him. One was Villaverde's über-efficient personal assistant, Carla, to whom I'd initially entrusted him. They'd been joined by a younger, dark-haired agent in a white shirt and a charcoal skirt suit by the name of Julie Lowery. Their attention was totally focused on him as they were chatting with him, trying to comfort him as he half-heartedly picked his way through a box of nuggets and some fries. Villaverde had already asked for a child psychologist to be brought in to help us out, a woman who'd worked with the bureau before, but they'd only been able to get through to her voicemail and were waiting to hear back.

"Does he have any family he can stay with? He's going to need some serious TLC," Villaverde added. "You need to think about that."

He was right, of course. I was so focused on wanting to get my hands on the sons of bitches who had gunned down Michelle that I wasn't thinking clearly about the other victim they'd left in their wake.

"I know."

"So what are you going to do with him?"

I wasn't sure why he was asking. "He's my son. What do you think? He'll live with us."

"Well, that's great. But you're going to have some paperwork to deal with. You'll probably need to run some blood work to establish paternity. It's a process." He paused, like he was already playing it out in his mind, then asked, "You know of any next of kin who might contest it? Are Michelle's parents around? These things can get messy."

She'd said there was no one close by when I'd asked her on the phone. I thought back to what I knew about her family. We were only together for a couple of months, and, intense as those months were, peripheral details like that had faded away.

"I'm not sure. No brothers or sisters that I know of. I think her dad's out of the picture, and her mom wasn't doing too well back when we were seeing each other, Alzheimer's I think, but . . . I'm not sure."

"Okay, we can look into that." Villaverde's expression softened up. "Look, all I'm saying is, you've got your hands full with this kid. You need to get the red tape sorted out and take him home, get to know him and start laying the groundwork for his new life. And that's not going to be easy. Not after everything he's been through today. I mean, he just watched his mom die, for Chrissake. That's gonna be tough to come back from. You've got a mammoth task facing you, my friend. And that's what you need to focus on right now. The rest of it, we can handle."

I wasn't with him. My mind was still locked in a replay loop, and I was watching Michelle buckle over as she dived into the car and hearing the sound of her grunt when the bullet hit her.

I just said, "I want these guys."

"Hey, I do, too. I already spoke to the head of SDPD's criminal intel unit. It's priority one for all of us, believe me. But there's nothing you can add to the mix. This isn't New York. It's not your beat. You'd just be a drag on our resources." He blew out a lungful of air, pushed off the edge of the desk, and joined me by the glass wall. "Look, Michelle's dead. Her boyfriend's dead. Whether the shooters were out to grab her or not, it doesn't matter anymore. It's over. These scumbags, they're gonna crawl back into whatever cesspool they came from. And we'll just have to keep on working the leads until we find them. Go. Be with your son. Take him home. Let us deal with this."

I balled my fists and felt my jaw tighten as his words sank in. Alex. Alex was now my priority, and, much as I hate to admit it, there wasn't much I'd be able to add to the investigation. Not out here. Not as an outsider with no local insights and no real contacts to work. I'd only be a burden to them.

The fact that it was true didn't make it any less toxic.

I glanced at my watch. It was just after ten—way past any four-year-old's bedtime. I needed to get Alex out of here and into a warmer, more comforting environment, get him to bed, let him get some rest. I'd always heard that kids were incredibly resilient, and Alex was going to need to draw on a full life's quota of resilience if he was going to get through this. I was going to have to learn some new tricks real quick, too, starting with the fact that I needed to figure out what I was going to tell him, how and when I was going to break the grim new reality to him. I was totally unprepared for this. I knew I'd need help and need it soon, and it didn't look like the child psychologist was going to be around before morning.

"I should get him out of here," I said.

"We'll get a couple of rooms set up for you at the Hilton. We use it a lot," Villaverde offered. "Might be a good idea for Jules to tag along and help put him to bed and get him settled," he added, indicating the brunette agent with a nod.

"Sure." I nodded somewhat absentmindedly, knowing that the help I really needed would have to come from elsewhere, but more thinking that I had an important call to make, one I could no longer avoid.

I checked my watch again and, for a split second, considered the time difference between California and Arizona before remembering that the Grand Canyon state didn't observe daylight saving time and was therefore also on Pacific Daylight Time, same as San Diego.

Which meant it wasn't too late to make that call.

"Give me a few minutes," I told Villaverde as I stepped out of his office and reached for my phone.

10

COCHISE COUNTY, ARIZONA

Tess couldn't believe what she was hearing.

At first, she'd been elated to get Reilly's call. It was never easy when he was out on a live assignment, not knowing where he was or how much danger he was really in. And at those times, his name showing up on her caller ID never failed to make her heart soar. She'd felt the same anxiety tonight, not knowing why he was out in San Diego, not knowing what level of threat required his immediate presence, and she was about to call him when his call lit up her screen. She'd felt the same visceral uplift at hearing his voice, the same surge of relief and joy—only this time, the surge proved short-lived.

She knew he was doing his best to massage her feelings and, to his credit, the words he used were carefully chosen and sensitively delivered, but it was still one hell of a bombshell, and despite all his efforts, she couldn't help feeling torn and pulled in all directions and dragged through a wringer of sadness, heartache, sympathy, melancholy, pain, and, yes, much as she hated the feeling—a touch of jealousy.

By the end of it, she felt dazed, emotionally pummeled, and physically exhausted, and her heart broke into even smaller pieces at the thought that however low she was feeling, the man she loved was surely feeling far worse.

And at the top of that whole tower of heartache, of course, was a young mother who'd just lost the rest of her life and a four-year-old boy who'd just watched his mother die.

There was really only one thing she could think of saying.

"I'll fly out in the morning," she told Reilly, her tone even and subdued and not really leaving any room for debate.

He didn't argue either.

"You all right?" Villaverde asked me as I stepped back into his office.

"Yeah," I said, feeling an unfamiliar, cold hollowness inside. I glanced out the glass partition at Alex and said, "Let's get the kid out of here. But after we get him tucked into bed, I need to do something."

"Shoot."

"Michelle's place," I told Villaverde. "I want to see it."

11

✦

The street outside Michelle's house was comatose-quiet, the tranquil residential neighborhood even more so that night, like it had clammed up from shock. A solitary police cruiser was parked out front and yellow crime tape was strung out around her property, the lone, faint echoes of the bloodstorm that had struck earlier that day.

The only ones on the outside, that is.

Inside, the echoes were much louder.

A large, congealed puddle of blood was the first thing that greeted Villaverde and me as we walked in. A messy streak broke off from it and arced sideways, away from the doorway. I visualized how it must have happened, when Michelle's boyfriend's body was shoved sideways by the shooters as they rushed out of the house with their wounded, or dying, buddy. Another trail of blood—the wounded shooter's, presumably—snaked deep into the house and disappeared into a dark hallway, accompanied by the bloody boot prints of at least two others.

I advanced into the hallway, trying to avoid the red stains on the ground. The place was littered with crime scene debris—black fingerprint dust, discarded index cards, rubber gloves, and empty tape dispensers. I've always been struck by how quickly death takes hold and imposes itself on whatever territory it's invaded, how quickly it can suck the life and light out of a victim's home and make it seem like they've been gone for years. This was no different, and the brutal finality of it was all the more striking given how close I had once been to Michelle.

I followed the macabre trail deeper into the house and down a narrow corridor. At the end of it, where it opened up into the kitchen, was another bloody mess, this one all over the floor and the walls. A frenzy of images rocked me, ones my mind was throwing up based on what Michelle had described. I pictured her plunging the kitchen knife into the shooter's neck, matching it with the red spurts lining the walls. I imagined the shooter collapsing to the floor, by the big puddle of blood, then being hustled back out of the house, almost if not already dead, his feet dragging behind him like twin paintbrushes and leaving a snaking red trail.

I stepped into the kitchen. It was relatively undisturbed. I could see the ghost of Michelle going around it, going about her Saturday morning routine. I noticed the dishwasher, open and with its trays out and still half-full, but what drew my eye was the fridge.

I moved closer to it.

Every square inch of its door was covered with photographs, drawings, and other personal mementos, like a montage of her life. I couldn't stop my eyes from feasting on them, and as I did, I felt my lungs shrivel. It was a shrine to happier days, a testament to a woman and her son and the abundance of good times they'd shared—good times I'd not been a part of, good times Alex would never enjoy again with his mother.

I lingered there as the images took root inside me, pictures of Alex from when he was a baby, of him and Michelle in parks and swimming pools and at the beach, all of them lit up by big smiles and laughing faces. My throat tightened as I took in Alex's drawings, crude and colorful creations of stick people and trees and fish and misshapen letters, enchanting expressions of an innocence that the boy was unlikely to enjoy ever again. Throughout it all, my mind was vaulting ahead, dropping me into those scenes like a digital special effect and taunting me with endless what-could-have-beens.

"Seems like she had a nice life."

Villaverde's words broke through my reverie.

I gave him a slow nod. "Yeah."

Villaverde stepped closer and took in the mementos on the fridge in silence. After a moment, he said, "Forensics have been over everything, so if you want to take something . . ."

I looked at him. He shrugged. I turned back to the fridge, took another long look at it, then peeled off a photo of Michelle and Alex posing next to a sandcastle on some beach.

"Let's check out the rest of the house," I told Villaverde as I slipped the pic into my breast pocket.

The rest was more or less undisturbed. Framed photos of Michelle and Alex kept calling out to me as I went through the living room and the master bedroom, but apart from accentuating the cold feeling in my gut, nothing in either room seemed out of place or looked to be of use to the investigation. Alex's bedroom was more of a challenge—I knew it would help him to have some of his favorite things with him, but I didn't know where to start or what to choose, and that only made me feel worse. It was cluttered with all kinds of toys, books, and clothes, and its walls were a colorful mosaic of cartoon posters and more of Alex's drawings. I thought that a good place to start would be to bring back the cartoon-covered bedsheets with me, as well as the three plush animals that were scattered on them. I pulled them all off the bed and rolled them into a ball, and I also grabbed some clothes from his closet.

The last room we checked out was a third bedroom, the smallest of the three. It was set up as her study, with a dark wood desk, well-stocked bookshelves, and a deep sofa laid out with a bunch of velvet throw cushions. Again, framed photos were nestled among the books and memorabilia from Michelle's past. I saw that, along with all the big novels and travel guides I remember she enjoyed, she also had plenty of the New-Agey tomes she was into, mind and spirit stuff I used to poke fun at. It was all warm and cozy and bathed in Michelle's eclectic taste, and it drove home even more how much Alex was going to miss her.

As I scanned the bookshelves, I also noticed a small, black wireless router that sat inconspicuously on top of a plastic storage box. I edged closer to it and saw that its green LED lights were on, indicating that it was broadcasting. I turned and saw a small inkjet printer on a low side table by the desk. It had a wireless logo on it. I swung my gaze across to the desk itself. There was no computer on it. There was, however, a small white cord that snaked down the side of the desk and led to a small, white power adapter with an Apple logo on it that was plugged into a wall socket.

But no computer.

I turned to Villaverde. "Did anyone log in a computer? A laptop, or maybe an iPad?"

"Hang on," he replied as he pulled out his phone.

I looked around. I couldn't see one anywhere. I went back and checked the master bedroom, the living room, and the kitchen.

Nothing.

Villaverde's call yielded no positive news. The homicide detectives who'd worked the house hadn't come across a computer. If they had, they would have logged it and sent it over to the crime lab.

"She didn't have one with her at the hotel," I told Villaverde. "Which means it was probably still here when she ran out of the house."

I checked the router again. It was a Netgear device and not Apple's own Time Capsule, which was a bummer. Apple's box automatically backs up the household computers' drives wirelessly, which would've been a boon in this case, but then again, maybe the guys who came for her would have taken that, too.

"So the shooters took it," Villaverde said.

It wasn't a huge help, but it told me something.

The killers weren't just after her.

12

✿

Raoul Navarro loved it here.

Just standing there, on his favorite among the many shaded terraces of his hacienda's *casa principal*, enjoying a fine Cuban and taking in the view as the lush moon teased the surface of the ceremonial pond, a soft breeze rustled the bougainvillea, and countless cicadas lulled his world to rest.

Life was good for Raoul Navarro.

Better than good, given that another fine Cuban, this one of the leggy female variety, was asleep, naked, in his bed. For although Navarro was single, he was rarely alone. He had a voracious appetite for all things carnal, and given his fortune and the handsome features that had been sculpted into his face by a very talented though sadly now deceased plastic surgeon, that appetite wasn't hard to quench.

His current playmate was the spa manager of a nearby luxury hotel who, to his great delight, had surprised him by proving to be more ravenous and adventurous in bed than he was, and as he looked out across his landscaped gardens, he craved being with her and tasting her skin between his teeth. He'd be doing that right now if it weren't for what was taking place in San Diego, events that had consumed his mind all day and still required his close attention. For although life was better than good for him, if all went according to plan—*his* plan, for Raoul Navarro wouldn't have it any other way—it was going to get a whole lot better.

Raoul Navarro usually saw his plans through.

Even after things had spiraled out of control five years ago, he was still around, living and breathing with a new name and a new face, free to come and go as he pleased, free to enjoy fine Cubans on a fine night such as this at the fine home that was his escape, an escape from the dangers of the past, an escape that had been forced upon him and that, as it turned out, was the best thing that ever happened to him.

He'd bought the dilapidated estate around two years after his supposed death, and it had then taken another two years and several million dollars to bring the seventeenth-century estate back to its former splendor. Not surprising, given how huge it was, spread out over close to fifteen thousand acres. It had originally been built as a cattle ranch, then in the eighteen hundreds it was converted into a *henequén* plantation, where its rich fields of agave cactus—the "green gold" that created immense fortunes—were farmed and turned into the sisal fiber that ropes were made of. Almost all the haciendas in the Yucatán had fallen into disrepair after the twin whammies of the land reforms of the Mexican Revolution and the invention of synthetic fibers, but after almost a century of neglect, the last few years had brought about a renewed interest in restoring these magnificent estates, with some converted into small luxury hotels, others into museums, and a select few into private domains.

The rebirth of the haciendas had coincided with his own.

Navarro loved the symmetry of it.

Standing there and basking in the serenity of his dominion, he knew he'd got it right. Given his situation and the savagery that was plaguing most of the country—a savagery in which he'd been not just a participant, but a highly innovative one at that—he'd thought about living abroad. He had the money and the squeaky-clean passport that would have allowed him to settle down anywhere, but he knew he wouldn't be happy anywhere else. It had to be Mexico. And if he was going to live in Mexico, Merida was the place to be. Nestled in the

Yucatán Peninsula on the southeastern tip of the country, the "City of Peace" was as far as one could get from the U.S. border, far from the orgies of blood the north of the country was drowning in. It was a place where the biggest concerns were aquifers that needed attention, overcrowded public schools, and a local cop who'd been bitten by a snake, and that suited the new, laundered version of him just fine.

It never failed to astound him how so many of his peers—ex-peers, really—just didn't get it. The richer and more powerful they got, the lousier their lives became. Never sleeping in the same bed on consecutive nights, changing phones every day, constantly fearful of betrayal, surrounded by an army of bodyguards. Prisoners of their own success. Before them, the Colombian drug barons had all met bloody deaths. Pablo Escobar, the granddaddy of them all, had occupied the number seven spot on the *Forbes* rich list, but he'd still lived like a rat, scurrying from one grubby hideout to another before being gunned down in a shantytown at the ripe old age of forty-four. The Mexican narcos weren't faring much better. It seemed like every week, the president's damned *federales* were claiming another big scalp—although ironically, all it did was trigger more bloodshed and mayhem as violent succession struggles and territorial grabs played themselves out. The kingpins who hadn't yet been killed or arrested were holed up in their fortresses, moving around like the fugitives they were, waiting for that unexpected bullet that would end their pointless lives.

Lesson learned.

He wasn't going to end up like them, and his life certainly wasn't going to be pointless. Not if everything went according to plan.

The plan that was currently in the thick of play.

He grinned inwardly at the thought of his fellow kingpins' miserable, pathetic lives, and it gave him even more pleasure to think that it was them who had given him the way out, that the reason he'd bailed on the narco high life in the first place was that they had come after him guns blazing, all because of his trespass, because he'd dared go after what was rightly his, even if that involved some blood-soaked face time with the sacred and untouchable *yanqui* himself, the DEA's head honcho in Mexico.

Well, El Brujo had shown them.

He'd managed to outsmart those two-faced *maricóns* and ride off into his palm-ringed sunset with three hundred million dollars of their money. In the meantime, the illiterate peasants were still busy amassing fortunes they'd never get to enjoy while slaughtering each other for the privilege. Then *la providencia* had smiled on him yet again. It had opened an unexpected door and presented him with an opportunity to finish what he'd started and claim his place in history.

It wasn't something he was going to let slip.

He checked his watch. As if on cue, his untraceable, pay-as-you-go phone buzzed.

It was Eli Walker, his man in San Diego.

"Do you have what I want?" Navarro asked.

The brief hesitation told him all he needed to know. Then came a flat and far-from-contrite "No."

Navarro said nothing.

"The woman," Walker fed into the pause, "she—"

"*Mamaguevo de mierda*," Navarro hissed. "The damn woman again? I told you about her. I told you she used to be a DEA agent. You knew she was trained."

"Yeah, but—"

"What did I tell you, after you screwed up at the house? What did I say?"

"What is this, fucking kindergarten?" Walker shot back gruffly.

"What did I say?" Navarro insisted, low and slow.

Another pause, then his contact came back, sounding annoyed and impatient. "You said not to consider her a priority anymore. You said she was expendable."

"I said kill the *puta* if you have to, but get me what I asked you for."

"And your words were heeded, *amigo*," Walker replied. "In fact, we're pretty sure the bitch took a round in the chest."

Navarro felt a slight ruffle at the American's use of the Spanish word. It wasn't so much the word itself as the way he said it, which had a condescending, racist tinge to it. "So what's the problem?"

"She had someone helping her. Some guy she called after she got away from us at the house."

"She called someone?"

"Yes. After we last spoke."

Intriguing.

"Who?"

"I don't know yet. All I know is, she called him Sean."

Navarro's pulse flared.

"It seems he's the kid's dad," Walker added, his words bathed in mocking contempt. "Something that asshole didn't know, not until now."

The flare went red-hot, igniting every nerve ending in Navarro's body.

Sean Reilly, he thought. *He didn't know.*

He kept his tone measured. "What else? What else did they say?"

"He gave her some instructions, to avoid detection. I'm thinking he's a cop, or maybe another DEA agent."

Navarro didn't bother correcting him. "And what else?"

"He said he was flying out here to meet her."

Navarro felt light-headed.

Perfect.

He'd probably experienced a wider variety of highs and hallucinogenic trips than anyone on the planet, and yet, right now—this was right up there with the best of them.

"So he was with her? When you found her, he was with them?"

"Yep. It took us some time to track her down, and he was already with her by then. And this guy turned out to be a serious pain in the ass. I lost another one of my boys."

Navarro didn't bother inquiring about that. His mind was busy

elsewhere, processing the update and strategizing his next move, doing what it did best when it wasn't busy figuring out new ways of
inflicting pain to put down any challenges to his little world.

"Well, I'm afraid your task just got significantly more . . . challenging, *amigo*," he finally told his contact. "The man's name is Sean
Reilly. He's an FBI agent. And I'd really like to meet him."

"Whoa whoa whoa, back up there. The guy's FBI?"

"Yes."

The man blew out a small whistle, then said, "That wasn't part of
our deal."

Hijo de puta, Navarro thought. Here it comes. "You want more
money, is that it?"

"No, I'm just not sure I want any of this," Walker snapped testily.
"Some broad and a kid, that's one thing. This guy . . . you're talking
about a whole different ball game. FBI, ATF—last thing I need is
those guys crawling up my ass. Especially when I don't know what
the whole story is."

Navarro fumed inwardly. "I thought you were someone I could
rely on to get the job done."

"Yeah, well, what can I tell ya? There's jobs and there's jobs. Thing
is, you start getting up close and personal with our *federales*, and
things get real messy real quick."

Something Navarro knew well, from personal experience.

He ruminated over it for a long second and realized he might have
to get his hands dirtier than he'd expected.

"Where are they now?"

"I don't know. We lost them after the hotel. We've got the scan-
ners on and me and the boys were gonna recon some local ERs, but
now I'm thinking maybe it's time to pull the plug on this mother and
call it a day. If she dies, this is gonna get red-hot. So maybe this is a
good time for us to say *vaya con dios*, you know what I'm saying? And
maybe we can do business some other time—like when it doesn't
involve a fucking fed and his family."

Navarro kept his fury bottled. He tried to remind himself that

Walker wasn't a useless worm. Navarro had hired him and his men on a handful of previous occasions, years back when he was still Navarro as well as more recently, in his new guise as Nacho, one of Navarro's lieutenants "from the old days." The American had always come through. Navarro needed to keep him on track just a little longer—at least, until he could take over himself, which he now realized he'd need to do.

"All right, you want to pull out, I understand. But I still have the second half of your payment, which I'm sure you'd like to collect."

"And I have a package here I'm sure you'd also like to collect, *amigo*. Am I right?"

Navarro bristled at the man's insolence, but Walker was right. He had something Navarro wanted, something he wanted badly. "Agreed. How about this then? Do one last little thing for me, and you'll get paid in full."

The man didn't take too long ruminating over it. "What?"

"Just find them. Find out what happened to the woman, and find Reilly. I don't need you to do anything more than that. Just find them and tell me where they are. I'll take care of the rest. Do we have a deal?"

Walker demurred for a moment, then said, "Fine. I'll have a lock on their location by tomorrow night."

SUNDAY

13

The pickup was, well, awkward.

Tess's plane landed pretty much on time, and I was there waiting for her after leaving Alex with Jules, who turned out to have the gentlest of manners with him, no doubt aided by a smile that should be designated as a global warming hazard, and spending most of the morning at SDPD's shiny headquarters on Broadway, going through their mug shot database and working with a police sketch artist to come up some visual cues to put out there. Tess was one of the first off the plane, walking briskly and trailing a small roll-on, and although she looked like a summer breeze on legs in her light linen dress and with her bouncy hair, it only took our eyes to meet for me to see the tense undercurrent that was bubbling underneath.

We hugged and kissed quite perfunctorily, like a couple whose marriage had passed its sell-by date. We limited ourselves to some superficial chit-chat about Nevada and the flight as we made our way out of the terminal, where I got hit by a combo of the furnace-blast midday heat and the memory punch of, yet again, treading the same sidewalk Michelle had died on less than twenty-four hours earlier.

It was all still too raw for me. I'm pretty sure Tess caught the look on my face as I glanced at the pavement, but she didn't ask about it and just stayed with me as I led her to the parking lot. The bureau had arranged a loaner for me to drive around in, a Buick LaCrosse that, if you could overlook its unfortunate name with its oh-so-idiosyncratic capital C, was a pretty decent car.

I was stowing Tess's bag into its trunk when I felt her hand on my arm.

"I'm really sorry for your loss, Sean."

Her hand slid up my arm and guided me around to face her. I pulled her close and kissed her, a sudden, deep, starved kiss that just as quickly felt a bit weird to me. I found myself pulling away gently and hugged her instead, avoiding her eyes and cradling her head against my shoulder. We stood there like that for a long moment, without saying anything, then I finally said, "I'm really glad you're here."

"Wouldn't have it any other way," she half-smiled.

I gave her another kiss, still too brief, and we were on our way.

She asked me about Alex, about how he was doing. The kid was in bad shape. He'd spent the night next to Jules, waking up intermittently with night terrors every couple of hours, one of which had caused him to wet himself. Much as I was desperate to be with him and help him through this, I could still see his discomfort every time I tried to get close to him, and I'd decided to pull back and let Jules comfort him as best she could.

The Hilton was easy to get to, perched conveniently at the crossroads of the Cabrillo and Mission Valley freeways. We walked past families with excited kids running around with SeaWorld caps and T-shirts and small huddles of conventioneers trying to look like they were happy to be there and made our way to the one-bedroom top-floor suite and the additional connecting bedroom that Villaverde's people had booked us into.

Alex was huddled in front of the TV in the living room, with Jules sitting next to him and being as attentive as ever. I wasn't sure how Alex would take to Tess—yet another new face butting into his life at a time when the only one he wanted to see was his mother's, but it all went down better than I expected. For her, anyway. Me, I was still on his boogeyman list.

Tess spotted it instantly.

After a moment, she turned to me and, out of Alex's earshot, whispered, "He really does seem scared of you."

I nodded ruefully. "I told you. It's really frustrating. I don't know how to get him past it."

She reached out for my forearm. "He just needs time. You were there when she died. He associates you with what happened to her."

"Yeah, but this is something else . . . it started before."

Tess's face scrunched up with confusion, then she turned to look at Alex.

"Why don't we get him out of this room? Take him out somewhere nice, give him something to smile about." She didn't wait for an answer and went up to Alex. She kneeled down so her face was level with his.

"How about that, Alex?" she asked him. "Would you like to go out and get some pizza or something? What's your favorite food? Anywhere you like, just say the word."

It didn't take long for Alex to succumb to her charms, and she coaxed the first quasi-smile I'd seen out of him when she said the Cheesecake Factory was her favorite, too. I watched from a distance as they debated the relative awesomeness of Key lime versus Oreo, but then the glowing kindling in my stomach got snuffed out when Alex asked the killer question he'd asked so many times before.

"What about my mama? Is she going to come with us?"

Tess glanced at me, then turned to Alex, reached out and held his hand, and said, "No, sweetheart, I'm afraid your mommy won't be coming with us."

"Why not?" Alex asked. "Where is she?"

Tess hesitated, then I saw her take in a deep breath and she said the words. "She's in heaven, sweetheart."

I felt my chest wall cave in.

The three of us ended up taking Alex to SeaWorld after that heart-wrenching chat, and throughout it all, Tess was nothing less than remarkable. She'd even managed to get him to eat something, which was more than Jules or I had managed. Alex was still clearly wary of me, avoiding eye contact and using Tess as a buffer between me and him. I decided the best I could do was to give him some space and let Tess keep on working her magic. We had a whole life ahead of us to work things out.

We got back to the hotel at about six, and Tess went off to try to put Alex to bed. Our setup was a one-bedroom suite, which had a separate living room, and an additional bedroom connecting to it. I went down to the bar and got myself a beer. I was feeling real antsy. A whole day had passed and I'd done nothing to try to get to the bottom of what happened to Michelle beyond streaming through a few hundred cold, troubled, or just plain vacant stares. I wasn't used to being this passive, and it was killing me. Problem was, it was now Sunday evening, and I was kind of helpless, waiting for Villaverde to come back with news from the tech guys or from the homicide detectives who were investigating the shootings. I was also aware of the need to make sure Alex was being looked after, and having Tess around had certainly helped make him feel better.

Still, I needed to do something. But I was drawing a blank at what I actually could do.

I was debating whether or not to order another beer when Tess showed up and slid onto the stool next to mine.

"You come here often?" she asked, a tired smile struggling to break out.

I managed a brief smile back. "My girlfriend's in our room. We'll have to use yours."

She raised an eyebrow and said, "You know what? That line came to you way too easily." Her eyes lingered on me for a mock-scrutinizing couple of seconds, then she turned to the barman and used her fingers to indicate we needed two more bottles.

"Is he asleep?"

Tess nodded. "Jules is with him. She's great, by the way. A real find. You were lucky to have her here."

I shrugged and stared away into nothing. "Yeah, it's been a lucky weekend all around."

She moved in closer and ran her hand through the hair at the back of my head. "You okay, baby?"

I wasn't sure what I was feeling. I stayed silent for a moment, just staring at the monster collection of bottles behind the bar. "It's weird," I finally said. "I haven't thought about her for years. I mean, literally. And then she calls up and . . ." I turned to face Tess. "She's gone, and I have a son. Just like that."

"I know," she just said, the strokes of her hand tightening somewhat. "It's horrible, what happened to her. It's beyond horrible. And yet . . . you have a beautiful baby boy, Sean."

I heard a crack in her voice and saw her eyes glisten. She blinked away a tear, and I couldn't help but reach out, right there at the bar, and pull her close, and kiss her. We stayed like that for a long moment, then I just kept her right up against me, feeling her breathing against my ear and the flutter of her eyelashes against my cheek.

"You gonna be okay with that?" I mumbled.

"More than okay, baby," she whispered back. "More than okay."

We stayed like that for a few minutes, just breathing each other in and finding our compasses again, then I gave her another kiss and edged back. I raised my bottle in a silent toast. Tess met my eye and, softly, clinked her bottle against mine. We each took a long swig.

"I spoke to Stacey this morning. You remember Stacey Ross?"

The name rang a bell, then it came back to me. Stacey was a psychiatrist who specialized in treating kids. The two of them had become friends when Stacey was treating Tess's daughter, Kim, after they had both got caught up in the bloodbath at the Met the night we first met. Kim was nine at the time, and Stacey had really helped her work through the emotional fallout from that night.

"She gave me a few pointers. For Alex."

"What'd she say?"

"She said he'll go through the five stages, same as an adult would. You know . . . denial, anger, bargaining, depression, acceptance. But she also said boys and girls deal with these things differently. He's likely to be more locked in than a girl would be in his situation. And it might set back his maturity a bit. That's what we'll need to help him with. Talking things out and not keeping it all in. But we'll get him through this," she insisted, a film of moisture making her eyes glisten again. "We'll get him through. And she's there if we need her."

I nodded as she took another swig, and I could tell that this was hard on her. We'd talked about her fears in the past, about how the thought of something bad happening to her and leaving Kim behind terrified her—it was a major factor in her turning to writing her novels and trying to leave the call of the wild behind.

"What else did she say, in terms of right now?"

"Well, he'll cry a lot, obviously. He'll be prone to waking at odd hours and he'll sleep intermittently. Maybe some bedwetting. Beyond that, she said we shouldn't lie, which is why I talked to him about heaven. He needs to believe that she's happy, that she's fine, even if she can't be here with him. She also said we needed to give him as much continuity as possible. I imagine going back to Michelle's house is off-limits for him."

I nodded.

"And it wouldn't be great for him anyway, without her there. But he needs some favorite things around him, wherever he is. Transitional objects, she called them. Toys, maybe his pillow or his blanket. His favorite drinking cup. That kind of thing. Maybe even Michelle's nightgown or something that smells of her. Would that be okay with you? I could ask Alex about what he's missing and go there tomorrow and get them for him."

Michelle's house was still a crime scene, and I wasn't too thrilled about having Tess go there, but I could see the need for it. "Sure. I'll take you there tomorrow."

"Great. Also, do you know if any of Michelle's close relatives are around, people Alex was comfortable around? Her mom maybe, or a sister?"

I told Tess the little I knew about Michelle's family, and said I'd find out what I could in the morning. She drew in again and kissed me, then kept her hand cupped on my cheek. "We're going to help him get happy again, Sean. I promise you that."

I gave her a small nod and a smile, and she squeezed my arm before heading back up to check on Alex. I stayed there alone, nursing another beer and spiraling back into my darkest thoughts, until my cell rang.

It was the cavalry.

Not only that, but Villaverde sounded upbeat.

He asked about Alex, but there was nothing much to say on that front. I knew it would be a while before I'd ever be able to answer that question with a cheerful and casual, "He's fine." Then he got to the reason for his call.

"Ballistics came back with a match for the nine-mil Michelle took off the shooters. You remember that armed double-kidnap up at that research center near Santa Barbara, about six months ago?"

My mind flashed to vague snippets from the news footage. "Some kind of medical facility, right?"

"That's the one. The Schultes Institute. Anyway, we got a match. Your shooter was one of the crew that did the hit."

This was solid.

I remembered that, apart from the missing scientists, people had died that day. "Was the match from a kill shot?"

"Yep," Villaverde confirmed. "A security guard. It also matches the slug from Michelle's boyfriend."

I got a small uplift from the fact that Michelle had, most likely by her account, not just taken out the guy who'd shot Tom, but that he'd also killed before. It wasn't going to bring her back, but right now, I was happy to grab any satisfaction I could get hold of, no matter how small.

"But that one's still unsolved, right?" I asked.

"I'm waiting for some callbacks, but as far as I know, it's cold."

"Whose case is it?"

"It's joint DEA-FBI."

"LA offices?"

"Yep."

I frowned. The inevitable beckoned. "I guess we're definitely going to need to talk to my good old buddy Hank Corliss."

"Yep," Villaverde repeated. "I already put a call in. We're seeing him in the morning."

14

≈

Less than three miles north of the hotel, a chartered Embraer Legacy private jet was touching down at Montgomery Field. It had taken off a little less than five hours earlier from Merida International Airport in the Yucatán and was carrying four passengers, all male.

The lone customs agent who boarded the small aircraft verified the passengers' identities and cleared them for immigration in under two minutes.

He had no reason to subject them to any further scrutiny. The charter company was one of the most reputable around, and he'd met the crew on several previous occasions. The passengers, all Mexican, were well groomed, smartly dressed, and soft spoken. The plane's paperwork was impeccable, and the men's passports bore the stamps of several European countries, as well as a few in the Far East. It all reeked of quality and, more importantly, had that intangible, disarming aura of integrity.

Shortly after the customs agent's departure, the four men disembarked and got into two chauffeured Lincoln Town Cars that had already been there long before the plane landed. Comfortable beds were waiting for them in a luxury six-bedroom oceanside villa that had been rented for them on a quiet street in Del Mar.

They would need a good night's sleep.

They had a lot of work ahead of them.

MONDAY

15

I left Tess, Alex, and Jules at the hotel and went to meet Villaverde at his office. Our sit-down with Corliss was set for ten thirty, allowing us to dodge Los Angeles's brutal morning rush hour traffic and giving us a chance to sample its delightful mid-morning snarl-ups instead. Tess was eager to go to Michelle's house and collect the stuff that her friend had recommended to give Alex a measure of comfort, and Villaverde had arranged to have an SDPD squad car drive her to the house while we were away and watch over her while she did her thing.

The first half of the drive was easy enough, a straight run up the interstate with the sun at our backs and nothing but the ocean to our left and sand dunes and rolling hills to our right for a good chunk of an hour. Then we hit San Clemente and its pastoral settings helped ease us into the less attractive aspects of human colonization and the chaotic asphalt cauldron that was downtown LA.

We drove past the building and turned in to take the ramp that led down to the underground parking. Outside the building's entrance were four huge fifty-foot metallic sculptures, flat cutouts of male figures leaning into each other like they were in a huddle. They were pockmarked with hundreds of small round holes and looked like they'd been shot up by a crazed army of gangbangers. I wasn't sure that was the best imagery to have outside a federal building, but then again, I never claimed to get modern art, and the symbolism that eluded me was probably much deeper and more sophisticated than anything I could hope to grasp.

We went up to the twentieth floor and were ushered into Corliss's office, and I got two small shocks.

The first was seeing Corliss after all those years. I knew what he'd been through, of course—it had happened after I'd left Mexico, but it was big news at the bureau back then, in all of its gory detail—yet I was still surprised by how much he'd aged. Not so much aged as worn out. The Hank Corliss I knew back in the day was a tough, hard-headed, and generally unpleasant sonofabitch with a crafty set of neurons firing away behind a pair of vigorous eyes that didn't miss a trick. The guy who greeted us from behind his desk was an antique-mirror reflection of the guy I remembered. His face was gaunt, his skin was lined and ashen, and he had black bunkers under his eyes. He moved with a slow step, and my grandmother, in her eighth decade, had a handshake with more of a kick to it.

The second was seeing Jesse Munro there with him. Two blasts from the past, two revenants from an unpleasant chapter of my life. Munro, however, hadn't aged a day. Hell, I knew he spent enough time at the gym looking after his finely preened image to make sure of that. He was pretty much as I remembered him. Thick blond hair gelled straight back, deeply tanned, unbuttoned shirt over a deep-V-necked white T-shirt that showed off his upper pecs, bright solid-gold chain. And that cocky, shit-eating grin, of course, that was never too far from the surface.

Corliss motioned us all into a seating area across from his desk.

"So," he said as he scrutinized me like I was there for a job interview, "I hear you're doing some good work out in New York. Looks like the move back there sure did you a world of good, didn't it?"

The wry smile that flitted across his lips confirmed the subtext in his words, not that I thought for a second that he'd forgotten the heated exchanges we'd had in Mexico. At the time, I was livid at myself at having killed—executed—an unarmed American citizen, Wade McKinnon, whom I knew little about beyond that he was a chemistry whiz who had developed some kind of superdrug for a narco named Navarro. Munro was with me on that ill-fated mission, and he'd done even worse things that night—things no one should be allowed to walk away from. And whereas Munro didn't seem to have qualms about it after we got back, I had a lot of trouble dealing with what I'd done. It kept gnawing away at me until it got to a point where I felt I had to do something to make amends—see if I could find any relatives of McKinnon's, let them know what had happened, come clean, get some kind of absolution or face whatever punishment I was due. Corliss and the rest of the suits, on the other hand, had no such misgivings and couldn't give a rat's ass about my inner demons. Most of all, they didn't want me out there blabbing about it either. So they dangled a carrot for me—a transfer to the New York City field office with a primo seat at the antiterrorist desk, a trophy position they knew might hit the spot. After endless deliberations and torturing myself over it for days, I'd ended up taking the carrot—not my proudest moment, I admit—and here we were, five years later, with the ghost of Corliss past looking all smug about it.

Anyway, I was going to answer that it did us both a lot of good, but given what he went through after I left, that would have been a seriously uncool thing to say. Instead, I went with a middle-ground peace offering.

"It's been a real hoot."

He watched me, like he was unsure about how to respond to that, then adjusted his seating position and got down to it.

"I'm very sorry to hear about Martinez. She did some good work for us, even if her leaving the agency was a bit, um, abrupt." He looked at me as he said it, like I had something to do with it. Which, as it turned out, I did, though I was pretty sure he didn't know about that. I mean, he knew we were seeing each other—it wasn't exactly a secret—but Michelle had told me that she hadn't made her pregnancy public knowledge within the agency. "Tell me how we can help."

He and Munro listened attentively as I took them through what I knew, then Villaverde filled them in on the ballistics match, which they were already aware of and was the part of the story that piqued

Corliss's interest, given that it was a live lead into a dead investigation of his.

"So," he said when we were done, "you got any other handles on the crew?"

"Not yet," Villaverde said. "That's why we're here."

Corliss pursed his lips and spread his palms out. "Hey, I was hoping you were coming here with something more for me, something that'd help us nail these fuckers."

"Right now, that's all we've got."

Corliss frowned. "Well that makes two of us then. We hit a wall on our end. These guys showed up, did their business, and got away clean. They had face masks. The cars they used were stolen, we found them wiped clean and burnt to a crisp. Ballistics and CCTV footage didn't get us anywhere either. No word on the street, no jackass shooting his mouth off in some bar, nothing. And six months later, it's all gone beyond cold."

I'd been hoping for something, anything, but not this. I glanced over at Munro and back at Corliss. "That's it?" I asked.

"That's it." His features sagged with a distant, dejected finality. "Look, what can I tell you? You think I'm happy about that? It's a goddamn embarrassment. I've had so much heat over this thing, I had the governor barking down my phone so bad I could smell his cigar breath through the handset. I didn't mind. I was just as pissed off as he was. I wanted to fry those sons of bitches, but they didn't leave us much to work with."

The room went silent for a moment while we digested the downer, then Villaverde asked, "What about the line of inquiry into them being three-patchers?" He was referring to members of outlaw motorcycle gangs and the three patches—the two rockers with the name of the club and its location, and the central patch with its logo—that they wear on the backs of their jackets and cut-offs. "Where are you at with that?"

Villaverde and I had talked about that on the drive up. He'd told me about the "biker types" reference from one of the survivors of the raid at the institute, and the comment didn't sit too badly with what I'd seen either. The crew that had come after Michelle at the hotel were hard-asses with alcohol-and-dope-corroded faces who could well have been bikers, but it was hard to tell given that they weren't wearing their colors, and too much of them was covered up to expose any telltale gang ink, biker or otherwise. Outlaw gangs, though, were acting more and more as enforcers for the cartels north of the border, that much we knew. It wasn't a stretch to imagine that if some narco from Michelle's past wanted to get to her for some reason, like recovering money she'd helped confiscate or just plain revenge, using a biker gang was an easy option. Villaverde and I had agreed that I needed to spend some more time going through some mug shots, with a more focused range this time. The ATF—the Bureau of Alcohol, Tobacco, Firearms and Explosives—were the experts on the bikers, and Villaverde had already put in a call to his contact there to get some sheets readied up for me to look at.

"We're chasing it up," Munro told us. "We're still leaning on every lowlife on our books and working it with ATF, but it's like getting blood from a stone. These gangs, they're all very tight-knit. The only time those dickwads let anything slip is to mess us around and screw with our heads by putting out rumors that it's the dirty work of some rival. So you've got the Desperados saying it's the Huns, the Huns saying it's the Sons of Azazel, the Sons of Azazel saying it's the Aztecas. It's a fucking nightmare. The only way to get any kind of traction is to have someone in there undercover, and that takes time. Besides, we don't even know what gang, let alone what chapter, we're talking about."

"What about the cartels?" I asked. "Any luck working it the other way around, from the top down?"

Corliss chortled. "Good luck with that. Our friends from the south have an even more rigid code of silence."

"But if they are bikers, you still think they were hired muscle and not end users," I pressed.

"My read? Yes. Absolutely." Corliss hunched forward. He gestured at Villaverde and said, "We've all had great success in shutting down plenty of local meth labs, but you know as well as I do that all it's done is move the production part of the equation south of the border. And that's where these white coats are needed. Not here. Our narco friends down there, they're now running superlabs where each one of them's churning out three, four hundred pounds of meth a day. *A day.* That's a lot of product, and it has to be done right. So when they get their hands on some hotshot chemist who can streamline their processes and give them a better quality product without blowing up their labs, they're not letting him go."

I felt like I was still missing a big piece of the puzzle. "I still don't get what any of this could possibly have to do with Michelle. It's been five years."

"Who knows," Corliss said, brushing it off casually, his tone growing weary. "She worked the cartel money trails. She caused some bad guys a lot of pain by taking away their toys and wiping out their bank accounts. Maybe one of them wanted some payback. These guys . . . they go to prison for a while, then they bribe or shoot their way out, they move around and stay under the radar . . . Maybe it took this long for one of them to track her down. Especially since she worked undercover."

It didn't sit straight with me, but right now, I didn't have much else to go on.

"They did take her laptop," Villaverde offered, giving me a sideways glance as if reinforcing Corliss's point. "Maybe they're looking for a way to reverse a trade? Get her to make some transfers their way?"

Corliss didn't take too long to chew on it—a dubious eyebrow spiked upward as soon as Villaverde mentioned it.

I tensed up, knowing where this was heading.

"Her laptop?" Corliss asked.

Villaverde nodded.

Corliss shrugged, not saying it but signaling it clearly enough with a wry, skeptical expression.

"What?" I pressed.

"Well, she took away a lot of money from some of these guys," he said, his mouth bent downward like he'd just sniffed some sour milk. "Maybe she kept some of it for herself. It sure as hell wouldn't be the first time that happened."

I felt my face flame up. "Michelle was clean," I said in no uncertain terms.

"And you know that because you two had a fling?"

"She was clean," I insisted.

"She's a trained undercover agent, remember? She knows how to keep secrets. Even from whoever's sharing her bed."

I saw the look he and Munro exchanged and could feel the veins in my neck go rock hard. I had to fight to keep myself under control. Michelle wasn't even in the ground yet and this damaged, bitter prick was already soiling her memory.

I flicked a glare across at Villaverde and back at Corliss. "She was straight. One hundred percent. No question."

I waited to let the words sink in, ready to pounce on any retort from any of them, but none came. Corliss just held my gaze with his tired, vacant eyes, then shrugged, the edges of his mouth still sagging dismissively.

"Maybe she was," he said. "Either way . . . it's something that needs to be looked into. It could lead us to our shooters."

I didn't like the suspicion hanging there, but nothing I could say was going to change that. But there was something I could throw back at him. "If it's about narcos tracking her down, you've got a leak in here. It's the only way they could have found her."

Corliss wasn't moved. "Big fucking surprise. You know how much time and resources we spend trying to keep our house clean? It's a constant battle."

"Was there anyone in particular that you can think of who'd be looking to get back at her?" Villaverde asked Corliss, adroitly moving on. "Anyone with a vendetta that was so strong it could resurface after so long?"

"A couple," Corliss replied. "No one likes being taken for a ride, especially not by a woman." He looked like he was running a list of possibilities in his mind for a second, and Munro chimed in.

"I'll need to look into her case history, but the last case she worked was a big one. Carlos Guzman. She did him some serious damage. Almost half a billion's worth. And as you know, he's still out there." Munro shrugged. "Probably richer than ever."

Villaverde and I exchanged glances. Neither of us had anything else to add. It looked like we weren't going to get much more from them either when Corliss turned to me and asked, "Why'd she call you? I mean, after all this time, why you?"

Given what Corliss had floated about Michelle possibly being dirty, I didn't feel like bringing up the fact that we'd had a kid together, not to him.

"She was scared and didn't know which way to turn," I replied. "And maybe she still believed in something old-fashioned called trust."

He blew out a long, rueful hiss, then nodded, slowly. "Trust, huh?" He paused, then his expression clouded and he seemed to travel to somewhere far and dark.

"My wife trusted me when I told her my work would never put her or our daughter in harm's way," he said, then his distant gaze racked focus and settled on me. "Didn't work out too well for either one of them, did it?"

There wasn't much to say after that.

16

❧

Tess felt uneasy as she crossed the threshold and stepped into Michelle's house.

She'd left Alex with Jules at the hotel, happily drawing at the small dining table in the suite's living room. Since Reilly needed to drive up to LA, he'd arranged to have a couple of PD guys escort her over.

It felt weird being there. On several fronts. It was weird being in the empty house of someone who'd just been murdered. That was a first for Tess, and it weighed heavily on her, with every hesitant step. It was also weird being at the home of Reilly's ex-lover, the home of the mother of his son. Tess felt like she was intruding, like she was some kind of parasite picking at the carcass of the newly departed. It was nonsense, of course—Tess tried to remind herself that, really, Michelle would probably be nothing if not grateful that she was opening her heart to Alex. But the discomfort was hard to shake.

She didn't plan on sticking around too long. She would just get what she thought would help Alex, then she'd be out of there.

She felt a shortness of breath as she stepped around the blood-stained floor and made her way into the living room, where some picture frames on a shelf drew her eye. She approached them almost solemnly and picked up a photograph of Alex and a brunette she knew had to be Michelle, given that she was also in several of the other pictures. It was the first time she saw what Michelle looked like. She was more than attractive. There was something highly appealing about her, a magnetism that shone through her eyes and jumped off the prints. Seeing her brought up another knot of conflicting emotions within Tess, a deep, heartfelt sadness and an empathy corrupted by a touch of jealousy.

She chose two frames that showed Alex and Michelle beaming with great smiles and slipped them carefully into one of the hotel laundry bags she'd brought with her. She knew it would be good for Alex to have them around. Then she advanced slowly through the house, trying to get some kind of idea of what Michelle was like and what Alex's life there was like. She checked out the kitchen and scrutinized Alex's drawings on the walls and the mosaic of postings on the fridge door, even looking inside the fridge to see what kind of things Michelle stocked, what Alex was used to.

As the fridge closed, she glanced out the French doors into the backyard, where something snagged her attention. Small patches of color, on the lawn. Alex's toys. She went outside, and a bittersweet smile dimpled her cheeks. The small, four-inch Ben 10 figurines Alex had asked her for were all lying there, untouched. She knew they were them, as Alex had shown her the images he called up on the tiny screen of his Omnitrix wristband, and she'd also done a web search and had Alex point them out to her online. Tess visualized Alex playing with them when the intruders had burst in, and felt a pang as she pictured Michelle and Alex running frantically, trying to escape. She shook the image away and picked up the toys, then went back inside.

She checked out Michelle's bedroom, then her study, where she found herself looking around the bookshelves, inspecting their contents to try to form a mental picture of what Michelle was like, what interested her. She had a lot of work ahead of her. If Alex was now part of her life, Tess knew that she owed it to him to try to get to know as much about his mother as she could. She would need to find ways of doing that, but a start would be spending more time going through her things and talking to her friends and family.

Not yet, though. It was all too soon for that.

Her eyes drifted across to Michelle's desk, where Reilly had told her the missing laptop had probably sat. The desk was fairly tidy, with a couple of stacks of papers and bills arranged on either side of the empty, central space. She was about to step away when she noticed a drawing sticking out of one of the piles. She moved the other papers off it and found a small stack of drawings, more of Alex's works, four of them.

Tess studied them curiously, trying to figure out what they depicted.

The first one showed some kind of tribal setting, with dark-skinned figures and huts and lush greenery around them under bright blue skies. The second was of another dark-haired figure surrounded by what looked like cacti that had red flowers sprouting out of them. The third was of a figure walking on ground that was bright orange, like it was on fire.

The fourth one showed two figures, one on either side of the sheet, drawn in the comedically surreal style young children had: an elongated, jelly-bean-like shape for a torso, sticks for arms and legs, circles for hands and feet, short stick-like lines for fingers and toes. She smiled and was about to put it down when something about it kept her from doing that. One of the figures, the one on the left, seemed to be holding something, aiming it at the one on the right. It was barely recognizable, but it read like a gun. The figure's torso had been colored in darkly. The figure on the right, though, was what had caught her eye. It was smaller and had brown hair, wide eyes, and a big, open mouth, like it was shouting. It was also holding something in its hand: something that looked like a tiny stick figure. Tess pulled the drawing into the light for a clearer view. The figure had a squiggle that looked like a depiction of brown hair, and green over its legs.

Something about the image seemed oddly familiar, while the overall effect was, for some reason, unsettling. Then she understood. With the drawing in hand, she went back into the hall, found the bag she'd put the toys in, and rummaged through it before pulling out the figurine of Ben himself. He was a young teen with brown hair and wore a white shirt and oversize green cargo pants. Tess eyed the drawing again and felt pretty sure that the object in the hand of the figure on the right was the Ben figurine. Which meant the person holding it had to be Alex.

But if that was the case, had he also drawn a larger, dark-clothed figure holding what could be a gun at him?

Tess felt a prickle of concern as her imagination shot off in all kinds of directions, then she forced herself to stop and brushed the thought away, chiding herself for letting the setting and the circumstances of her being there get the better of her. He was a kid, and kids played with toy guns. She was reading too much into it.

She put the toy back in the bag and went about collecting the things she and Alex had talked about: more toys, his blanket, and his pajamas—Ben again, of course—some clothes, his Buzz Lightyear toothbrush, and a few picture books. She also took the four drawings with her.

Half an hour later, she was back in the police cruiser, heading back to the hotel.

17

It was around three in the afternoon by the time I left Villaverde in the parking lot outside his office on Aero Drive, got into my trusted LaCrosse, and headed downtown to look at some more tough-guy stares. Villaverde had called one of the SDPD homicide detectives from the car during our drive back from LA and given him the heads-up about what we were looking for so they'd have time to coordinate with ATF and have the database keyed in accordingly and ready for me by the time I got there.

The more I thought about it, the more I thought this could be a real opening. It felt right—these guys weren't black or Latino, and if you were looking for a crew of white bruisers in Southern California, a biker gang was a good place to start. I was starting to feel pretty good about our chances, despite the face that SoCal was rampant with one-percenters, which was what members of OMGs, to stick to the hip abbreviations—outlaw motorcycle gangs, not the more popular OMG that's usually followed by four exclamation marks or a smiley face—called themselves. Most even wore a "1%" patch on their colors. The term was supposed to refer to something some upstanding official from a national motorcycle association had once said, something about ninety-nine percent of motorcyclists being law-abiding citizens, but the association in question had long since denied anyone there ever having said that and it seemed to me that it was the outlaws themselves who had just plucked the number out of their own ass and were using it to talk up their mystique and their exclusivity. Given the swamp of mug shots I was about to trudge through, I thought that term had to be way off the mark, at least as far as Southern California is concerned.

The ride downtown looked pretty straightforward, as per Villaverde's instructions—south on the 15, then west on Route 94. I didn't even bother using the in-car GPS. The freeway was running smoothly, with sparse traffic in both lanes. Barring the unexpected, the drive didn't look like it was going to take more than half an hour.

The unexpected, though, wasn't about to give me a break on this trip.

Its latest incarnation came in the shape of a maroon sedan with two silhouettes inside that seemed to be maintaining too constant a gap behind me. Now I don't usually abuse my badged status by storming down freeways at autobahn speeds just to pick up my dry cleaning, but on this occasion I was keen to get to the mug shot gallery and see how generous a mood it was in. I was probably running fifteen miles per hour or so above the speed limit, and the car—a decade-old Japanese model, possibly a Mitsubishi, though I couldn't really tell—was keeping up with me, although holding back about five or six car lengths. The good thing about traveling at that speed is that if someone wants to follow you, they're going to have a tough time putting a small buffer of cars in between them and you, and so it was with these guys. I've had cars innocently trail in my wake before, of course, their thinking being that if there were to be a speed trap, I'd be the sacrificial lamb that would hit it first and get stopped while they'd sail on, but this didn't feel like one of those. I guess my inner goon-dar had been cranked up to eleven ever since Michelle and I walked out of that hotel room, and over the years, giving it the benefit of the doubt hadn't served me too badly.

I slid into the slow lane and eased off the gas a little, and sure enough, my two groupies suddenly didn't seem like they were in such a rush anymore and followed suit. Again, some of my harmless tailgaters tended to do the same, usually because they worried I knew something they didn't and had slowed down for a good reason. In those circumstances, though, the cars usually crept up closer to me—basic wave theory, but let's not go there right now—but in this case these guys hung back and kept the same big gap between us. Again, not conclusive, but something about these guys didn't sit well with me.

I sped up again and changed lanes, and so did they.

The goon-dar was blaring away in my ears.

I felt a small kick of excitement. If anyone was following me, it had to be the same crew, although it didn't make much sense to me why they'd be doing that. I did a quick run-through of what we knew about their actions so far. They'd grabbed a couple of scientists. They'd come after Michelle, twice. Why follow me? Michelle was dead. I wondered if they were after something she had, something they think I might be able to lead them to. They'd taken her laptop. Maybe they hadn't been able to get past its password. But then something much more likely occurred to me. Maybe they didn't know she was dead. Maybe they didn't even know that she was hit. If so, then maybe they were still trying to find her to get whatever it is they want from her. And if that was the case, then that was one way to flush them out—although if these guys were part of the original gang, which seemed to make sense, flushing them out was no longer a problem. They were right there, within reach. I just had to make sure I didn't screw up on the nabbing.

By now, I'd reached the ramp that banked off to the right and linked up to the Martin Luther King Jr. Freeway. I took it. The sedan did the same.

I stayed in the slow lane.

One guess as to what they did.

My mind raced ahead, sifting through my options. I was pretty sure they were tailing me, and if so, I wanted them. Badly. I could see two immediate problems I'd need to overcome. First off, I needed to find somewhere quiet to make my move. These guys had shown repeatedly that they didn't mind spilling innocent blood, and there was no way I was going to risk doing anything where some bystanders could get hurt. This was exacerbated by my second problem, which was that I didn't know San Diego at all, and this wasn't something my GPS was going to solve for me. It would help, though, and I jabbed it on and hit the Map button before pulling out my phone and calling Villaverde.

I kept the phone low and out of sight and put it on speakerphone just as he picked up.

"I think I've got a tail," I told him. "Two guys in a maroon sedan. I'm on 94."

Signs for the airport loomed ahead, and only stoked my anger.

"Can you get a read on their plates?" he asked.

I glanced in the mirror. "No, they're too far back."

"Okay, um," he stammered, "let me—how do you wanna play this? We can set up a roadblock and—"

"No, it'd take too long," I interjected. "I don't want to risk losing these guys or scaring them off."

"I hear you, but you can't face off with them on your own either."

"Agreed, but right now we need to figure out where I'm going."

I caught a glimpse of the road signs flying past and they confirmed what Villaverde had told me at the onset, about the freeway ending and morphing into F Street. The SDPD's headquarters was now only a few blocks away. I thought about sticking to the plan and pulling into the department's parking lot and sneaking around to surprise my guys while they waited for me to leave again, but the thought of making my move with armed backup on a crowded downtown street wasn't working for me, not with these trigger-happy cyborgs. It didn't look like I was going to have much of a choice in the matter anyway as I was about to run out of freeway. I was desperate to avoid getting into slower city streets and traffic lights—too many pedestrians and fewer options—but the only off-ramp was onto the San Diego Freeway, heading north.

I glanced at my GPS screen. The freeway ran north for a mile or so, then banked left and went west briefly, toward the airport, before turning north again. I couldn't risk taking it, not after having driven all that way south from Villaverde's office. It would make me look like I was doing a weird big loop, which might tip off my guys and make them bail. So I just sailed by the off-ramp and motored ahead.

The maroon sedan stayed with me.

"I'm about to hit F Street," I informed Villaverde, still playing out the notion of somehow faking them out and doubling back to ambush them while they waited for me to resurface. It was taking root nicely. I quickly explained my idea to him and asked him to think of somewhere away from the crowds where I could face off with them without worrying about collateral damage.

I was now on F, a wide, one-way street that cut across the downtown area east to west, and I could almost hear Villaverde's mind whirring away as he processed my request.

"There's the Coast Guard facility on Harbor Drive," he finally said. "I can call ahead and make sure the guard at the gate lets you through and get some of the guys ready to back you up."

"No. No Coast Guard or Navy, nothing like that. It might spook them." I was worried my stalkers might not want to lie in wait for me outside a military base, not in these terror-alert-heightened times, and I really didn't want to lose them. "Come on, David," I pressed him. "I'm running out of road."

"Hang on." He went silent for another moment, then said, "Okay, how about the Tenth Avenue Terminal area, down at the harbor? There's container yards and warehouses and storage tanks, that kind of thing. What do you think?"

It seemed like a decent option. "Does it make sense that I would have left the freeway where I did if I was originally going there?"

Villaverde thought about it for a second, then said, "I wouldn't have necessarily come off the fifteen, but yeah, why not? You're not way off base. Besides, you're a visitor here, you're not expected to know the ideal route to take."

I didn't like hearing that. Plus, I wasn't sure what they were thinking, or expecting. But the downtown area didn't look like it was going to offer me what I was looking for, and the harbor sounded better.

Also, Villaverde's suggestion of the gate at the Coast Guard facility gave me an idea.

"Is there a bonded warehouse facility there with a security gate?"

"Yep, I know where it is."

I glanced at the street signs on the next corner. "Okay, I'm just crossing Thirteenth. I need you to guide me to the terminal. And see if you can call the gate and let them know I'm heading their way."

Villaverde got to it and told me to take the next left. I tensed up with expectation and turned the wheel while eyeing my rearview mirror.

Sure enough, the maroon sedan turned in behind me.

18

As he sat on a tattered and cracked leather couch across a stained coffee table from Eli Walker, El Brujo felt the rumbling of an oncoming storm echoing through his veins.

He tried to stay positive as his eyes wandered around the spartan interior of the gang's clubhouse and the five other bike brothers who were sitting around the room while his ears and his mind remained locked on the phone conversation their leader, the club's president, was having. The man had, Navarro reminded himself, come through for him before. Several times, in fact. They'd done good business together years earlier—back in the days when Walker and the rest of the narco world knew him as Raoul Navarro, back when he was scheming and scything his way up the kingpin ladder of power and notoriety—and they'd done business of a different kind, also without a hitch, in the last few months. There was no reason to expect Walker to fail—again—this time, but somehow, Navarro couldn't help but feel the man was going to let him down.

The clubhouse was next door to the club's business front, the shop where Walker and his boys built, sold, and serviced motorcycles of all kinds. Navarro knew these guys had a nice little business going, what with the garage out front gleaming with rich lacquer and expensive chrome. He knew how passionate bikers felt about their rides, especially out here in California, and he knew how much some people were prepared to pay for the outrageous custom bikes people like Walker created for them. Only last week, he'd read about a Hollywood screenwriter whose stolen bike had just been recovered in the Philippines, of all places. It was worth close to a hundred thousand dollars. Navarro knew that a lot of what he saw out front were also worth big bucks, and given that the bikes' main cost component was labor and that the markups on what went into them were huge, it was an ideal setup through which Walker and his gang could launder the money the gang made from trafficking and selling drugs and guns and the rest of their illegal enterprises.

The clubhouse itself was not to Navarro's liking. It reeked of cheapness, what with all the mismatched furniture and tattered walls, to say nothing of the overflowing ashtrays and the stink of stale beer. It was the first time he'd actually been there—Navarro had steered clear of the United States until his rebirth—and he found it odd that for people who were clearly generating a serious amount of cash, Walker and his gang were living like slobs. Navarro understood that it was part of who these guys were, part of their ethos, of the only life they knew, but it was the opposite of what he was used to, the *banditos* back home who sought to surround themselves with luxury and project wealth and status as soon as they could afford it—wealth that they inevitably lost, wealth that possibly contributed to their downfall. Maybe these guys had it right, living less ostentatiously. Maybe it kept them off the ATF's radar. Either way, it didn't matter, he thought. Not if they can deliver what he needed from them.

He'd know soon enough.

He glanced at Walker and saw the big man grunt into his phone, and their eyes met. Walker's expression was still locked somewhere between stone-faced and grave as he fingered his furry goatee with his meaty, calloused fingers and gave Navarro a slight nod of reassurance. Navarro returned the nod, cool and supportive, but in truth, he'd already lost a big chunk of whatever respect he'd ever had for the biker's abilities from the moment Walker hadn't recognized him when he'd shown up there with his two aides in tow. Navarro was fully aware that this was an unfair judgment on the big man. The plastic surgeon had done such a great job on Navarro's face that the narco's own mother, had she ever stuck around to see her son after giving birth to him, wouldn't have recognized him. No one did, which was the whole point of going through the long and painful process in the first place. Still, in some perverse way, he'd expected more from Walker. He'd wanted him to recognize him. That would have been a strong testimony to the sharpness of the man's mind. But Walker, like the handful of people from Navarro's past that he'd shown himself to, hadn't caught on to the deception, and given that his stock had been plummeting ever since that first failure at the woman's house, it didn't bode well for the biker.

Navarro hoped the big man wouldn't sink any further.

"All right, good work," he heard Walker say. "Stay on his ass and keep me posted."

Walker hung up and looked across at him.

Navarro met his gaze with a raised eyebrow, inviting an update.

"My guys are on your fed's tail," he informed him. "He's driving into the city."

Navarro nodded his approval, slow and thoughtful, then just said, "*Muy bien.*"

19

Villaverde's directions were flawless, and it wasn't long before I reached the huge marine terminal complex and spotted the gate to the bonded warehouse.

"I'm here," I told him, still on my BlackBerry's speakerphone.

"Okay, you're all set."

There were few cars around and zero pedestrians, which was what I was hoping for. I put my turn signal on early intentionally in order to see how the goons in the maroon sedan would react. They receded in my mirror as they slowed right down to give me some space to let a container truck pass before I could turn in to the storage facility's entrance, which was across the street from us. As I did, I watched them pull up to the far curb and stop.

It looked like they were going to wait for me. Which meant they needed me to lead them to something. It had to be Michelle. They were definitely still after her.

As I waited for the truck to pass, I scanned the facility's outer perimeter. There was an eight-foot-high chain-link fence around its frontage that wouldn't be too hard to climb over. I pulled up to the gatehouse and rolled my window down as the security guard lumbered out to meet me. I knew his name was Terry since, moments earlier, I'd listened in to Villaverde on the phone with him. Terry was in his fifties and wasn't the fittest or the most nimble guy I'd ever seen—the term *mammoth* did spring to mind—and it was just as well I hadn't been counting on his being my wingman during my planned sneak and grab.

"Terry, right?" I showed him my creds, both as a matter of procedure and for the benefit of the watchful eyes up the street. I saw his expression go a bit jittery and quickly added, "Keep your eyes on me and act natural, okay? Just make like you're asking me what this is all about before you let me in."

"Okay." His eyes were throbbing with tension and he was visibly having a tough time resisting taking a peek over the roof of the La-Crosse to check out the bad guys.

"Stay with me, Terry," I reminded him, slow and calm. "Just keep your focus on me and answer my questions without looking their way."

"I'm sorry," he said. "Okay, um—so, what do you want to know?" An Oscar was definitely not in Terry's future.

I gave the place a quick sweep and settled on a warehouse to my right. I indicated it with a discreet nod. "I need to leave my car behind that building over there so it'll be out of sight while I go over the fence and sneak up on the guys who were following me. Okay?"

He took a second to calm his nerves, then said, "Sure thing."

I figured this was enough of a show for my stalkers. "Good." I flicked a glance at the holstered automatic almost buried under his paunch. "I'm assuming you know how to use that."

He grinned, and his hand dropped down to give its grip a small pat. "You bet your ass."

The *bet your ass* was a bit too gung-ho for my liking, but better that than having him go all wobbly-kneed on me if things went sour. "Well, backup's on its way, so don't you go and play hero or anything. Just stay sharp, all right?"

His jowls sagged with disappointment at that, and he gave me a glum, "I hear you."

"And don't look at them when you let me in."

Terry nodded again and stepped back to roll the barrier aside for me. I gave him a small nod back as I drove in.

"I'm in," I told Villaverde.

I pulled in behind the warehouse and continued all the way down to its far end, where I parked alongside its wall.

Villaverde's voice came back. "I've got a Harbor Police black-and-white about three minutes out and another on the way."

I picked up the phone and killed the speaker function as I got out of the car. "Keep them back and tell them not to approach until I say so," I insisted firmly. "Make sure they understand that, David. I don't want my guys to bolt and I don't want this to turn into the OK Corral either. These guys like to shoot stuff up."

"Copy that. And keep the line open."

"Will do."

I had to move fast.

I took off my jacket and chucked it into the car, then pulled out my gun, chambered a round, and flicked the safety off before slipping it back into its holster. Then I set off.

I trotted down the back of the warehouse until I reached its corner, making sure I couldn't be seen from the street. There was some tall grass growing at the base of the wire fence that provided a small measure of cover. I'd seen my guys pull up on the other side of the street, but this wasn't the kind of street people parked on and I didn't think they'd still be there.

I peered out and surveyed the area.

I couldn't see them at first—then I spotted them. They were parked in the small lot of a marine supplies store, almost directly across from me. The spots were slightly angled, herringbone-style, and the sedan was nose-forward facing toward Terry's gatehouse— which meant I needed to move farther down the fence before climbing over it if I didn't want to be scaling it almost in direct view of my goons.

There was a second warehouse sitting behind the one I was hugging. I nipped back along the wall and away from the street, made sure the goons weren't looking my way, then sprinted across the gap between the two buildings, staying low. I kept running all the way down until I reached the far corner of the second building, took a cautionary peek behind it, then went around and kept going until I was crouched close to the fence again. I figured there were now a couple of hundred feet between me and them. It was enough.

As another truck rolled by outside, I crept up to the fence and gave it a little tug to test its rigidity. It was solid, and the diamond shapes formed by the crossed wires were just wide enough to accommodate the tips of my shoes. I stayed low and waited for another truck to trundle by, then I got something even better—a big eighteen-wheeler coming out of the bonded warehouse facility itself. I reckoned it would snare my goons' attention, and I tensed up, ready to move— and as the truck rumbled past, I took three big strides and leapt onto the gate. I was up it in four quick moves and launched myself over it, landing hard on the sidewalk in a low crouch before scurrying for cover behind the slow-moving truck and rushing across the street in its dusty wake.

I dove behind a parked car about a dozen cars down from the maroon sedan and paused there to catch my breath, then I peeked out. I could see the guy in the passenger seat, in profile. He was looking dead ahead, toward the gate. I pulled out my gun and darted out, hugging the cars and ducking from one to another in quick, stealthy bursts. I tried to minimize the risk of being spotted by timing my moves to coincide with trucks rolling past, knowing the eyes in the maroon sedan would be distracted by them when they weren't otherwise fixated on the gate, waiting for me to reappear.

I paused about five cars away, where I got a decent view of the guy riding shotgun. He had a shaved head with what appeared to be a flame-like tattoo pattern running along its side, above his ear, and was wearing metal-framed shades. He was just sitting there, smoking in silence with his elbow on the windowsill and his gaze locked on the warehouse's entrance. Although I hadn't seen the tattoo under the cap he wore at the hotel, I recognized him now—he was one of the three hard-asses who'd come up in the elevator, the guy I'd slammed into in the lobby.

I couldn't really see the other guy's face.

My entire body tightened up in anticipation and I nipped out again. With my gun hand leading the way, I tucked in behind the car that was parked closest to theirs. There was an empty spot between them. I crouched low, steeled myself with a couple of deep inhales, and, with another truck passing, I scurried fast and silent around the back of the car and sprang up alongside the sedan's passenger side with my gun barrel about four feet away from Flamehead's cheek.

"Hands on the roof where I can see 'em. Both of you, right now."

They both flinched and spun around to face me, stone-faced behind their shades.

"Do it."

To press my point, I flicked my gun to the left and aimed it just inches from Flamehead's elaborate skull and let off a quick round into the rear window as a warning, blowing up the tempered glass and showering them with its granules.

I swung the gun right back into Flamehead's face.

"Okay, okay," he grumbled as both his hands shot up and reached for the top of the window frame.

I saw a stir deeper in the car as the driver twisted around, his face locked with angry resolve as his right hand dived for something—the grip of a gun sticking out by his waist. I didn't have time to shout out another warning and just took my shot.

The guy let out a loud yelp and screamed out "Fuuuck!" as his left hand flew up to the bloodied hole in his shoulder that my round had punched.

"You fucking nuts, man?" Flamehead moaned, his eyes flicking from his groaning friend to me and back.

"I'm not screwing around," I yelled back. "Now give me those hands and get out of the fucking car."

I watched intently as the passenger door swung open and Flamehead climbed out of the car, slowly, with his arms up. He was wearing a black Windbreaker over a dark T-shirt, baggy jeans, and a bulky pair of work boots. I couldn't tell if he was carrying or not.

"You got a weapon?" I asked, bending down a bit so I could keep an eye on the guy behind the wheel.

"Yeah," Flamehead grunted. "Belt holster."

"Two fingers. Easy. On the ground."

He nodded grudgingly, then pulled an automatic out and set it down by his feet.

"Now kick it under the car. Gently."

He did so.

"Okay. I want both hands on the roof and your legs spread," I ordered him, then turned my attention to the driver. "You, out."

I took a few steps back and edged around the front of the car so I could keep an eye on the driver. I held my Browning in my right hand while my left hand fished out my phone.

"I've got them," I told Villaverde. "Send in the troops."

The driver was cursing and groaning his way out of the car. He was shorter and stockier than Flamehead and sported a soul patch—a smidgen of beard beneath his lower lip—and long, straight hair that he wore tied back. He rounded the door to face me and looked mad as hell as he scowled at me before spitting at the ground.

I held his glare and told him, "Easy, tiger. I think one hole's enough for today, what do you say?" I nodded at the gun on his belt. "Two fingers. You know the drill."

He spat again, then did it.

"Kick it under the car," I told him. "And I don't mean all the way to the human torch there."

He bent down and did as directed—and that's when Terry decided to make his appearance.

"Ho-ly shit, buddy, you okay?"

My eyes flicked across to track his booming, breathless voice, and I caught a glimpse of him waddling across the wide street with his gun out, his face all sweaty, his fleshy jowls rippling with the ebb and flow of each heavy step—

—and that split-second diversion was enough for the two goons to try to make their break.

They bolted almost simultaneously, like they were joined by some freaky mind-meld, the two of them charging at me while unleashing demonic yells. Flamehead reached me first, coming at me from the left, but I managed to deflect his first punch with my left arm and pound him with a flat strike from my gun hand that landed flat across his nose and upper lip and sent him staggering sideways all rubber-kneed, but the move had left my right side exposed and Soulpatch was on me in a flash, tackling me around the waist and shoving me down to the ground. The Browning and the BlackBerry tumbled out of my hand as I hit the asphalt hard and I lost sight of them, my attention focused on Soulpatch's left arm, which was flying down for a hammer punch. I caught it with my forearm and swung his arm away before jabbing his bloodied shoulder with my left fist, causing him to wail out in pain—then Terry shouted, "Stop!"

I saw Soulpatch look up and swung my head sideways and caught sight of Terry standing there, about twenty feet away, with his face all scrunched in concentration and his gun out in a two-handed stance, and he yelled again, "I'm warning you!"

I heard Flamehead blurt, "Fuck this," and flicked my head to my left to see him run off—then Soulpatch sprang off me and onto his feet and tore off after him.

Terry yelled, "Stop!"

And just then, just as I was shouting "Don't!" he squeezed the trigger, once, twice, then again, three quick, loud bursts that whipped through the air between us.

"Nooo!" I barked as I pushed to my feet, my eyes rocketing away from Terry to look down the road where I saw Flamehead stumble and hit the asphalt like he was a toy that had his power switch flicked off.

I yelled out to Terry, "Stop firing!" my arms out wide and my hands splayed open. His face flooded with confusion, then he nodded, and I added, "Call nine-one-one and get an ambulance down here," jabbing an angry finger at the fallen man in the middle of the road, then I turned away from him and scanned the ground for my

Browning and my phone. I glimpsed the phone with its back off and its battery scattered by an adjacent car, decided they could wait, and tore my eyes across to focus on recovering my gun, which was lying by some weeds at the edge of the sidewalk.

I scooped it up and ran down the street.

Soulpatch had veered off to the right, and I caught sight of him weaving through some parked cars in an adjacent lot as I got to Flamehead, who was just sprawled on the ground, wheezing with labored breathing and barely moving. With all his dark clothing, I couldn't see where he'd been hit at first, then I saw it, a small hole in his Windbreaker by the base of his right shoulder blade.

I glanced across and saw Soulpatch disappearing behind more cars, and decided I needed to lock him down fast.

Terry was making his way over, his step slow and deflated. I yelled out to him, "Stay with this guy till the ambulance shows up and send the uniforms after me."

He nodded. "You got it." And I was off.

I snaked through more parked cars and hurtled into the next lot, past another messy boatyard and a meat warehouse, but I couldn't see him anymore. The bastard was moving fast, even though he was wounded. I'd only hit him in the shoulder, in an area I knew didn't have major arteries that would make him bleed out nor, obviously, any vital organs. I knew my slug wasn't going to slow him down too much, although from the puff of car seat stuffing I'd seen when I'd shot him, I knew the bullet had been a through-and-through, which meant he had two holes in him and he'd be losing blood from both.

I swung my gaze right and left, searching for any sign of him as a cold, hollow space grew in my gut. All around me, I could see a mess of low-rise structures that housed shipping- and auto-related businesses with big yards of scattered equipment and lots of places to hide—or lots of cars to jack. I advanced again, keeping to the same direction I'd seen him heading in, but with each aimless step, the hollow feeling grew like a black hole and consumed my insides with the doomed realization that the bastard was probably gone.

20

"Where are you?" Walker barked into the phone.

"I'm in the Barrio," Ricky "Scrape" Torres replied. "It's all gone to shit, man. I'm hit."

Walker could hear the strain and the desperation in his bike brother's voice. "What? What the hell happened?"

"The fucker just came out of nowhere and jumped us. One minute he's behind the gates in the warehouse, next thing you know he's got his gun in Booster's face. I was going for my piece and he shot me in the shoulder, man. I'm bleeding bad."

"What about Booster?"

"He's down, man. This fucking security guard put one in his back when we made our move. I don't know if he's dead or what."

"Goddamn it," Walker spat, his veins swelling with fury. "How the fuck did he get the drop on you?"

"I don't know. We messed up, all right? But I need help here, I'm losing blood, I need someone to fix me up."

Walker thought for a second, and as he did, he saw the rest of his guys staring at him, concern and anger burning in their eyes. Then his gaze settled on the Mexican, who was also watching him—the goddamn Mexican and his fucking fed from hell. He cursed inwardly at having brought this down on the club, at not having pulled out as soon as he became aware that an FBI agent was involved. He'd been blinded by the easy money he'd been paid for grabbing the others for the Mexican, and he'd had no reason to suspect that this last snatch would turn out to be such a disaster.

Regardless, they were in it now, and he had a man down in the field. And Eli "Wook" Walker always took care of his men.

He asked, "You said you're in the Barrio?"

"Yeah, I just crossed under the bridge."

"What, on foot or you driving?"

"On foot, man. The car's history."

Walker wasn't worried about that. It was stolen anyway. "Can you drive?"

"Yeah, I think so. But I need to jack me a ride."

Walker thought it over quickly, then said, "Okay, get yourself some wheels and head out to the grotto. Think you can make it there?"

"I guess."

"Do it. I'll send someone around to sort you out."

"You gotta do it fast, man," Scrape pleaded. "I'm wasting here."

"Just get your ass over there as soon as you can and sit tight. You'll be fine."

Walker hung up and found himself facing a wall of questioning stares. Before he could start filling them in, the Mexican spoke up.

"Is there a problem?"

Walker was in no mood to cajole the man. "Yeah, I'd say there's a fucking problem," he growled. "I've got one man down and another with a slug in his shoulder because of you."

The Mexican got up from the couch, calmly, and took a step toward Walker, sending a ripple of tension across the room. The rest of the bikers straightened up and inched forward threateningly, clearly ready to rumble, as did Navarro's two aides.

Navarro stilled his men with a small, calming gesture without even looking at them while studying Walker with a curious smile on his face. "Because of *me?*"

"You should have told me the bitch had a goddamn fed for a boyfriend from day one," Walker hissed.

Navarro remained calm. "Well, you did know she was ex-DEA. And if you and your *babosos* hadn't been so pathetically incompetent, the boyfriend wouldn't have been around, would he?"

Something about the way the Mexican spoke tripped a small circuit deep inside Walker's brain. He wasn't sure what it was, but it made him uneasy. Still, the man was standing there, mouthing off in front of Walker's own crew and doing it in his own fucking clubhouse. Not too many people had done that and lived long enough to brag about it.

"Listen to me, you wetback sonofabitch. I don't know what you've got yourself into or what the hell this is all about, but I know we're done here. So how about you get that chickenshit shrink of yours out of my basement, give me the rest of my money, and get the fuck out of my face while I'm still feeling charitable."

Walker stared down the Mexican as a loaded silence choked the room. From the corner of his eye, he could see that his men were ready to deal with any threatening move. There were six of them facing three Mexicans in the room and one outside, odds that Walker was more than comfortable with. He knew the Mexican's heavies had to be packing, but his own guys weren't exactly there to play bingo and their guns were also ready to rip.

The Mexican seemed to read the situation the same way and after a few seconds of deliberation, his body language eased off. Then he spread his arms wide in a brotherly, conciliatory gesture, and shrugged.

"I understand you're angry right now. I would feel the same way. But we've done good business together in the past, and it seems a shame to me for us to throw that away and kill the chance of doing more good business in the future because of this. So how about we shake hands and conclude this unhappy experience and move on without poisoning our relationship with any further disrespect? Deal, *amigo?*"

Walker eyed the man curiously. The Mexican just stared at him with a cordial, even expression.

The man had indeed paid them good money in the past for relatively easy work, and the pragmatist within Walker agreed that there was no need to kill off any future prospects between them. And given all the heat that the club would probably be facing after the shootout, Walker preferred not to have four more bodies and a whole lot of forensic evidence to bury, to say nothing of a potential Mexican shitstorm from the wetback's *compadres* south of the border.

Walker nodded. "Deal."

The Mexican spread his arms wider and gave him a look that was part reproachful and part relieved, then stepped toward Walker and brought his arms together, his hands inviting a handshake.

Walker shrugged and took a step in himself, and extended his hand.

Walker's gaze locked onto the man's eyes, and the same circuit in the biker's brain tripped again as the Mexican's hands wrapped themselves tightly around his right hand. And in that instant, the Mexican's eyes hardened, giving Walker a peek into an abyss of darkness he knew he'd encountered before as he felt something sharp cut into the inside of his wrist.

His skin lit up with a burning sensation, and Walker flinched and tried to yank his arm back, but the Mexican's grip stayed solidly locked on his wrist and held it there for a moment longer while his icy stare dug deeper into him—then Walker tugged back and pulled himself free.

He studied his wrist with confused, angry eyes, saw the small spouts of blood appear from where he'd felt the cuts—then he looked up to the Mexican's hands.

"What the fu—"

Walker didn't have time to finish the word. From either side of the Mexican, the two *sicarios*—professional gunmen—were whipping out their silenced handguns and unleashing a torrent of rounds with deadly accuracy.

Three seconds later, Walker's men were all dead or dying where they stood.

Walker's jaw dropped an inch as he stared in disbelief at his fallen brothers and watched in dumbstruck shock as the two enforcers went around calmly pumping confirmation slugs into their heads, then he tore his gaze off the slaughter and swiveled it back onto the Mexican— and then two things hit him.

The first was who the Mexican really was.

The second was a complete and sudden loss of feeling in his arms and legs.

He just fell to the ground, collapsing on himself like someone had turned all his bones to Jell-O.

Walker couldn't move anything. He couldn't even twist a shoulder or lift a finger to straighten himself out. Nothing worked. The realization sent a rush of terror through him as he just lay there, on his side, his cheek and nose squashed up against the wood flooring, his eyes locked at a disturbing sideways angle and giving him no more than a close-up view of the dust and the scrapes that littered it.

The Mexican's boots edged closer until they were right up against Walker's face, and from the corner of one eye, he could see the man towering over him and looking down at him like he was no more than a cockroach.

Then he saw the Mexican's boot rise up.

21

I got back to the street outside the bonded warehouse to find a black-and-white pulled up where I'd left Flamehead. One of the Harbor Patrol uniforms was talking to Terry while the other was busy on his radio. Within seconds, another cruiser swerved in and discharged two more officers. I gave them all a quick description of Soulpatch, and one of them radioed it in and asked for an immediate BOLO to be sent out. The uniforms then jumped back into their cars and tore off to look for him just as an ambulance screamed in.

Flamehead wasn't doing well. He was still lying in the middle of the road, sprawled on his belly. I couldn't see much blood under him, but although he was conscious, he was just staring vacantly at the asphalt and barely responsive. I stood back with Terry and watched as the paramedics went to work on him, hard and fast.

I was livid with myself. I'd started off with two potential living, breathing leads into finding out who had targeted Michelle and why, and I was down to one half-dead extra from a Mad Max movie who didn't look like he was going to be doing any talking anytime soon.

I put my BlackBerry back together and watched as one of the paramedics checked his blood pressure while the other used some trauma shears to cut through Flamehead's Windbreaker and T-shirt to reveal an oval entry wound in his right upper back.

"BP's one hundred over palp," one of them announced.

"I've got one GSW through the lung. Let's roll him over."

They moved together expertly like they'd done this a thousand times before and used the shears again to cut through the front of his shirt. There was a two-and-a-half-inch sucking-air chest wound just below his right nipple.

The lead paramedic, a striking brunette with steel-blue eyes, a lush mane of wavy hair that she wore tied back, and the name Abisaab embroidered across her chest, examined him with agile, calm hands, then told her colleague, "He's hypoxic, his oh-two sat is eighty-nine percent and it looks like the bullet punctured his lung. I think he has a pneumo. Get the mask."

They quickly strapped a high-flow, non-rebreather oxygen mask over his mouth and nose, then ran a couple of IV lines into his forearm as my phone's software finally finished its interminable reboot. I felt my spirits sagging as I dialed Villaverde to bring him up to speed.

I heard the other paramedic, a short, muscular Latino by the name of Luengo, say, "Systolic's down to eighty," sounding more alarmed than before, then Abisaab said, "I've got frothy blood coming out of the wound, we need to seal it now," and within seconds they were at full throttle, taping a seal tightly across the wound while keeping one side open. When they were done, Luengo broke away and prepped the gurney.

"Guys, I need an update," I told them.

Abisaab replied without taking her eyes off Flamehead. "His lung's down and he's very hypoxic and tachycardic. He can hardly breathe. We need to get him back to the ER to put in a chest tube."

I asked, "What are we looking at here?"

She got my drift and turned to face me, and her eyebrows rose up with a doubtful look, but she didn't say anything—standard procedure given that the victim was still conscious and quite possibly hearing everything going on around him.

I stepped back to give them some room and gave Villaverde her read. I heard him blow out a frustrated sigh, then he said, "There's not much more you can do out there. Why don't you head on back up to Broadway and look at some faces?"

Villaverde was right. It was pretty obvious that even if Flamehead made it, I wouldn't be able to go near him for days. Which infuriated me to no end. For some reason that I still couldn't figure out, these goons were tailing me, and I didn't fancy sitting around looking over my shoulder while waiting for this bastard to get his vocal cords back. I needed to find out who these guys were.

I watched as Abisaab and Luengo lifted him onto the collapsible gurney, then strapped him in.

"I need to check his pockets," I told them as I moved in.

Abisaab stayed on task. "We've got to go."

"I'll be quick," I insisted, my fingers already rifling through his pockets.

"Sir—"

"Just give me a second!"

He had nothing on him—no wallet, no ID. Not that I expected to find anything, but sometimes you get lucky. He did have a cell phone, though, a cheap prepaid, which I pocketed.

I stepped back to let them take him away, and as they did, I noticed something on Luengo's arm. The bottom of what seemed like an elaborate tattoo, just peeking out from under the edge of his sleeve.

An idea slapped me.

"Hang on, hang on." I rushed right back up to them and pushed through to get to Flamehead.

"We have to move him now," Abisaab objected.

"I know, just—" I moved the cut fabric of his T-shirt aside, one side, then the other. I couldn't see anything. I turned to Abisaab and said, "Give me your scissors."

"What?"

"Your scissors. Give them to me."

"We have to move him, agent," she insisted, her eyes drilling into me.

"So stop wasting his time and give me the goddamn scissors."

Abisaab looked at me and must have read the utter seriousness on my face as she shook her head and rummaged in her medical kit before handing them to me grudgingly, like I'd just snapped the neck of her pet cat.

I went to work on the rest of Flamehead's jacket, using the scissors to cut lengthways up the sleeve that was closest to me.

"What the hell do you think you're doing?" she asked.

I kept going. "You're wasting his time, not mine, you hear me? His time."

I pulled the sleeve apart carefully, exposing his forearm, then the rest of his arm all the way up to his shoulder. His skin was bare.

I scurried around to Flamehead's other side and did the same to his left arm, working carefully around the IV lines that were plugged into it. There was nothing on the forearm, but as I peeled back the rest, I saw the tattoo on his shoulder.

I peeled the fabric away to get a clear view of it. It depicted an eagle holding two crossed M16s in its claws, positioned like crossbones under a skull. Curiously, the eagle was wearing sunglasses and a bandana, and its wings were drawn like they were made of flames.

I stared at the shades and the bandana.

Maybe. Just maybe this would be something.

I pulled out my phone and took two quick snaps of the tattoo, checked to see that they were clear, then glanced up at Abisaab.

"He's all yours," I said, giving her a contrite look. "I'm sorry, it's important." It didn't seem to soften the brunt of her uncompromising glare much, but she managed to grace me with a small nod.

I was already dialing Villaverde as they wheeled him away.

"I got a tat off the guy's shoulder," I told him. "The guy could be a vet, but it could also be a club patch."

"Send it over," he said. "I'll shoot it across to ATF."

I was stoked. If this was a club patch, the guys at ATF were bound to have some record of them, and we'd soon know who they were.

I emailed it to him and sprinted back to my car, feeling a small tug of hope.

22

Walker watched aghast as the man's right boot kicked down on his shoulder and flipped him onto his back.

The Mexican was still looking down on him with cold bemusement. Walker felt an onslaught of blood in his temples and as he stared into the man's eyes, a sudden realization speared through him.

This was no "ex-lieutenant" of Navarro's, no "Nacho" or whatever the hell he'd called himself.

It was Navarro himself.

The sonofabitch wasn't dead.

The ramifications of that realization sent his already turbulent thoughts into a tailspin as he just lay there helplessly while Navarro held up his hand and adjusted a big silver ring that, oddly, bridged across two of his fingers, the right middle and the fourth next to it.

"Works like magic, doesn't it? The tribe it comes from, that's what they believe—that it's magic. Which in a way, it is. A potent little neurotoxin cocktail that denervates the motor neurons at the level of the upper spinal cord and causes quadriplegia," he said with genuine exuberance, like he was marveling at its effects for the first time—something Walker knew firsthand was definitely not the case.

He'd seen its effects before, in Mexico. On someone they'd suspected of being a snitch.

The memory drenched him with fear.

"You'd need a pretty capable anesthetist and some decent equipment to achieve that in an operating room," Navarro added, "and yet, here it is, just a simple toxin from a jungle spider . . ."

Navarro got down on his haunches for a closer look at him, and his eyes suddenly lost their wonder and turned more predatory. "The great thing about it is, it doesn't cripple all your muscles. You may have noticed that some of your nerves—the ones from your neck and above—they still work, don't they? Which means you can talk. So tell me, *amigo*," he said softly, almost in a whisper now. "What is this 'grotto' you mentioned, and who is this 'Scrape' you were talking to?"

Walker steeled himself and spat into the Mexican's face.

"Fuck you."

The Mexican's face brightened, almost as if Walker's reply was the one he'd been hoping for. He stared at the biker like he was proud of him again while swinging his arm out behind him without turning back.

Walker strained to see what he was doing. He saw one of Navarro's enforcers hand him something but couldn't see what it was. Then Navarro smiled at him and brought it out, like a magician pulling out a rabbit, holding it up in front of Walker—a pair of garden shears, the one-handed kind with a spring between the blades.

He snapped the blades together as a demonstration, then turned his attention farther down Walker's body.

"Let's see . . . what shall we start with?"

Walker tensed up and tried to lean his head up to see what Navarro was doing, but he couldn't see much beyond the back of the Mexican, whose arms were busy with something. Then he heard a sickening crunch and a snap, and Navarro turned back to face him. He looked gleeful as he brought something up for Walker to see.

A finger, held in his blood-soaked hand.

Walker felt his stomach shoot up to his throat.

"One down, nineteen to go. Shall we try again?"

Walker felt rivers of sweat seeping out of him. "Like I said," he grunted. "Fuck. You."

He heard another crunch.

Another snap.

He couldn't stop himself from retching, and although he knew he shouldn't be feeling any pain, his mind was still conjuring some up for him. He felt his consciousness seeping away.

Navarro asked, "Well?"

Walker summoned up the little strength he still possessed and spat at the Mexican. He couldn't manage anything more than a weak, pathetic spit that missed its target and sank his spirits even further.

Navarro looked at him like a disappointed parent, then turned away.

"I don't have that much time, so . . . how about we forget about the rest of them for now and skip to something much more . . . convincing?"

He saw Navarro nod to his enforcers, and a perverse, surreal mix of terror and fascination burned through him as he watched the Mexicans bend down and pull his belt and jeans down.

Then Navarro went to work again.

23

The Babylon Eagles.

That's what the bastards called themselves.

Kudos to the guys at ATF—it took less than ten minutes for them to come back with the name after Villaverde sent them the shot of the tattoo I sent him. They also had an address for the Eagles' local hangout, which was the mother chapter of the club. The gang's clubhouse was adjacent to a bike garage that acted as their front, on a side street off El Cajon Boulevard in La Mesa. That address didn't mean much to me, but I punched it into my GPS and was already on my way there. Villaverde would be meeting me there, along with backup—SWAT, ATF, and local PD.

I was back on the freeway, charging north with a full clip in my Browning, a blue light spinning on my car's roof, and the gas pedal crunched down as far as it would go.

Hoping I'd get there before everyone else.

24

Walker felt a dizziness he'd never experienced before.

The bear of a man had been wounded in battle, years ago. Bullets and shrapnel had cut into him, but he'd soldiered on and returned to the field. Then, since getting back from the Gulf and founding the Eagles, he'd seen his fair share of scrapes. He'd met up with all kinds of blades and seen batterings from brass knuckles and baseball bats. Walker could take a hit. They didn't call him "Wook" just because of his thick, wild hair and the bushy goatee he wore.

This was different.

He was spiraling away, bleeding out. He knew that. But it wasn't accompanied with any normal pain. It was a weird, far more uncomfortable sensation, an odd pain that came from within. Navarro had told him that this was visceral pain, pain that emanated from an organ itself, pain that doesn't travel through the spinal cord.

Pain that ate you away from the inside.

He hadn't been able to hold out. He'd told Navarro what he needed to know. And now, he was ready to die. Hell, there was no point in living.

Not like that.

"What the fuck is this all about?" he wheezed, his mouth barely able to form the words. "What are you after?"

Navarro stared down at him as he wiped his hands on a wash cloth. "Something I'm afraid you won't ever have the chance to enjoy, *amigo*. But who knows? Maybe in another life . . ." He handed the towel to one of his enforcers, and when his hand came back, it was holding a gun. "*Vaya con dios, cabrón.*"

Without flinching, he pressed the barrel of its sound suppressor between Walker's eyes and pulled the trigger.

Navarro stood up, pulled his jacket straight and brushed it with his hand, then handed the gun back to the *sicario* closest to him.

"Go bring our guest out," he ordered him in Spanish, "then let's go find this Scrape."

25

I didn't get there first.

Far from it. And judging by the barrage of pulsating emergency lights that greeted me when I turned off El Cajon, I got a sinking feeling that we were all too late.

Two squad cars and a couple of unmarkeds were already there, scattered outside the bike shop, with another black-and-white and an ambulance pulling in behind me. A couple of police officers were hopelessly undermanned as they tried to put up yellow crime scene tape around the block while struggling to keep back the growing crowd of gawkers.

I ditched the car as close to the action as I could and briskly walked the rest of the way, flashing my creds to one of the uniforms who was moving to block me. I found Villaverde across the forecourt of the shop, standing outside what I took to be the clubhouse's entrance, talking to some sheriff's department guys and a couple of grease monkeys in blue coveralls. He peeled off when he saw me and came over.

"What happened?" I asked.

"In here," he just said as he led me away. He pointed back at the bike mechanics with his thumb. "One of the club's prospects found them and called it in. It ain't pretty."

Prospects were hangarounds who'd graduated to prospective members of the club, brother-wannabes who were on probation and hadn't yet earned their patches.

He ushered me through a door around the side of the single-story structure and let me into the gang's clubhouse.

More like their slaughterhouse.

I counted six dead bodies in total, scattered around the big room's perimeter. Five of them had been gunned down and just lay there, bent in various grotesque tableaux of death. A quick, professional job, each of them with two or three holes in them and an additional round between the eyes to finish them off. The bodies and the wounds still looked fresh. They had all died wearing their cuts.

The sixth was something else altogether.

He was a big guy, bushy goatee, long greasy hair. He was sprawled on his back in the middle of the room. Like the others, he was in his cuts and had taken a round between the eyes. He also had a couple of fingers missing from one hand. I spotted them across the room, discarded like cigarette butts. The part that drew the eye, though, was his crotch. His pants had been pulled down, and his dick had been cut off. An ungodly, pulpy mess was in its place, and a large puddle of blood had pooled between his legs, spreading down to his feet.

My gut twisted around itself and coiled up like a boa, and I didn't bother looking around to see where that body part had ended up. I glanced over at Villaverde instead.

He gave me a look that mirrored my feelings.

There was a new player in the game.

And what we were dealing with needed to get reclassified on a whole new level.

I took a second to let my insides settle, then asked, "The guys in the shop see anything?"

Villaverde shrugged. "The guy who reported it saw a car driving off just before he came over. A dark SUV, black, tinted windows. Big car, like an Escalade, but he didn't think it was a Caddy." He paused, then added, "You need to see this, too."

My eyes surveyed the room as he led me across it. On the side wall, behind a leather couch, was a poster-size mural of the club's patch, the one I'd seen on Flamehead's shoulder tattoo. There was a bar, an upright piano, and what looked like a meeting room beyond it, and, oddly, a row of baseball bats hanging by a doorway. Then something else caught my eye. On the far back wall, behind a pool table. A whole bunch of framed photographs.

"Hang on," I told him.

I crossed over for a closer look.

There were several war poses, the kind of pictures we'd become all too familiar with, of battle-weary soldiers smiling to the camera, flashing V signs with their fingers in a stark desert setting. One of them showed the chopped-up biker and a couple of other grunts standing proud against an apocalyptic background of tanks gutted by depleted uranium shells and burning oil fields. It was obviously Iraq, which means they were either out there in the early nineties or a couple of years after 9/11. Next to the vet gallery were about a dozen similar shots laid out in two rows. Each shot was a black-and-white eight-by-ten mug shot of what I assumed were the club's full-patch members.

I immediately recognized several of them: the one who'd just been Bobbitted; the guy who shot Michelle and who I crushed in half; Flamehead; Soulpatch was also up there, all brooding and defiant. Like the others, he was grudgingly holding up a black tablet that displayed his booking number and where he'd been arrested—in this case, the La Mesa Police Department. It was a local arrest, so if he wasn't already on the club's ATF file that was now sitting on Villaverde's smartphone, getting his name wasn't going to be an issue.

"These are the guys who were tailing me," I called out to Villaverde, tapping the frame with the back of my fingers.

Villaverde joined me for a look.

"This is the one the security guard shot," I said, indicating Flamehead. "And this is the guy who ran off."

"Okay, let's get a name and put an APB out on him." He pulled up his ATF file and called over one of the cops to get the alert out.

I had mixed feelings about what we'd walked into. On the one hand, the entire club seemed to have been wiped out. At least, all the full-patch holders. Six dead here, Michelle's killer, the one she'd stabbed, Flamehead, and Soulpatch. Ten in total. There were twelve portraits on the wall, but the missing two could have been long-dead members who still had their faces on the wall for posterity. If these were the guys who'd kidnapped the scientists from the research center and come after Michelle, they were no longer a threat to anyone. However, an even more savage group seemed to have taken their place, and they were still out there. And with the bikers dead, we were back where we started in terms of figuring out who we were dealing with.

Unless we could find Soulpatch.

Before they did.

"Ricky Torres," Villaverde announced, "road name Scrape." He showed me the image on his phone. It was a different mug shot from the one that was up on the wall, but it was the same guy, no question.

I nodded, and he gave the uniform the go-ahead to spread the word. As the deputy headed off, Villaverde flicked a nod toward the side door and told me, "Over here."

He led me through the door and down a narrow staircase to a basement. It was one big, messy, windowless room. All kinds of crates and boxes were lying around it, and the air was stale with dust and rot.

"Check this out," Villaverde said, pointing at some pipes that ran along the bottom of one of the walls, by a far corner of the room.

There were nylon cuffs on the ground by the pipes. They'd been cut open. Two of them. The corner was also littered with empty fast food wrappers and soft drink cups. I leaned in for a closer look. They looked and smelled relatively fresh.

Whoever had been tied up down here hadn't been gone long.

I stared at the plasticuffs. "Maybe this is where they brought the two scientists."

"Maybe. But I can't see them keeping them here for months."

"Maybe this is where they hold them before handing them over. Which means they might have grabbed someone else more recently."

I turned to Villaverde. "We need to look at missing persons reports. Maybe another chemist."

I glanced around again, and something by one pair of cuffs glinted in the light and caught my eye. I edged closer to it. It was a contact lens.

I pointed it out to Villaverde, and—given that he had gloves—he collected it and slipped into an evidence bag.

I thought about the timing, and despite the fact that whoever was tied up down here could well turn out to have nothing to do with Michelle or the kidnapped scientists or the shoot-out upstairs and that they could all be separate deals that the bikers were involved in, the timing was troubling me. These guys seemed to have too many balls in the air for these events not to be connected. I found myself wondering if the massacre upstairs didn't have something to do with whoever had been living off the cheap burgers down here, and, if so, how it could possibly relate to Michelle. There were still too many unknowns, which was frustrating me. The key was figuring out who had hired the bikers. Which got me thinking about who else might know that.

"You said this was the mother chapter of the club?" I asked Villaverde as we made our way back upstairs.

"Yeah, why?"

"So there are other chapters?"

"A few," he said, scrolling through the ATF file again. "Here we go. The club has three other chapters scattered across the state and, weirdly enough"—he looked up—"one in Holland. As in Holland, Europe."

"We need to talk to the nearest ones, the ones they might be closest to. They might know who these guys were working for."

Villaverde's brow furrowed with skepticism. "Sure, but club business like this—it's usually compartmentalized. I doubt other charters would be in on what these guys were up to. And even if they were, they wouldn't talk to us about it."

"Maybe after what just happened here . . ."

Villaverde still seemed doubtful. "It's not in their DNA."

I nodded in the direction of the bike shop. "What about the prospects? Even if they weren't in the circle of trust yet, one of them could have heard something. And one of them might know who was being kept down here."

"Absolutely. They seem pretty shaken up as it is, so it should give us a leg up into scaring any leads out of them."

As we got back to the main room, I saw the bloody corpses again and it made me think about Soulpatch/Scrape. I was getting a bad feeling about him, and an uncomfortable urgency was goosing the hairs on the back of my neck.

"We need to find Scrape," I told Villaverde.

"His jacket's got his last known address, last known girlfriend, parents. We'll have something soon."

I thought about the bullet hole in his shoulder. "He would have called in to give these guys a heads-up on what happened at the terminal. Which means the psychos that did this might know about him. They might even know where he's headed. If they wiped these guys out, they might have the same thing in mind for him. We need to move fast."

I felt a mounting frustration. We needed to find him, like, now. There was a solid chance he'd be able to tell us what we needed to know about what this was all about—and who these new players were.

Just then, I heard some commotion outside the clubhouse's entrance.

"No, ma'am," a man was insisting with a raised voice. "I said you can't—"

"Don't tell me what the hell I can and can't do," a woman cut him off forcefully. "This is my husband's place and I want to see him."

Two uniforms appeared in the doorway, visibly trying—and failing—to stop a woman who was pushing and shoving her way past them. She slipped through and barged into the room. She looked like she was in her early forties. She was curvy and had auburn hair that was streaked with highlights,'and she was in low-cut jeans, snakeskin boots, and a denim shirt that was tied in a knot around her midriff. She wasn't someone you'd describe as pretty, but she had something else going, a kind of raw, savage appeal that was hard to ignore.

Her eyes immediately latched onto the butchered biker, and she stopped in her tracks and just froze, dropping her bag, her hands rushing up to cup her face.

"Wook!" she screamed, tears bursting across her face. "Wook, oh Jesus, no, Wookie baby, no no no . . ."

She wobbled and looked like her legs were about to give out from under her. I rushed across the room to help her, with Villaverde close behind.

"Ma'am, you shouldn't be here, please," I said as I reached her, placing myself between her and the biker's body. "Please," I repeated, putting my hands on her shoulders.

"I don't . . . ," she muttered, the words trailing off as tears streamed down her face now. Then her voice came back, full of rage. "What happened? What did they do to him?"

I pulled her in and held her for a moment, trying to calm her and give her a chance to catch her breath. "Let's go over there," I said, guiding her into the meeting room while making sure I stayed between her and the dead body. "Come on."

I couldn't avoid passing close to two of the other dead bikers and did my best to shield her eyes from them, but she still caught sight of them and flinched with each new shock.

I pulled up a chair for her, facing away from the main room. "Please, sit down, ma'am."

I asked her if I could get her some water—I don't know why we always do this, as if water has some magical curative power that lets people just brush away the most traumatic events. In her daze, she nodded a yes. Villaverde went out to get some from the bar.

I had to tread softly, but I also needed to get anything useful from her, fast. I felt the clock was ticking on Scrape, and we were playing catch-up. She said her name was Karen, she was Wook's wife—Wook being Eli Walker, she informed us, the club's president. One of the prospects had called her as soon as the grisly discovery had been made, and she'd immediately rushed over.

I tried to answer her questions as gracefully as possible, within the limitations of what I could actually tell her, but very quickly, I had to steer her away to what we really needed to know.

"We need to find Scrape," I told her.

She looked at me in total confusion, like I was suddenly discussing the weather.

"Why?"

"He's still out there," I replied. "He's wounded, and I think the guys who did this might be after him. We need to find him first or he might end up dead, too."

She looked at me, jittery and nervous, then asked, "Wounded?"

"He's been shot." I let it sink in, then pressed on. "Do you know how to contact him? Do you have the number of his cell?"

Her eyes darted away and she blinked a few times, finding it harder now to keep eye contact with me.

"It's okay," I told her. "This isn't about you. This is about keeping Scrape alive. I just need to know how to reach him."

She hesitated again, then shook her head. "I don't have his number. But if he was out doing something for the club," she added with a look that made her subtext about it being something illegal clear, "he wouldn't be carrying his cell anyway. He'd have a fresh prepaid for the job."

I turned to Villaverde. "You find a phone on Walker?"

"No."

I frowned, feeling time slipping away from us, like a sea that was receding before a tsunami. "What about a safe house, somewhere Scrape might go to wait for help. A doctor the club works with, someone's house maybe? A girlfriend?"

She was still visibly nervous and kept shaking her head like she didn't know anything.

"Please, Karen," I insisted, gently. "We need to find him."

"We've got a friendly doc at St. Jude's who doesn't ask too many questions, but Scrape wouldn't go there, not if he has a bullet in him."

"Where then? Think, Karen."

She looked at me and her eyes narrowed with concentration, like the answer I was looking for required a physical effort.

Then she said, "The grotto."

26

❧

"**I**'ve got him. Suspect in custody, I repeat, suspect in custody."

Todd Fugate, deputy sheriff with the San Marcos Sheriff's Station and part of its Gangs and Narcotics squad, felt good radioing in the news. The call had come in from the San Diego office and was a high-priority request from the FBI—not exactly a daily event at the station. Fugate was just pulling out of the Grand Plaza Mall when the call had come in, and he'd jumped on it. The target's location, a downtrodden warehouse complex tucked in off La Mirada, aka the grotto, was less than five miles down the parkway. Knowing he'd be first on the scene, he hit the gas and rushed over.

Once he got there, he didn't even wait for backup to show up. The alert had said the suspect had been shot in the shoulder and was probably traveling alone. It didn't specify that he was armed. Fugate didn't need more than that, and, as it turned out, he'd been proven right. The suspect was unarmed and weak and looked like he was about to faint. He gave himself up with zero fuss. Hell, by the looks of it, he was probably relieved that his ordeal was over. Fugate would drive him to the hospital himself—faster than waiting for an ambulance to come all the way out there—and the sonofabitch would soon find himself sitting in a cushy hospital bed with flirty nurses fussing all over his bad-boy ass, which had to be way better than bleeding out in some dingy warehouse all on his own.

Fugate felt good as he herded the suspect into the backseat of his Crown Vic. He didn't bother to handcuff him to the steel loop on the floor of the backseats. The man was pretty out of it already. Yes, the deputy sheriff was pleased with himself. The San Diego County Sheriff's Office had been, as per the slogan on his black-and-white's fender, "keeping the peace since 1850," and right now, on this fine summer's evening, Todd Fugate felt proud to be making a solid contribution to that noble tradition.

He was dead less than a minute later.

He was pulling away from the warehouse when a big SUV appeared at the gate and suddenly, unexpectedly, charged at him. Fugate spun the wheel to avoid the collision, but the SUV's front bumper clipped his tail and spun him around like a toy and sent him careening sideways before diving nose-first into a ditch by the warehouse's gates. The deputy looked out through shaken eyes to see the SUV do a quick U-turn before storming back and pulling up so it was blocking his way. Before its wheels had even stopped turning, its doors were flung open and two men were climbing out.

Fugate threw the car into reverse and hit the gas pedal, but the tires just shrieked and spun aimlessly as the jammed car rumbled in its spot and refused to budge. He gave up and drew his weapon, but he was too late—the men had already sprinted over and had beaten him to it. The first slug hurt like hell as it punched into his lungs, but the pain lasted only a second. The second bullet took care of that as it went through his brain and turned his lights off.

He wasn't alive to see them drag his charge out of the car and shove the wounded man into the back of their SUV, nor to see them drive off unchallenged.

Which was just as well.

27

We were back at square one.

Soulpatch—sorry, Scrape or Torres or Dickhead or however you want to refer to him—was gone. Flamehead—or, more accurately, Billy "Booster" Noyes, as it turns out—was in ICU at Scripps Mercy with a big tube down his throat. The rest of the bike brothers were in permanently suspended animation on aluminum trays down at the morgue.

We also had a dead deputy who probably had no idea that this morning was going to be his last.

And we had plenty of questions.

Questions that hounded me as night fell and I finally made my way back to the hotel, ready to toss the memory of this crappy day into the incinerator section of my mind and move on to tomorrow.

I was tired and bummed out, and seeing Tess was like a tonic to my senses. She had Alex already asleep, which was a good sign, although I knew he wouldn't be out for the night. I checked on him, saw him curled up in his kiddie sheets and with a bunch of plush and plastic toys crowding him, and I got the impression that he looked more restful than he had the night before.

Tess was a tonic all around.

I sent Jules home for the night and saw her out, giving her a breather to catch up with her life after she'd been drafted in all weekend. Then I ordered a club sandwich from room service, relieved the minibar of a couple of beers, handed one to Tess, and hit the couch with her.

I gave her the short version of my day while wolfing down the club, filling her in about what we'd discovered at the clubhouse while leaving out the gorier details. Telling her about my days always helped in that the storytelling exercise allowed me to step back and look at what was going on from a broader, clearer perspective. It also highlighted the questions that were key to figuring out what was going on.

Questions like, why were they following me? Why did they take Scrape and not shoot him on the spot? The one that trumped them all, of course, was, who killed the bikers? Was it someone who had hired them to come after Michelle and/or whoever was being held in the basement, or were the killings unrelated? Timing, and my gut, suggested the former, and that's what I was going with. So the question, beyond the who, was why? Did they get greedy and fall out over the money? Had they become a liability to whoever hired them, and if so, why? Did they mess up—in which case, was killing Michelle a mistake? But then again, maybe they didn't know she was dead. Then I thought, maybe their employer felt they'd outlived their usefulness—given that they had a tail on me yesterday, they clearly didn't have what they were after. Maybe whoever it was had decided to take matters into his own hands. Which, given what Eli Walker went through, wasn't a reassuring thought.

Tess then took over and told me about her day, and I let my mind throttle back to idling speed and just glide along as I listened to her voice and watched her face light up with animation. Then her face crumpled up with that inquisitive look that I had a real love-hate relationship with—love, because being doggedly inquisitive was part of the allure of Tess Chaykin, and hate because, well, it usually meant trouble—and she got off the couch and went into the bedroom and came back with a few sheets of paper that she showed me, drawings she said she'd found on Michelle's desk, among her papers.

"Alex's?" I asked.

"Yeah, must be. They're similar in style to others at the house."

I flicked through them. Not to put too much of a Louis C.K. spin on it, but yeah, they were cute, but that was pretty much it as far as I was concerned. Then, animated Tess came to the forefront and took over.

She pulled one of them out and put it on top of the others. "What do you see?"

I struggled a bit. "Two vaguely human-like figures. Or aliens maybe?"

She flashed me the look. "People, doofus. Two people. And I think this one's Alex," she said, pointing at the one on the right. "This thing, in his hand. That's his Ben toy, his favorite. He asked me to bring it back from the house."

I couldn't see it. "Did you ask him?"

"No."

"Why not?"

The nose crinkled. Again, part of the allure. "It's not a happy drawing."

"Not a happy drawing. Why, because there aren't any rainbows and butterflies in it?"

I do love the winding up part.

"Look at his face," she insisted. "See the open mouth, the big eyes. It looks to me like he's scared. And this guy, facing him. The dark clothes. Something in his hand."

"Voldemort? Oops. Forgot. Not supposed to say it, right?"

The look again, only cranked up to eleven. Yes, this is our foreplay. Sad, but, hey, it works.

"I'm serious. I think there's something there. Maybe a gun."

I gave it another glance. It could be a gun. Then again, it could be pretty much anything you wanted it to be, given that the blob-like entity holding it was so far removed from what humans really look like, it made Picasso's figures look like Normal Rockwell's.

"Kids play soldier and cowboy and alien hunter all the time; that's what boys do. So even if it is him . . . maybe that's just him and something from some cartoon show or a friend of his, who knows. Could be anything."

"So why was it on Michelle's desk, among her papers, not on the kitchen wall or in his bedroom like the others?"

I didn't have an answer for that—or, rather, I had way too many answers to that. Also, my brain was pretty much maxed out by real life. The fanciful flights of Alex's imagination, sweet and charming as they were, would have to wait.

"I have no idea," I simply replied, taking the drawings out of her hand and setting them down on the coffee table. I rolled over and crowded her against the back of the couch, and kissed her hungrily. Then I remembered where we were and pulled back. I stood up and held out my hand to her.

"Why don't we discuss this in my office?"

As Tess followed Reilly into the bedroom, she couldn't stop thinking about the drawing.

Maybe Reilly was right. Maybe she was reading way too much into it.

Problem was, the annoying little curiosity demon that lurked in the dark recesses of her mind was all restless and clamoring for her attention.

The demon was still bouncing around inside her as she locked the door behind her and felt Reilly turn her around and pin her against the wall. It definitely wasn't on her mind for the next hour or so, but after that, as she fell asleep in his arms, it was back, front and center, running amok and demanding an audience.

28

Farther up the coast, a very different kind of demon was hurtling across an entirely different landscape.

Navarro was back at the secluded beachfront villa in Del Mar, sitting cross-legged on a polished teak deck beyond the pool house. The sea was a stone's throw away directly in front of him and the low moon was bearing down on him like an interrogator's spotlight as he just sat there, quiet and serene—on the outside, that is.

Inside, things were radically different.

He'd been at it for over an hour, sailing through tunnels of fire and abysses of endless darkness, diving and soaring and spinning through kaleidoscopes of color and fields of surreal visions from his past and his future.

He'd done it before, of course.

Many times.

For those who weren't accustomed to it or who didn't know how to tame it, the brown, sludgy concoction he'd ingested could have disastrous consequences, both immediate—vomiting, pissing on themselves, an utter conviction that they were dying, screaming and begging to be saved from a terror that seems unending—and longer term. But not for Navarro. He knew what he was doing.

He'd first taken this particular psychoactive brew in the highlands of Peru, long ago, and had been coached through its usage by a blind shaman. The lucidity it instilled in him was overwhelming at first, but he'd learned to focus it, and with each use it grew more effective.

He pulled back from the edge and burst into a field of blinding white light, and felt incredibly clear-headed. His breathing slowed right down, calmed by the inner peace that bloomed from deep in his core, and he opened his eyes.

Magnificent.

He breathed in a big lungful of sea air and held it in for a long moment, relishing a newly awakened super-sensitivity to everything around him. The waves lapping against the shore, the crickets in the trees—he could even hear the crabs scuttling across the sand. And in his mind's eye, he could now see things, ones he'd missed or hadn't noticed, with exhilarating clarity.

The drug had worked like magic. Just as he knew it would. He'd been taught by the best, ever since his lifetime fascination with what ethnopharmacologists called the "sacred spirit medicine" had started in his early teens.

It was a fascination that had served him well.

For like all kids, Raoul Navarro grew up believing that magic existed. The difference was, he never stopped believing in it.

He grew up in Real de Catorce, a village of steep cobblestone streets and rundown Spanish colonial houses that sat perched on the side of a mountain in the one of the highest plateaus of Mexico. Built up and then abandoned after a silver-mining rush a century ago, Real's saving grace was as the gateway to the Wirikuta desert, the Huichol Indians' sacred peyote harvesting ground. It was a place where a penniless kid like Navarro could scrape together a few dollars by finding the elusive little peyote buttons that hid under mesquite bushes and selling them to *primeros*—tourists who were seeking their first peyote high. He wasn't, however, content with just selling it. He was curious about what the peyote actually did, and he didn't have to wait too long to find out. It wasn't long after his thirteenth birthday that he was blindfolded by a Huichol shaman and led into the desert, and became a *primero* himself.

The experience was life-changing.

It taught him that the spirits were everywhere, watching his every move, and he decided he wanted to learn their ways.

He hung out with the shamans and taught himself to read, eventually devouring everything he could get his hands on, from the works of Carlos Castaneda to the writings of the great psychopharmacologists and ethnobotanists. But as the real world proved to be a heartless, unforgiving place, he embraced the inevitable career option of so many of his peers and got sucked into the violent climb up the drug-trafficking totem pole—and found out he liked it. He didn't only like it—he had a talent for it. And so, as his power and his wealth grew, he was able to indulge his fascination even more.

With his growing resources, he traveled across Mexico and then farther south, into the jungles and rainforests of Guatemala, Brazil, and Peru, where he befriended anthropologists and sought out isolated peoples that devoted as much time and energy to understanding the invisible realms of gods and spirits and the time-bending pathways to our pasts and futures as we devoted to figuring out the mysteries of global warming and nanotechnology.

Always seeking to open channels to new dimensions of consciousness and reach new heights of enlightenment, he spent a lot of time and money endearing himself to and worming his way into the trust of secretive tribal healers and shamans. Under their guidance, he experimented with all kinds of psychoactive substances and entheogens—mostly plant-derived concoctions that played a pivotal role in the religious practices of the tribal cultures he was exploring. He started with more easily accessible, local mind-altering substances like psilocybin mushrooms and *Salvia divinorum*, under the guidance of Mazatec shamans in the isolated cloud forests of the Sierra Mazateca, then he moved on to more obscure, and more intense, hallucinogens like *ayahuasca*, the vine of the soul; *iboga*, the sacred visionary root; *borrachero*; and others that few outsiders had ever been offered. He even went as far as Africa, venturing deep into Gabon and Cameroon to take part in Bwiti *ngenza* ceremonies, where he learned to communicate with his ancestral spirits. But he was starting out from a dark place. His soul was already enthralled by the violence it had tasted, and as these drugs altered his consciousness and gradually disintegrated his ego, he found himself venturing into the more sinister depths of his subconscious and finding things there that most people wouldn't want to look at.

But then, Navarro wasn't most people.

With each new experience, he was dragged further down by the demons that skulked in the abysses of his astral realms. But he couldn't stop, and he grew more fascinated by the doors each journey opened up in his mind and by the psychospiritual epiphanies they triggered.

Epiphanies that sometimes went beyond the spiritual.

Epiphanies that helped him navigate dangerous real-world situations and rise among the ranks of narco kingpins with remarkable ease.

Epiphanies that earned him the nickname El Brujo.

The sorcerer.

And it was one of these epiphanies that had steered him onto a new course, a new sense of purpose. It was the root of what was now driving him on.

Navarro had long known that the game was changing. For anyone who took the time to notice, the drug world was constantly evolving. He knew that the current staple of the trade, cocaine, was on its way out. The future, he knew, was in a new type of experience, one that didn't require cumbersome needles or flames or snorting, one that anyone could access by popping a pill that was no bigger than an aspirin. This was the great appeal of synthetic drugs and amphetamines, regardless of how destructive they were.

If Navarro was out to shape the future, nothing was going to stand in his way.

He emerged from his trip with his imagination and his powers of perception greatly enhanced. Observations and obscure details were shooting out of previously ignored corners in his mind and bursting into focus.

One of them rose above all the others.

He focused on it, cajoled and nurtured it until it shone with pleasing clarity.

He went inside and hit the shower, cleansing his body, allowing the water to wash away the sweat and usher him back into the world others called real. Then he dried himself off, slipped on his nightclothes, and checked Reilly's file.

It was all there.

He picked up his phone and called Octavio Guerra. The man who supplied him with his bodyguards. The man who got him all the background information on the Americans that Navarro was interested in. The fixer who usually got him anything he needed. And although it was late, he knew Guerra would pick up his call at any time, day or night.

"The FBI agent, Reilly. His file says he has a woman, in New York. Tess Chaykin." He paused, then told Guerra, "Find her."

TUESDAY

29

It was under another impeccable blue sky that I drove to La Mesa to interview Karen Walker.

We arranged to see her there, at the local police department's brand-new digs on University Avenue, since it was closer to the Eagles' clubhouse and to where she lived. My thinking was that given what she'd just been through, it would be more courteous than to have her drive all the way out to Villaverde's federal offices out by Montgomery Field. To her credit, she arrived on time, and although she looked shaken up and on edge, she seemed to be holding up reasonably well. She didn't bring a lawyer with her either.

I greeted her along with Villaverde and Jesse Munro, who'd driven down from LA that morning. After I'd left him, Villaverde had called Corliss to fill him in on yesterday's developments, and Corliss had offered to send Munro so we'd have direct access to DEA resources now that the investigation was ramping up. The four of us were in a conference room on the second floor, which I figured would be more conducive than one of the smaller, and windowless, interview rooms downstairs, where the club's prospects were to be questioned.

ATF records showed that she and Walker got married in 2003, shortly before Walker had been shipped out to Iraq. They had two kids, an eight-year-old boy and a girl of three. Karen ran a nail bar in La Mesa. She also had a prison record, a brief stint for aggravated assault, which didn't really mesh with the more composed woman before me, but then again, maybe there was something to be said for prisoner rehabilitation.

We'd barely sat down when she asked about Scrape and whether or not we'd found him. The deputy's murder had been on the news, but we hadn't released details of why he was there to the press. Karen had put two and two together given the location of the shooting, and I decided telling her something the press hadn't been privy to would help establish some kind of rapport between us.

"They have him," I told her. "They shot the deputy and took him with them. We don't know where they are and we don't have any leads on that either."

Her eyes darted around each of us. They were brimming with confusion and unease. I could see fear there, too.

"You don't have anything?"

"That's why you're here, Mrs. Walker—"

"Karen," she interrupted brusquely, without a smile.

I took a breath and nodded. "Okay, Karen. Here's the situation. Your husband and his buddies were doing some work for someone. I'm not talking about building custom rides here. I'm talking about armed kidnappings that go back several months. I'm talking about shoot-outs that have left several people dead. But that's not why we're here right now. We're not here to try to tie you to any of those events. We're here because of what happened at the clubhouse. We're here because we need to find the guys responsible and take them off the streets. Okay?"

I waited for her to give me a little nod, then pressed on.

"Now, you saw what these people are capable of. We don't know who they are or what they're after, but it looks like whatever it is, it's still in play. Which means that as long as they're out there, anyone who was close to the club is potentially at risk. And that means you, Karen. More than anyone."

I paused, letting my warning sink in. For the record, I wasn't pulling her chain. I genuinely did feel that she was at risk. But whether I really cared or not right now, given what her husband's gang had done to Michelle and all the others—that was open to debate. Maybe deep down, I wasn't as ambivalent about her as I thought. She didn't inspire a gut dislike inside me, and yet, although I didn't know how much she knew about her husband's activities, I assumed she knew enough. But I also knew from experience that partners of violent criminals are often also victims in their own way.

"We need to know who the Eagles were working for and what they were doing," I added.

Her gaze bounced around us again, like she was being pulled in opposite directions. I knew she was uncomfortable just being inside this building. I'd seen her sheet, and she'd spent some time behind bars. She was no fan of law enforcement. She pulled out a pack of Winstons from her handbag, fished out a cigarette, and held it tightly between her fingers, then started tapping it against the table. She wore big silver rings on strong, well-manicured fingers. I also noticed she had tattoos on her wrists, though I couldn't see how far up they went.

"You do want us to nail whoever did this to your husband, don't you, Karen?" I pressed.

"Of course I do," she shot back.

"Then help us."

The tapping intensified, then she blew out a long, frustrated breath and looked away before letting her gaze settle back on me.

"I want immunity."

"Immunity? From what?" I asked.

"From prosecution. Look, I'm not new at this, okay? Assuming I did know something and I tell you about it, I'm an accessory. At best. And while I really want you to get the sick fucks that did that to Wook, doing time isn't high on my bucket list."

She stopped there and just stared at me, then at the others, then back at me. She was trying to project indifference and defiance, but I had been around enough people in her situation to know that behind the tough biker-chick façade, she was shaking. Still, what she was asking for made sense, from her point of view. And as pissed off as I was about what her husband and his gang had done, I couldn't be sure she knew every detail about what they were up to, nor that we'd ever be able to successfully prosecute her even if she did. More to the point, there was a strong chance she could help us figure out who was behind it all, and right now, ending this black run and getting my hands on whoever had sent the bikers after Michelle was worth making a deal that kept Karen Walker's tattooed wrists out of prison.

I slid a glance at Villaverde. Given her record, we'd anticipated her demand. We'd also agreed that we couldn't afford to refuse it.

"Okay," I told her.

Her face flooded with surprise, like she was not sure how to take that. "What, just like that? You don't have that authority. Don't you need to get it approved by the DA or something?"

"It's already done. We've already discussed it with the San Diego County DA's Office. They're on board. LA County won't be a problem either." I indicated Munro with a nod, and he gave her a small confirmation nod back. "The paperwork's being done as we speak." I leaned in. "This isn't about you, Karen. You have my word as a federal agent that nothing you say in here will be used against you in any way. But if we're going to get these guys, we need to act fast. They could be making a run for it. So if you know anything, now's the time to speak up."

I saw her jaw muscles clench, and she resumed the tapping while debating what to do.

"How long for that piece of paper to get here?" she asked.

"Not long, but it might be more time than we have."

She exhaled again, her eyes narrowing. Then she sat back, threw a glance out the window for a long second, and turned to face us again. She nodded to herself, short quick nods, like she was convincing herself that she was making the right move.

"They were working for some Mexican scumbag," she told us. "I don't know his name. Wook just called him 'the wetback.'"

I felt my synapses perk up. We were rolling.

"What were they doing for him?"

"It started about six, seven months ago or so. He hired them to grab a couple of guys."

"The scientists up by Santa Barbara?" Munro asked.

She nodded. "I didn't hear anything else about that for a while. Which was good, given how badly it had turned out. Then a few weeks ago, he came back with some other jobs. More grabs."

"Who was it this time?" I asked.

"I don't know. I really don't. The first one wasn't a local job either."

"Where was it?"

"Up the coast. Somewhere around San Francisco, I think. Look, Wook didn't tell me everything. Sometimes he didn't tell me anything at all, not up front anyway. I'd hear about them because things got ugly and he'd get all worked up about that."

I wondered what Wook did when he got all worked up about something.

"You don't know anything else about who they went after?" I pressed.

"No," she insisted. "Only that it was another brainbox. Then a few days ago, they went after someone else and it all went bad again."

I felt my face flare up and my muscles stiffen. She was talking about Michelle. "Who did they go after?"

"I don't know," she said. "But from what I heard, I think it was a woman."

I was studying every pore in her face looking for a tell about how much of this was true, but I couldn't say for sure, either way. More importantly, I didn't need to hear the rest of that story, not right now anyway, so I asked her the more pertinent question.

"This Mexican. What else do you know about him?"

She opened out her palms, and her voice ebbed. "Nothing. Wook didn't tell me anything else, I swear."

Something still didn't compute. "So your husband and his boys, they just met him six, seven months ago? And just like that, they agree to do some pretty high-risk stuff for him? Doesn't seem like the wise course of action, does it?"

"Wook said they'd worked together before. Years ago."

"Where?"

She sighed, like she was annoyed at herself at having to give it all up. "A few years ago, Wook and the boys used to run shipment security on this side of the border for a Mexican drug baron. This new guy was one of the head honcho's lieutenants. Wook didn't remember him, but he said the guy knew stuff, stuff that only someone who was there would have remembered."

"Like what?"

She stared at me for a moment, looking increasingly uncomfortable. "The Mexican suspected one of his crew was working for a rival cartel. Plotting to take over their turf. Wook was there that day. So was Guru."

"Guru?"

"Gary. Gary Pennebaker. He and Wook founded the Eagles when they got back from Iraq."

I thought back to the two faces on the clubhouse wall that weren't among the dead.

"Anyway, they're there and the Mexican starts cutting the guy up to get him to talk. I don't know the details, but it was bad. Hannibal Lecter bad. Wook said the guy was a real sicko. And Guru and Wook are watching this, and Guru pukes his guts out in front of everybody. Wook couldn't stop laughing." Her expression darkened with what I read as embarrassment, that this upstanding citizen was her man. "Anyway, this new guy, he was there that day. He was one of the head honcho's enforcers. Wook said the way he described it to him, he had to be there. Which was enough to get them started."

She'd already told us she didn't know the new Mexican's name. "Did Wook mention the honcho's name to you?"

She shook her head ruefully. "No."

"What about Pennebaker? Where is he? How come he wasn't at the clubhouse?"

Villaverde was already deep into the ATF file on the Eagles. "It says here he left the club after a stint in prison?"

He looked up at Karen for confirmation.

"That's right."

I was buzzed. This Guru could be the key to ID'ing our bad guy. If he was still alive.

"Where can we find him?"

She just shrugged and said, "Your guess is as good as mine."

30

Tess felt restless as she stood by the door to Alex's room and watched him play with his figurines on the floor by his bed.

They'd already been down to the breakfast buffet, and they were now back in the suite, waiting for Jules, who was on her way. Alex had spent most of the day before indoors, and Tess felt they ought to take him out for some much-needed distraction. Jules had suggested they take him to Balboa Park, which was nearby. There was plenty there to keep him entertained: one of the world's greatest zoos, the Air and Space Museum, the Natural History Museum, and a whole lot more. The idea had excited Alex who had, predictably, chosen the zoo.

Tess couldn't wait to get him there. She was hoping the animals and the shows would take his mind off what had happened and help him find his smile again, even if it was just for a little while.

A smile that bringing up the drawing probably wouldn't inspire.

Tess couldn't get the damn thing off her mind, and she felt bad for obsessing about it. She couldn't help it. And as she turned away, her gaze drifted across to the small dining table by the windows and a bunch of drawings Alex had done the day before.

She had an idea. One she knew she ought to resist, but couldn't.

She went into her bedroom and retrieved the drawing she'd brought back from Michelle's house, then went back into the living room and chose two of the new drawings from the table. She then slid the older one under the two new ones and joined Alex in his room.

She sat on the bed close to him and held up the drawings.

"These are great, Alex. I love them. You did these with Jules, right?"

He nodded but didn't look up, his attention lasered on the alien battle he was orchestrating.

She looked at the first drawing. It showed a jelly-bean-shaped figure and a big marine creature, either a dolphin or a whale. SeaWorld, obviously. The figure had brown hair and was holding a small stick figure, similar to the drawing she was curious about.

"Is that you and the dolphin at SeaWorld?"

Alex didn't respond.

"Alex, tell me—is this you and one of the dolphins?"

This time, Alex flicked a quick, disinterested glance at the drawing, then he shook his head.

Tess felt deflated. "It's not you?"

Alex shook his head again. Then, without looking at her, he said, "It's not a dolphin. It's Shamu."

She felt a twinge of excitement. "Ah, so it's you and a whale."

He nodded.

The next drawing showed Alex with his take on leaping dolphins. He was still lost in his fantasy world, and Tess was finding it hard to engage him. She felt guilty about trying to draw him out of it, especially given what she was about to foist on him. But she also felt she had to do it. The little curio-demon was insisting on it.

"Alex, I found another drawing at your house yesterday and I wanted to ask you about it. Can I ask you about it?"

He didn't answer.

"It's this one," she pressed on, holding it out.

"It's one of yours, isn't it, Alex? I mean, that's you, right? With Ben in your hand?"

This time, he glanced furtively at it. Tess was ready for it, studying his face, trying to read his reaction when he saw it.

The unease flashed through the instant he looked over.

Still, she couldn't stop herself.

"So if this is you, who's that with you?" She pointed at the mystery figure.

Alex didn't reply.

"Alex, who is that? I'd really like to know."

He didn't turn.

"Alex?"

Nothing.

Tess decided she had to try something else. "Alex, tell me something. Did your mommy ever ask you about it, too?"

This time, she got a reaction. A slow, hesitant nod.

"So what did you tell her?"

Grudgingly, without looking at Tess, he said, "We talked about it a little."

"And what did you talk about?"

"Mommy also wanted to know who it was."

"So what did you tell her?"

"I said I don't know."

He seemed to be telling the truth.

"That's all you told your mommy? That you don't know?"

"Yes," he insisted, softly. "That's what I told them."

Them. Not her.

" 'Them'? Who else did you talk to about the drawing, Alex?"

He didn't answer.

"Alex? You said you told your mommy and someone else that you didn't know. Who was it? Who else did you talk to about it?"

He hesitated, then he said, "Dean."

Tess felt the back of her neck sizzle. "Who's Dean, Alex?"

Alex frowned, then he said, "Mommy's friend."

Tess felt lost. Reilly had told her about Tom, but nothing about a Dean. "Where did you see Dean, Alex?"

"At his office. He has a fish tank. He let me feed the fish."

Tess was floundering.

"Why was Mommy asking you about this drawing, Alex? What's special about it?"

"Nothing."

Tess's mind was shooting off in all kinds of directions, none of them clear. She decided to revert to her original question one last time and pointed at the jelly-bean figure with the toy in its hand. "But that's you, right?"

Alex slid a sideways glance at the drawing and, reluctantly, nodded.

"Okay, so . . . who's that?" she insisted softly, pointing at the other one. "Tell me what you told Dean, Alex. I'd really like to know. Who is that?"

Alex didn't reply at first, and without looking at her, he said, "No one."

Tess could see that he was holding back. She could also see that he was scared to tell her who he'd drawn.

Which confirmed what she'd suspected. This was important.

The question was, who was Dean and why did Michelle take Alex to see him?

She didn't want to press Alex any harder, already feeling bad about what she'd asked. But she didn't know who else to ask. She didn't know who Michelle's friends were, if she had any family she was close to, and even if she did, she didn't know if Michelle would have talked about it with them.

There was only one place for her to start finding out.

"Alex, what school do you go to?"

31

Whe needed to find Guru.

Problem was, it looked like he didn't want to be found.

Between Karen and ATF records, we had a decent, if incomplete, bio on the man. Pennebaker and Walker—Guru and Wook—were both local boys who ended up together at Camp Pendleton, where they joined the 1st Marine Division. They both saw active duty in 2003 and 2004 in Iraq, first against the Iraqi Republican Guard, then against the far more combative and deadly insurgents, a mutually loathing mishmash of local militiamen and foreign mercenaries whose only bond was their common hatred of the American and British troops there. Most significantly, Pennebaker and Walker fought side by side in Fallujah during Operation Phantom Fury, a down-and-dirty weeklong street fight that left a heavy mark on all its participants. They managed to make it back home to California with all their limbs intact and with solid service records, but by all accounts, they left Iraq as changed and disillusioned men. Angry, bitter men, according to Karen. They resigned their commissions and bailed on the Marines as soon as they landed on home soil and moved back to San Diego County. Soon after that, they formed the Babylon Eagles. Interestingly, it seemed that Pennebaker was the one who had coined the club's name.

A couple of their war buddies joined them. So did Pennebaker's younger brother, Marty, who'd been floating around aimlessly and barely scraping by. The two missing faces in the photo gallery at the clubhouse—those were the Pennebaker brothers. Then, about a year into the club's life, a scuffle with a rival biker gang left Marty bleeding to death on the street. Pennebaker went ballistic. He found the guy who killed his brother and beat him to a pulp. He then did something unexpected and turned himself in.

At the trial, two things worked in his favor. The biker he'd killed was a scumbag who had a rap sheet as long as his arm. Also, Pennebaker's story resonated with the jury at a time when there was a general feeling that our government wasn't really looking after the returning veterans with the care they deserved. Guru was given a seven-year sentence for manslaughter. He ended up serving only four of them at Ironwood, getting out early on good behavior. That was about fifteen months ago.

Then he disappeared.

The ATF didn't have a take on that. According to Karen, he came out of prison with a new mind-set and didn't want to have anything to do with the club anymore. He saw Walker one time—Karen didn't see him—then he was gone.

No records. Nothing. The man had gone totally off-grid.

I was now twice as interested in finding him. He could potentially help us track down our Mexican bad guy by telling us who he and Walker used to ride shotgun for. Beyond that, the "dropping out" business got my curiosity pinging. He disappears and all kinds of bad stuff starts happening to his ex-bike brothers. Could be a coincidence. They did happen—occasionally.

I couldn't know until we found him.

32

As he took the I-95 up to Mamaroneck, narcotics detective Andy Perrini wondered why Octavio Guerra was so keen to locate the archaeologist who'd turned to writing hokey novels. Obviously there was an angle—the Mexican fixer always had an angle—but Perrini had several of his own irons in the fire right now, so he had decided to not try to second-guess his paymaster on this occasion.

He already knew Tess Chaykin's address; it was in the file he'd prepared for Guerra a few weeks back. The house belonged to Tess's mother, Eileen, though the widowed Mrs. Chaykin appeared to no longer live there. He hadn't been asked to discover where she was, and if Perrini had one rule when he was working for someone else, it was always to do the bare minimum necessary, unless extra effort somehow meant he could skim a bit more wedge off the deal.

Chaykin's boyfriend, an FBI agent assigned to the Counter-Terrorism Task Force who had been the primary subject of his report, had moved in a couple of years ago and the pair of them were now playing house with Chaykin's teenage daughter, Kim. Perrini cringed at the thought of having to live with someone else's kid. But even worse than that was the thought of having to combine family responsibilities with pleasure. He always kept the two strictly compartmentalized. Rachel and the boys in Greenpoint, and Louise in the apartment on Second Avenue, which he paid for with what he euphemistically called his nontaxable income.

Perrini turned onto Mamaroneck Avenue just after two P.M. and flicked on his GPS's soporific female voice for the final part of the journey.

He'd read up on Mamaroneck before he'd set out. The whole civic setup seemed to be unnecessarily complex, with both a village and a town using the same name, but only part of the Village of Mamaroneck was in the Town of Mamaroneck, although all of the Village of Larchmont was considered part of the Town of Mamaroneck. The town's website even had a page to help you determine whether you lived there or not. Apparently "Santa Claus Is Coming to Town" had been written and first performed in the town, which seemed to be its proudest moment. All of this reminded Perrini of why he generally never ventured north of Mount Vernon.

He arrived at his destination and immediately wiped the GPS's memory. He drove along the tree-lined street just within the speed limit and took a good look at the target house and at those on either side. Over the years he'd learned to take in a huge amount of information with only the smallest of glances. As he turned off the street and started to circle back, he already knew that Tess's house had no car parked outside, that the mailbox hadn't been emptied in a couple of days, and that the drapes had been left half open in that ridiculous way that people think sends a signal to passers-by that they're at home when they're really out of town. The feature of the property in which he was most interested was plainly accessible from one side but shielded from the other by a large rhododendron bush. And it was of the perfect type, though he was, of course, prepared for every eventuality.

The neighbors to the left had two boys who were still too young for summer camp—a fact he'd gleaned from the two boy's bikes of different sizes left casually on the grass—but appeared to be out at present. The neighbors on the other side appeared to be retired, which he deduced both from the immaculate garden and the selection of walking sticks leaning against the inside of the porch. The gleaming Lexus in the driveway told him that at least one of them was home. Which suited Perrini perfectly.

Now back where he started, Perrini pulled in about a hundred yards short of the Chaykin house and parked behind a blue Prius. He then called Chaykin's home number again—he'd programmed it into the throwaway he'd bought with cash a few hours earlier. He let it ring for the maximum time allowed by the network, then re-pocketed the phone once the line had gone dead. It was just as he had called it.

No one home.

He fished out a clipboard and a Phillips screwdriver from the stakeout detritus on the backseat and loosened the laces on one of his patent leather shoes, then he climbed out of the car and set off. He walked casually down the street, straightening his tie and sweeping his fingers through his mane of onyx-black hair, a feature that had served him well over the years with both female interview subjects and the still-delectable Louise, who'd been barely twenty when they'd first hooked up.

As he approached the front of Chaykin's property he looked down, noticed his shoelace was undone, and knelt beside the rhododendron bush as if to retie it. He laid down the clipboard, took out the Phillips head, and quickly loosened the screws holding the street number to the gatepost on the near side of Chaykin's driveway. When he had them sufficiently free of the wood, he angled the Phillips head down behind the screw heads, pried off the faux-iron plaque, and quickly put it and the screws in his pocket. Then he tied his shoelace, picked up his clipboard, and continued on his way.

He walked confidently across the driveway of the retired couple, past their immaculate Lexus, and rang the doorbell, holding his clipboard in that officious manner that filled most ordinary citizens with preprogrammed discomfort.

A woman in her sixties opened the door, wearing a well-cut pantsuit and a string of real pearls. A ripple of satisfaction ran through Perrini's chest. This was almost going to be too easy.

"Good afternoon, ma'am," Perrini said in the tone he normally reserved for Rachel's mother and the precinct captain's wife. "I'm from the Fire Prevention Office down on Weaver Street. We're currently going around making sure everyone has their house number clearly displayed from the street, as stipulated by town law."

The woman immediately looked over Perrini's shoulder at the painted china disc stuck to her low picket fence. It was still there. She swung her eyes back to Perrini with a quizzical look.

He smiled.

"You are of course within regulations yourself, ma'am. And a very pretty sign, I might add. Looks lovely against your mimosa."

It was the woman's turn to smile.

Perrini cast his eyes onto his clipboard, on which rather incongruously sat that week's roster for the Ninth Precinct's narcotics squad.

"No, ma'am. I am inquiring with regard to the house number of your neighbor"—Perrini tapped his clipboard with a pencil—"a Tess Chaykin?" He gestured over to the gate post from which he had only just removed the number and gave her an apologetic wince. "No number visible."

The woman gave her pearls a small, anxious tug. Clearly, the thought of anyone on her street being in contravention of town laws was somewhat troubling.

Perrini had to suppress his smirk.

"We've already written to Miss Chaykin regarding this matter, but so far we haven't heard back. Now, we don't like to fine people unless we absolutely have to. Maybe Miss Chaykin is away for the summer and there's no one to check her mail?"

The woman nodded. "She's out of town. But her boyfriend's here," she added, with a pointed little grimace of disapproval to go with *boyfriend*, of course, "though I haven't seen him since Saturday morning. Maybe he hasn't been opening her mail?"

Guerra had told Perrini that Sean Reilly was in San Diego, so no surprise there.

"Is there any way you could reach her?" said Perrini, in such a way as not to suggest the slightest note of aggression. "I can hold off on the fine, but I can't do it forever."

"Well, I'm not sure I can," she said, apologetically. "She's in Arizona with her daughter. They're out at her aunt's place. Can't it wait till she gets back? I think she's only there for a couple of weeks."

And with that Perrini had got exactly what he'd come for, so he decided to ease off and leave the Town of Mamaroneck's laws where he'd found them. He held up the pencil, then wrote a meaningless scribble on the top sheet of the clipboard. "I think I can hold off till then. I'll make a note to come around again in a couple of weeks. Thank you so much for your time."

The woman smiled at him and retreated into her house.

Perrini went back to his car and called Guerra's secure line from his own cell phone. He knew Guerra wouldn't answer unless the Mexican fixer's firewall could identify exactly who was calling and authorize the call.

Guerra picked up immediately.

"Did you find her?"

Guerra's military-like bluntness always grated on Perrini, though he knew that the man had at one point been a full colonel in the Mexican army, before he had retired under something of a cloud.

"She's not here. She's in Arizona, at her aunt's place."

Guerra paused for a second, then he said, "I need confirmation that she's there. Call me when you have it." Then the line went dead.

Perrini had to admire Guerra's brutal efficiency, if nothing else.

He pulled out of the side street and headed back to the city. As he turned onto the thruway, he called Lina Dawetta, a clerk at the Ninth Precinct with whom he had his own brutally effective relationship. She did whatever he asked her to, in order for him not to report her cocaine habit to her boss—a habit he had done everything to encourage and now fed.

He knew she wouldn't cross him. The last person to do that had been dragged out of the East River with half a face. And that back-stabbing scumbag had been a cop.

"I need something," he told her, before telling her what it was and agreeing on a time and place to meet.

33

By midday, we were firing on all cylinders.

The three of us were still at the police station in La Mesa, finishing up our interviews with the prospects. Villaverde had as many bodies as he could muster out at the bureau's office working on tracking down Pennebaker. Munro was doing the same with his people in LA. ATF was also in on the act, which was where I was putting my money, but the breakthrough I was waiting for was playing hard to get.

The prospects didn't have much to say. In more mundane circumstances, that wouldn't have surprised me. Biker clubs prized loyalty and commitment more than anything. In outlaw gangs, it was like a blood oath. Patch holders did not discuss club business with anyone outside the club, ever. So, normally, I would have put the prospects' lack of chattiness down to them seeing it as an opportunity to showcase their worthiness to the club they were trying to join, but in this case, there was no club. Not anymore. Everyone in its mother chapter had been wiped out. So I didn't see why the prospects would still want to protect their sponsors, given that they were all dead. Which told me that what they were telling us was the truth. Walker and his crew knew how to keep things quiet.

None of the local missing persons reports coming in threw up anyone whose profile matched the previous kidnap victims—scientists, chemists, pharmacologists. We were spreading the net up to San Francisco and beyond, across the whole state, but so far, nothing.

We did get one lead, though. Nothing major, but it was some-thing.

It was from the squad car of the deputy who'd gone to pick up Soulpatch/Scrape from the grotto.

These days, more and more squad cars were being equipped with in-car video cameras. It made sense on a whole bunch of levels. Drunk drivers overwhelmingly pleaded no contest when told they were be-ing filmed, resulting in less paperwork and court time. Municipal bean counters loved them—the cameras, not the drunk drivers—since they helped cut down on the tens of millions of dollars paid out in lawsuits on unsubstantiated claims that couldn't be effectively thrown out without the video records. They were also a great boon in proving probable cause for vehicle searches and seizures, resulting in more confiscated drug money. And cops loved the fact that hard-heads were far more reluctant to throw punches at them or even turn belligerent while on camera.

Unfortunately, the cameras didn't stop the thugs who came after Scrape.

They did, however, allow us a glimpse into what had happened, despite the fact that the shooters had thought of pulling out the re-writable DVD from the overhead-mounted console inside the car. What they didn't know was that the video system in Fugate's patrol car also included an integrated hard drive that not only backed up anything that was on the DVD, it also added ten minutes of pre- and post-event footage to it.

It was all there for us, downloaded, cued up, and ready for viewing in high-res color.

We started with the footage from the front-facing camera. It was brief, but intense. The deputy's car is heading toward the gate of the warehouse. No one else is around. Then a big black SUV, a Chevy Tahoe, turns into the complex and just charges at the squad car. We barely get a glimpse of it as the deputy curses and swerves to avoid it, and the camera angle swings away—then the picture rocks wildly and spins around as the SUV rams the deputy's car and sends it sliding into a ditch.

Fugate curses again, but from that point on, the footage from the front view camera is useless. Nothing is going on in front of the stalled car. But that's when the backseat camera comes into play.

The footage from it was far more disturbing.

It starts with Scrape, sliding across the seat, his hand pressed against his shoulder, muttering "Easy" and wincing with pain as he settles back. He doesn't look great. Then the car drives off and he's bouncing around back there—then his face goes wild with alarm, the SUV plows into them, and he's thrown around like a puppet before he pitches forward and slams straight into the impact-resistant glass partition as the car hits the ditch and comes to a standstill.

And that's when the footage got real bad.

With Scrape looking on, his face tight with terror, a gunshot rips through our ears and a splatter of blood hits the partition as, off camera, the deputy is shot through the head at point-blank range. Then Scrape starts to scream as he frantically squeezes as far away from the door as he can while a figure—unclear at this point—reaches in to drag him out. We hear the scuffle and the banging of Scrape's boots against the partition and we see the dark figure's gloved hands latching onto the yelling and screaming biker before yanking him out of the car by his legs. Then the image stays fixated on the ghostly backseat while in the background, faint but audible, some car doors slam shut and the Tahoe screeches off.

After a moment of stunned silence, I said, "Let's see that again. The part where the shooter goes for Scrape."

We watched the grim sequence again, looking for a tell that would help us track down the killers. I was hoping we'd get something on the guy who leaned in to grab Scrape—a glimpse of his face or maybe just a reflection of it on something in the car. But most of his head was blocked by the bulky metal frame of the partition. Then I spotted something and hit the Pause button.

"Right there. What is that?"

I went back a few frames and held it there, on an image of the killer struggling with one of Scrape's legs. He was wearing something dark and long-sleeved, but as he fought to hold down the biker, his left sleeve had ridden up and I could see something around his wrist, between the top of his glove and the edge of his sleeve.

I got the tech to zoom in and enhance it as best he could, and we got a clearer look at it. It was a leather wristband. An elaborate one, about half an inch wide. It seemed intricately tooled, with silver strands and some tiny blue gemstones.

Not exactly a fingerprint, I grumbled inwardly, staring at the screen, puzzled by why they had taken Scrape and not shot him on the spot, and wondering what state he'll be in when we finally catch up to him.

My deliberations were interrupted by our point of contact at La Mesa PD knocking on the door. Villaverde gestured through the door's glass inset for the cop to enter and he quickly joined us, his body language telling us that whatever he had to say was important.

"Karen Walker wants to talk to you. She's on hold. Line four."

I duly pressed the button and put the call on speaker.

"Karen? This is Agent Reilly."

"I thought of something else. About Guru's kid brother, Marty. I don't know why I didn't think of it yesterday, but maybe it can help you find him."

She was obviously serious about earning her immunity.

"Shoot."

"Marty had a girlfriend. Dani—Danielle Namour. He and Dani were really close and she was devastated when he died. So devastated I wondered if there was more to it, if I was missing something, and I asked her about it. Turns out, she was newly pregnant. The kid was Marty's. I don't know, maybe it's nothing, but maybe it's not, you know?"

"Everything helps, Karen. Where can we find her?"

"We lost touch not long after the shooting. Maybe she was following Guru's lead, I don't know. She didn't want to have anything to do with us either. I heard she did have the baby. A girl."

"Karen, where can we find her?" I pressed again.

"Last I heard, she was living down in Chula Vista, working in a high-end fashion store at the Chula Vista Center. But that information's a couple of years old."

"Thanks, Karen, that's great. We'll talk to her."

I could hear some relief in her tone. "Like I said, I want you to get the bastards who did that to Eli."

I ended the call and looked at our POC, who was already heading for the door.

"We'll get right on it," he said as he left the room.

I stared at the phone and played the call over again in my head. It might turn out to be nothing, but then again, blood is the thickest of all ties, especially when tragedy strikes. A fact I had just experienced at first hand.

Pennebaker clearly had a conscience.

Maybe it extended to his niece.

34

Tess felt uneasy as the color drained from the principal's face.

The woman, Marlene Cohen, hadn't heard the news about Michelle's death, and Tess hadn't relished being the one to break it to her, but she didn't have much of a choice. What she did, though, was avoid going into too much detail about what had happened, limiting herself to telling her that there had been a break-in at Michelle's house, and that the intruders had shot her, fatally.

They were in the principal's office at Merrimac Elementary, a smart and cheerful preschool-to-grade-six school that sat at the end of a cul-de-sac by San Clemente Park, close to where Michelle lived. Tess had checked out the website of the school before heading out there, and the first thing she'd noticed was how glowing its reviews were. Clearly, Michelle had done her homework and had chosen a highly regarded school for Alex. It made Tess think of the exercise she'd soon need to do herself on that front—school selection, admissions, and everything that went along with being the parent of a young child in today's manic, highly competitive world. It had been years since her daughter, Kim, had been in grade school, and the thought of going through it all again was daunting. Surfing through the website of Alex's school had made her stop and think, in more gritty detail, about how very different her life was going to be from now on.

The website informed her that the school ran some summer camps, which meant there'd be staff there for Tess to talk to. It also had a list of faculty members, but there were no Deans on it. Tess hadn't been able to get anything more out of Alex about who he was talking about. In fact, most of the faculty were women. So she'd taken a cab out to the school and asked to see the principal.

Cohen, a tall, elegant, gray-haired woman who reminded Tess of a figure from a Modigliani painting, took a moment to collect herself before inquiring about Alex, how he was doing, what would happen to him. She told Tess she didn't know the boy personally, but she thought she remembered seeing him and Michelle at school events.

"What can I do to help you?" she finally asked.

"I found a drawing that Alex had done that I was curious about, and when I asked him about it, he said his mom took him to see someone called Dean. I'm thinking maybe it's some kind of counselor. Does that name mean anything to you?"

Cohen pursed her lips and shook her head. "No, not really. We don't have any Deans on staff here. What was the issue with the drawing?"

"I'm not really sure. It shows Alex and someone else, kind of an ominous-looking figure. And when I asked him about it, he didn't want to talk about it. He seemed scared by it. What about his teachers? Maybe they know something."

"Alex was in prekindergarten," Cohen said as she checked her computer. "He was in room two. Miss Fowden's group."

"And she never mentioned anything to you about him?"

"Nothing."

Tess frowned. "Is she around? I'd love to talk to her."

Cohen's nose crumpled apologetically. "She's not working this summer."

"I really need to talk to her. Can I call her? Do you know if she's around?"

Cohen looked at her, uncertain.

"Please. It's important."

Cohen smiled. "Sure. Let me try her."

She picked up her phone, glanced at the computer screen to get the teacher's number, and dialed. Tess watched anxiously as the call seemed to go unanswered, then Cohen spoke up.

"Holly, it's Marlene. I've got a woman here who needs to talk to you. It's about Alex Martinez."

Tess's heart deflated. From the principal's tone, she'd evidently reached the teacher's voicemail.

Tess gave Cohen her cell phone number, which Cohen included in her message. Then she thanked her and left.

As she walked back to the waiting cab, she felt the midday sun weighing down on her, draining and oppressive. She relived her chat with Alex, and the fear she saw on his face was still there, like a wraith, stalking her through the heat haze.

It was still there as the cab drove off, and she pulled out her iPhone to let Jules know she was on her way back. Her hand stopped and she stared at the phone for a moment.

The edge of her mouth cracked with a small grin and she hit two on her speed dial. Reilly's number.

"Everything okay?" he asked, picking up promptly, as he always did.

"Yeah. I'm at Alex's school. I just had a chat with the principal. It's a great little place. Nice people." She didn't really want to mention the drawing again. "Tell me something. You guys have Michelle's phone, right?"

"We do."

"Could you check and see if there's a Dean in her contacts list or in her calendar?"

"Why?"

"Alex mentioned something about Michelle taking him to see someone by that name. I don't know who he is, but . . . might be good to have a chat with him, don't you think?"

Reilly went silent for a second, then said, "This is about the drawing, isn't it?"

She cursed inwardly. He knew her way too well. "Yes. I asked him about it, okay? He was scared, Sean. He was definitely scared and he didn't want to talk about it. All I could get out of him was that Michelle was also curious about it and took him to see this Dean to discuss it. That's worth checking out, isn't it? I mean, what if someone was threatening him? What if it's related to what happened to Michelle?"

Reilly went quiet again. "Dean."

"That's it."

"Okay," he relented, clearly not convinced. "I've got to go."

"Love ya, big guy."

"Right back at ya."

She put her phone away, stared out the window, and exhaled heavily, trying to ignore the prickles of impatience that were stabbing away at every pore of her body.

35

Sitting at the solitary booth in the back of the Black Iron Burger Shop on East Fifth Street, Perrini wiped the last traces of the burger and the side of onion rings from his mouth and stretched his arms out lazily. As freelance jobs went, this one was almost embarrassingly easy. He knew this was a rarity, especially after one of the previous year's jobs for Guerra had turned from strictly an information-gathering exercise into shutting down the local operation of a particularly aggressive Mexican cartel that was trying to muscle its way into the city.

Initially he had balked at turning off one of his newest suppliers of cash-stuffed envelopes, but the rival cartel that had hired Guerra in the first place were so pleased with how things had turned out that they had given Perrini a rather sizeable bonus, albeit one from which Guerra had creamed off a hefty twenty-percent commission. Nevertheless, it would be enough to put Nate, Perrini's eldest son, through college, and a good one, too.

Perrini had taken no chances with the fallout. Within a week of the entire upper echelon of the incoming cartel's New York City contingent being sent to Rikers, Perrini had ensured that his sometime contact had been fatally stuck with a rather nasty shank by an up-and-coming lieutenant of the incumbent African-American gang in the South Bronx, a favor arranged by an old friend at the Forty-first. The killing had been marked down to a racial slur and had therefore been logged as having nothing to do with a turf war between competing Mexican gangs.

It was a win-win for Perrini, as the freshly triumphant outfit was from then on more than generous with both their cash and their product. In fact, he had a twenty-gram bag of their finest uncut cocaine sitting in his left trouser pocket at this very moment.

He waved over the waitress to ask for another vanilla malt and saw Lina Dawetta walk into the restaurant. He watched her glance around edgily, clearly making sure there was no one she knew in there. She then walked over to the booth and sat on one of the vacant stools facing the detective.

Seeing as the restaurant was just a couple of blocks from the precinct house, bumping into somebody one of them knew was an occupational hazard, though the only time it had happened to date, Perrini had calmly fielded a sly smile from a homicide detective with whom he was on no more than corridor-greeting terms. Let them think he was screwing a lowly PAA. Though the powder was gradually taking its toll, Lina was strikingly attractive in an olive-skinned, auburn-haired Sicilian way, and Perrini knew that the unspoken code between male cops would keep his wife from ever hearing about it.

"You want something to eat?" said Perrini, smiling at the young police administrative assistant as though she were his favorite niece or beloved sister, rather than a civilian who earned a third of his detective's basic salary.

"No. Just a Diet Sprite."

She set down her open purse on the vacant stool beside her.

Perrini relayed the order to the waitress, then without taking his eyes off Lina or changing the smile on his face, nonchalantly removed the bag of cocaine from his pocket, stretched his hand underneath the bar-height table, and dropped the bag into Lina's purse.

It was a point of principle with Perrini always to go first in any exchange. It promoted trust and reduced his risk should the meeting be compromised before the end. He never understood why so many people insisted on the kind of ridiculous ballet you saw in movies. He was happy to trust the other party to make good, just as the other party should trust that he would not be amused if they tried to fuck him over.

Lina took out her lipstick and compact from the purse in a practiced movement that included moving the cocaine bag to a side pocket where it couldn't be viewed by a passing customer.

The waitress delivered their drinks as Lina ran the lipstick across her pale lips, returned both objects back to where they'd come from, then took out a folded sheet of yellow legal paper and opened it on the table in front of her.

"Hazel Lustig. Born July 18, 1947. Sister of Eileen Chaykin, nee Lustig. Never married. No children. No federal warrants. No local traffic violations. Taxes all in order. Qualified as an equine veterinarian in 1971. By 1985 had her own practice in New Jersey specializing in race horses. Sold it in 1998 and retired to Cochise County, Arizona, where she owns three hundred acres and cares for about forty retired racehorses. The ranch isn't open to the public. Two bank accounts, both in the black. One significantly so."

Lina slid the sheet across the table.

"Phone number?" asked Perrini after draining half his malt in one long slug.

"Home number is right there. She doesn't have a cell phone. I also checked the cell reception in that area like you asked. It's spotty at best. Locals and the press out there have been making noise about that, but the mobile carriers don't give a crap." She took a sip of her Diet Sprite as Perrini scanned the sheet. "Anything else?"

Perrini folded the sheet and pocketed it. "Not that I can think of right now, but that could change. I'll be in touch. As always."

"Thought you should know. They're purging all the unused NCIC accounts. I'll have to create a spoof login if they delete them all."

"As long as you keep me out of it I don't care what you do." Perrini flashed Lina an arctic glare. A split second later, the smile with which he'd welcomed her was back.

"I'd better get back to my desk. Got a mountain of cases to key in." She lifted her purse off the stool and turned to leave.

"Enjoy your little present," said Perrini, gesturing to her purse. "You know there's plenty more where that came from."

He shot her a wink, then dropped his eyes to his malt and drained it down to the foam.

When he looked up, she was already out the door.

Twenty minutes later, Perrini was back in his car, across from Tompkins Square. He had toyed with a few different approaches, but decided to go with an angle that usually worked wonders: appealing to a person's natural vanity, even if it was at one step removed.

He pulled out his throwaway and dialed Hazel Lustig. She answered after five rings.

"Hello?"

"Hi. Is that Hazel Lustig?"

"Yes. Who's this?"

"My name is Daniel Shelton. I'm calling from the Historical Novel Society. I understand from Friedstein and Bellingham Literary Management that Miss Chaykin is staying with you at the moment?"

It was a gamble that Chaykin had left her aunt's number with her agent, but if she was there for a month and the cell reception was bad, then the odds were surely stacked in his favor.

"I'm afraid she's not here. Can I pass on a message?"

Her tone was defensive. Protective. Too late to change tack now though.

"Oh, that's a shame. We're running a review of her latest book—and, well, it's a rave. I just got it, and the reviewer really, really loved it. And I thought it would be great to get an interview to go alongside it, do a little feature on her, but I'm playing catch-up here with a lot of people off on vacation and I've got a deadline coming up fast. Do you know when she'll be back? We could do it over the phone, or even by email."

The woman went quiet for a moment, then said, "The thing is, I'm really not sure she's got much time to spare right now, she's—she's tied up on a family matter." Her tone had softened at the mention of a rave review. Seemingly an appeal to vanity by proxy was almost as effective as direct praise.

"I'm real sorry to hear that. We're all huge fans of her books here. I hope it's nothing serious."

Perrini waited for the reply, but Hazel wasn't biting.

"No," she said, "nothing major, thank you. If you give me your number, I'll be sure to pass on your message."

He gave her the number of his fresh throwaway plus an email address he'd created while sitting in the car digesting the double-patty delights of his recent fix. Then he thanked her politely and ended the call.

Miss Chaykin was playing hard to get. And although Perrini enjoyed twisting sixty-year-old women around his little finger—a feat he still couldn't achieve when it came to his mother, who always seemed to know exactly what he was thinking—it was clearly time to apply a more straightforward approach.

He wondered about what the woman had told him. Tess Chaykin was "tied up with a family matter." Her aunt would "pass on" his message. Perrini wondered about that, and it sounded to him like Chaykin was out of town. He thought about Guerra's request and about Chaykin's boyfriend being out in San Diego and what Perrini had found out about him, and he wondered if that was the family matter she was dealing with.

Problem was, Guerra had no interest in probabilities. He demanded facts. Which left Perrini with little choice but to spend a bigger chunk of his fee than he would have liked on a third party, an option he avoided as much as he could—not just due to the expense involved, but also because it involved using people he didn't know and required them to do something that could land them with federal-level problems if they were found out.

He took out his phone and called Lina. She answered immediately.

"I need a fix on a cell phone. The full workout."

"Ouch."

Lina knew the ramifications, too.

"I need it. I'll text you the number."

"Okay," she relented. "Ship it over."

Perrini knew the drill. It would take anything between thirty minutes and five hours for Lina to come back with a location. There were several variables involved: the make and model of Chaykin's handset, what carrier she was with, the cell coverage at her location, the number of masts there, and whether her phone was GPS enabled or not. On the plus side, Lina had a few tricks of her own. A combination of geek-level expertise in using the data at her disposal, plus contacts she'd nurtured at three of the big cell phone carriers, meant that Lina had not once failed to provide an accurate lock on any number he'd given her.

Perrini decided to have a quick nap before he returned to the station house. By the end of the day, there was a good chance he'd know exactly where Tess Chaykin was, and so would Guerra.

What the Mexican chose to do then was no concern of his, though Perrini was pretty sure that, given the kind of clients Guerra usually worked for, her best days were now probably behind her.

36

We left the La Mesa station house in Munro's Yukon, taking
Spring Street to the South Bay Freeway, then heading south.
Villaverde had opted to go back to Aero Drive and brief his team
on everything we'd learned to date. He said he'd include Jules on the
briefing, via speakerphone. Also, one of his guys had volunteered to
drive my LaCrosse back to HQ so that I wouldn't be without a vehicle later in the day, which was something I don't think anyone in
the New York office would've thought of offering.

The run down to Chula Vista was a breeze, with the early evening
traffic still several hours away and Munro driving with the urgency
that we both felt. La Mesa PD had done a great job locating Dani
Namour, and they'd sent us the name of the store where she worked.
I'd asked them not to tip her off that we were headed down there,
since although it was clear that she'd severed her ties with the Eagles,
we didn't know what else was going on in her life and I couldn't be
sure she wouldn't bolt at the first sign of law enforcement. So they'd
had one of their female officers call the boutique from her cell phone
and ask what days Dani worked because she'd been "so helpful" on
the last visit. Not only was Dani working today, but she was mid-shift.

Maybe we had finally caught a break. I was feeling optimistic,
thinking it would be pretty unlikely that whoever had all but wiped
out the Babylon Eagles knew about her.

A few blocks out from our destination, Dani's rap sheet came
through on Munro's handset. From the looks of it, and against all

odds, she'd managed to keep her nose clean. Apart from a couple of minor traffic violations, she seemed like a model citizen. Which boded well for her daughter.

We parked in the lot outside Macy's and walked over to the main entrance, which was marked by an octagonal tower sporting a faux cupola, a far cry from the domes of Vatican City that had probably inspired it. A quick glance at the store locator had Vanessa—the boutique where Dani worked—on the south side of the mall facing a CVS, and we headed there after Munro had stopped to grab a couple of sodas, reminding me that I'd been running on empty since that morning.

The store was one of those up-market fashion outlets that sold a small selection of items, all from big-name designers. There was an elegantly dressed and heavily made-up woman somewhere in her forties serving a customer, and a younger blonde in her mid-twenties standing farther back, at the cashier's desk, leafing through a glossy magazine—Dani. Unsurprisingly, she didn't look anything like what I imagined, given the image I had of her as a biker chick. Her clothes, hair, and makeup were all immaculate. She'd clearly left the biker life well behind, although I was hoping just a little link to that world remained, a link that was as thick as blood in this case.

Munro waited by the entrance while I went inside.

"Miss Namour?"

She had already looked up when I walked in and was now gazing straight at me. She knew there was no way I was there to buy a dress.

"Yes?"

She was scrutinizing me and starting to show the unmistakable signs of someone who knows that their day is about to take a turn for the worse. I flashed my creds discreetly at her, making sure the older woman wasn't looking over.

"Could we step outside for a minute?"

Dani smoothed down her jacket and glanced over to her boss. "Suzie, I need to go out for a sec and help this gentleman out with something."

Suzie nodded uncertainly, then got back to her customer. Dani gestured me through the door and followed me out of the shop.

"There's a food court on the next level up. We can talk there."

I tilted my head for Munro to follow and the three of us headed for the escalator, Dani leading the way.

She obviously had a steady job and had successfully moved on after her time around the Eagles went sour, and I felt bad about having to stir up all that pain again, but we were way behind the curve and needed something to get us back on track. We sat outside one of those Mexican restaurants that are a step up from Taco Bell but still the wrong side of the real thing, and got down to business.

"I'm Agent Reilly, FBI. And this is Agent Munro."

"DEA," he added.

She cut us off before I got any further with my introductions.

"This is about the clubhouse, right?"

I nodded.

"I saw the news, and you're wasting your time. I don't know anything about that," she said, her tone firm and defensive. "I've had nothing to do with those guys for years."

The anger and bitterness erupted so quickly it was almost a shock, though I'd learned over years of interrogation that the bad stuff always lurks right up against the surface, whether you can see it there or not.

"Your daughter, Naomi," I told her. "She's Marty's kid, right?"

At her daughter's name, Dani's face hardened with a mother's protective instinct, but then when I mentioned Marty, her face softened and her eyes flicked away for a moment as memory took over.

"Why are you here? Look, Naomi has no clue who her father was, and I want to keep it that way."

Munro stepped in with perfect tag-team timing. He laid both hands palm-up on the table in front of him and gave Dani a wide smile. "We can see you've got a life here. We're not interested in doing anything to hurt that. When people leave a bad life behind, get a job, raise a kid, pay taxes . . . it makes our job a whole lot easier. One less wasted life is one less violent death to write up. If all the girl-friends, wives, and mothers just got up and walked away from the gangs, how long do you think the guys would last before reassessing their life choice?" He gave her his patented gotta-love-me grin.

Dani relaxed visibly at that. Munro had hit just the right chord. The bastard was good at his job.

It was my turn. "We're here 'cause we're looking for Gary." I watched for her reaction to the name, and I got the surprise I was expecting. "We think he can help us nail the guys who wiped out the club. I don't blame you for not wanting to get involved, but these guys, they're seriously bad. They also killed a deputy up in San Marcos. Guy had a kid. Same age as Naomi." I let that percolate for a moment. "We think Gary knew one of them back in the day, and given what they did to the guys, I think he'd want to help us track them down. Thing is, we don't know where he is and we need your help to find him."

She took a deep breath, then sighed, suddenly resigned to the incontrovertible fact that one never truly leaves the past behind.

"He doesn't want to be found and that's okay by me. I'm doing just fine without any of them." She looked at Munro as she added, "Just like you said."

He nodded at that, clearly appreciating that she'd been listening.

"My parents near disowned me when I started hanging out at the club, but they helped out when Marty got himself killed. I think they were grateful I was still alive. They still look after Naomi so I can work. I paid for my father's laser eye surgery last year. He says he can see better now than when he was twenty."

She was proud of how far she'd come. And rightly so. But it was becoming clear that we'd made the trip down to Chula Vista for nothing. Dani's eyes wandered off. Munro and I had been in the job long enough to let her go wherever she was going. After a long moment she landed back with us. I leaned forward, sensing that she might have brought something back with her.

"I don't know where he is. He told me how much he'd miss hanging out with me and Naomi and said maybe things would change one day, but that day hasn't come yet."

I had to keep pushing, to keep prompting her in the hope that something would rise to the surface. "People rarely manage to disappear completely," I told her. "They often miss something. Some detail, some contact, something they might have mentioned. Think about it, Dani. If this were a life-and-death situation and you needed to reach him, how would you do it?"

"I don't know," she said, visibly trying to come up with something. "He just wanted a new life." Then something sparked on her face. "Maybe . . . You could try one thing. After I got pregnant, Marty and I once talked about what we'd do, if things ever got too hot. If we ever had to get out. I was thinking about the baby and worrying about the kind of life Marty was into. And he told me about this guy that Gary knew in the Marines. A real wizard for fake IDs. Marty said we'd use him before heading for the border. Maybe that's what Gary did. Maybe he used the guy to get himself a new life."

I shared a quick glance with Munro. This could be something. When people dropped off the grid they often used fake or stolen IDs, and knowing the source of the ID would be a huge boon.

"Did he tell you the guy's name?"

She shook her head. "No. Maybe he did, but I don't remember. Sorry."

Another wall. Easy come, easy go, right?

"If you find him," she added, "say hi from me. Tell him I think it'd be good for Naomi to get to know her uncle."

She stood, smoothed down her jacket, and turned to go. After a second she looked back.

"Bear in mind, he probably wants to be found even less than I did."

Then she headed for the escalator and was gone.

I called Villaverde and gave him the update. He needed to look for Marines from Walker and Pennebaker's days who had done time for fraud, or had criminal records before they joined up. I also had another idea. Something more specific. Something that would fit with the two bikers' feelings about the military. It was a long shot, but at this point we had to try anything that might move us forward.

"Look for soldiers over the past ten years that were listed as MIA, but then came back onto the grid. Start at Camp Pendleton and work out from there."

Villaverde immediately grasped what I was suggesting. "So Pennebaker walks out of prison and somehow assumes the ID of a missing soldier?"

"Yeah. And most likely one with no living relatives. I get the impression that the new Pennebaker wouldn't have wanted to hurt a soldier's family, but would have no qualms about deceiving the government."

"I'll get my guys straight onto it. You coming back here?"

I said we'd head straight up to Aero Drive.

By the time we got back to his office, Villaverde was sitting at the main meeting room table with two other agents, going through army service records. I joined the party while Munro found an empty desk and put in a call to Corliss.

He told me he'd made contact with the USACIDC—the United States Army Criminal Investigation Command—at MCB Quantico and requested the service histories that we needed. With both the FBI and the DEA pressing for access—and adding into the mix that both San Diego PD and the SDSO wouldn't back off until they found whoever killed Deputy Fugate—he hadn't had to face any jurisdictional stare-downs.

There were seventeen soldiers who fit our profile. All of them had been listed MIA at some point over the past ten years, but only five of them had returned to the fold in one way or another in the last two, which was our window for Pennebaker. Of the other twelve, nine had been confirmed dead and three were still listed as missing.

We were trying to find someone born between 1970 and 1985

who looked enough like Pennebaker for him to assume his identity. There was one name that stood out. Marine Sergeant Matthew Frye. Born 1982. Listed as missing in 2003. Came back on the grid in 2009. Missed three psych evaluation appointments but had finally been discharged at the beginning of 2010. He still had his tags and had been identified by a sister, who was his only living relative. Placed side by side, Frye and Pennebaker could have been brothers, notwithstanding their choice of optional mustache.

"Where's Frye now?"

One of the junior agents pushed a few keys on the laptop facing them, then spun it around to face Villaverde, who shared the details.

"Social Security has him in Los Angeles. Works at a private rehab clinic up in Montecito Heights. Sleeps there, too, by the looks of it. His work address and residential address are the same."

Call it instinct, call it fifteen years on the job, but I knew this was our man. Pennebaker walks out of prison a changed man, but almost certainly still bitter about the past. Feels more like a soldier than anything else, but has seen and heard too much ever to go back to active service. Needs to leave his recent past behind because those years were notable for some serious criminal activity. We knew that Walker and Pennebaker had a reputation for getting the job done. Why else would someone want to hire them years after they last worked together? That kind of reputation works both ways. It all fit. The only way to know for sure was to meet him. Any kind of contact before then risked putting him back on the missing list.

I turned to Villaverde. "We need to get up to LA."

"This time of day, you'll need to go by air."

He had seemingly crunched the facts the same way I had.

He picked up a phone and told the other end that he needed a chopper.

Twenty minutes later, we were airborne in an LAPD JetRanger on the way to have a chat with a man I hoped would turn out to be our own guru.

37

Tess hated waiting.

She was impatient from minute one, as her mom never failed to remind her, often adding that it was a small miracle that Tess had had the decency to stick around inside of her for the full nine months and not kicked and screamed her way out prematurely.

She was back at the hotel, with Jules and Alex. They'd gone downstairs for a light lunch, and they were now back in their rooms. Jules was on a conference call with her office while Tess was on the couch with Alex, reading *Tikki Tikki Tembo* with him. It was one of his favorites, one he'd asked her to bring back from the house. It was also a book she remembered reading to Kim years ago, but even with that added emotional kick, its charm and its amusing tongue-twisters still weren't enough to drag Tess's mind off the drawing or calm her bubbling impatience.

Then her phone rang.

She picked it up, saw a number she didn't recognize, and her pulse vaulted. She never answered a call that fast.

It was Holly Fowden, Alex's teacher.

Tess thanked her for getting in touch as she sprang off the bed and slipped into her bedroom, closing the door behind her. She then explained who she was and what had happened. Fowden also hadn't heard about Michelle's death, and her voice broke as she struggled to find the right words to say. Tess helped her by moving the conversation along and told her about what had prompted her visit to the school and her chat with the principal.

"Alex's mom did come to see me," Fowden told her. "She showed me that drawing."

"Why?"

"She didn't explain much. She just said Alex seemed to be troubled by something and wanted to know how he was in class."

"And how was he?"

"Normal. Happy. I didn't notice anything wrong with him."

"But she did?"

"Well . . . yes." She sounded a bit uncomfortable discussing it with Tess, but carried on. "She said he hadn't been sleeping well and having nightmares . . . She also said he'd been saying things she didn't understand, things she was surprised he knew. She seemed confused by it all and wanted to know if I'd talked about them in class."

"Like what?"

"Names of places. Cities and towns in South America. And animals like boas and piranhas, I remember her saying."

"And you hadn't taught them that?"

"No."

Tess wasn't sure why this was surprising to Michelle. He could have easily picked those things up while watching television.

"Did he say anything like that to you?"

"After she mentioned them, I noticed that some of his drawings had a different feel than what other kids would normally draw, but again, nothing too out of the ordinary. But there was one thing he did say that surprised me. I didn't really think much of it until after his mom called."

Tess felt a spark of anticipation. "What was it?"

"We were out in the park and I had the kids draw some of the flowers that were there. And Alex drew this white flower that was really gorgeous. But when I asked him which one he was drawing, he said it wasn't one of the ones in the park. And then he said something else. He said, 'They say it fixes your heart, but actually it kills people.'"

Tess wondered what kind of TV shows he'd been watching. "A flower that kills people?"

"I know, weird, right? But when I asked him what he meant, he didn't want to say. It's odd, though, 'cause lately, he's been more articulate and seems to have a richer vocabulary than his classmates. But on that occasion, he didn't want to say more."

"So how did you leave it?"

"I told his mom I'd let her know if he said or did anything unusual or if he seemed at all unhappy about anything. I saw her when she dropped him off a couple of times. She said she was taking him to see a specialist but didn't really go into detail."

"What, like a shrink?"

"Yes. A child psychologist. Privately. She didn't want to involve the school in it. She didn't want Alex to be labeled in any way. You know how it is."

Tess was familiar with that kind of pressure. "Do you know who she took him to see?"

"No."

"Did she say anything about him?"

Fowden thought about it, then said, "No, I'm sorry. I got the feeling she was kicking herself for even mentioning it to me."

Tess had to get more. "Was it a man or a woman?"

Fowden paused, then said, "A man. Yeah, I'm pretty sure she referred to him as 'he.'"

Tess thanked her, got her number, and ended the call.

She didn't have much. A first name that may or may not relate to a local shrink.

Tess left her room and saw that Jules had ended her call and was now playing with Alex. She hesitated to interrupt them, then picked up her iPad, went back to her room, fired up Safari, and started trawling the online listings for psychologists in the San Diego area named Dean.

38

We landed at Hooper Heliport at five thirty, took the elevator down to the street, and got straight into a Bureau Suburban that was waiting for us. Our destination was only five miles out. As we drove north toward the hills, the agent riding shotgun briefed us on the clinic.

"The place was founded about twenty years ago by Ursula Marshall, on an endowment. It's got twenty beds. Day center caters to another ten. The patients don't pay a dime, and the waiting list runs over two hundred. Ursula's daughter was a runaway. Died of an overdose at nineteen. Ursula's dad owned a big slice of Washington State at one point, and Ursula was an only child. This is one of the things she used her inheritance for."

I asked, "And Frye is there full-time?"

"He runs the place, apparently. Does a bit of everything, including counseling. The place tends to cater to ex-military personnel."

"Love the soldier, hate the war," Munro said, with more than a hint of sarcasm.

He obviously hadn't changed his stance since the last time we worked together, his stance being that the war isn't over till every single enemy combatant is dead, whether it's the wars in the Gulf, the War on Terror, or the War on Drugs. At this point, as long as he didn't rile Pennebaker, I didn't really care what he thought.

We left Griffin Avenue and climbed deeper into the Monterey Hills. The views were breathtaking, the houses few and far between.

If you wanted somewhere secluded but still within reach of a city, the area was perfect. The last place recovering addicts needed to be was in the middle of downtown with all the treacherous distractions and lethal delights on offer.

The clinic was a sprawling three-floor building, hacienda style. A handful of palm trees edged the property on two sides, and a steeply sloping lawn ran down to the road. We climbed out of the Suburban and walked up to the main entrance. The door was open. We stepped into an atrium that was dominated by several tall indoor cacti. To the left was a common room filled with armchairs and sofas. To the right was a huge open-plan kitchen with a mess-style table dead center and running the room's entire length. At the rear was a wide wooden staircase.

A young woman dressed in a T-shirt and faded jeans and sporting a long blonde ponytail walked down the stairs toward us.

"Hi. Can I help you?" She tucked her bangs behind her left ear. I bet the soldiers melted when she did that.

"We're looking for Matthew Frye."

She turned back up the stairs and called out.

"Matt? There's some people here to speak to you."

She turned back to face us and I immediately recognized the glint in her eye. She and Matthew were an item.

"This about Donaldson?" she asked.

"No, why?"

She waived it aside with a shrug. "One of our patients. He's suing the army for compensation. Lost an arm in Afghanistan, got addicted to painkillers, but they didn't cut it, so he switched to heroin. Failed a mandatory drug test and was fired. Didn't work for three years. He's been here three months, been clean for six weeks."

This story certainly wasn't going to change Pennebaker's mind about anything. If Frye was indeed Pennebaker. But they do say that in time you tend to find yourself where your environment echoes your beliefs.

Our conversation was halted by a tall, wiry man descending the stairs.

"You guys from the Military Review Board?" he scoffed. "Not surprised you're not in uniform. Probably never seen a day's action in your lives."

He came to a stop in front of us. He looked surprisingly like the photo of Frye. But it was definitely Pennebaker.

Munro couldn't let his dig go by unchallenged. "We've seen action. Plenty of it. Just not in BDUs."

Pennebaker cast a more analytical eye across the pair of us. I could see him revising his opinion, deciding whether he could take both of us if he were so inclined.

Munro took a couple of steps toward the door in case Pennebaker decided to charge for the exit.

The agent who had driven us out there would already be covering the rear. And the local FBI car was parked a couple of hundred yards down the street.

For a moment, Pennebaker rocked back onto the balls of both feet and tensed his limbs—the instinctive reaction of a soldier—then he relaxed his entire body and cocked his head to one side.

"You know who I am. Good for you."

I walked toward the common room and sat down, and gestured for Pennebaker to join me. "Come on. Sit. We need to talk. It's about the club."

He took a deep, annoyed breath, then followed suit and grabbed a chair facing me. Munro joined us but stayed on his feet.

"I've got nothing to say about that. I'm out. Been out for years. End of story."

There was no guilt or paranoia or rage on display. His words were calm and assured. Whatever path Pennebaker was on had turned potentially self-destructive feelings into confidence and what appeared to be a strong sense of self-worth.

"In fact, why should I talk to you guys at all?"

I thought of mentioning that the last time I looked, identity fraud was a criminal offense and we could make his life miserable because of it. Instead, I took out my phone and showed him a photo of his mutilated ex-brother-in-arms.

"I don't think Walker's gonna mind you talking to us."

Pennebaker gazed at it, unblinking. His stomach had got stronger, too.

"In fact, given what they did to him," I added, "I'm pretty sure he'd want you to talk to us."

39

Lina Dawetta came through for Perrini, as he knew she would.
She told him that the target was using a new Verizon iPhone,
which had helped. Her contact at that carrier was über-efficient,
highly pliable, and far from insensitive to the appeal of a small batch
of crisp hundred-dollar bills and the charms of her dark Sicilian skin.
Also helpful was the fact that Chaykin had her GPS location service
switched on. Most people did, without realizing it. In Chaykin's case,
it showed, as Perrini had suspected, that she was currently in San
Diego.

Perrini chuckled to himself as he wondered if there had been any
domestic fireworks following her undoubted discovery that her boyfriend had a kid he didn't know about.

Ah, the wicked web we weave.

"I just emailed you the tracking app," Lina told him. "Your client's
Android-based, right?"

"Correct," he told her. "You done good, darling. I'll be in touch."

He hung up, checked his email to see that he'd received what she
sent him, then he dialed Octavio Guerra's number.

An hour later, Tess still hadn't found any Deans in her online search.

She quit her browser and tossed her iPad onto the bed, then sat
up. The day was wasting away, and she wasn't getting anywhere.

Her thoughts turned to Alex, and she felt they could all use a
change of scenery. Balboa Park, with its open spaces and its museums,

was a short hop away. The zoo had been great in terms of keeping him occupied and giving him a distraction from the reality checks that, she knew, were hounding him at all hours. There were plenty of other attractions there to provide him with more of that.

She peered into the adjacent room, where her suggestion was greeted with enthusiasm by both Alex and Jules.

A few minutes later, they were all in Jules's car and on their way there.

Twenty miles north of their position, the black Chevy Tahoe emerged from the gates of a beachfront villa and breezed down the quiet residential street, headed for the freeway.

In it were three well-groomed, casually dressed men in combinations of chinos or cargo pants, sports shirts or polos, and Timberlands or Merrells. They also all sported sunglasses that masked the resolve in their eyes and light Windbreakers that hid the silenced handguns in their upside-down underarm holsters.

One of them, the one riding shotgun, had his eyes trained on the Android-powered HTC phone that he held in his hand.

He'd just downloaded a custom app that had been emailed to him, one that worked off the phone's embedded Google Maps feature. The phone's browser was open on a live map of San Diego, and the map had two live markers blinking on it: a standard one that used the phone's built-in GPS function to display its current position, and a second marker—a white, blinking one that the app had overlaid onto the map.

The marker, they'd been told, was accurate to within ten feet of the target's true position.

The three men were about to put that claim to the test.

40

Pennebaker waved away the duty nurse—who was wearing a look of genuine concern now that she knew we were there to talk to her boyfriend—and handed me back my phone. He closed his eyes and took a breath, clearly still of two minds about whether he wanted to go back to the part of his life that Walker's death evoked. After a moment he opened his eyes again and looked straight at me.

"What happened?"

I told him about how we found Walker and the Eagles. How the two bikers had tailed me. How they kidnapped scientists from the Schultes Institute. And how Torres had been taken, most likely by whoever killed Walker.

When I was done, he said nothing for a long moment. Then a look of righteous anger took hold of his face and his calm demeanor evaporated in an instant.

"You don't care about what happened to them. No one gives a shit about any of us. You fight an unwinnable war and kill innocent civilians for your country, then you come home and people are either terrified of you or they hate you for what you were ordered to do."

I shot Munro a look. He kept his mouth shut, though I could tell it was a struggle. Last thing we needed was a pissing contest. However vehement Pennebaker turned, it was crucial I kept things even. We couldn't afford to alienate him any further or risk him clamming up completely.

"It can't have been easy. Adjusting to civilian life after Iraq."

He ignored me and plowed on, his tone growing more bitter with each sentence.

"We had to rely on each other. But we couldn't do that either, because the pain and the violence ran so deep we just didn't know how to leave it behind. If anything, putting together the Eagles just magnified it. Turned it inward. Each one of us ended up fighting himself. And losing. And you want to drag me back to all that? Drag me back to the shit that killed Marty and almost got me killed? Screw you."

He sat there, with a look of total defiance in his eyes. The kind that could be backed up by physical force if required. In that moment, I saw how Pennebaker and Walker had become the go-to guys when they worked together. The pairing of Walker's blunt force with Pennebaker's more coherent rage must have been a formidable combination.

"But you got out, and by the looks of things"—I couldn't resist turning my head back to the space that Pennebaker's girlfriend had recently vacated—"you're doing okay, right? Look, we have no interest in messing with what you've built here."

"But we will if we have to," chipped in Munro, having designated himself bad cop whether I liked it or not.

"We need to catch these bastards; that's all we care about," I countered. "Whoever they are, they're out of control. And you know what that's like. You know how destructive that can be."

Pennebaker's eyes narrowed as he studied me for a moment, but said nothing.

I held up my phone to him. "You like having these guys running around out there? Killing others? Maybe someone else's kid brother?"

I caught a twitch in his expression as my words dug in, and waited for them to settle in deeper. After a couple of seconds, he let out a rueful breath and his shoulders sagged, then his expression softened a touch.

"Marty wasn't cut out for the three-patch life. But I couldn't talk him out of it. I saved Wook's life in Iraq, that's why he let me walk away, but I couldn't save Marty. I could hardly live with myself the first few months. If I hadn't done time, if I hadn't been forced into that structure, hell, I'd probably be dead by now."

"But you found a purpose."

"I've been through some shit. And I know there's a way to get past it. But you need to be strong. And you need people to care. And to keep caring. A lot of these guys come back from Afghanistan or Iraq and the first thing they do is stick a meth pipe in their mouths. No better friend, no worse enemy."

He chortled at the irony.

I knew where that haunted grin was coming from. *No better friend, no worse enemy* was the motto of the Marine division Pennebaker and Walker served with in Iraq.

"Anything to dull the pain," he resumed with a slow shake of his head. "But it just makes the problem worse. Covers up what's broken so you don't have to face it. So we get them off the drug and then we try to deal with why they're on it in the first place. It's a long road, and there's no quick solution."

"And now that the Eagles have been wiped out you can never go back. Even if you want to."

"It was only a matter of time. That's why I turned my back on them when I got out."

"I can see the why. Just can't see the how. Matthew Frye is watertight. How did you manage that?"

"When I got out of prison, I needed a fresh start. Wanted to leave the past behind. A new name will do that for you. Someone owed me a favor is all. He even arranged to get me vouched for. Hired someone to play the part of Frye's sister. Frye's sister—the real one—is a crack whore. She doesn't even know what day it is, let alone whether her brother's alive or dead. If I could force her here, I would, but she doesn't want to get clean. That's the killer. You have to *want* to get clean, even if you don't think you'll make it. Some of our patients go back, but most of them make it. Eight out of ten, in fact. Better than any government program."

"Looks like you're winning your own little war on drugs, huh?" This time Munro made no attempt to hide his sarcasm.

Pennebaker cocked his head. He could do sarcasm, too.

"Walker and me, we were part of a total bullshit war. And this War on Drugs is no less bullshit than the war for oil. Criminalization and incarceration don't work, but no one has the guts to change anything. A quarter of our prison population is doing time for minor drug offenses, but no one gives a damn, do they?"

I'd heard all these arguments before, but I didn't have an answer for him. It was the kind of moral conundrum that could really make your head hurt. All I knew, all I was convinced of more and more each year, was that the system we had in place wasn't working and that the so-called War on Drugs was unwinnable. There was way too much demand and too many people making easy money by supplying the stuff, and no matter how many of them we put away, there were always going to be plenty of others ready to step into their shoes. It was an undefeatable, omnipotent beast. I knew this as someone who'd been a foot soldier in that war. It was as if we didn't learn any lessons from Prohibition. More money than ever was being spent on fighting this war, and yet the production, distribution, and consumption of drugs like coke, heroin, and particularly meth were increasing every year. I knew the statistics—the real ones—and the sad irony was that the global War on Drugs—God, I hated that expression—was now causing more harm than drug abuse. All we'd done was create a massive international black market, empowered armies of organized criminals, stimulated violence at home, wrecked a few foreign countries, and destroyed countless harmless users' lives. Which isn't to say that I wanted everyone to be out there shooting up and ruining their lives with crack and meth. Then again, I didn't much like the pain and suffering that alcohol or oxycodone were causing either. Someone needed to step up and acknowledge that this prohibition wasn't working. Someone needed to break that taboo and put it firmly on the table and lead an open-minded, clear-headed, unprejudiced discussion about alternative approaches. But I wasn't holding my breath on that one. History didn't look kindly on those who acknowledged losing a war, even when it was already long lost.

Pennebaker scoffed and threw up his hands in resignation.

"We had a woman in here who spent six years in prison for selling thirty bucks worth of weed. Her kids were taken away from her and she fell into crank as soon as she got out. Her way to drop out. Chalk one up for the system, right? Even the UN's Global Commission on Drug Policy is now admitting the ban has been a failure and calling for legalization. That's the same UN that sent us out to the Gulf. You think anyone in Washington's got the balls to listen? The only way to deal with it is to confront why we do it and educate people about their options. Then maybe they can make better choices. I'm happy with my choices now. First time ever I can say that."

I figured now was a good time to prompt Pennebaker to tell us what we'd come here to learn.

"Help us with one thing and we'll leave you in peace. We know you and the boys ran security for some Mexican narco back in the day. Who was it?"

Pennebaker's expression clouded. "Why?"

"Might be the same person that hired the Eagles to do the grabs— then burned them."

Pennebaker grimaced. As though this memory was somehow worse than all the others put together.

"Guy was a real whackjob. You could see it in his eyes. I know that look. He always hired ex-soldiers. American and Mexican. Thought it gave him an edge. And I guess it did. We did what he asked and he paid us well. Our government may be deluded, confused, incompetent, badly advised, and sometimes just plain stupid, but this guy was just pure evil."

"What was his name?"

"Navarro. Raoul Navarro."

41

They were back in Balboa Park—Tess, Alex, and Jules, wandering across the plaza, hordes of people all around them, out making the most of another gorgeous Californian scorcher and taking in the wealth of attractions the park had to offer.

Tess hadn't found any psychologists in the area called Dean. So she'd given up and decided Alex could use another excursion, this time to the Air and Space Museum.

They left Jules's Ford Explorer in the lot behind the Starlight Theatre, and as they walked alongside a bank of colorful flowers that bordered the walkway, Tess's mind drifted back to her chat with Alex's teacher and the flower that kills. Her first thought when she'd heard it was that it had to come out of some cartoon Alex watched, maybe something some dastardly alien with a Dr. Evil laugh was trying to unleash on an unsuspecting world, only to be thwarted right in the nick of time by Ben and his wondrous Omnitrix. But here she was, still thinking about it and wondering why her earlier easy dismissal of it wasn't staying down for the count.

"Alex, do you remember that flower you drew for your teacher, in the park? The white one?"

He nodded, not really interested. "Uh-huh."

"Where did you see it? Was it in the park?"

"No."

"Where then?"

He slid her a curious sideways glance. "I don't know . . . I just . . . I know it."

"But you said something about it. Do you remember?"

He nodded.

She stopped and crouched down so her face was level with his, and put her arm softly on his shoulder. "Tell me why it's special."

He stared at her like he was sussing her out, then said, "It can fix people. But it kills them. So it's not good." He paused, then he added, "I told them that."

"Who, Alex? Who'd you tell that to?"

"People. Brooks, and the others. But they didn't like it." Tess felt completely lost by his words—then something behind her seemed to catch his eye and his face lit up like a bank of stadium floodlights. "Look!"

Tess followed the direction his little finger was pointing in. Up ahead was the Air and Space Museum, with two sleek fighter planes flanking its entrance. Alex slipped out of Tess's grasp and scampered off.

She couldn't compete with that.

She glanced at Jules, shrugged, and they both trotted off behind him.

The murderous flowers would have to wait.

42

N*avarro.*
   The name hit me like an arctic wave.

Pennebaker and Walker ran drugs for Navarro?

I was swept up by a storm of colliding thoughts, associations, theories—and unease, and I was only half-listening as Pennebaker went into more detail about the bikers' work for the Mexican.

It was pretty much as Karen Walker had told us. They used to ride shotgun on drug shipments—Navarro's shipments—once the goods had crossed the border. It was easy money until the day they got wind of a rival cartel that was plotting to move in on the Mexican narco's territory via a mole within his inner circle.

"Navarro, he sets up a meet with us all to talk about a new shipment, so's not to tip the guy off," Pennebaker was telling us. "So we head south of the border and all meet up in this quiet bar down in Playas. And it was just weird, man. One minute they're talking and it's all cool, then the guy just falls to the ground like he just got the Spock nerve pinch, only he's still wide awake. He's just, like, paralyzed. Navarro's *pistoleros* use the surprise to whip out their guns and take out the guy's two bodyguards. Then Navarro brings out this knife and just calmly goes to work on the guy. He cuts his belly open, he starts pulling out intestines and shit and cutting them up in front of him, telling him in detail how he's going to die while chucking the pieces he was cutting out to a couple of dogs. It was insane."

Munro smirked. "And you threw up."

Pennebaker shook his head with a combination of discomfort, embarrassment, and awe. "Yeah, I puked my guts out. The guy was gutting him like a fish. I mean, that was some weird shit, right? They didn't call him El Brujo for nothing."

"The wizard," Munro added.

"Wizard, sorcerer, whatever," Pennebaker shot back. "El Loco would have been more appropriate. The guy was a total freak. I could see the writing on the wall and started to think we needed to end our little arrangement with him and seek greener pastures, but then I didn't have to 'cause Marty got killed and that was that."

I wasn't really focusing and was just getting bits and pieces of it. My mind was elsewhere, hurtling down some dark trenches.

I had to interrupt.

I told Pennebaker, "Just give us a second, all right?" and motioned for Munro to join me. Pennebaker looked at me with a mix of disinterest and confusion as I led Munro out of the room.

"This is about what happened in Mexico," I told him once we were out of earshot.

Munro frowned, thinking about it. "I agree, but—how? And why now?"

It didn't help having the bastard here with me. I never really liked him anyway, and it only got worse after the bloodbath in Mexico. Looking at him now, I could feel a sting in my finger from pulling that trigger, and even though the blame was entirely mine, I still resented him for it, too.

Still, I had to put that aside and stay focused.

"I don't know, but think about it. We took out a chemist who was developing a new superdrug. The guys who came after Michelle grabbed two chemists, maybe more." My brain was racing ahead, playing a speed-game of mental connect-the-dots, and I was already sensing what the final picture was going to look like. "The drug McKinnon was developing. We didn't get it that night. What happened, after I left? All I heard was that it was never recovered."

Munro nodded. "His laptop—"

"I know, that I heard. Two strikes and it fried itself."

That night, we'd managed to bring back the two things McKinnon had packed: a laptop and a tattered old leather-bound journal. The journal had apparently proved worthless—according to Corliss and some agency analyst, it held the ramblings of a Jesuit missionary called Eusebio something from God knows when, handwritten in Spanish and half-faded. The laptop, where his research was presumably stored, turned out to be not only password- and fingerprint-protected, but with some heavy-duty 256-bit Blowfish protection software on top. The software fried its hard drive at the second incorrect password attempt. Two attempts. Not five, not ten. Talk about ruthless. The agency's top techies couldn't break it beforehand or recover anything off it after it was wiped. That level of security wasn't surprising, given that these chemists are often working on new drugs that can be worth billions of dollars—but it didn't help our cause.

"But you guys went after Navarro in a big way after he came at Corliss," I told him. "You didn't get anything then either?"

"Dude, Navarro didn't have it either. Why do you think he came after Corliss? The formula for the drug died with McKinnon. That's what made Navarro freak out. That's why he went berserk and moved on Corliss—a move he knew would bring the DEA down on him like a ton of bricks and make him the cartel enforcers' number one target at the same time."

It was all crystallizing, but I could also feel something urgent close by, clawing away at me from some deep crevasse in my mind, desperate for my attention.

"Okay, so the formula is gone—but they think we have it," I said. "Someone does. That's why Navarro came after Corliss back then. That's why whoever's behind all this got the bikers to kidnap the scientists. And that's got to be why they went after Michelle."

"But Michelle wasn't part of our task force," Munro reminded me. "She had nothing to do with the raid on Navarro's lab."

"No, she didn't," I told him. "But I did."

The realization tumbled down to the pit of my stomach like a cluster bomb, then ripped me apart from the inside out.

"They didn't want anything from her," I added, the tumblers in my brain falling into place and lining up with brutal clarity. "They wanted me. That's why they came after her. They knew I was the guy who took out McKinnon. They must think I know something."

I saw Michelle get hit again, saw her looking at me with death closing in around her, saw her lying there on the sidewalk with life seeping out of her, saw her mouth those last words to me with her dying breath—and I wanted to tear myself apart.

It was me they were after, all along.

They came after her to get to me.

She died because of me.

My blood turned to acid, a torrent of it rushing through my body and scorching everything in its path. I guessed that they must have come after Michelle because they didn't know about Tess. Or maybe New York was too far out of their reach, and they needed to draw me here, to their turf, a short hop from the border.

And if that wasn't enough, I then realized something else.

Alex.

"They weren't just after Michelle," I hissed, feeling short of breath. "They were after Alex. They must know he's my son. That's why they came after them. To grab him. To use him as leverage. To get to me."

Which had to be why they were still following me. Not because they didn't know Michelle had been hit. Because they wanted me. They wanted something from me, and they wanted to use Alex to make me get them whatever the hell they're after.

Which meant Alex was still a target.

He was at risk.

As was Tess.

My vision went all blurry at the edges as the whole plan played itself out at fast-forward speed in my mind, and I pulled my phone out and stabbed Jules's speed dial.

43

❧

"Wow, look at that one," Alex screeched and pointed excitedly as he stared at the planes outside the Air and Space Museum.

They were standing under the Lockheed Blackbird that towered over them from its mount on three metal columns at the museum's entrance.

"This is the fastest one. It's like a rocket," he said, marveling at the sleek black spy plane that had first taken to the air from the salt lakes of Area 51 in Nevada. He was all bouncy and animated, his gaze darting back and forth from the Blackbird to the smaller Convair Sea Dart that also flanked the entrance.

Jules saw the delight on Tess's face as they watched him run around, and she couldn't help but smile, too. She knew how Tess felt. Seeing Alex happy like that after everything he'd been through, even if for a fleeting moment, was as warming and intoxicating as a tumbler of fine aged single malt.

Tess glanced over and flashed Jules a smile that was loaded with gratitude before turning to Alex and asking, "How about we go inside?"

He was already scooting off ahead.

The circular museum was made up of an outer ring jam-packed with aircraft of all shapes and sizes that were set around a central pavilion, the entire display dominated by a huge, World War Two–era seaplane. Alex had told Tess he'd been to the museum before, but he hadn't yet seen any of the 3-D animated films that were showing at its Zable Theater, films that had added physical effects that some marketing wiz had decided to call 4-D, even though, strictly speaking, all 3-D movies were already being screened within an Einsteinian four-dimensional manifold.

They walked around the exhibits, with Alex leading the way, gesturing excitedly from one aircraft to another, the excitement spilling out of him effusively. The place was buzzing, as busy inside as on the promenade outside, and as they ambled through, Jules found herself unconsciously surveying the scene around them. People from all walks of life seemed to be there—families, couples, locals, foreigners, old, young, a hugely diverse cross section of humanity that had converged around an outstanding sampling of man's genius at conquering his primal urge to fly.

They'd been in there for about half an hour and were waiting to go into the screening room when a man caught Jules's eye. He was a Latino with dark olive skin and wore jeans, a Windbreaker, and cowboy boots. A hands-free cell phone cord dangled from his ear, and he was talking into its mike. Jules wasn't sure why her eye lingered on him for that extra little beat. Something about him just struck her as odd, but she couldn't put her finger on it. He just seemed out of place. Didn't look like a tourist. Seemed uncomfortable in his surroundings, like he wasn't really there to check out the planes. But after watching him for a few seconds, Jules decided that she was overthinking. He hadn't looked over at them once. He was probably just taking a work call. Or maybe he'd been forced to go on an outing by his new girlfriend and her kid and he didn't want to be there. Whatever his story, Jules decided he didn't merit more of her attention and chose to ignore him.

She chided herself about the episode. Yet another demonstration of how she could never relax, not entirely. She'd been at the job too long to allow her guard to drop completely. She could picture her friends rolling her eyes at her, but the fact was, she loved being an agent for the Bureau. Her college roommate and best friend, in particular, took great pleasure in goading her about marriage and children, but Jules laughed off both her barbs and her encouragement. She kept promising she'd work on lightening up and allowing the rest of what life had on offer to seep in, but they both knew it was just wishful thinking.

The line for the showing moved along, and as Jules headed into the theater, she took a second to note the exits—other than the main door, there were two doors at the back of the tiny thirty-six-seat space leading to the Education Center—before realizing she'd made the sweep entirely from instinct.

Even out for a day's fun with a four-year-old, she couldn't leave the job behind.

She saw Tess and Alex don their 3-D glasses and sit down to soak in the delights of *Jet Pack Adventure*, and decided to wait for them outside the theater, where she could download the most recent case updates to her phone. For a second, she even contemplated having a go in the flight simulator—she'd been in plenty of helicopters and small aircraft, but never in an F-18 fighter—but before the idea could take root, her phone vibrated.

She confirmed the caller ID—it was Reilly. Probably calling to check up on his son.

"Where are you?"

He sounded agitated.

She tensed up as she told him, her eyes instinctively surveying the ground around her.

Reilly bypassed the pleasantries and said, "I need you to get Alex and Tess out of there without alarming them. David's organizing a safe house."

An icy finger slid down her spine. "Why, what's happened?"

"They're after me. That's why they came after Michelle and Alex. To use them to get to me. Which means Alex is still in danger. Tess too."

She listened as he ran through what it was all about—Mexico five years ago, Raoul Navarro. She sensed a mixture of frustration and thinly veiled unease as he said the name, and it chilled her further. In the little time she'd been around Reilly, she'd been impressed by his clear-headedness and his drive, possibly even developing a pointless little crush on him. To hear him rattled like this was unsettling.

He also told her that the goons who took out the Eagles were probably ex-military, that it was Navarro's MO.

When he finally took a breath, she asked, "Shall I call for backup?"

He hesitated, then said, "No need at this point. I don't want to freak out Alex any more than he already is. Just take them back to the hotel and pack everything up. I'm heading back to San Diego now."

"You got it."

She ended the call, edged across to the cover of a low-slung plane, and did a quick 360-degree sweep of the museum. She didn't see anything suspicious at first—then she saw the Latino again. Just inside the central pavilion. Only this time, he was standing next to another guy who also had a hands-free cable dangling from his ear. The second guy was holding some kind of handheld device, and both of them were looking intently at the screen. Then one of them looked over in Jules's direction and gave the other a discreet nod aimed at the theater, and as he did, she saw it. A small dimple under his Windbreaker, one she knew was from a handgun that was slung in an underarm holster.

The back of her neck went all fuzzy with the sense of something bad about to happen.

Jules's eyes locked on them, but the men stayed put. They looked straight past her and didn't seem to register her. Her mind leapt ahead, as it had been trained to do, instantly assessing options. Best case, the guys were playing Angry Birds or checking sports scores. Worst case, they were hostiles. Which is what she read in their eyes and in their body language.

Meaning they were there because they were tracking Alex and Tess.

Meaning somehow, they had a GPS lock on them—with the most likely suspect being Tess's phone.

But if that were the case, they didn't seem to be looking to make their play now. They seemed to be waiting for Tess and Alex to come out, maybe to move out into the open—or to be in transit, in the car—before they took action.

Dammit.

Jules had no idea how many of them were deployed, but she knew that the last thing anyone needed was a gun battle in a crowded public place on a summer afternoon. And if the recent past was anything to go by, it was clear that this Raoul Navarro had no compunction about the loss of innocent lives and that he was set on getting to Reilly in any way he could, including through women and children.

Her mind scrambled for options, then it hit her—if the men were indeed cartel enforcers tracking Tess, she could use the GPS lock against them. She might be able to move Tess and Alex to safety with zero casualties. Her only doubt was whether to call Reilly back—as an agent he'd want to be kept up to speed, but as a father the last thing he needed was the play-by-plays. Villaverde had already taken her aside the day before and told her that although Reilly was right in the middle of whatever was going on, they needed to be careful that his personal involvement in the case didn't cause any problems, not least for Reilly himself. Her priority was Alex. Taking down the bad guys could wait until the boy was safe.

Still, she had to call him.

She speed-dialed Reilly and described what she was seeing.

"What do you want me to do?" she asked.

He went silent for a quick second, then said, "Don't engage them, okay? Do not engage them in any way. Like you said, we don't know how many of them are there. There's got to be cops in the plaza or close by. I'll get you some backup."

"Sean, I don't want a shoot-out here. Not with all these people. Not with Alex and Tess in the middle of it." Instead, she ran through her idea with him.

He exhaled with frustration, then said, "You'd be leaving them unguarded."

"Yes, but with a bit of luck, they won't have anyone on them."

He went silent again, clearly juggling between unattractive options.

"I can do this, Sean," she insisted. "It'll work."

"Okay. But be safe, Jules. No heroics. I mean it."

She cracked a nervous smile and was suddenly aware of how quickly her heart was beating. "I'll keep you posted." Then she hung up.

44

Jules turned casually, walked over to the theater, and slipped inside. She spotted Tess and Alex immediately. They were sitting at the edge of a row, with Tess on the aisle seat and Alex beside her, his face all lit up with wonder.

Jules crouched down beside her.

"There's a couple of guys outside. I think they might be bad news."

She looked at Tess, making sure the information sank in calmly, before adding, "We don't have much time. There's a chance they're tracking you through your cell, so I need you to give it to me. I'm going to use it to lead them away from you."

"But—"

"I spoke to Sean," she insisted, keeping her tone calm and low. "It's the safest option. Give me your phone."

Tess took out her iPhone and passed it to her. Jules guessed that the novelist had been through her share of potentially lethal situations and probably knew that efficiency was often the key to survival.

"Stay here for ten more minutes," she told Tess. "Then meet me by the exit of the lot where we parked."

She handed Tess the keys to her car. Jules reckoned it would take Tess and Alex no more than ten minutes to walk to the parking lot they'd left it in. Once the three of them had regrouped they could drive straight onto Park Boulevard and slip away.

"Good luck," Tess said, before putting her hand on Jules's forearm. "And thanks."

Jules nodded, then skulked back toward the doors.

She turned off the iPhone, slipped it into a pocket, then left the theater. She hated leaving Tess and Alex alone, but the risk of staying with them and being overpowered was even worse.

She emerged from the darkness into the brightness of the museum's main exhibit area and scanned her immediate surroundings. The two hostiles were now over by an unusual, boomerang-shaped plane. If they were pros and they were tracking Tess's iPhone, then they were going about it the right way—anticipating the movement of the target, but positioning themselves so they could change direction if they needed to. Staying close, but not too close.

More confirmation that they were what she suspected.

Using a group of museum visitors as cover, Jules ducked low and walked briskly toward the main entrance. She figured she had maybe half a minute or so before the hostiles knew they'd been made. GPS tracking was pretty good, but it wasn't perfect. The signal had a massive bounce before it got to the phone company. Then there was the latency between the signal itself and whatever cell network the hostiles were using to track it. As long as she had the iPhone turned back on within thirty seconds, she'd buy herself the time she needed to put some distance between them, and the hostiles wouldn't ever know they'd lost signal lock.

Jules left the museum by the main rotunda entrance and switched the iPhone back on. She ensured the slide-lock was active, then headed north toward the Museum of Art. The plaza was still heaving with summer-camp day-trippers, groups of tourists climbing in and out of buses, parents helping their toddlers out of SUVs, and lovers holding hands and carrying picnic baskets—all of them enjoying the gorgeous weather. Jules knew she couldn't allow herself to walk any faster than an excited four-year-old, but she used every bit of cover available: gaggles of retirees, oversize vehicles, and families arguing over what they should see first. As she stepped onto the wide sidewalk that ran alongside the parking lanes, she joined a large group of tourists and allowed them to swallow her.

She tried to avoid looking back. The hostiles would certainly know what Alex looked like—they might even have a picture of Tess—but there was no way they knew Jules by sight. To pick out one four-year-old boy from a moving crowd wasn't going to be easy for them. Jules just had to trust that the men wouldn't notice they were following a false trail until it no longer mattered.

After another hundred yards, she ducked behind some trees, found cover, and peered back the way she'd come. Sure enough, the hostiles were following, eyes darting between the handheld and the large group of tourists moving slowly away from the museum.

As Jules worked her way through the trees and up the ramp toward the Marie Hitchcock Puppet Theatre, she saw the perfect move. Crawling at a snail's pace heading away from the theater was an electric buggy carrying two elderly ladies. Emblazoned on the side of the cart were the words SAN DIEGO ZOO.

The zoo was all the way at the other end of the park, and the cart was obviously heading that way. Jules glanced back, assessed that she was out of sight of the hostiles, and sprinted up to the buggy.

She slowed right down when she reached it and caught the driver's eye.

"Excuse me," she asked, motioning for him to stop.

He hit the brake.

"Will you be coming back this way?" she asked him, smiling. "I've got my grandparents here and they could use a ride to the zoo."

The buggy's driver told her he'd come back for them in about twenty minutes. Jules thanked him and stepped aside, and as the buggy started up, she dropped Tess's iPhone into one of its rear baskets, then ducked back into the cover of the trees and waited.

Barely twenty seconds later, the two hostiles passed within ten yards of her as they tracked the iPhone's GPS signal. She stayed put and watched them, every nerve pulsing, then slipped out from her cover and started walking back.

After a few seconds, she glanced behind her and saw them rounding the curve. She was now out of their sight line. She jogged back toward the museum, her jog quickly turning into a sprint as she put more distance between her and them. Soon the Air and Space Museum was just a couple of hundred yards ahead of her, and she was about to take a pathway down to the lot where she'd left her car, along a service road that ran between two large administration buildings, when she stopped in her tracks.

There was a third hostile.

Another Latino, no more than thirty yards away, standing right at the edge of the lot, next to a black Chevy Tahoe SUV—the one she'd seen on the clip from the dead deputy's in-car video. He also had a phone cord going up to his ear.

He turned around just as she noticed him, and for a split second they locked eyes, both of them knowing instantly that each had made the other. Which meant he'd probably guess that Tess and Alex weren't where his compadres thought they were.

She had no way of calling Tess to warn her because her phone was by now halfway to the zoo.

Jules didn't have time to think about it any further. All she knew was that she couldn't let the bastard warn the others, and that if she drew her weapon, the situation would immediately spin out of control. So she did the only thing she could think of.

She threw her whole body forward and charged.

She saw his eyes narrow and his head pull back with a look that was somewhere between amusement and disbelief a split second before she slammed into him with her right arm bent tight against the front of her body, crushing him against the side of the Tahoe, forcing the air from his chest and breaking three ribs before using the tail end of her momentum to shove him to the ground.

She fell on top of him and scrambled to get her cuffs out while trying to keep him pinned down, but he was too strong for her. He spun her arm back and caught her across the shoulder, then twisted on himself and shoved her back viciously against the car, her head thudding heavily against its door and jarring her vision. Her eyes recovered just in time to catch an unmistakable flash of steel as the enforcer pulled a vicious-looking stiletto from his left boot.

She dove at him again, clamping her left hand around the hostile's wrist while she jerked the heel of her right hand full force into his nose. He grunted with pain and momentarily lowered the blade before flicking it right back at her stomach. He was stronger than she anticipated, and Jules knew she wouldn't get much more of a chance to survive the fight.

She kicked the knife arm away and threw herself at it with both hands, smashing it against the tarmac, but the enforcer refused to relinquish his grip on the knife. He lashed out with his right knee, catching Jules in the kidney full force. She allowed the momentum to topple her from him, but held onto his right wrist with both hands as she rolled off him and onto the ground. He went with her, trying to maneuver his weight on top of her, but with a final surge of adrenaline she twisted his arm around and used all her body weight to spin the blade around and drive it into his midsection.

His eyes shot open and he gasped heavily as Jules rolled him right over her and flat onto his back. Not wanting to take any chances, she pulled out her Glock and slammed it into the side of his head, knocking him out cold. She patted him down, pocketed his phone and his stainless steel handgun before throwing a pair of cuffs on him as an added safety. She pushed back to her feet and noticed several tourists staring at her with expressions ranging from terror to *You go, girl*.

"FBI," she shouted as she flashed her badge to them. "Stay back. This man is dangerous." She quickly pulled out her phone and called it in, asking the dispatcher to radio local PD and get them to send as many uniforms as they can to the lot.

Her entire body was sizzling with trepidation. Tess and Alex were in serious danger. She couldn't be sure how much the guy she took out had told his *compadres*, but she had to assume they now suspected they'd been duped, and that Tess and Alex could be closer to where Jules was. She charged off to meet them and was heading toward the lot when she glimpsed the two hostiles entering the parking lot at the north end. They hadn't seen her, but they knew where their buddy was and they'd soon find him. She turned and sprinted down the service road toward the parking lot and saw her gray SUV immediately, sitting across the lot, by the exit.

Jules was moving as fast as she could, weaving through people, trying to make it to the car before they saw her. She skirted around the lot's south side, throwing looks over her shoulder every couple of seconds—then saw one of the enforcers spot her and alert his buddy.

The two men were moving now, coming fast, drawing their guns as they cut across the lot to intercept her.

She pulled out her weapon as several rounds sliced through the air and whistled past her. A couple of kids who were climbing back into their family car started screaming as a nearby windshield shattered, and the lot turned to mayhem with people yelling and taking cover. Jules was leveling her gun at the lead killer, looking for a clear shot, when, to the right, a black-and-white drove into the lot. The hostiles saw it, too, and as one of them slowed to fire at it, Jules stopped, crouched and let off five shots in quick succession, missing him but forcing him to take cover behind the corner of the building on the west side of the service road.

The other kept going, staying low, ducking for cover behind successive cars, heading straight for the lot's exit—and the Ford Explorer.

Jules's body ignited with alarm.

She bolted forward again as the black-and-white screeched to a halt. Two SDPD cops jumped out and went to take up positions behind their car, but the driver was hit and dropped to the ground before he could make it. Without coming to full halt, Jules took aim at the hostile who had taken down the cop, but there were civilians all around the lot and she couldn't fire. She had to keep going. The hostile heading for Tess was still rushing down the side of the lot, closing fast on the parked SUV.

Jules looked right and left. There was no way she was going to get to Tess first. Not without running straight into to the hostile's path.

The hostile was now beelining for the car—he seemed to know Tess and Alex were in it, possibly because Tess wasn't in a parking spot but waiting by the exit. As their trajectories converged on the Explorer, Jules saw him train his gun on it—but she couldn't shoot at him, not with all the people and parked cars between them.

Instead, she veered right and leapt up onto the hood of a parked car, climbing quickly onto its roof, where she could get a clearer shot at the man. She lined him up, gripping her gun with both hands, about to pull the trigger when shots cut the air past her from the right, from the shooter farther back. A round grazed her shoulder, throwing her off balance, and she fell off the roof and hit the asphalt hard, her gun skittering out of her fingers.

The shooter she'd tried to take out was now barely twenty yards away from her and charging in for the kill.

Jules was on her hands and knees, looking for her gun, eyes darting from under the cars and back to catch glimpses of the killer closing in, seeing a wicked grin creep over his face as he anticipated the kill—then she heard a wild screech from behind her and turned to see the Explorer lurching backward, wheels spinning, coming right at her.

She rolled out of its way as it drew level with her, its tires squealing as it slewed to a stop.

She didn't need an embossed invitation.

She pulled the back door open and leapt inside.

"Go!" she yelled.

Tess threw the car into gear and floored the gas, and as they blew out of the exit, Jules caught a glimpse of the receding gunman who was already pulling back and disappearing into the crowd.

As Tess swung onto Park Boulevard and pulled away from the park, Jules knew the area would soon be crawling with cops. They'd deal with the shooters. Still, she wasn't sure she'd made the right call. She closed her eyes and tried to calm herself as she wondered about it.

Either way, Alex and Tess were safe.

That had to count for something.

45

I could breathe again.

Tess and Alex were now out of harm's way, tucked away in a bureau safe house that Jules had driven them to, straight from Balboa Park and bypassing the hotel. Villaverde had sent a couple of agents to the hotel to pack up their stuff and take it over; one of them would stay with them to beef up security. I promised Tess I'd be there as soon as I could. Until then, I was in Villaverde's office with him and Munro, chewing over what Pennebaker's little news flash meant.

"It's got to be someone who was close to Navarro," Munro speculated. "Someone who knew what he was working on and is now trying to get his hands on it, one of his lieutenants who climbed up the ranks after he was killed."

That's how it works down there. Every time some kingpin is arrested or killed, you get a bunch of his underlings going to war with each other over who's going to take his place, all while trying to fend off takeover attempts from other cartels. The violence spirals and is often far worse than it was before the takedown. It's like we can't win either way.

We weren't going to get anything out of his shooters. The one Jules had knifed was DOA before he reached the hospital. The other two had melted away into the crowd and disappeared.

Villaverde asked, "What is this drug anyway? What was so special about it?"

"We don't know," Munro told him. "All we know is that it's a very powerful hallucinogen that McKinnon found through some godfor-saken tribe in the middle of nowhere."

I remembered the recording I'd heard of McKinnon's distress call. It had come in unexpectedly, via a cell phone that had been smuggled in to him.

His message was brief, chaotic, and intense.

He gave his name and said he'd been kidnapped several months earlier by armed bandits while bioprospecting in the rainforests down in the south, near Chiapas. The *banditos* had thought to ransom him to whatever big pharmaceutical company he was working for—a common occupational hazard for researchers working in the hinter-lands in that part of the world. When it turned out McKinnon wasn't working for anyone but himself, they debated killing him before coming up with another way to monetize their catch. They offered him to Navarro, figuring El Brujo would be interested in the kid-napped chemist's talents.

They had no idea.

In a desperate attempt to stay alive by proving his usefulness, Mc-Kinnon made the mistake of telling Navarro about something he'd discovered, something he'd been searching for for years, something the shaman of a small, isolated tribe living deep in the rainforest had shared with him: a radical hallucinogen that was, according to him, unlike anything else out there. Navarro tried it, loved it, and became obsessed with it.

"McKinnon was very cagey about giving us any specifics," Munro told Villaverde. "It was like pulling teeth. He said it was an alkaloid that would be irresistibly popular, and described it as '*ayahuasca* on steroids.' But Navarro had a problem. With most of these tribal hal-lucinogens, like *ayahuasca*—taking them is like drinking mud. Liter-ally. Thick horrible sludge that tastes like shit and makes you puke your guts out for days. No one would want to try that. Navarro needed McKinnon to turn his discovery into an easy-to-pop pill that didn't have the horrible side effects—and once it was a pill, Navarro could easily add chemicals into the mix to make it highly addictive.

He threatened McKinnon with a slow, drawn-out death—we know how convincing he can be on that front. So McKinnon got to work. And he did it. He told us he figured out how to synthesize it into pill form, but he hadn't told Navarro—not yet. He wasn't sure how long he could hold out. We looked into McKinnon and he checked out. He had the profile and all the know-how he needed to come up with something like that. So we had to do something. We couldn't afford to let that drug hit the streets. That's why we had to get him out."

Or kill him, I thought.

"But you don't know what its effects are?" Villaverde pressed.

"McKinnon wouldn't say. I guess he thought it was too damn dangerous to say more. That's why he called in his SOS. And that's why he didn't leave any record of it behind. At least, nothing we've found."

Villaverde nodded, soaking it in. "So now we've got another player after it, whoever hired the bikers." He turned to me. "Why you? What do they think you can give them?"

I said, "I have no idea. But they must know I was there"—I turned to Munro—"*we* were there, and maybe they think I found McKinnon's notes and still have them." I looked at Munro, curious about something. "You were there, too. Why is this about me and not you?"

He gave me a nonchalant shrug. "No fucking clue."

Bottom line was, we needed to know who we were dealing with if Tess and Alex—and maybe I—weren't going to spend the rest of our days boxed up in some kind of witness protection wonderland. And something was bothering me about that very question.

I turned back to Munro.

"What do you know about Navarro's death?"

From the knowing half-grin on his face, it was clear he knew exactly where I was going with this.

"I can't tell you for a fact that the bastard's dead, if that's what you're asking."

I felt a little charge go off inside me. "It is."

Again with the shrug. "We went after him, as you know. DEA

doesn't take an attack on any of its agents lightly, least of all some coked-up *maricón* coming after someone like Hank Corliss."

Any narco, Navarro included, had to be well aware of that. It was gospel, ever since Enrique Camarena was yanked out of his car and tortured to death in Mexico in the mid-eighties. The DEA had pulled no punches in bringing his killers to justice, even going so far as to kidnap suspects that were proving hard to extradite and smuggling them into the United States to face trial. And yet, Navarro had come after Corliss himself, brazenly and in plain sight.

A bad move.

A mad move, even.

"The narcos beat us to it," Munro continued. "Navarro had brought down so much heat on them all that they decided it was in their best interest to end the witch hunt themselves. But they weren't about to hand him over to us alive, not with everything he knew. So they invited him in for a chitchat. He wasn't buying."

"So they took him out with a car bomb," I threw in. I remembered going over an interdepartmental report on that. "How solid was the coroner's paperwork?"

"Come on. You know what we're dealing with here. Mexico." He pronounced it *may-hee-koh*, the sarcasm loud and clear. "But we did what we could. We had our own guys run DNA tests and ask the right questions. And their take was, it was him."

"But you were basing that on, what?"

"Whatever we could get our hands on. Stuff we found at his house—his toothbrush, hair, spunk on his sheets. General height, weight."

"Fingerprints?"

"Yes, on two fronts. They matched ones we found at his house. And they matched a file the *federales* had on him, one that had prints from an arrest early in his career."

None of that was foolproof. If he had enough money and the right connections on whom to spend it—which someone in his position had to have—Navarro could have staged the whole thing.

Which is where my suspicions was converging.

There was no way of knowing for sure. Not yet, anyway.

Either way, it didn't really matter. Whether it was Navarro or one of his ex-lieutenants, what mattered was that one of them was after something they thought I had. Because of a mistake, an error of judgment I made—a crime I committed, let's not mince words here—five years ago. What goes around comes around, right? I'd heard that piece of twaddle all my life. I never gave it much thought—until now. But if that was the case, if my take on this was correct, it meant the bad guys' game plan was to get hold of me. It meant I was their golden goose.

And that was something I could definitely use.

46

The safe house was a three-bedroom ranch-style house close to the top of the hill in El Cerrito. It was pretty much what I expected. Someone with a more generous predisposition might use the terms *minimalist*, *vintage*, or *functional* to describe it. I'm thinking it came out of the gulag section at Home Depot. I wasn't exactly expecting Four Seasons–level comfort, but I felt bad for Tess and Alex, more so since I didn't know how long we'd need to keep them holed up here. The place was just grim.

Still, its living room faced west and afforded a pretty decent view of the city's skyline and the ocean beyond, especially now, with the sun melting into the horizon. Tenants who weren't here for the reasons we were would probably find it inspiring or uplifting. I didn't. I was just standing there, alone, somberly taking in the passing of another day, thinking about Mexico, about Michelle, and about how pulling that trigger had somehow created some kind of cosmic ripple that, five years later, had sent a similar bullet ripping into her.

"Nice view."

Tess sidled up next to me, looking out, her hand brushing up against my back before snaking around my waist.

"Only the best is good enough for my gal, you know that."

She smirked. "You spoil me, kind sir."

I glanced back toward the bedrooms. I could hear Jules and the new guy, Cal Matsuoka, chatting quietly in the kitchen.

"How's Alex?"

"Not great. He's still shaken up about what happened," she told me, her tone dejected. "Moving here wasn't great for him either." She cast her eyes across the room. "I don't know what to tell him anymore."

I nodded. "We'll figure some way out of this."

She shrugged and looked out, her eyes lackluster and failing to mask the frustration and unease that were engulfing her.

"What happens after you get these guys—the ones who got the bikers and the deputy? What happens then? How do we know whoever sent them won't just send others after us?" She turned to face me, and she really looked spooked. "How do we know it's ever going to end?"

This was the moment to look squarely into her eyes and say something heroically reassuring and supremely confident like, *Don't worry, we'll get them.* But Tess knew me better than that, and she knew the world didn't really work like that. The thing is, standing there beside her, I couldn't imagine not getting these guys. I was going to see to it that they were out of our lives for good. So I actually did say, "We'll get them. Them, and whoever's behind them." And to her credit, she didn't scoff or even show any hint of doubting it. She just nodded, and her face tightened up with resolve.

She looked out at the sunset again.

"Tell me what happened," she said. "The guy you shot. The scientist. Tell me about it."

I'd given her a quick summary of the Eagles' ties to Navarro and—in broad, intentionally vague strokes—told her how it all linked back to the mission in Mexico. I'd never told her about it, just like I hadn't told Michelle at the time. And this time around, I hadn't gone into detail because I didn't want her to know the whole story.

"Talk to me, Sean," she pressed, reading my hesitation. "Tell me what happened."

And something shifted inside me, and I decided I didn't want to make the same mistake I'd made with Michelle. I should have told her, just like I should have told Tess about this, too, ages ago.

I looked out, the sun no more than a golden sliver getting swallowed up by a ravenous sea, and I could still see those events unfurling in my mind's eye, like it was yesterday, although you never know, do you? The mind plays tricks. I've found that some memories people remember so vividly, the ones we're sure we know so precisely, are sometimes not as accurate as we think. Over time, the mind massages the truth. It distorts and adjusts and adds in small increments, making it hard to tell what actually happened from what didn't. But in this case, I think my memory was razor sharp.

I'd have been happier if it wasn't.

It wasn't easy to get to him.

Navarro's lab was in the middle of nowhere, high up in the lawless and impenetrable Sierra Madre Occidental, a volcanic range of tall mountains that were cleaved by steep gorges, ravines, and plunging canyons known as barrancas, *some of which were deeper than the Grand Canyon. Neither the Aztec emperors nor the Spanish conquistadors had ever been able to impose their authority on the violent and fiercely independent villagers who lived in the Sierra's folds, and the Mexican government hadn't fared any better. The mountains, rife with marijuana and poppy fields, were controlled by regional strongmen and warring drug mafias. Gangs of armed bandits and renegades still roamed around the wild hinterland on horses and mules, like they did a hundred years ago and more. Navarro had chosen his compound's location well.*

We didn't have that much to go on. McKinnon's position had been pinpointed by homing in on the signal of the cell phone during his call. After that, the mission had been planned hastily, and in the interest of not alerting any bought-and-paid-for Mexican law enforcement personnel in Navarro's pay, we put together the intel we needed ourselves using one of the Air Force's Predator drones, without involving the local authorities.

The plan was for us to be choppered in, but the landscape around our target wasn't doing us any favors. The compound sat on a high mesa, and the terrain around it was too hostile and inhospitable for a ground infiltration. Given its high altitude setting and its commanding all-around views, chopper approaches were also highly vulnerable to detection. The best we could do was land about three miles away and cover the rest of the journey on foot over rough terrain that, we knew, was home to scorpions, rattlesnakes, mountain lions, bears, and weird, mythical mutant cougar-like beasts called onzas *to boot.*

A cakewalk.

We hit the ground about three hours before sunrise, figuring that would give us enough time to get to the compound under cover of darkness, get McKinnon out, and make it back to the chopper by dawn. We moved fast and sleek across steep, rocky slopes and rushing creeks, through pine forests and thickets of oak saplings, juniper, and cactus. There were eight of us in the strike team: me, Munro, a couple of DEA combat troops, and four Special Forces soldiers. We knew we were venturing into a well-guarded compound, so we were armed to the teeth: Heckler and Koch UMPs with sound suppressors, silenced Glocks, Bowie knives, body armor, night vision goggles. We were also wearing head-mounted video minicams that were sending a live feed back to the DEA's field office inside the embassy in Mexico City, and we had a Predator flying overhead, giving us real-time visuals via the drone's operators at Peterson Air Force Base in Colorado. The plan, obviously, was not to engage. We were meant to sneak in and get our man out before they knew we were even there.

Didn't happen.

Munro and I made it through the sleepy security without too much trouble. There was only one guard we couldn't get around stealthily, and Munro had used his knife to put him down. We found McKinnon where he said he'd be, in his lab. He looked like he was in his late fifties and was of average height, a bit on the skinny side, with a silvery goatee and clear blue eyes that were shot through with intelligence. He was wearing a white straw cowboy hat with a silver scorpion clipped onto it and a snap-button Western shirt, and he had a battered old leather satchel on the counter beside him. He seemed scared and thrilled in equal parts to see us there, and was all raring to go. But there was a wrinkle.

He wasn't alone.

He had a woman with him, someone he hadn't mentioned in his call, a local who'd been cooking and cleaning for him during his incarceration. A woman he'd bonded with. Deeply, evidently, since she'd risked her life to sneak in a phone to him, the one he'd used to call us. She had a kid with her, her son, a boy of three or four—that thought now made me feel like I was swallowing my fist. She was also pregnant. With McKinnon's baby. She had a pretty big bump on her.

He wasn't leaving without her. Or the kid.

Which was a problem.

A huge problem.

We didn't exactly have a limo waiting outside. We had to get around the guards again. Quietly. Then there was the three-mile trek back to the chopper. Over rough ground. In total darkness.

Munro refused.

He told McKinnon there was no way the woman and the kid would be able to make the trip. Not without seriously slowing us down or unwittingly giving up our presence, which would blow the mission and possibly get us all killed. There was a small army of coke-fueled, trigger-happy pistoleros *out there, and the last thing Munro wanted was for them to know we were around.*

McKinnon was incensed. He flat out refused to leave without them.

Munro wouldn't budge and got angry.

Then it got ugly.

McKinnon said it wasn't negotiable.

Munro told him he wasn't the one dictating the play and mocked his naïvete, asking him how he even knew the woman's baby was his and mocking him by saying he'd probably been duped by the woman who saw him as a ticket out of that miserable hellhole and into the United States.

I tried to mediate and interceded on behalf of the woman and her kid, telling Munro we could carry the boy and the woman probably knew the terrain better than we did. Munro turned on me and growled about how this wasn't a mission to rescue innocent hostages, but rather to bring back a scumbag who was working on new ways to wreck people's lives. We didn't owe him anything, Munro hissed. We weren't rescuing him—we were there to make sure his work never saw the light of day, period.

McKinnon told him to go fuck himself and said he was staying.

And Munro just lost it.

He pulled out his Glock and, without so much as a blink, pumped a bullet into the kid, then another into his mother.

I couldn't believe my eyes. I can still see the shock and horror on the woman's face for that split second after the bullet hit her kid and the way her head snapped backward like it had been punched by a blast of wind when he shot her before she collapsed onto the floor, already dead.

McKinnon just lost it.

He started shouting, hurling abuse at us, moving around frantically, just incensed and raging and out of control. Munro was yelling back at him, ordering him to shut up while jabbing his gun angrily at his face. I tried to calm them both down, but they were beyond that. McKinnon started throwing things at us, lab equipment, stools, anything he could get his hands on.

Then he ran.

We scambled after him, but he was at the lab's door before we could get to him, flinging it open and storming out while screaming from the top of his voice.

And everything went haywire.

I was on him first and just managed to grab him when the first shots crackled in the night. Shouting echoed in the darkness around me, the guards snapped to attention at his outburst and rushed out from all directions. Bullets ate up the timber walls around me as I dragged Mc-Kinnon back inside, wild, nonsilenced bursts from the Mexicans' AK-47s flying all over the place while, from beyond the perimeter of the compound, short, three-bullet snaps were coming in from our guys who were positioned in various spots to cover our exit, the whole chaotic mess mixed in with urgent, clipped commentary coming through the earpiece of my comms set.

Between the weed, the lechuguilla bootleg tequila, and the coke, the pistoleros weren't thinking straight, and it went manic. I was hustling

McKinnon back through the lab, my left arm around his neck, the other leveling the snub-nosed UMP at the doorway, when the first guards burst through, three of them. I cut one of them down and saw another get hit by Munro's fire, but the third took cover behind a counter and started spraying gunfire recklessly from behind it.

I pulled McKinnon and we both dove for cover behind another cabinet, landing heavily under a shower of debris from the torrent of bullets blasting everything around us, while Munro slipped out of sight, his voice in my earpiece telling me he was going to secure McKinnon's files, which were farther back, at the very back of the lab. Then another pistolero *charged in, laying down more gunfire randomly, firing at everything that moved, tacking left, away from his* compadre, *snaking his way farther down the lab, and before I knew it I was separated from Munro and pinned down by the two gunmen.*

Then I heard McKinnon curse and groan, and noticed his thigh.

He'd taken a slug there, right through the middle of it halfway up from his knee. I couldn't see if it had gone through, and while it didn't look good, at least blood wasn't gushing out, which meant maybe his femoral arteries had been spared. His face was taut with pain, his eyes bristling with fury, his hands covered with blood, and I immediately knew there was no way he was going to make it back to the chopper. I wasn't sure I was either—not with the two shooters doing a pincer move on me.

Munro was in a bind of his own, cornered by more shooters, and I heard him growl through my earpiece that he was pulling out and heading for cover.

I was left alone with McKinnon, pinned down, with the scientist cowering next to me and two half-crazed Mexicans closing in.

Outside, the battle was raging. Life was cheap down here, and Navarro had a small army based in the compound, a small army that was now coming out of the woodwork, full force, guns blazing. Our guys were racking up the kills, but the sheer number facing them meant that we were taking losses, too. I heard one, then two of them get hit—and knew I had to pull out, too, and fast.

I wasn't sure I could get out of there in one piece, but if I managed it, I sure as hell couldn't do it with McKinnon in tow. Even if I cut down the pistoleros, I couldn't take him with me, not in the shape he was in.

But I couldn't leave him there either.

Not with what he knew.

Munro was in my ear, haranguing me, pushing me to do what needed doing.

I can still hear his words, crackling in my head. "Just cap the sonofabitch, Reilly. Do it. You heard what he's done. 'It'll make meth seem as boring as aspirin,' remember? That's the scumbag you're worried about wasting? You happy to let him loose, is that gonna be your contribution to making this world a better place? I don't think so. You don't want that on your conscience, and I don't either. We came here to do a job. We have our orders. We're at war, and he's the enemy. So stop with the righteous bullshit, pop the bastard, and get your ass out here. I ain't waiting any longer."

I was running out of time. Fast.

And maybe it was a horrible mistake, maybe it was an inexcusable murder of an innocent civilian, or maybe it was the only thing to do—I really don't know which one it was anymore—but, either way, I turned my gun on McKinnon and put a bullet through his brain. Then I lobbed a couple of incendiary grenades at the banditos and got out of there just as the whole place went up in flames.

47

Tess was looking me like I'd just strangled her pet cat. Not just strangled it, but chopped it up and tossed it in a blender. It's a look I'll never forget.

She was quiet for a torturously long moment. I didn't say anything more either. I just waited for her to digest it in her own time.

After a while, I couldn't deal with the silence anymore.

"Say something," I told her, softly.

She let out a weary sigh and did, her voice subdued.

"I just . . . I don't . . . It's the second time in a week you've hit me with stuff from your past, and this . . . I can't believe you never told me about it." There was hurt in her eyes, and I hated seeing it there, knowing I'd caused it.

"It's not something I'm proud of."

"Still . . ."

"I . . . I was disgusted with myself. I could barely live with what I'd done. And I didn't want to lose you because of it either." Looking at her now, I wasn't sure we'd ever recover from this.

It didn't help that she didn't say anything to contradict my feeling. She just looked away, nodding to herself with a hint of resolve in her expression, like she was looking for something, anything, to limit the fallout.

"Why was it so important to stop him?" she finally asked. "What was this drug he was working on?"

I frowned. It was something that made the whole feeling even worse. "We never found out," I told her. "The secret died with him. And with Navarro, I guess. But someone out there wants it, and they want it real bad."

I told Tess everything I read about McKinnon after we got back from there. I had wanted to know everything about him. He'd become an obsession. So I'd got hold of the file the DEA had put together on him and followed it up with a few inquiries of my own.

McKinnon was a quiet, unassuming, and well-respected anthropologist and ethnopharmacologist from northern Virginia. He held a PhD from Princeton, and after teaching there and at the University of Hawaii at Manoa for a number of years, he obtained a grant from the National Geographic Society to explore the medicinal plant usage of indigenous peoples in remote corners of Central and South America. He went there seeking out traditional cures that were typically passed down orally from one healer to another, and the fascination blossomed. He'd turned into a medicine hunter and ended up dedicating his life to living with isolated tribes in the Amazon and the Andes, researching and cataloguing their use of plants and funding his ongoing bioprospecting from lecture fees and by selling articles and photographic essays to newspapers and magazines.

His life was his work, and he'd never married or had kids.

Tess asked, "So how'd he end up coming up with a superdrug?"

I reminded Tess that in many cultures, particularly in the Far East, the mind and the body were considered to be one entity, unlike in Western medicine. Curing a problem in either one of them invariably meant dealing with an underlying cause in the other. Amazonian shamans, I had discovered, pushed this approach to another level. They believed that true healing involved healing the body, the mind, and the spirit. Some of them believed that bodily disease, as well as mental illness, were caused by noxious spirits that needed to be expunged in religious rituals that often involved psychoactive substances—hallucinogens such as *ayahuasca*, which has been documented to cure both depression and metastasized cancers. This meant that for someone like McKinnon, studying the cures that healers and shamans administered involved learning and understanding the properties of the complicated brews the healers had perfected over centuries of usage and of the psychoactive plants they put in them.

"His medicinal work involved participating in religious rituals and taking all kinds of hallucinogens," I told her. "And somewhere on that path, he came across this drug."

"You don't know where he discovered it, with what tribe?"

"No. And, obviously, Navarro didn't either, nor does whoever is after it now, whether it's Navarro or someone else."

"But clearly, it's something really powerful—otherwise they wouldn't be doing all this now, five years later, and still be this desperate to get their hands on it, would they?" She looked at me with an expression that somehow injected a touch of hope in me that maybe we weren't completely toast. "Maybe you did the right thing. Maybe . . . maybe if he'd lived, things would be much worse."

Michelle had said that, too. I'd tried to convince myself of that for years, and hearing her say it as well, thinking about what was happening now—maybe there was some truth in it. Right now, I was just pleased Tess was still in the same room as me.

"But what the hell is it?" she asked. "There are plenty of hallucinogens out there and they're not as bad as something like meth, right?"

I'd asked the same question, back then. "Three reasons. One, he said it was something that could be hugely popular, that it had such a kick in it that people wouldn't be able to resist, that it would make meth look like aspirin—his words, not mine. Two, he'd managed to turn it into a pill. Which means it's easy to take. And the right drug at the right time can spread like the plague. Three, since Navarro would be the only one supplying it, he could make it as addictive as he wants. Which would be a disaster since we're talking about a heavy-duty hallucinogen."

"Why?"

"Most human brains," I explained, "are not wired to deal with the effects of a hard-core hallucinogen. They're just not. The brain can deal with the effects of weed or coke or heroin, but a hard-core hallucinogen is very different. It runs a serious risk of destroying a big chunk of the psychological fabric of its users. That's why these drugs have always been seen culturally, in pagan religions and such, as something that is by the few and for the few, meaning it's meant to be taken only after a proper initiation. It's part of a ritual, a ceremony, a rite of passage . . . you do it once in a lifetime, maybe when you come of age, when you enter adulthood, when you reach a certain milestone of maturity—or when you're in bad shape and you need to be healed. The only people who are allowed to do it regularly are the shamans and the medicine men, and there's a reason for that. They can take it on a regular basis because they're trained to deal with its effects, their whole lives are devoted to coping with the ramifications of what you see and what you experience when you're tripping. Biologically and, more importantly, psychologically, the average person is just not equipped and not trained to deal with something this intense, and from a social point of view there isn't time for the average user to do that. There's a real risk that if a drug like this were to become mainstream—based on what we know about it—it could cause a lot of problems. People using a pill like that wouldn't be able to function. They could easily develop long-term depression and mental instability and suffer breakdowns. Psychiatric wards would have to deal with an onslaught of hundreds of thousands of patients. Look at how devastating and debilitating meth is, how it takes over lives and turns healthy, successful people who had everything going for them into zombies—and we're only seeing the beginning of it.

"This could be much worse," I added. "Meth and crack, as bad as they are for you—they don't rewire your brain. They get you high, you'll get addicted to them, and they'll ruin your body, but when you're not tripping, your brain's essentially back to what it was even if everything around it is falling apart. Hard-core hallucinogens work differently. These drugs can—and will—rewire your brain. Someone who takes stuff like what McKinnon was talking about runs a real risk of coming out of it as a different person with potentially different moral views, a different psychological take on the world, a completely different perception of the world that you live in, how you relate to it . . ."

Tess looked confused. "What, like *ayahuasca*? 'Cause that's a hardcore hallucinogen, right? But I remember reading about people who'd suffered from depression all their lives who went deep into the Amazon and spent, like, a week there with shamans taking it and coming out of it saying it had cured them."

"Yes, but they did that within a ceremonial setting with an expert healer by their side. And they took it *to get healed*. The problem with stories like that is that you read them and you think these drugs are an easy cure to all our problems. You'd be thinking *ayahuasca* is a magic bullet for depression and *iboga* should be given to all heroin addicts to help get them off it. But the thing about these hallucinogens is that it's as much about you as it is about the drug. It's about what state of mind you're in when you take it, what you're hoping to get out of it, about having the right physiology—and the right guidance. That's crucial. The guidance, the ritualized, sacred framework with others around you and shamans looking over you and guiding you through your trip. If this becomes a street drug, the average junkie or suburban teen tripping on this in some squat or in a basement den or in some loud, strobe-lit nightclub isn't going to have any of that. Where's the guidance going to come from? Where's the highly experienced healer who's going to help them interpret all the repressed stuff they might see as they see it and tell them they're not going insane and help them understand what their psyche is telling them?"

"Okay, but if it's going to give such a bad trip and be that dangerous, it'll put people off taking it, won't it? It doesn't sound like something that's going to be popular in nightclubs."

I shook my head with a slight scoff. "Drug user psychology has very little to do with common sense. You know that. People seek out what's dangerous. Like with heroin. Every once in a while, a new batch that causes a lot of overdoses hits the street. And guess what? That's the brand everyone then wants. They pay more for it. They seek it out. Hearing that people died from it only makes it more popular. Same with AIDS and needles, or the *krokodil* heroin substitute that's raging through in Moscow these days. People who have an appetite for this stuff don't react rationally, by definition. They're looking for the strongest thrill they can get their hands on. They'll love the dark side of it—more intense than a 3-D horror movie. And if it's as easy as popping a pill . . ."

Tess let out a weary, ponderous sigh. "Okay, so . . . what now?"

"You and Alex will need to stay here for a while. I'm sorry. I also think you ought to call your mom and Hazel and give them some idea of what's going on so they can keep an eye out for anything suspicious."

Her face tightened with alarm. "You don't think—"

I cut her off, knowing she didn't want to say it. "No, I doubt they're in any danger. But I'd rather make sure we cover all the bases. I've got the local sheriff keeping an eye on the ranch already. Discreetly."

"You sure?"

I reached out and put my hand on her arm. "They're safe, Tess. I've made sure of that."

Her expression sank into gloom. "Okay, I'll . . . I'll call them tomorrow. But . . . whoever's after this . . . they think you've got it, right?"

Her look clearly telegraphed what she was worried about.

"It's what I do, Tess. And I've had a lot of practice." I gave her a half-smile. "We now know what they're after. They want it, we have it. Which means we're in the driver's seat. And we can use that to try and force a mistake out of them."

I needed to boost her confidence, though I wasn't sure I bought it myself. We still didn't know who we were dealing with. I found myself thinking again about McKinnon's own words, the ones that had started it all.

It'll make meth seem as boring as aspirin.

The words that sealed his fate.

And many others', since.

One way or another, I needed to put an end to their poisonous sting.

And I knew that, to do that, I'd have to draw them out. Using the one thing I knew they wanted.

Me.

48

Hank Corliss parked his car in the single garage of his house, climbed up three small steps, and went through the narrow doorway that led to his quiet, empty home.

Like he did every night.

He set down his attaché case on the couch and plodded across to the kitchen, where he got a clean tumbler out of a cabinet. He filled it using the fridge's ice maker, then retrieved a bottle of Scotch from another cabinet and filled the glass slowly, his weary eyes staring through the ice cubes as they cracked and popped and settled in. He carried the glass into the living room, set himself on the couch, and flicked on the TV. He didn't change the channel. He didn't adjust the volume. He just looked dead ahead as the random images unfurled on the screen and raised the glass for that first sip, rolling it around his mouth, feeling the burn tickle his throat, letting the golden potion work its magic.

Like he did every night.

Only tonight, things were a little different.

Tonight, there was a glint of hope breaking through the desolate numbness in his mind.

Hope that the beast who'd wrecked his life might finally be made to pay for the horrors he'd caused.

It wasn't likely. It wasn't probable. But it was possible. And right now, that was worth something. It was a hell of a lot more than he'd had in years.

His thoughts coasted back to that time, five years earlier, when he was running the DEA field office in Mexico City, fighting an unwinnable war against a well-armed, ruthless enemy that was everywhere and had the power to corrupt anyone. There was a reason why the posting had been nicknamed "the greatest laxative in the foreign service." Beyond being insanely dangerous, it was also a thankless task. Few Mexicans wanted him or his agents in their country, even though the cartel's turf wars were claiming thousands of victims every year. The locals blamed his countrymen for what was happening to their homeland, lambasting the insatiable appetite for drugs north of their border that had created the market in the first place while condemning the unlimited supply of easily bought weapons that were flooding south across the Rio Grande and spilling Mexican blood with increasing savagery.

"Poor Mexico . . . so far from God, so close to the United States," the dictator Porfirio Díaz had quipped in the nineteenth century.

For most of Díaz's countrymen today, the quip still held.

Despite all that, despite the difficulties he knew he'd face on the ground, Corliss had thrown himself into his assignment with the steely resolve and unflinching commitment he was known for. The posting was a badge of honor for him, the ultimate challenge for someone whose entire career had been devoted to the War on Drugs. It was a chance to take the fight to the enemy's backyard, to disrupt the poisonous scourge at its source, before it reached American soil.

To show those gutless *cabróns* how it was done.

Right off the bat, he and his men had notched up some decent successes. Against a rising tide of severed heads dumped in coolers, mass graves, and spiraling corruption that reached the very highest levels of government, Corliss's agents had led successful raids on several labs, torched many tons of narcotics, and put their hands on millions of dollars of illegal earnings.

Then the call had come in.

The call that changed everything.

Corliss tried not to think about that night, but he couldn't help it.

Even if he wanted to, even if he could somehow overpower his mind and force it to forget, his body wouldn't let him.

The pain and the scars left behind by twenty-three bullet holes would see to that.

He hadn't expected the attack. No one had. Not at his house. Not in the gated compound, not at the home of the head of the DEA in Mexico. But that's where it had taken place. And the barrage of painful images that battered his mind whenever he relived it was so intense and so surreal that he didn't know what was real from what was imagined, not anymore.

The men had burst in on them in the middle of the night, rousing him and his wife, Laura, from their sleep. Four men in balaclavas, four soulless demons that rose out of the pits of hell, dragged them out of their bed, and threw them into the living room to face their worst fear: the sight of their nine-year-old daughter, Wendy, sheer terror crippling her face, in the clutches of one of the men, the one who was their leader. The one who didn't bother with a mask.

Raoul Navarro.

The man who'd hardly ever been photographed, the one of whom the agency had no more than a couple of grainy, out-of-date photographs. And yet, here he was, in Corliss's own living room, not even bothering to hide his own face.

Which didn't bode well at all.

The Mexican had one hand clasped around Wendy's neck, anchoring her in place. In the other, resting against the other side of her neck, he held a thin, small knife. Its compactness wasn't any source of comfort. Not when its smooth, sleek blade glinted with such ferocity.

"You took something from me," Navarro announced. "I want it back."

At first, Corliss's frazzled mind didn't register any of it. He didn't understand what the man wanted. He pleaded with him to let his daughter go, saying he'd give him whatever it was he wanted and asking him to explain what he was talking about.

"McKinnon," Navarro added, coldly.

In a blinding flash that seared right through him, Corliss understood.

"The journal," he muttered. "I have it. It's right here." He pointed to a corner cabinet in the living room, his eyes begging for permission to retrieve it.

Navarro gave him the smallest of nods, and Corliss scurried across the room, his breath coming short and fast, his fingers twitching as he rummaged through a drawer before pulling out the old, tattered leather-covered book.

The book he'd had translated by an analyst at the agency.

The one whose contents he hadn't shared with anyone else there.

He held it up to his captor like a trophy.

"Here," he said, edging closer to him, one hesitant step after another, a supplicant approaching his executioner. "Now, please. Let her go."

Navarro nodded to one of his men, who stepped in and took hold of the journal, tucking it into his backpack.

"Please," Corliss pleaded.

Navarro smiled—an awful smile, a smile that chilled the bone more than any frown.

"Do you take me for a *baboso*?"

Corliss was lost.

"That's not what I came for," Navarro added, fixing him with a murderous stare while tightening his grip on Wendy and pressing the blade against her skin.

Corliss could see Wendy's artery straining against the edge of the blade. "No, please. I don't know what—" Then, in a stomach-wrenching flash, he got it. What Navarro had come for. And the realization hit him like he'd been stabbed with live wires.

"I don't have it," he told the Mexican. "We don't have it. We couldn't access it."

"Bullshit." He pressed the blade in even tighter.

"I'm telling you, we never got it. The laptop, it had a password, we couldn't crack it. The hard drive got wiped. I'm telling you we don't have it."

"I'm not going to ask you again."

Corliss's mind was scrambling for answers, but he couldn't think of any. "Please. You've got to believe me. I'd give it to you if I had it. I'd give you anything you want. Just don't—don't hurt her. Please."

And then he saw it. A narrowing in Navarro's eyes, a hardening of his jaw muscles. A seething exhale. And the fingers, tightening their grip on Wendy's neck—and on the blade.

"Okay, well, if that's how you want to play it," Navarro said—

And Corliss bolted.

"No!"

He lunged forward, arms outstretched to grab his daughter and pull her to safety, with Navarro's men leaping at him while the startled Mexican lurched backward—

And in the flash of chaos, in that instant of madness, Corliss saw the blade nick Wendy's neck, saw the blood shoot out, saw her eyes shoot open with fear, saw her mouth go wide and heard her scream tear into his ears—

And she slid to the ground, holding her neck, blood spurting relentlessly through her fingers, her terrified gaze locked on her father—

He was on her in a flash, cradling her, pressing down against the cut on her neck, caressing her hair, telling her she was going to be all right—

His wife, sobbing and out of breath, now alongside him, desperately trying to do something to stem the life gushing out of her and bring some measure of comfort to their daughter—

"Help us," Corliss shouted, tears streaming from his eyes. "Help us, damn you."

Navarro and his men just stood there and watched as, in a few brutal seconds, Wendy lost consciousness. Then her breathing stopped and she just lay there, in Corliss's arms.

Dead.

He looked up at Navarro, drowning in fury, sorrow, and confusion.

"Why?" he mumbled between breathless sobs. "Why? I told you . . . I told you we didn't have it."

And in that instant, he thought Navarro finally believed him. But it was too late.

It didn't matter anymore.

"I told you I didn't have it," he wept. "Why did you have to do this?"

"Perhaps you'll understand," Navarro replied, coolly. "In another lifetime."

Three words that Corliss would never forget.

He roared as he leapt to his feet and launched himself at Navarro.

He never made it, never even laid a finger on the Mexican.

The bullets had stopped him.

Twenty-three of him.

He didn't remember much else about that night.

He'd spent days in a coma. Weeks in intensive care. Months in a hospital. Years in rehabilitation. Three months into his ordeal, he'd been told that his wife had taken her own life. Which hadn't surprised him. He'd seen how Wendy's death had affected her, how she couldn't live with the memory of that night. And now she was gone, too.

They were both gone.

But Navarro was still out there. Roaming the land, carefree, no doubt causing more horrors, inflicting more pain and suffering wherever he went.

A monster on the loose.

At first, Corliss couldn't understand why he'd survived. He couldn't understand why he hadn't died from the hailstorm that had ripped through his body. After leaving the hospital, he'd considered ending his own life and joining his girls in the hereafter. He'd thought about it a lot. He'd come close to doing it a few times. Then, one day, he understood.

He understood that he'd been spared for a reason.

He realized he was still alive to do what had to be done.

To put the monster down.

To make sure his evil was extinguished.

To make sure he paid.

And right now, it seemed like there was a chance that the monster was finally out in the open. Not just out in the open, but here. In America. In California.

Within range.

Corliss's arm slid down to rest on the couch, the empty tumbler slipping out of his fingers and rolling into the cushions. And as he drifted off to sleep, he held onto one thought: that if the monster were ever caught, that he'd be the one to slit his throat and watch him die, one slow breath at a time.

Hasta la vista, motherfucker.

49

On the smooth timber deck of the stucco-and-terracotta-tile pool house, the monster was busy scouring the deep folds of his consciousness for some answers of his own.

The day hadn't gone well.

He was now one man down. His target was nowhere in sight. And he couldn't see a clear way forward that would bring him what he was after.

He needed a more enlightened view.

An epiphany.

The blind Peruvian's brew would see to that. It always did.

He needed to find Reilly, but that wasn't going to be easy. He couldn't have his men tail him as he left the only location he was sure to go to, the local offices of the FBI. Not after the fiasco of the last attempt. Not after the bikers had been eliminated. The enemy was on high alert. They'd be looking out for anything suspicious. And the last thing Navarro needed right now was to lose more men.

Guerra and his techie snoops wouldn't be useful either. Reilly's phone, like that of any FBI agent, had sophisticated anti-hacking software installed on it. There was no way to track him through it. And his woman's phone was also no longer an option. That door had been slammed shut at the museum.

He sat there, naked, cross-legged, and completely still, as he dived and soared through breathtaking landscapes and rapid-fire sequences of imagery, some he recognized, others he didn't, the real blending with the surreal as his synapses burst into unexplored territory and linked up through previously unmapped connections.

And then it came to him. The simple realization that his answer was well within his grasp.

In fact, it lay within the walls of his gated villa.

A living, breathing answer that was calling out to him, beckoning for his attention.

The sorcerer's face broadened into a peaceful smile, and he shut his eyes.

Tomorrow, he knew, would be a far better day.

WEDNESDAY

50

I didn't get much sleep. My mind had been churning away all night, scheming and plotting, stress-testing different routes forward— anything to escape thinking about Tess and where I stood with her. I hadn't come up with anything even remotely foolproof, but some were less harebrained than others. All the paths I had explored, though, had one thing in common: They were all centered around me setting myself up as bait to flush out our Mexican aggressors.

As you can imagine, I wasn't exactly jumping up and down with glee.

By nine, I was showered, dressed, and walking into Villaverde's office to go over our options. Munro arrived at roughly the same time. I knew Villaverde wouldn't be thrilled about my thinking. I wasn't looking forward to putting myself out there as a lure for a bunch of psychos who took pleasure in snipping off people's privates, but I couldn't think of anything else that might work. Unless Villaverde or Munro had a brilliant alternative to put on the table, I was pretty much committed to putting my plan in motion.

Maybe it was a half-assed way of trying to make up for what I'd done. I don't know. All I knew was, I wanted the bastards gone and I wanted to know that Tess and Alex wouldn't have anything more to worry about.

We started off by going through a round-up of whatever updates had come in concerning the previous days' events. There was nothing in them that led to a eureka moment. The guy Jules had taken out at

Balboa Park had nothing on him that would help ID him, and his prints didn't get a hit either. The SUV they'd abandoned there was a dead end, too. So far, all we knew was that it had been stolen a couple of days ago. Detectives were on their way to interview its owner as a matter of procedure, but I knew it would prove to be a waste of time.

The follow-up reports on the multiple homicide at the Eagles' clubhouse the day before didn't give us anything to jump about either, although I'd had an idea about that.

"One thing worth doing," I told them. "The guy Pennebaker told us about, the one Navarro went to work on. Pennebaker said one minute he was fine, then he just dropped to the ground like he'd been hit with a tranquilizer dart. Only he was still awake, just paralyzed."

"What are you thinking?" Munro asked.

"Given that I don't believe in voodoo, I'd say Navarro slipped him some kind of mickey. Which got me wondering about Walker. He was chopped up and left to bleed out, and yet there weren't any signs of a struggle there. Like he didn't resist. Which doesn't make sense."

"Unless he was drugged," Villaverde added, getting my drift. "Okay. I'll get the coroner to run a full toxicology workup."

I'd already pretty much made up my mind on that one, and I knew what the tox report would confirm.

This wasn't some lieutenant of Navarro's.

It was him.

I just knew it.

Villaverde was picking up his phone when he handed me a sheet of paper.

"Michelle's phone records," he said. "There's a Dean there, like you thought. Take a look."

I looked at the printout. Several calls were highlighted, all made in the last six weeks to a number that was registered to Dean Stephenson. It had a 510 area code.

"It's not local," I asked.

Villaverde shook his head. "Berkeley."

"And he's a shrink?"

"Yes and no," Villaverde replied. "He teaches psychiatry. Runs the department up at UCB."

Which surprised and kind of worried me. Of all the shrinks Michelle could have taken Alex to see, she'd chosen someone who was undoubtedly a big hitter, despite the fact that he was basically an hour and a half's flight away.

I called Tess and gave her his name and number while Villaverde spoke to the coroner, thinking she could run with it while we focused on figuring out how to get the bad guys to step into the limelight, ideally without my laying down my life in exchange.

Something else was nagging at me, but I couldn't quite put my finger on it. In any case, I barely got a chance to float my proposal when one of Villaverde's men burst into his office, his face all alight with urgency.

"You've got to see this," he announced as he beelined across the room to Villaverde's desk, grabbed a remote control, and used it to turn on the TV that sat on the bookshelves.

It was a local news channel. The banner read "Armed hostage situation in Mission Valley," and the screen was showing some grainy footage that someone had filmed using their phone. There was a guy with a gun, holding someone by the neck, shouting and waving his gun around frantically while backing away from the camera.

I recognized him immediately from the small tuft of hair under his lower lip. It was Ricky "Scrape" Torres, aka Soulpatch—the biker with the bullet wound in his shoulder who'd been yanked out of the dead deputy's car.

In living, breathing color.

51

Ricky Torres didn't know what the hell was happening to him.
He'd been duct-taped like a mummy and held in some room somewhere for what felt like forever. His wound had been treated and stitched shut, but it still hurt like hell. Then a little while ago, he'd felt a prick in his arm—some kind of antibiotic, no doubt—then, still with a duct tape blindfold over his eyes, he'd been untied, dragged to his feet, thrown into a car, and driven away.

And then this.

Thrown out of the car onto hard asphalt before his captors screeched away.

Had they let him go?

Hesitantly, he stood up and tore the tape off his eyes. The sun assaulted his vision instantly, and it took him a long moment before he could make things out clearly. When he did, he realized they'd dumped him in Mission Valley, right by the main parking lot of the Westfield Mall. He felt drowsy and disorientated, and found himself staring curiously at the Hooters across the road. His face contorted into an odd smile as a weird thought dropped into his mind. Right now, a few beers in the company of some scantily clad hotties would really help him forget everything that had happened to him in the past—how long was it? Forty-eight hours? More?

He didn't know.

He stood there for a moment, still unsure as to why the bastards had let him go. During the drive over, he'd asked himself whether they were taking him somewhere isolated so they could kill him there and dump his body. Clearly, that wasn't the case. But he felt like crap. His head was throbbing, his eyes felt like they weren't focusing properly, and although the pain in his shoulder had eased off after they'd stitched him up, it was now back with a vengeance. Although he'd felt the bullet being removed, he now found himself wondering if his wound was infected. He knew from his days fighting in Iraq that infections to bullet wounds were often more lethal than the bullet that made the hole.

He needed to get it checked. Fast.

But a quick beer sure sounded good.

He took a couple of uncertain steps into the street—then heard a loud blast from a horn that stopped him in his tracks. He spun around to find that he was looking directly at the driver of a truck that was screeching to a halt, only narrowly avoiding hitting him. The guy was gesticulating and swearing loudly in what sounded like Spanish, but Torres couldn't be sure. The sound reaching his ears was distorted, and there was a disconnect between what he was hearing and the movement of the guy's mouth. There was also something *odd* about the driver. Torres squinted and tried to focus against the sun. Then he saw it.

The guy had yellow eyes.

Torres blinked, shaking his head before taking another look. The eyes were still yellow. Not only that, but fangs were now protruding from beneath the guy's upper lip, and his skin was shimmering like the skin of a snake.

What the—?

Torres staggered back onto the sidewalk, violently shaking his head as he retreated, unable to tear his eyes off the horrific sight. The driver swore at him and hissed through his sharp fangs as the truck rumbled off. Torres watched it go in total confusion, wondering what the hell had happened just then. He'd barely slept since he'd been nabbed and was clearly starting to hallucinate, but he needed to hold it together and get his head straight if he was going to have any chance of staying clear of the cops. He decided that the last thing he needed right now was wasting precious time on boilermakers and trying to get into the pants of some buxom waitress.

He turned to head the other way when he felt it. A weight, tugging against his belt. He glanced down and pulled back the Windbreaker they'd put him into and saw it: an automatic handgun, tucked into his belt.

His jaw dropped, and he quickly covered the gun up again. He glanced around nervously, hoping no one had spotted him, and noticed that he was facing a CVS, which took up most of the first floor of the building in front of him. What he really needed were some kick-ass painkillers. Something to take the edge off the throbbing pain in his shoulder so he could get somewhere safe and figure out his next move. Yes, that was the right move. For sure.

He set off across the parking lot and headed for the pharmacy. But as he made his way along the parked cars, he heard the unmistakable sound of a magazine being clicked into the body of an AK-47.

He spun around, his hand instinctively slipping under his jacket to grip the gun. A woman was loading shopping bags into the trunk of her car while her kid screamed that he didn't want to go home. As she leaned into the car's open tailgate, Torres realized that she must have hidden her weapon inside the car so he couldn't see it. He thought about going over to the woman and demanding that she give him her weapon, but the sound of the kid's screaming suddenly spiraled to an unbearable level, piercing his skull like a battery of bayonets.

He covered his ears as he turned and ran into the mall.

People seemed to avoid him as he staggered into the building. As he passed the Macy's, he looked down at his shirt and noticed that he was drenched in sweat. Or was it blood? Maybe he'd been hit and the pain from his shoulder had stopped him feeling it? He wiped his fingers across his face then looked at them. No, it was just sweat. His mouth felt horribly dry. He needed water. And those painkillers. He set off again, but a searing pain ripped through his abdomen, causing him to double over. He leaned against a wall and retched several times. He felt like he wanted to throw up, but he didn't think there was anything in his stomach. The pain was so bad he leaned his back against the wall, and although he was desperately trying to stay on his feet, after a moment he had to just let himself slide to the floor.

Something was wrong. Inside him. Something was seriously, seriously wrong, he knew it. And it was starting to scare him.

He raised his head and saw an older woman staring at him with a concerned look on her face. That's how the suicide bombers got you. He knew that. They pretended to be a friend and then they took you to hell. He had lost three friends that way, blown to bits in the middle of a crowded street as his unit went door-to-door, trying to flush out insurgents. A woman had offered to show his sergeant a house in which some of them were hiding. He'd stayed behind to cover the street, and seconds later, there were pieces of his buddies scattered across the road.

He wasn't going to let them get him that way.

He steeled his eyes and looked at the woman and went for his gun, but his hand froze as he stared at her face and saw it start to bend and change, her gentle gray eyes turning black and threatening, her nose morphing into the sharp beak of a bird. He tried to move, but the pain in his gut was too severe. The woman's arms were now covered in black feathers, and her hands had been replaced by razor-sharp talons. And she was edging slowly toward him, her claws outstretched.

With a huge effort he pulled the SIG out from under his jacket and waved it at the harpy-like beast.

"Get back! Get away from me!"

The beast didn't need telling twice. It turned and skittered away.

Torres couldn't understand what was happening. He stuck the gun back under his belt, hauled himself to his feet, and slipped around the corner toward the entrance of the CVS. It was only a couple of hundred yards away and he was sure he could make it as long as he didn't stop again.

He was halfway there when he heard a voice behind him.

"Sir? Sir? Are you all right? Do you need any help?"

Torres ignored the voice and kept going. It was a trick. A trick to keep him from getting the help he needed.

"Sir?" The voice turned into a rasp. "I'm going to need you to stop so I can talk to you."

Torres spun around—much faster than he meant to, considering the agonizing pain in his abdomen—and found himself looking at another goddamn insurgent. The man had his hand resting on a sidearm that was hanging from his belt. Torres couldn't exactly make out what uniform the towelhead bastard was wearing, but whatever it was, he'd probably taken it from the body of a dead American soldier.

It *was* a trap.

They were going to take him hostage, torture him, and cut off his head. That's what these sickos did. Torres's eyes darted around. Thirty yards away—too great a distance for him to do anything other than shoot him—a younger man was holding a cell phone that was pointed straight at him. They were already filming their hostage video. He wanted to shoot the bastard, but his captain had told him not to use his weapon unless his life was in immediate danger. Or was it someone else who had said that? He couldn't remember. But he knew he should obey his orders if he could.

He felt another presence and turned around. Another man—this one disguised in jeans, tennis shoes, and a polo shirt—was walking toward him. Jesus. They had sent a whole team for him.

He had to do something or he was screwed.

He put out one hand, palm upward, in a gesture of surrender, but at the same time took two steps to the left. Then, as the man in the polo shirt drew level, he grabbed him by the neck, pulled out his gun and pressed it against the insurgent's head.

"Stay away," he yelled. "Everyone stay the fuck away from me."

The insurgent in the fake uniform had already pulled his sidearm and was pointing it at him, but Torres had the upper hand now. He backed away, toward the CVS, dragging his hostage with him, moving faster with every yard despite the pounding pain in his head and the burn in his gut. As he shot another look toward the insurgent—

who was staying put for now—he saw the bastard's eyes turn yellow and horns sprout from his head. He blinked and shook his head, but when he opened his eyes, the horns were still there, gleaming like black obsidian, sharp and menacing. Sweat was now streaming down his own face and he screamed, "No," before shoving his hostage away. The man scurried off, but not before giving Torres a sideways glance—he too had yellow eyes and horns, only his mouth widened to reveal a horrific set of fangs and an angry, forked tongue.

Torres felt a surge of terror as he realized something was allowing him to see the motherfuckers for what they really were. Demons, agents of Satan, soldiers of the antichrist. He'd always known they were evil; he'd just never seen them show their true forms before. He needed to survive, to tell everyone about this. People needed to know. But first he had to deal with the agony ripping through his stomach.

He reached the CVS's entrance, where another insurgent came out of the store and tried to grab him. Torres swung his elbow into the guy's face, then kicked a boot right through his shin bone. The demon collapsed to the ground. He crouched down beside his groaning victim and grabbed his gun, then he spun around with a weapon in each hand, one pointed at the insurgent on the ground, the other one at the guy in the fake uniform, who was now standing twenty yards from the store entrance. He saw that more of them had appeared, a horde of snarling, clawing beasts closing in on him.

He felt light-headed, and his vision was swaying in and out of focus as he yelled to the fighter he'd just overpowered.

"Shut the doors. Now!"

At least if he were locked inside, they couldn't get him. And maybe he could get the painkillers he was now really desperate for.

The store's security guard got up, scurried over to the main doors—two big glass panels with chrome handles—and proceeded to close and lock them.

"Where's the pharmacy?" Torres shouted.

The guy gestured into the back of the store.

"Give me the keys."

The guard handed them over.

"And your radio."

He complied.

Torres stuffed the keys into his pocket, then dropped the radio to the ground and smashed it under his boot. He looked around him. Several customers—or were they two-faced enemy combatants?—were backing away from him with their hands up, some of them crying and whimpering. For a moment he wondered what the hell he was doing. Wasn't he supposed to be getting out of town? Away from the cops? How had he got himself locked into a mall? It didn't matter right now. At least he was still alive. Yes, the fuckers hadn't managed to get him. Not like the rest of his unit, who'd been blown to smithereens by that towelhead bitch. It was just him now. And he wasn't going to let them fuck with him.

He needed a plan.

Step one: Deal with the pain.

Step two: Talk to the ranking officer and make a deal.

He knew something they needed to hear about. Maybe he was the *only one* who knew.

Covering the store with both guns, he crept slowly toward the pharmacy.

52

I was already halfway out of the SUV before Villaverde had thrown it into park. There were at least ten black-and-whites scattered across the main lot, plus a SWAT truck and two incident response vehicles parked off to one side. A couple of uniforms had already thrown up a tape barrier about fifty yards from the mall's main entrance. On the other side of the lot were four local news trucks. A fifth pulled in as I jogged over to the command-and-control truck, Villaverde a few paces behind me.

I waved my creds and climbed into the truck. The SDPD incident commander was expecting us and introduced himself as Captain Jack Lupo. In turn, he introduced Sergeant Alan Schibl, who was the ranking SWAT officer, a civilian hostage negotiator by the name of Tim Edwards, and Belinda Zacharia, a sharp-suited lady from the sheriff's office, which made sense considering Torres was a witness to the killing of their deputy. There were also a couple of uniforms and a comms technician.

Lupo brought us up to speed. As far as they knew, there were nineteen hostages in the CVS—seven staff and twelve customers—though they couldn't be a hundred percent sure about the number of customers. No hostages seemed to have been harmed—yet. Torres seemed to be acting alone. The witness who had shot the camera-phone video had stated that Torres was acting bizarrely, obviously in pain, and had been sweating profusely. Edwards had tried calling the store's fixed line, but once they got past the automated answering system the number rang unanswered. Torres wasn't picking up.

Schibl, who had been itching to chime in since we'd entered the truck, couldn't contain himself anymore.

"I've got a pair of marksmen on either side of the store's main entrance. They can't see him at the moment, but if he moves into their line of sight without our move endangering a hostage, I've given them the order to shoot."

Zacharia jumped on him before I had the chance. "Hang on there a second, sergeant—we need this guy alive. He's our only solid lead. The sheriff's consulted the mayor on this and he has his full support. We can't let whoever murdered Deputy Fugate get away. Not under any circumstances. So I suggest you tell your men to stand down."

There was a good chance things were going to get ugly very quickly. I'd spent a decent chunk of my professional life locked in these interdepartmental pissing contests. Although Villaverde was officially in charge, he'd still have to fight the others every step of the way in order for his orders to be given priority. I looked at him and he flashed me a subtle, wry smile. I knew that look. He was going to sit back and wait for the loudest voices to burn themselves out, then calmly assert his authority. It wasn't my way of dealing with a situation like this, but I was on Villaverde's turf and far too close to the case to risk trying to shout down the natives. Against all natural inclination, I decided to give them a couple of minutes to reach the correct conclusion on their own.

Schibl puffed out his chest—the most he could do in the present company to show his intense displeasure at being ordered around by a woman, and not even a cop at that—and gave her both barrels.

"We need to take him down at the first opportunity," he shot back. "End of story. He's an ex-Marine with a history of violence. I've dealt with siege situations before where the hostage-taker is a soldier with PTSD. He might as well be high on meth. The outcome's always the same anyway. The grunt ends up dead one way or another. So how about we put an end to this as soon as we can and avoid any additional casualties."

He turned to Lupo, as though Zacharia didn't exist.

"I hear you," the incident commander told him, "but there's a bigger picture here. This perp's right in the middle of a major federal case and he's the only witness to several major crimes, crimes in which at least ten people have lost their lives. If there's any way we can talk to him, we need to take it. So I'm afraid I have to agree with Belinda here. Tell your men to hold their fire unless one of the hostages is in immediate danger."

Schibl grimaced. He had obviously hoped that Lupo would back him up, but instead, the ranking cop had told him in no uncertain terms to do what he was told. It was my turn to shoot a quick smile at Villaverde, who finally took the opportunity to say something.

"Before the day is out," Villaverde told Schibl, "there's a good chance we're going to need you to ask your men to take that shot. But right now, I think we do need to balance the need for action with the benefits of restraint." He turned to the hostage negotiator. "Hand me the comms link, will you? Let's try calling him again."

Edwards dialed the number then held out the handset to Villaverde, who gestured toward me.

"You want to take this?"

I nodded and took the handset. After about twelve rings, someone picked up. Edwards's face lit up with anticipation, and the comms operator nodded to signal that the call was being recorded.

"Ricky," I spoke into the silence, "my name's Reilly. I'm with the FBI."

"Are you one of them, too?"

It was Torres. He sounded agitated, desperate, and absolutely terrified.

"One of who, Ricky?"

"Those things."

"What things? I'm with the FBI, Ricky. Is everyone okay in there?"

"Just keep those things away from me, man. I saw them outside the entrance. I won't let them take me, whatever they do, you hear me? Any of them come near me, I'll blow their fucking heads off."

I didn't know what he was talking about. He was obviously having a bad trip, and was far more scared than someone who still had the chance to give themselves up before the shooting started. It was pretty obvious which tack I needed to try.

"Listen to me, Ricky. Whatever it is you're scared of, we can protect you. We wanted to protect Wook, but they got to him before we did. We know who you and the rest of the Eagles were working for. Guru told us. We just need you to help us find them. Then we can lock them up and keep you safe."

"Guru?" he blurted. "Guru's gone, man. How'd you talk to him? You're lying. You're one of them, aren't you? You want me to come out so you can sink your claws into me. Well fuck you, man. Fuck you all to hell." Then he hung up.

"The guy's totally lost it," Schibl said.

I had to agree. Which didn't bode well for Torres. Not with a SWAT sergeant who was itching to fast-track him to join up with the rest of his biker buddies.

I, on the other hand, wanted him alive and talking. But I didn't think I was going to get that chance.

At the westernmost edge of the parking lot, under cover of a line of trees, Navarro and his two surviving *pistoleros* sat in the air-conditioned cool of their Toyota Land Cruiser. They had doubled back after releasing Torres into the wild and taken up their surveillance point just as he had disappeared through the mall's main entrance.

Navarro had a pair of binoculars trained on the area of the parking lot that had been overrun by the police, and a slight grin tugged at his cheek as he tried to imagine what kind of hell Torres was probably going through. The drug, a gray powder that he'd rubbed into Torres's open wound, was a particularly insidious one. He'd been taught it in Vanuatu, in the South Pacific, by a shaman with a fully tattooed body who was referred to as the Black Vulture. Navarro had used it on several captives over the years, and it had never disappointed him. It would scour its victims' unconsciousness, dredge up their deepest fears and paranoias, and bring them bursting to life in heightened, surreal ways, turning the most mundane settings into the stuff of Wes Craven movies. Left unchecked, it had the uncanny ability to send one's soul spiraling into self-destruction in the most unexpected ways, something that never failed to entertain Navarro, although this was one implosion he knew he wouldn't be able to enjoy in person.

He watched Reilly and Villaverde dash out of their car and into the melee, and the sight caused him further disappointment. He'd been expecting them to arrive separately. This was a twist he'd thought possible, but he'd been hoping things would work out differently.

Still, he knew that they had a good opportunity to put the rest of his plan into action. It was obvious from the spectacle that was now unfolding at the other end of the parking lot that the first half of his plan had gone exactly as he had imagined it would. That was another thing the blind Peruvian's drug had taught him. What was real in the imagination—whether under the effect of drugs or not—was just as real as what you held in your hand or put in your mouth. Maybe more so. He had imagined himself as the sole dispenser of a drug that no one would be able to turn down. And soon—after years of waiting—it would be true. The thought didn't excite him unduly, as he'd known that this moment would come, sooner or later. He had imagined it, and soon it would be happening, for real. Indeed, who could say that the imagining was not as real as the events that it brought about?

He inclined his head toward the gunman in the back, who was watching live coverage of the siege on a 3G-enabled tablet.

He nodded to the man.

The *pistolero* nodded back, set the tablet down, and climbed out of the car.

53

Torres waited nervously as the pharmacist hunted through the meds behind the counter. He'd already given Torres a couple of codeine-laced painkillers, but they only seemed to have made things worse, and he was now hunting for some antibiotics.

Torres raked his eyes back and forth across the store. He knew the place was far too big for him to control for any length of time. He just had to hope that the rest of his unit would come and rescue him before the creatures tore him to pieces. He felt lost and confused, unsure about whether the insurgents were being controlled by the monsters, or if they were simply one and the same. His head felt like it was going to burst open, and his skin was so itchy he wanted to slice it off. The pain in his stomach had eased off a bit, but his shoulder was now hurting so bad it felt like he'd only just been shot.

The pharmacist returned from behind the counter carrying a square cardboard box, from which he removed a strip of pills. He pressed out two into his palm and offered them to him.

"This is the strongest penicillin we have. Take them. It's still the best thing for infections."

Torres reached out to take them, but as his fingers were about to touch the pills, he saw that they weren't pills at all, just two shiny beetle-like insects with serrated legs ending in vicious-looking hooks and long antennae that waved back and forth trying to feel their way toward him.

The pharmacist stared at him. "They'll help. Trust me."

Torres blinked, but the beetles were still there, squirming around in the palm of the pharmacist's hand.

He swatted the man's hand away viciously and reared away from him.

"You're trying to get those inside me?" he screamed. "So they can eat me up from the inside? What did you give me before?" He swung his gun into the pharmacist's face. "Is that why my shoulder hurts so bad? Have I got them inside me already?"

The pharmacist raised his hands to calm him, and Torres saw the yellow eyes, the twisted and sharp horns, the long fangs, and the shimmering skin that he knew was the way that all of them *really* looked. The beast was coming right at him—

And he pulled the trigger and just watched as the monster's head exploded, spraying blood across the pharmacy counter.

A ripple of panic spread across the lot, and the *pistolero* didn't know what had caused it. The news crews had sprung to action, talking animatedly on live feeds, while cops and agents were moving to and fro with a sense of renewed urgency.

He guessed that something must have happened inside the mall. This was good and bad. Good, because it provided him with a measure of diversion, distracting everyone around and making his task potentially easier. Bad, because it could mean that the situation his boss had engineered was coming to a head, which could lead to his window of opportunity closing sooner than expected.

It wasn't a problem. He didn't need that much time.

He picked up his step marginally, making sure he didn't attract attention, and kept moving through the tangle of parked cars.

Twenty seconds later, he was by the SUV he'd seen the agents arrive in.

And before anyone could take notice of him, he was heading back the way he came, a slight grin of satisfaction pinching the edge of his mouth.

Screams erupted from the other side of the store, the noise cutting deep into his head as he staggered backward, waving the guns wildly from side to side.

"Stop! Stay back! Keep away from me!"

His throat was parched and burning now. He still hadn't had a drink. He'd meant to have one when he first entered the store, but he'd forgotten. He couldn't seem to keep a thought in his head.

"Someone bring me some water. Please."

No one moved. Why wouldn't they listen to him? He wasn't being unreasonable. He just wanted some help. Wanted the searing pain in his shoulder to stop. Wanted his head to stop throbbing. Wanted his mouth to stop feeling like it was slowly filling with sand. Wanted to stop sweating like he was in Nasiriyah. He couldn't work out why no one would help him and was suddenly overcome with violent rage.

"Bring me some water. Now!" He waved the guns around to reinforce his point.

After a few seconds, an older man approached him. He must have been at least sixty. He was holding a bottle of water.

"You a soldier, son?"

The man sounded friendly. Like he wanted to help.

"I was," Torres replied, shivering now. "Not now. Not anymore."

The man took a few steps toward him, holding out the bottle as a peace offering.

"My brother was in the army," he told Torres. "Got himself killed in Kuwait in ninety-one." He held the water just a few inches from Torres's hand. "Here. Drink this. You look like you need it. Just don't hurt anyone else, son."

Torres stared blankly at the bottle. After a long moment, he took it. He unscrewed the lid and raised the bottle to his lips, but as he was about to drink, he noticed a weird black shape inside the bottle near the bottom. He held the bottle up to the light and saw a snarl of black snakes writhing around in the water. They were grotesque, with bulbous eyes too big for their bodies and sharp spines along their backs. One of them thrashed against the side of the bottle and hissed at him.

They were trying to poison him. They'd do anything to get the creatures inside his body so they could rip him up from the inside.

He hurled the water across the room and pointed both guns at the old man, who nonetheless took a step toward him.

"Give me the guns, son," the man said, calmly. "You need to give me the guns so you can get the help you need."

He knew the man was lying, trying to trick him. He was going to take his guns, then drag him to some dark basement where they'd cut him up and feed on him. Is that what they did? He couldn't make sense of it anymore. It was all jumbled up in his head. Was he back in the army, or was he dreaming? Monsters weren't real. He knew that. But there was one standing right in front of him. And no way was he imagining this. It just was there, yellow eyes and fangs staring back at him, drool oozing over its bottom lip, talons outstretched.

He realized he had to get out before they ate him alive. There were too many creatures for him to defeat alone and he was locked in here with them. He had to leave. To run the gauntlet and escape. Shut in with the creatures, it was only a matter of time before they devoured him. Outside, at least he had a chance. And maybe they wouldn't want to lose any more of their number. He'd soon find out.

He backed away from the treacherous monster and made for a small group of the creatures that were still pretending to be human. He grabbed a young woman around the neck and dragged her over toward the main entrance, pulling the keys from his pocket. He unlocked the doors and maneuvered the woman so she was in front of him, then opened one of the doors a few inches and peered out into the plaza.

"I'm coming out," he shouted. "Let me go and I won't kill this one."

The mall was empty other than for two of the creatures waiting for him about sixty yards down the main plaza.

Torres took a step forward, but then he felt his hostage's weight shift, as though it were trying to stop him from going any farther. He turned toward the creature. Giant razor-edged bones were breaking through the skin of its neck. Elongated talons were sprouting from the ends of its arms. Feathers were covering its body. Its face was melting as a serrated beak burst through the flesh. He let go of the disgusting creature, raised his gun and fired. Or he thought he did. He'd definitely meant to pull the trigger, but somehow he hadn't managed to. Maybe it was something to do with the darkness flooding his head.

He felt his legs buckle underneath him.

The floor felt like quicksand under his boots, and as he fell, he wondered whether now, finally, he would be allowed to sleep.

I held my breath as I watched Torres go down on the feed from the lead marksman's helmet-mounted video camera. The bullet hit him square in the side of the head, just in front of his right ear. The woman he'd been using as cover only seconds before was hysterical, but alive.

Which was the prime objective.

I had no idea why Torres let go of her, but in doing so he had given the sniper a clear shot. A shot he'd had to take, since it was clear that Torres was about to kill his hostage.

I was fully aware of the probability that the siege would end with Torres dead. But knowing it didn't make things any better. Navarro had yet again caused a bloodbath, and our only lead to him was dead.

I wondered why Navarro had opted to send an armed ex-Marine on a bad trip into a crowded mall. But then going from everything I'd learned over the past few days, it was clear that Navarro enjoyed the chaos and death that he caused. And that this almost certainly wasn't going to be the last of it.

54

Tess hadn't slept well. She was all wired and angry, with a horde of powerful emotions warring inside her. It didn't help that she also felt like a caged animal, straining against the confines of the safe house, unable to go out for a jog or a therapeutic cup of coffee.

She'd already called her mom and spoken to Hazel and to Kim, too, putting a gloss on what was really going on before asking them to keep an eye out while trying not to alarm them too much. She failed, of course, and she knew it. It wasn't the first time she'd got herself into a sticky situation, even though this one wasn't through any fault of her own. Still, she was glad the call was behind her. It needed to be done.

Jules was with Alex in the living room, keeping him busy. She'd hit gold by signing him up to Club Penguin on her laptop. Given his giggles and squeals, he was having a blast. Tess had left them alone after breakfast, feeling a need to some time on her own, and was out in the back garden of the house, sitting on the grass with her back against the trunk of a lone sycamore tree, deep in thought.

She was still reeling from what Reilly had told her the night before. At first, she'd been horrified by it, no matter what spin she put on it. Then she'd spent a lot of the night trying to put herself in his place, reliving it from his point of view, wondering what it was like and what she would have done in his place. And what she'd realized was that she couldn't know. She knew it was easy to come to a rash judgment, as a passive outsider. It was very different from being there, on the ground, in the thick of it, with bullets flying and men intent on killing you swarming around you and the pressure of having to make a split-second decision weighing up your own moral instincts against a threat to the greater good. It wasn't about excusing what he'd done. It was about trying to understand it, knowing that in his line of work, in the kinds of situations he willingly put himself into in the line of duty, impossible choices sometimes had to be made.

She was also locked on one other thought. She knew that, sooner or later, McKinnon would have been killed by Navarro. She knew this was a self-serving rationalization, but she still found some solace in it. Then she reminded herself of something else that had given her a small uplift. After they'd talked late into the night, she'd asked Reilly if there was anything else he hadn't told her. If there would be any more bombshells to rock their world. He'd assured her there weren't, and she believed him.

Her thoughts migrated to the reason all this was going on, and to Alex. She found herself wondering about the drawing, about what his teacher had told her, about what he'd said about the plant. She went back inside, picked up her iPad, grabbed the firewalled cell phone Jules had given her to replace her iPhone along with the piece of paper on which she'd scribbled the number Reilly had given her, and went back outside.

She called the number in Berkeley.

The phone went to voicemail, its standard message informing Tess that she'd reached the office of Dean Stephenson, that neither he nor his assistant, Marya, were available, and to leave a message.

She waited for the requisite beep, then introduced herself and said, "I'm calling for Professor Stephenson. It's about Alex Martinez. It's . . . I really need to talk to you. Alex's mother has . . ." She hesitated, unsure about how much to say on a cold message. "She passed away, and I was hoping to talk to you to find out what we can do to help Alex through this difficult time." She ended the message by asking him to call back, leaving her phone number, and thanking him.

The call made her uncomfortable, but she wasn't sure why. She focused instead on moving on with the other question that was on her mind: what Alex had told his teacher, and her, about the plant he'd drawn.

She brought up Safari and Googled "Brooks," the name Alex had mentioned, along with "plant" and "heart." She got more than thirteen million hits, and after trawling through the first couple of hundred of them without coming across anything that struck her as relevant, she decided she needed to narrow her search and try again.

She tried it again, spelling the name with an "e" this time—Brookes. Thirty-four million hits and change.

She frowned, went back to the original spelling, and typed in "Brooks," "plant," "flower," "heart," "medicine," "treatment," and "death," then deleted a couple of names that had cropped up in her first search to avoid useless hits.

She was down to a slightly less daunting three hundred thousand hits, so she waded in.

An hour later, she came across something.

It was a news item on the WebMD website about a promising new heart treatment a pharmaceutical company had been trumpeting that had just had its testing suspended. The drug, which was based on an extract from a rare flower, had initially shown a lot of promise. Although the sap of the plant itself was poisonous, more than twenty useful alkaloids had been identified from it, and early testing had shown the drug they had synthesized from them to be a powerful cholesterol inhibitor. The company's stock price had soared based on those early tests. Two years into the testing phase, however, everything had gone wrong. Several patients had developed cardiac complications that were traced back to the use of the drug, and the test phase was shut down.

Tess Googled the plant the article mentioned.

It was a small, unremarkable white flower. Then something else snared Tess's attention. The plant's natural habitat.

It was indigenous to the Amazonian rainforest.

Her skin tingled with unease, as if tiny, invisible ants were crawling all over her.

She wondered how Alex knew about this. Sure, he could have seen it on a news broadcast. But to understand what it did, at age four? And register the name of Brooks? And then, there was the way he said it. In the first person. *I told them about it. They didn't like it.*

The ants were getting more agitated.

She chewed it over, her mind bouncing from one thought to another without managing to line them up into a coherent whole. After a while, she grew frustrated and decided to go inside and have another go at seeing if Alex would elucidate things for her, and her eyes caught sight of the note she'd written down when Reilly had called. She found herself pausing to stare at the name that was on it with a sense of intrigue that wasn't there before.

Dean Stephenson.

Why did she know that name?

It was there, she was sure of it, tucked away in the attic of arcane tidbits her mind was prone to hoard, taunting her—but she couldn't quite put her finger on it.

She decided to cheat and typed his name into the search box—and in the 0.15 seconds it took for the results to flash up, it came back to her.

There were more than four hundred thousands hits. She skipped the Wikipedia entry about the professor and went straight to the third result, his own webpage. It redirected to the University of California at Berkeley's Department of Psychiatry and Neurobehavioral Sciences, and specifically, to a specialty subsection called the Division of Perceptual Studies.

She felt her insides shrivel up with dread as the unthinkable started to fall into place, and within seconds, she was gone, losing all sense of place and time as she read page after page, immersing herself in Stephenson's work and the endless stream of information rushing at her while tying it back to what had been happening the last few days.

And then an impossible thought struck her.

Impossible, and yet . . . she couldn't ignore it.

She went back to the news item about the heart treatment, noted the name of the plant it had been derived from, and ran a new search around the suspended cure. This time, she added the name Wade McKinnon to the mix.

Her finger was trembling as she tapped the screen to initiate the search.

The result drove a spear through her senses that pinned her in place, and she understood.

55

We arrived back at Aero Drive feeling shell-shocked and with morale sinking fast. The body count had risen still further, a viable lead had been wiped out before we could make any use of it, and Navarro had yet again proven himself to be both lethally effective and spectacularly audacious, with seemingly no sense of a line that he would not—or could not—cross.

I followed Villaverde into the large meeting room that had become the de facto operations center since Michelle's death three days earlier. A couple of junior agents were co-coordinating with local law enforcement, trying to see whether Navarro had left behind any kind of trail before the siege started. One was reviewing traffic camera footage; another fast-forwarding through video from the two security cameras that surveilled the main parking lot at the mall. As Villaverde sat down, he looked from one to the other. They shook their heads in turn. Nothing yet.

After a moment, Munro joined us. He didn't look any happier than Villaverde. In fact, if anything, he appeared to be even more frustrated than I felt myself. Villaverde hit the Intercom button and asked for sandwiches and coffee for everyone, then leaned back in his chair and closed his eyes. He was clearly gathering his thoughts, but there didn't seem to be too many of them to gather.

"The guy's a fucking ghost," he grumbled. "We've got *nada*, and the way things have gone over the past seventy-two hours, I don't expect that's going to change much." He turned to Munro. "Anything from your side?"

Munro shook his head. "No hits. We've talked to everyone from Border Patrol to informants on the street. Corliss is in direct contact with the PFM," meaning the Mexican federal investigators. "He's called in every favor he's owed on both sides of the fence and come up empty-handed."

There was only one hand left to play now. We needed to give the bastard exactly what he wanted. Or at least to make it look like I was within his reach for as long as it took to tighten a strategically placed net around him.

"I don't think we have any choice," I offered. "We need to flush Navarro out into the open. Or at least his soldiers. We know he thinks I have the information he wants. Let him come and get it."

"If it's him we're dealing with," Villaverde put in. "We still have no solid evidence that it is."

"It doesn't matter *who* it is for this to work. We just need to agree how to stage it so that he feels confident enough to make a play for me and I have some cover."

Villaverde's grim expression betrayed his lack of enthusiasm for my willingness to be the bait. He was clearly frustrated as hell—and unhappy at not being able to disagree with me on this.

"Anyone have any other ideas?" I let the question hang there for a long second. "Okay. So let's talk about how we hook him."

Munro—always the brutal pragmatist—jumped in immediately. "News conference. That woman from the sherriff's department can lead. Lupo. Fugate's widow. A psychiatrist, one from the army if we can get one. You can't sit on the panel, but they've got to know you'd be there for something like that. Hold it somewhere with at least three ways in and out. Ramp up the police presence at two of the three, but leave the third light to the naked eye. Then you pop out to take a call or something, he makes his move, and we spring the trap."

Villaverde shook his head, his face wearing a look of total disbelief.

I could see that his fuse had just burned all the way down to the explosive. "After what just happened? You want to put that many people in his line of sight? No way."

It was the first time since I'd met him that he'd looked anything other than totally calm.

The door opened, but instead of coffee, the junior agent who entered was carrying a thin brown file folder, which he held out to Villaverde.

"Tox report on Eli Walker." He handed it over, adding, "There's a rush on the same for Ricky Torres. The sheriff's office has already called the mayor. We should have it by the end of the day."

As he left, Villaverde opened the folder and scanned the single sheet inside. Then he glanced pointedly at me and handed it to me.

Walker had an organic paralyzing agent in his blood. A combination of spider and lizard venom, specifically the brown widow, *Latrodectus geometricus*, and the Mexican beaded lizard, or *Heloderma horridum* of the family Helodermatidae. Plus a third neurotoxin that the lab couldn't identify.

I chucked the file to Munro. "Now tell me it's not El Brujo we're dealing with."

Munro went over the sheet and, for once, kept his mouth firmly shut.

Closely on the report's heels, our refreshments arrived and the three of us used the well-rehearsed rituals of shaking sugar into coffee and rewrapping an overfilled ciabatta without dripping fat onto our clothes to take a step away from the case and be in our own heads for a second. I was used to these moments being almost exclusively filled with thoughts of Tess, but the person who catapulted to the front of my mind this time was Alex.

He didn't deserve any of this.

I finished a mouthful. "I'll go on the morning news tomorrow. Alone. They can talk it up, make a lot of noise about how they're going to have an exclusive with the FBI agent dealing with this investigation—whatever it takes to make sure Navarro has a chance to hear about it. I'll drive there on my own and leave on my own. Full police presence in the studio, but none outside. None that they can see, anyway. We run multiple tails. I'll be safe till he thinks I've told him everything I know and I'll be sure to keep my mouth shut before we arrive wherever it is we're going."

Villaverde sipped his coffee and again shook his head, but this time it was clearly in resignation.

We were all out of alternatives, and if nailing the sick bastard meant that I was walking directly into harm's way—tribal pharmacy and organ removal included—so be it. It was still, in real terms, nothing that hadn't already been aimed at Michelle, or Tess, or Alex, or countless others since this goddamn mess had blown up.

I was ready to do it.

After all, you could only die once, right?

56

Tess wasn't sure what to do.

She felt hyperalert, and her pulse was raging wildly. It was like an awakening, like her mind was suddenly unchained and set free to roam through uncharted territory. She'd spent a couple of hours roaming through Stephenson's website, and by the end of it, questions were accosting her from all sides while competing insights jostled for supremacy inside her, all of them demanding she push them through to their rightful conclusion.

She didn't know where to start. The one question that was foremost on her mind was the one she was too scared to ask—and yet, she knew she had to do it. She wasn't sure she could. It wasn't fair. It wasn't right.

He was only four years old.

As if to pry her out of her torment, her phone rang. She stared at it absentmindedly, then recognized the area code.

510.

Berkeley.

She leapt at the call.

It was Dean Stephenson's assistant, Marya.

"I just got your message," she told Tess. "I'm so sorry to hear about Miss Martinez. That's just . . . awful. What happened?"

Tess simply told her that Michelle had been killed by an armed intruder at her house, and that Alex was now in the care of his biological father. She then explained who she was.

"I've been talking to Alex's teachers," she added, "and they told me that he's been going through a tough time. I was hoping I could talk to Professor Stephenson about it."

"Given what's happened, I'm sure Dean would absolutely want to help you with Alex," Marya replied. "The thing is, he's away."

"Oh?"

"I'm afraid so." The woman sounded uncertain.

Tess paused, unsure about why she was perplexed by her tone. "Do you know when he'll be back?"

Marya's tone was still hesitant. "I'm not sure."

Tess's antennae spiked up. "Well . . . can I call him? Do you know where I can reach him?"

"No, I'm sorry. He . . . he didn't tell me where he was going, and his cell's just going to voicemail."

Tess was picking up all kinds of alarming signals. "How long has he been away?"

"About ten days, I guess. Since the beginning of last week."

"And he didn't tell you where he was going?"

"No. He just left me a message saying he had to go check out a new case and would be away for a while."

Which sounded odd. "Does he do that a lot?"

"Well, no, not really. He usually sends one of his researchers first. And it's not like him to be rash like that. He's got a full calendar and I've had to field some tough calls and reschedule everyone."

"Isn't there anyone you can ask about him? Does he have a wife, someone he lives with?"

"He's divorced," she said. "And he's not living with anyone."

Tess's mind was on fire. More insights were crashing in, more associations linking up.

She swallowed and asked Marya, "Tell me something. Does Professor Stephenson wear contact lenses?"

"Yes, he does." Marya sounded perplexed. "Why do you ask?"

Tess felt the pressure push up to her temples. She didn't know what to say. She needed to end the call. "Let me get back to you. I need to check a few things out. Thanks, you've been a huge help. And please let me know if you hear from him in the meantime."

She ended the call and took in a deep breath.

She couldn't avoid it anymore. It was kicking and screaming at her.

She steeled herself and went into the house.

She retrieved the drawing from her bedroom and found Jules in the kitchen, preparing Alex a peanut butter sandwich and a glass of milk.

"Is he in his room?" she asked.

Jules nodded. "Yeah, I was about to call him to give him these."

"Give me a second with him, will you?"

Jules gave her a confused look, then just nodded. "Sure."

Alex was on the floor of his bedroom, playing with his figurines. He glanced at Tess as she came in, but didn't say anything.

"Hey, what's Ben up to today?"

Alex shrugged. "He's helping his grandpa Max save Gwen."

"Sounds like he's got his hands full."

She sat down on the floor, next to him. "Alex, I need to talk to you about something."

He didn't look over.

"I've asked you about this before, but I really need to ask you again and I need you to answer me, Alex. It's really, really important." She hesitated, then added, "I talked to your mom's friend, Dean. He said it's okay. He said you can talk to me about it."

Her heart was kicking against her chest, her veins throbbing with tension as she pulled out the drawing and set it on the floor in front of Alex.

"I need to know, Alex." She pointed at the other figure in the drawing, the one that seemed to be threatening Alex. The one that now looked like it was holding a gun at him.

She tapped it with her finger.

"I need to know who this is, Alex. I need you to tell me who this is."

He just stared at it, without moving—almost without breathing.

"Alex, please," she insisted, gently. "I need to know. It's just between you and me. There's nothing to be scared of. Nothing at all. I'm your friend, Alex. You have to trust me on this."

His mouth slid open a touch, and he glanced at her sideways, his expression mired with hesitation.

She met his gaze and gave him a warm, comforting smile. "Tell me, Alex. I'm here to help you."

Alex's eyes were wide with fear. "But he's your friend," he mumbled.

The words tore through her.

She knew the answer, but she needed to hear him say it. She felt breathless, felt she could barely utter the words, but she steeled herself and asked, "Who, Alex? Who's my friend?"

He twisted his lips and curled in on himself, like it was the last thing on earth he wanted to say, then he said, "Reilly."

He looked up at her, fear and confusion playing across his face.

"Reilly killed me. He shot me." He raised his hand to his head and pointed his finger at the middle of his forehead. "Right here."

She nodded, her entire body numb to the world, like she was in a trance.

"Tell me what you remember, Alex. Tell me everything."

And he told her.

Everything.

When he was done, she edged closer and took him in her arms and hugged him. She kept him there, close, hugging him tight against her, caressing his hair gently, feeling his little heart beating against her chest.

After a long moment, she gave him a kiss, got up, and headed out of his room. She walked into the living room, slowly, feeling like she'd fallen through a crack in a frozen lake and was floating around aimlessly in the icy darkness.

She found her phone and dialed Reilly's number.

"Sean," she told him, "I need you to come over. Like, as soon as you can. We need to talk."

He said he'd be back as soon as he could.

She put the phone down and stared out into the fading light and wondered how she could have been so wrong about everything she thought she knew about her world.

57

As he drove home with the sun setting up ahead in lush pink and purple brushstrokes, Villaverde resolved to rise before dawn the following day and drive up to Black's Beach to hit the surf.

In the time before he was made Special Agent in Charge, he would go there at least three times a week. He would drive the six miles up to UCSD, park in an almost-deserted lot as the sun just started to glimmer over the mountains to the east, then take the steep path down the cliff to the best waves in the county. He would spend two hours riding the sometimes ten-foot breakers back to shore, stop on La Jolla Village Drive for breakfast, then head back south and still be behind his desk by eight thirty.

Since taking over responsibility for the San Diego field office, he was lucky if he got to surf once a week off Pacific Beach, which, although it had the benefit of being a mere eight blocks from his house, had erratic waves that never got over a couple of feet high. He still couldn't get his head around how anyone in the Bureau managed to have a family on top of the job and still have any kind of time to themselves. When he'd separated from Gillian three years earlier—she'd moved to Chicago with her firm while he'd chosen to stay in San Diego—he'd agonized for weeks over whether he'd thrown away his one serious chance at having kids, but as the days turned to weeks, he realized that he was actually much happier on his own.

He turned off Grand Avenue, drove the three blocks to his house, and carefully turned the Chevy Traverse into the driveway. It was always a tight squeeze maneuvering the SUV up onto the narrow, upward-sloping driveway, but he was well practiced and always managed just to clear the vehicle's rear end off the sidewalk.

He had stopped at Margo's Mexican Grill for takeout and picked up a six-pack of Corona from Vons, all of which he now gathered from the passenger seat foot well. As he swung the door shut, he did a quick subconscious sweep of the street, as he did every night when he returned home. Everything was normal. As it always was. He was looking forward to unwinding in front of his TiVo. Unlike the handful of cops he knew, he never took his work home. He'd seen one of his partners drive himself into the ground, obsessed with a particularly gruesome and labyrinthine gang-related murder case, but even before that Villaverde had always made it a rule to work at the office and relax at home. Of course sometimes it meant that he didn't leave the office till three in the morning, or sometimes not at all—there was a pretty comfortable sofa in one of the meeting rooms—but he'd always finish whatever he was doing before heading back.

Villaverde unlocked the door, collected his mail from the floor, flicked on the lights, and walked through to the kitchen. He unscrewed the cap off a beer and took a long swig. Tomorrow, he'd empty his mind completely at Black's Beach, get into work early, then supervise the sting operation at the KGTV news studio out on Air Way. He and Reilly had already taken a conference call with Channel 10's editor in chief and executive editor. They had agreed to put Reilly on the air, and they'd start trailing his interview from six in the morning, which should give El Brujo plenty of time to get his act together.

An act he hoped to break up.

Permanently.

He heard the doorbell ring. He took another gulp of beer, set down the bottle, and walked over to the door. He hadn't bothered to close it; the night was cool and he loved the feel of the breeze inside the house. On the other side of the screen stood a tall, dark-skinned man in a very well-cut suit. He was waving hello hesitantly and seemed confused.

"I'm sorry, this isn't the Prager house, is it?" the man asked.

Villaverde instinctively dropped his left hand to the Glock at his belt as he opened the screen door with his right, keeping his sidearm angled away from the open door.

"They're next door," Villaverde told him. "Fifty-eight."

"Oh, man, I'm sorry," the man said as he smiled at him sheepishly and rubbed a few days of growth on his chin with a well-manicured hand.

A hand that had something around its wrist.

A tooled leather wristband.

Villaverde's eyes locked on it, with the soft click of the door at the back of the kitchen reaching his ears at exactly the same instant that his brain matched the wristband to the video from Deputy Fugate's in-car video.

He took a step back and pulled his sidearm, but before he could raise it, the man at the door had charged in and grabbed his left arm with both hands, and he was now trying to twist it up behind his back.

Villaverde knew this move. He dropped his left shoulder, recentered his weight, then kicked out with his right leg, sweeping his assailant's legs out from under him. The man let go of Villaverde's gun arm with one hand, but still kept the other firmly clamped around his forearm. Villaverde threw himself on top of the man's lower body and followed through with a succession of punches to his abdomen while twisting his own gun around to face the second assailant, who he knew would reach him any second.

As he swung the gun out, he felt a sharp pain in his right thigh. He looked down to see a thin metal spike sticking out of his leg and understood, with sudden horror, that the man had let himself be brought down specifically so he could stab him.

Villaverde fired a couple of shots at the second assailant as the man approached from the kitchen, but his vision was already blurring and his muscles relaxing involuntarily. The bullets went wide and missed their target.

He felt himself sliding into sleep, and just before he lost consciousness entirely, he realized it was highly unlikely that he'd be riding the breakers the next morning.

58

Tess looked totally spooked right from the second I saw her. She seemed to want to jump right into things and just led me out into the garden as soon as I came in, away from the house. I didn't know exactly what was troubling her, but I assumed it was fallout from our talk the night before and suspected this wasn't going to be a fun chat.

She surprised me by saying, "I called the shrink, Dean. Dean Stephenson."

Not what I thought this was about.

I asked, "The one you think Michelle took Alex to see?"

"Yes. Turns out he's not just any shrink. He's a practicing child psychiatrist, but he also runs the Department of Psychiatry and Neurobehavioral Sciences at Berkeley. And, more specifically, he runs a subsection called the Division of Perceptual Studies."

I wasn't sure where she was going with this, or what the urgency was. But clearly, it was important. I tried not to be too flippant and said, "Okay." Though I might have stretched the word out a bit more than was wise.

"His central focus—his focus for more than forty years of study and field research," she told me, "is survival research."

She paused and gave me a look, like she was waiting to see if I'd heard of it. I made a face to indicate I hadn't. "What's that?"

"Survival research is about looking into whether or not any part of us can ever survive the death of our physical body."

Survive the death of the physical body? She was losing me. "What are you talking about?"

"People like Stephenson explore whether or not our souls might be able to survive the deaths of our bodies, and they do this by looking into things like near-death and out-of-body experiences, deathbed apparitions, after-death communications . . . and what they call 'transmigration of the soul.' And that's what Stephenson's speciality is. Reincarnation."

"So . . . you're saying the guy Michelle chose to take Alex to see is an expert on reincarnation?"

"Yes. And before you give me that roll of the eyes you're so fond of, try and keep one thing in mind here: We're talking about a seriously qualified, high-powered academic, okay? This isn't some turban-wearing medium in a fairground Michelle took him to see. The guy's a legend in the parapsychology community. Which isn't a big one, for all the reasons you can imagine, starting with its name. He's got impeccable credentials. He's got a PhD from Harvard. He's a fully qualified psychoanalyst who's had scores of papers on psychiatry published in all kinds of professional journals. He's written books on psychiatry that are required reading in classrooms. He's got fellowships at the most prestigious hospitals. The guy's a bona fide member of the medical elite of this country."

"And he studies reincarnation," I reiterated, trying to keep all cynicism out of my tone. Then I had to ask, in case I was missing something, "So he believes in it?"

"Yes. Well . . . in his own, guarded way. This is a guy who's studied thousands of claims over the years. He's got a team of researchers working for him. He doesn't deal with past-life regression, with hypnotizing adults—he doesn't believe in it. He only looks at cases where children are having what's called spontaneous recall. When they remember stuff. Out of the blue. And despite all the evidence he's collected over the years, he doesn't go around making claims he can't back up. He acknowledges the fact that he doesn't have any proof of reincarnation. What he says is that, in a lot of the cases he's studied, reincarnation is the best explanation he can think of. It's the one that fits best. He's got evidence, but not proof, if you see what I mean."

It still sounded to me like something James Randi would have a field day with, but if Tess was taking it seriously, I was all ears. I'd kind of learned that lesson the hard way over the years.

"Okay," I said. "So how's this related to Alex?"

"It seems Alex was exhibiting unusual behavior—behavior that points to reincarnation."

"Spontaneous recall?"

"Yes."

"Like what? Is this about those drawings you showed me?"

"Partly, yes," she said, fixing me intently as her hands went all animated. "Typically, in these cases, kids who claim to remember past lives start talking about them at a very young age, sometimes as soon as they can speak. They start saying things that they shouldn't normally know about—names of people they've never met and places they've never been, sometimes in a language they've never learned. They'll talk about stuff that's beyond their age, like technical details about, say, a World War Two plane, like they'll see a picture of one and they'll know whether the thing hanging under its wing is a bomb or a drop tank. Details. And when they talk about them, they're more articulate and more lucid than they normally are. More than would be expected at that age. Then, typically, these memories fade by the time the kids reach six or seven. The theory is that other memories— current ones—crowd them out."

I was doing my best to keep an open mind. "So you're saying Alex knew stuff about some past life?"

"According to his teacher, he started saying things that surprised Michelle. And a couple of things that surprised his teacher, too. And the drawings. And he was having nightmares. Michelle didn't seem to want to talk about it too much, but it must be why she took him to see Stephenson."

I tried to picture Michelle doing that. Weirdly enough, that didn't seem too outlandish to me, given that she was into a lot of New-Agey stuff that I used to like ribbing her about. I'm not saying I was buying it. I'm just saying I could see why she would think that and take him to see someone like Stephenson.

Tess obviously read the doubt on my face. "You think this is nonsense."

"No, I mean—hey, what do I know?"

She gave me a small, reproaching shake of the head. "Look, I'm as much of a skeptic about this as anyone. But after reading all this stuff about Stephenson and his work . . . It's amazing, Sean. These kids, the ones whose stories he examined . . . Stephenson and his people aren't fools. They pick at these claims like they're reincarnation CSIs. They interview the kids, they talk to everyone around them, to family members from both their present and past lives. They record everything and cross-check it all, word for word, and all the time, they're looking for reasons to dismiss them. They look for holes or for alternative explanations or for parents who are inadvertently feeding their own wishful thinking or their cultural predispositions—and, obviously, they also look for outright scams. But in some of these cases—dozens of them, over the years—Stephenson and his team ended up convinced that the kids could very well be reincarnated souls. And it's not just memories. Some of these kids have physical links to what they claim are their previous lives. His website's full of them—it blows the mind. One kid who started talking about a past life had been born with a serious birth defect where his main pulmonary artery hadn't formed completely. By the time he was three, he was telling his mother things like, "I never used to hit you when you were a little girl, even when you were really bad," and remembering all kinds of things about his grandfather—his grandfather who was a New York City cop who had died long before the kid was born, from being shot six times while trying to stop a robbery. And the bullet that finished him off had gone in through his back, through his lung and cut open a major artery that caused him to bleed out. Wanna guess which artery it hit?"

She didn't even wait for me to answer, her face ablaze with excitement. "The pulmonary. Another kid who started remembering a past life had this birthmark under his chin. The past life he was talking about matched that of a drug dealer who killed himself by holding a gun to his chin and pulling the trigger. When Stephenson and his team looked into it, they got coroner reports and eyewitness testimonies, then they checked the kid more closely and you know what they found? A hairless birthmark on the top of his head, exactly where the autopsy report said the bullet's exit wound was. Stephenson's website says that in many cases where they saw a birthmark that corresponded to the entry point of a bullet, they discovered another one that matched the exit wounds on the autopsy reports. It's mind-boggling."

My mind was definitely in a major boggle. Two tides were pulling at my better judgment. One was that it was Tess telling me all this, and Tess had a finely tuned bullshit detector, one I trusted. The other was Stephenson. The fact that a Harvard PhD with all his credentials could devote his life to researching hundreds of cases and end up being convinced by a significant number of them wasn't that easy to dismiss. I just couldn't believe I was actually sitting here entertaining this insane notion, but I was intrigued and found myself going along with her and asking, "Do all the past lives that these kids recall involve a violent death? Hasn't anyone remembered a past life that ended peacefully in bed?"

She studied me dubiously, like she wasn't sure if I was being serious or just a doof. I wasn't kidding. Either way, she said, "Actually, a vast majority of the cases he's studied, something like seventy percent, seem to involve previous lives that didn't end naturally, meaning they died either in a car crash or by getting shot or murdered or in some other kind of violent end. And his theory is that the shock of those deaths might somehow disrupt things and cause those souls to retain more memories than they normally would." She paused, gauging me again. "I don't know what to believe, but . . . you've got to admit, it's pretty compelling evidence."

"But not proof," I pointed out. Then I nodded. "Yeah, it's—

surprising. And a bit troubling. But what about Alex? What did he say about him?"

Tess looked uneasy. "I don't know. I only spoke to his secretary."

"And?"

"He's away. She doesn't know where he is." Tess's face tightened, and I could see she wasn't comfortable with what she was about to say. "I think he's your missing scientist, Sean. The guy in the basement of the bikers' clubhouse. The contact lens?"

That took me completely by surprise—and I was now seriously interested. "What makes you think that?"

"About ten days ago, he called her and said he had to go away. Didn't say where, didn't say for how long. He's not picking up his cell. He's never done that before." She paused, letting out a rueful breath, then added, "He also wears contacts."

Him and countless others. "What else?"

She hesitated.

"Tess, come on. The fact that you're sure Stephenson didn't slip off to Vegas on a bender means there's more. Tell me."

She was having trouble keeping her eyes on me, and I noticed she was also shivering. I suddenly flashed to something Karen Walker had said when we interviewed her. That the bikers' last kidnapping was in the San Francisco area.

Stephenson was at Berkeley.

I felt a chill crawl down the back of my neck as Tess edged closer.

"I don't think they were after you, Sean," she said. "I think they were after Alex all along. That's why they're still after us. And that's why they took Stephenson."

"Why?" I asked, feeling my core tighten up. "Why would they want Alex?"

She met my gaze, and a shadow crossed her face. "Because they think he's the reincarnation of McKinnon. Because it looks like your son could well be the reincarnation of the man you killed."

59

Villaverde awoke in a large, airy room.

He looked around and saw that he was in some kind of gym. An expensive, in-house one. In front of him, an elliptical trainer, a rowing machine, and a Power Plate were lined up facing a floor-to-ceiling glass wall. Beyond, he could see the sea shimmering in the moonlight, and realized he was in a beachfront villa. Which would have been great if he didn't have his wrists and ankles duct-taped to a set of steel wall-mounted gym bars.

He was also naked above the waist.

He closed his eyes and tried to remember what had happened, how it had happened. They'd drugged him, he knew that much.

El Brujo.

The loco prick had grabbed him from his home. Which wasn't easy. FBI personnel's home addresses are well protected. That information isn't easy to get hold of—not easy at all. Then he thought back to the rest of his day, and it all made sense. The mall in Mission Valley. Dumping Torres there, with a gun, all of which seemed pointless and random. It was all misdirection. They must have followed him from there, although he was always—by instinct—careful about that. Then he realized they must have tagged his SUV. Of course. Someone must have sneaked up on it and stuck a tracker to it. They didn't even need a tracker. They could have just taped a live cell phone to his SUV and tracked that.

But why him?

Reilly.

They were after Reilly. They'd hoped to put a tracker on his car, but they couldn't since he and Villaverde had both arrived together in Villaverde's SUV.

And that, he realized, had signed his death sentence. There was no doubt in his mind about that.

And at that moment, not having children—or even a girlfriend—made complete and utter sense to him.

He tried tugging at the tape, but it was solid. His arms were stretched out horizontally, his legs spread into a V—he was like a fly caught on sticky tape.

Something else, too. His head felt heavy. Heavy, and—slow. Like his reflexes were dulled.

He heard footsteps at the door, and twisted his neck to see who it was. The door to the gym opened, and a man stepped in. He was smartly dressed in a black open-necked shirt and some expensive-looking gray slacks. He wore dark leather loafers without socks, and his slick black hair was gelled back.

He had a fat, short, curved knife in his hand.

And as he positioned himself in front of Villaverde, the agent met the man's eyes and felt an odd shiver. They were studying him with an inscrutable intensity, the kind of eyes that were laser-focused but aware of everything around them, the kind of eyes that could casually dismiss anything they surveyed without the hint of emotion.

And in that glance, he spotted the tiniest of acknowledgements, as if to say, "Yes, it is me." And Villaverde knew, for certain, that it was Navarro.

"Don't think you're going to—"

"Ssshh," the man stilled him with two rigid fingers in front of his mouth. Then he raised his knife and, slowly, slid it across the surface of Villaverde's bare chest without pushing it in too deeply and opened up a vivid, red, circular gash across his entire torso.

Villaverde refused to scream. He wouldn't give the *pinche madre* the satisfaction. Navarro studied him dispassionately, then he slashed his chest again, and again, making horizontal and vertical slits that criss-crossed the circle in a symmetrical pattern. Then the man finally stepped back, admired his handiwork, took out a cloth from his pocket and began to wipe clean his blade.

Villaverde felt like he was going to black out from the pain. He was trying not to look at his lacerated chest, but couldn't help himself. His torso was a bloody, fleshy mess of cuts. He was bleeding profusely, his blood drenching his pants and dripping off his toes and onto the polished wood floor of the gym. None of the cuts, however, appeared to have hit an artery or an organ.

He didn't understand why he was being tortured before Navarro had even bothered to ask him what he wanted to know. He had always wondered how he'd react in a situation like this. He knew he wouldn't tell them anything, no matter how much pain he felt. He was going to die anyway, there was no way around that. But he had several choices regarding how he spent his last moments alive. He was in too much pain to get angry, and he felt it was pointless to vent by screaming abuse. But he still had to say something. Honor demanded it.

"Whatever you're after, you do know you're going to end up like all the others, right? Sooner or later, if we don't get you, one of your fellow narcos will and you'll be dog food like everyone else."

Navarro tilted his head to one side and gave Villaverde a thin smile. Then he removed a small leather pouch from his pocket and loosened the lace that held it closed. He held the pouch aloft, almost reverently, and whispered a few words in a language that Villaverde didn't understand. Then Navarro's eyes gazed directly into his own.

"Clear your mind, and enjoy."

He dipped a hand into the pouch, then pulled it out. His cupped palm was now full of a fine gray dust that looked something like human ash. He took a step forward, so he was up close to his prisoner, reached out, and—with his eyes locked on Villaverde's—he massaged the dust into the open wounds on Villaverde's chest. The powder burned—badly—but Navarro didn't flinch, even though Villaverde was screaming so loudly it felt like he was going to burst his own eardrums.

Then, just as suddenly as he'd started, he stopped. He turned and stepped away, grabbing a towel from a stand on the way and wiping his hands as he stood by the glass wall and stared out at the sea.

Villaverde felt the pain subside, then, very quickly, his pulse started to race. He thought of Torres and realized that in a few minutes he wouldn't be in control of his own mind.

After a few minutes, Navarro returned to face him and stood absolutely still, staring at him while muttering some more incomprehensible words.

And then he felt it. Much sooner than he had expected.

His temperature rose. Sweat broke out across his face. Stomach acid boiled in his abdomen and shot up into his mouth, making him retch and almost choke. He shut his eyes, only to see strange, primordial shapes glide across his vision. He opened his eyes again, but the weird forms were still there, swimming across his vision of Navarro and the gym behind him.

He closed his eyes again, trying to block out the confusion. Blinding colors took over, then suddenly, they disappeared, like someone had hit a switch in the back of his eyes. The blackness was intense, complete—a darkness he'd never encountered. He opened his eyes, suddenly terrified that he'd gone blind, and the creatures appeared. Horrible, hissing reptiles and snakes. Deformed, human-like shapes, snarling through fanged teeth, strafing him from all corners. And behind them, black walls, closing in, tightening against him like a giant vise.

He started to scream and shut his eyes, trying to block out the horror. He forced himself to think of something else, something calming, and thought of the last time he'd gone surfing at Black's Beach. He tried to focus on the waves rolling in from the submarine trench half a mile off the coast. On the raw ocean swells marching toward the shore, one after the other, before releasing their energy in big hollow peaks. He tried to remember the smell of the sea, the sound of the seagulls shrieking overhead, the feeling of the sheer power of the waves as he paddled out to join the lineup.

For a brief moment, it worked. He felt a blissful calmness as his turn came up. He jumped up onto his board. Bent his knees. Centered his weight. But something was rushing toward him. Not the beach. Not the ocean. Something else. Something from deep inside of him. He felt it slam into him with a force greater than the biggest wave he'd ever ridden. It knocked all the air from him. He couldn't breathe and was gasping for air. It seemed as though all his organs were jammed up against his heart—and then it burst out of the cuts on his chest.

A three-headed snake, thick as a boa and black and slimy, emerging from a field of flames, curling out, coming out of him and spinning on itself before it drew level with his face and snarled at him, its wide jaws filled with rows of fangs.

Villaverde could see flames jutting out of the cuts on his chest, he could smell his own skin burning and feel it sizzling and melting from the scorching heat. He knew he would be incinerated completely within seconds, and as he screamed and tried to turn away from the monster facing him, it followed his head around and moved right in so it was breathing into his sweat-drenched face and asked him, with an echoey hiss, "Where are they?"

60

My *son is the reincarnation of the man I killed.*

At least, that's what I thought Tess had just said. My head was still spinning from it, and I felt like I was the one having an out-of-body experience.

It was absurd, and all I could muster was, "What are you talking about?"

"The things Alex was remembering. Animals and scenes from rainforests." She pulled out Alex's drawings and showed them to me again. "These tribes, these settings. That's right from McKinnon's past. He spent his life in those places." She was getting breathless, her words spilling out more intensely. "These plants. They're medicinal plants. And this drawing here"—she pointed to the one of the man walking on orange, fiery ground—"that's fire walking. McKinnon's done it; I read it in a bio of his. Then there's that other flower Alex drew, the one his teacher told me about. He told me it was supposed to cure heart problems, but that it turned out to be harmful. McKinnon was the one who found it. I looked it up. He was working for a big pharmaceutical company at the time. They were funding his research and footing his bills down there. And he found this plant that showed a lot of promise as a cholesterol inhibitor. But then the tests went bad and he fell out with his bosses 'cause they'd built it up into this medical marvel and they didn't want their share options to implode. That's why he bailed on the big pharmas and struck out on his own. Alex told me about this. Not in full detail, but he gave me enough to want to look into it. All the pieces fit."

"Come on, Tess. Look at the drawings," I countered. "It's not like they're photographic evidence. They're pretty vague, maybe you're reading stuff into them *because* it fits . . . and they could be things he saw on TV or in some issue of *National Geographic*. And that cholesterol story? Maybe he heard about it on the news or heard someone talking about it."

"Maybe . . . but he remembers you, Sean. This drawing?" She handed me the one that showed Alex with someone facing him, and looked at me squarely as she tapped her finger against the dark figure. "He said this was you. He says you shot him." She tapped the center of her forehead. "Right here. He told me the whole story. Just like you told me. In detail."

She hesitated, and paused as I stared at the drawing again, giving it a proper look this time. And it was uncanny. Although it was a kid's drawing, I saw something in it. A raw truth, an emotion that brought that night cannoning back into my mind's eye. It was deeply unsettling to imagine that Alex had actually drawn me there, in the lab, but looking at it now with different eyes, it suddenly didn't seem impossible.

And yet, it had to be.

"He knew, Sean," she continued. "About the woman. About her kid. About the guy who was with you, how he shot them."

And that hit me like a sledgehammer. "What?"

"He told me about it. How they died. How angry he got, how he ran . . . He told me about the laptop and the journal, about Father Eusebio. He knew about it. He knew everything." Her eyes were glistening with moisture now. "How could he possibly know that, Sean? How could a four-year-old who wasn't even born back then know any of these things?"

I didn't have an answer for her.

I was having trouble coming to grips with the basic notion, let alone the details. I tried to step back, to go back to the beginning and track forward, to try to make sense of the sheer absurdity of what Tess had just hit me with. I racked my brain looking for another explanation, pulling her theory apart, but I kept butting up against one thing, one certainty that I couldn't bat away. Alex didn't get it from Michelle. I'd never told her how McKinnon had died, let alone what Munro had done. And it wasn't written up in any report either. Corliss had made sure of that.

I looked at Tess, feeling my own soul going into a tailspin. "It can't be . . ."

"How else could he know, Sean? How?"

And just like a moment earlier, I didn't have an answer for her. But I now understood. I understood what this was all about.

"Navarro's not after me," I said, my voice hardening with anger. "He's after Alex. Because he thinks Alex is the reincarnation of McKinnon. Because he wants the formula. Because he thinks Alex might remember it."

"Exactly," Tess concurred. "Alex is the target. Has been all along."

It fit.

It goddamn fit.

And if this was true, then for some weird, sick, karmic mind-fuck of a reason, whoever chose how these things happen decided he'd drop-kick the soul of the man I executed into the body of my own son.

Forget intelligent design.

This was perverse, sadistic design.

I slid down to the ground and leaned back against the lone tree, feeling as isolated as it was. I still wasn't sure I believed it. It was too insane, too surreal. It needed a major leap of faith, and I wasn't there yet. But I couldn't dismiss it out of hand either. Not with everything Tess had dug up. And if it were true . . . The thought of Alex seeing his murderer every time he looked at me, his own father, was too horrific to imagine. I went back to looking for ways to sink Tess's conclusion, fast, to rip it apart and shred it into nanoparticles so it would never come up again.

I couldn't.

I felt like my head was about to explode, like an astronaut in deep space whose helmet had cracked open. And I wish I was in space, where, if you believe the movie posters, no one can hear you scream. I'd have really belted one out. But I couldn't. Not here. Not in front of Tess, not with Alex and Jules and the other agent close by. So I just slunk back, leaned my head back, and shut my eyes.

Tess slid down and sat next to me.

After a moment, I asked her, "You really think it's possible?"

She took a long second, then said, "I don't know what to believe. And—honestly?—I'm torn. I'm torn between wanting it to be real and hoping it isn't." She reached out and put her hand on my arm and leaned in closer. "I don't want it to be real for your sake. For Alex's sake. It would be so . . . cruel. And unfair. And part of me is kicking myself for even having looked into it. But if it is real . . . we can't run away from it. It's better if we face it and deal with it and fix things so Alex and you can have the kind of father-and-son relationship you both so deserve."

She stared up at the night sky. I followed her gaze upward. It seemed more vast and endless to me than ever.

"And if it is real . . . Jesus. It changes everything. If this life isn't the end, if there's a chance that we come back . . . That's a whole other conversation and one I'm not sure we need to have right now."

I nodded, more to myself than to her. All of that could wait. "I need to make sure Alex is safe," I told her. "For good. If that's what Navarro believes, then Alex isn't going to be safe until that bastard is put away. That's what I need to take care of first. After that . . . we'll deal with the rest."

I had to find Navarro. But once I did, I needed to shut him up, permanently. I didn't want any of this to ever come to light—it would haunt, if you'll forgive the pun, Alex for years to come and would make his life very difficult. I also didn't want Navarro blabbing about this from some prison cell and inspiring a whole new wave of narcos to come chasing after my son like he was their golden goose.

I had to find El Brujo.

Little did I know that he'd find me first.

61

I didn't hear them come in.

It was late. Really late, or really early, depending on which way you look at it. I wasn't sleeping, but I guess my senses were so numb I couldn't say I was awake either. I was physically and mentally trashed, and sleep would have been very welcome. I did get some, initially. Maybe a couple of hours. Then somewhere around four thirty in the morning, my eyes flickered awake, and that was it.

Jules and Cal, the new guy, were alternating two-hour shifts on watch, but I'd offered to share the roster with them. My shift, though, wasn't till six. And yet, here I was, staring at the ceiling. Maybe I couldn't rest until I'd found a hole, some way of sinking Tess's theory. Or maybe it was something inside me—acutely sensitive hearing or some kind of ESP, depending on whether we're going for a strictly scientific explanation or, given where my head was at, a more esoteric one—that shook me awake because of the imminent danger. Either way, I was awake, just barely, lying there in bed with Tess next to me, trapped in that really irritating zone where you're too tired to think but too wound up to sleep.

I thought I heard a faint creak, like from a plank of flooring or a door frame. Could be Jules getting herself a cup of coffee from the kitchen—or was it Cal's shift? I wasn't sure. Jules, I think. The house was silent again for a moment. Then I heard another creak, followed by a metallic snap.

That one slapped me awake, but by then it was too late. I was halfway out of bed and reaching for my gun when the door to our bedroom flew open and two dark silhouettes swarmed in. My fingers never made it to the Browning's grip. I felt the hard, deep sting in my chest before I realized one of them had targeted me with his gun, but it didn't sound like a normal gun and what hit me wasn't a bullet. It came out with a whoosh, like you got from a compressed air cartridge, and what I had in my chest wasn't a gaping bullet wound. It was a three-inch-long syringe dart with a black tip at its back end.

I kept going for the gun, but one of the intruders was already on me and kicked my arm away from the night table before throwing me against the wall. I glimpsed Tess barely sitting up in the bed before she yelped as she was hit with another dart. I pushed myself off the wall to hit back at the intruder, but in mid-stride, my muscles turned to jelly and I just crumpled down to the floor like a rag doll.

I couldn't lift a finger.

I could only watch, a prisoner of my own body, as they walked around me like I wasn't even there. From the corner of my eye, I could see them lifting Tess off the bed and carrying her out of the room, and a rage like I'd never felt flared through me. My thoughts rocketed to Alex, and I hoped they'd used something else to drug him, something that didn't keep him conscious like I was, something that would spare him the horror of witnessing this. I thought of Jules and Cal, too, hoping they weren't deemed expendable, hoping they'd been spared. Then a face loomed into my frame of vision, upside down, from behind me. A new face, one I'd never seen before, but I knew it was him.

Right there, inches away from me. And I couldn't lay a finger on him or rip his damn heart out. Assuming he had one.

I just stared up at him, lost in my silent fury, screaming my lungs out in total silence, and I thought of spiders and lizards and what my tox report would look like when they did my postmortem.

THURSDAY

62

"Hey, come on, wake up. Please."
The words woke me up with a start.

It took a few seconds for my eyes to focus, but I already knew I wasn't going to like what they showed me. My head felt woolly, not quite like a hangover. More like my skull had been caught in a vise that was just loosened by half a turn.

I was lying on a thin cot and the first thing I noticed was that my hands weren't bound. The cot squeaked as I bent up, and I saw that my legs weren't tied either. I glanced around. My surroundings were spartan to a fault. I was in a windowless room, about fifteen-foot square. Its walls were old and made of stone that rose up into a low barrel vault. There was literally nothing else in the room apart from me and the cot and a guy who was just standing there, staring across at me like I was a stranded alien. Which, in a sense, I realized I probably was.

"Who are you?" he asked, his voice wobbly and bristling with racked nerves.

I looked at him, and clarity started to seep back into my brain. "You're Stephenson."

Surprise flushed through his face. "How'd you know? Who are you?"

I sat up, slid my feet to the floor, and rubbed some life into my thighs and arms as I looked around our cell.

"I'm Sean Reilly. FBI." My mouth felt like it was lined with sandpaper.

"What the hell's happening?" he asked. "Where are we?"

The air was cool, but there was a latent humidity in the room, like it was seeping in through the walls.

"I'd say we're somewhere in Mexico."

His jaw dropped, and he had trouble mouthing his next question. "Mexico? What? Why? Do you know what the hell's going on? I'm a college professor, for God's sake. They must have the wrong guy."

He told me they came for him one morning, early. He couldn't remember exactly how long ago this was. The days since had blended into each other. They'd made him call his secretary, then they'd gagged and blindfolded him and stuffed him into the trunk of a car. From there, he'd been driven somewhere, led down some stairs, and tied to a wall. He'd been held there by some bikers who hadn't bothered to keep his blindfold on, then he'd been taken by others—Spanish-speaking Latino types who, now that I'd mentioned it, were most likely Mexican. He'd seen the dead bikers littering the place where he'd been held.

Then it was my turn to explain. "I'm Alex Martinez's father," I told him. "And no, they don't have the wrong guy. You're here—we're all here—because of Alex."

His jaw dropped even further.

It didn't look like we were going anywhere for a while. So I told him what I knew.

And then I let him return the favor.

Tess woke up in a rather different setting.

Her room had vintage mahogany furniture, exposed timber beams, muslin curtains, and tall windows that bathed the room in streams of golden-yellow light. With the birdsong wafting in from the lush trees outside, she could have fooled herself into thinking she was in some sleepy boutique hotel if it wasn't for the man who was sitting in an armchair across from her bed and watching her with an unreadable frown on his face.

"Where am I?" she asked, though she already knew the answer to that.

"You're my guests." Then, pointedly, with the thinnest of smiles. "All of you."

She sat forward, ramrod straight. "Where's Alex? And Sean?"

"Alex is fine. He's still sleeping. I'll make sure you're with him when he wakes up."

She dreaded the next question. "What about Sean?"

He paused, as if thinking of how to answer that one—or maybe he was just letting her anxiety worm its way a bit deeper. "He's here," he finally confirmed. "He's fine."

She relaxed slightly.

His eyes narrowed as he studied her. "You know why you're here, don't you?"

Tess wasn't sure what to say. "I think so," she finally replied, "though I'm not sure I believe it."

"Oh, believe it, Tess. Trust me on this. It's all real. I know." His face relaxed into a hint of a smile. "I've been there. I've seen it. It's all very, very real."

Tess felt her nerves sizzle. "How do you know?"

He waved it off as he stood up and walked across to the window. "You'll understand. With time." With his back to her, he added, "The more relevant question you need to be asking yourself is, why are you still alive? And the answer to that is simple. You're here because I need Alex to feel relaxed and comfortable so that Doctor Stephenson can work his magic and get me what I need from the boy." He turned to face her, his face not betraying a hint of emotion. "That's your only value to me here, do you understand?"

Tess stared at him and, knowing everything she did about him, she just nodded.

"Good. So I strongly suggest that you help me. Not just for your sake. For Alex's. I'd prefer it if Stephenson can get the information out of him himself, without complications. If it proves difficult, there are other things I can do to jog Alex's memory. Things that might not be particularly pleasant for a four-year-old boy. So I would really urge you to help Stephenson and help Alex remember."

"And then?" she asked, again knowing what the answer—the honest answer—would be.

The slit of a smile came back. "We'll see. Help me get what I want, and who knows how things will turn out. Cross me . . . and the heroin-addict whore-hell I'll send you to will be worse than anything you can possibly imagine."

He kept his stare on her as the words shuddered in. Then he walked out, leaving her to stew in his turbulent wake.

63

⁂

Stephenson confirmed what Tess had sussed out.

The things he told me about other cases, the level of authority he conveyed about a subject he probably knew better than anyone on the planet—it was all staggering and shook me to my core. Despite the state we were in, he spoke with a calm eloquence and a coherence that commanded attention, and I couldn't imagine anyone, least of all well-educated academics, would doubt him. More troubling was the fact that every detail I gave him about what I knew about McKinnon, including his death, tallied with what he'd heard from Alex about his past life experiences, right down to the headgear I was wearing on that hellish night.

I couldn't see how this could be anything else than what still felt impossible to me.

I fell silent for a long moment, processing everything I'd heard. After a while, I asked, "How come people don't talk about this more? Why don't more people know about your work?"

He let out a small scoff. "You're saying you're surprised?"

From the look on his face, it was evidently a long-festering frustration for him.

"I can show you all kinds of polls that show that one in four Americans believe in reincarnation," he added, "but that's just an easy answer to a casual question. Dig into it a bit deeper and even the ones who say they do get uncomfortable. And that's really why my work is considered fringe science. No one wants to have to think about it.

Not seriously. Our political, academic, and religious leadership—they all have a built-in resistance to it. It goes against the grain of too many sacred tenets. Medical researchers won't consider it since they have this fundamental, nonnegotiable belief that consciousness can't possibly exist outside the brain. And for people of faith whose upbringing can't accommodate something that different than what they've been taught all their lives, this idea that there's an afterlife, but it doesn't involve heaven or hell, is blasphemous. But it's not what the whole world thinks. Buddhists and Hindus have believed in reincarnation from day one. And they're almost a quarter of the population of this planet.

"This is a new paradigm we're talking about," he continued. "And it makes a lot of people very uncomfortable. Especially—and this always surprises me—my peers. Academics who are supposed to have an appetite to explore new ground and uncover the secrets of this universe we live in. But despite all our credentials and all the care we put into our research, most of my peers wouldn't be seen dead agreeing with me in public. The problem is, even if we have a mountain of evidence that it does happen, we don't have any proof, and we don't have any way of explaining how it happens. There's no biological explanation, not even a tangible theory, for what we call 'ensoulment'— the moment when a soul roots itself into a fetus or an embryo, or even earlier." He shook his head with a pained, rueful smile. "But then, that's a whole other can of worms."

I thought back to all the IVF sessions I'd gone through with Tess, and dredged up everything that had been explained to us. "Well we know it can't happen in the first fourteen days after conception, right? 'Cause up until then, the zygote is still just a cluster of cells that can still split into two and give you two identical twins. If there was already a soul in there before that, how would that split work?"

Stephenson seemed impressed by this. "Scientifically, you're right, of course," he told me. "But a lot of people believe otherwise, as I'm sure you know. Still, the issue of how and when and where a soul embeds itself in that cluster of cells you're talking about—that's a question that's baffled the greatest minds in history. And the simple answer is, no one knows. The Japanese believe the soul is in one's stomach—that's why when they commit suicide by seppuku, they stab themselves there. Descartes and most scientists since his day believe the soul lives in the brain—that's why head injuries can cause personality changes. But where exactly, and what does that mean? We don't really know. Da Vinci ran experiments on frogs and concluded that the soul resided at the spot where the spinal column meets the brain. Some scientists have even tried monitoring dying patients' body weight at the exact time of death, claiming that there's an infinitesimal but observable weight loss upon death that they explain as being the weight of the soul that's leaving its dead host."

"Twenty-one grams?" I offered with a slight snort, citing the meme I'd heard time and again.

"More like twenty-one nanograms, if that." Stephenson shrugged. "The main question, though, is this. Can a soul live outside the body? Can consciousness survive outside the brain? Out-of-body experiences—for which we have a lot of evidence—would suggest that the answer is yes. Did you know that there are plenty of documented cases out there where transplant patients took on some of the personality traits and memories of their organs' donors? How's that possible? And what's consciousness if not memories and personality traits? But we still have a lot of work to do before we prove it—if that's even possible. And it's harder since, academically, this is a taboo subject in our country. They just think it's the stuff of horror movies and TV shows. But in many other cultures, reincarnation isn't taboo. It's part of the culture, part of their religion. It's just not in ours. People here—well, people back home," he corrected himself somberly, "they're just not predisposed to take claims like that seriously or investigate them. If a kid starts saying weird things, the parents' first instinct is to think that it's coming from their imagination, that they saw it on TV or something—or they'd just think their kid is abnormal and discourage him from voicing any more 'nonsense.' In other cultures, the parents' starting point would be to encourage the kid to tell them more about what he knows, and they'd be asking themselves if these are signs of a reincarnated soul. They'd look into that. And that's another issue I've tried to address in my work. Does this cultural appetite for the concept of reincarnation mean these people come up with links and explanations to fit their theory, or are they really solving something that needed to be solved?"

"I'm amazed you stayed with it all this time," I told him. "Given all the flak you've had to deal with."

He let out a long sigh, and his expression turned doleful. "It's just a shame, really. That we can be so prejudiced and closed-minded about what I think is the biggest question facing us. But that's the way it's always been, especially about anything having to do with the nonphysical world. That's why we don't know much about it. But then again, we didn't know much about the subatomic world not too long ago either. And just imagine, for a second . . . if we could prove it. If we had proof that reincarnation was real, beyond a doubt. It would change everything. A lot of people would fight it, of course. Bitterly. Angrily. But after it all sinks in, it would make us better. All the great revolutions in human thought did that. They made us more humble and more humane by giving us a better understanding of what we are, of our place in the universe. Copernicus took us out of this delusion that we were the center of the universe. Darwin showed us that we're only one small part of a big evolutionary system. Freud showed that there's more to us than an ego and showed us that we have unconscious impulses influencing us, and that pushed us to try and understand ourselves better. This would be another huge step in that tradition. Death is the biggest mystery we face. And if reincarnation were ever proven to be real, it could open the door to a whole new exploration of . . . everything."

I scoffed. "Not gonna happen though, is it? No matter what proof you might come up with, people will always find a way to shoot it down and say you're wrong."

He shrugged. "Doesn't mean I won't keep trying." He looked around the walls. "Assuming we ever make it out of here."

I left that hanging and came back to the most pressing question on my mind. "How'd Michelle take it? When you told her?"

"It troubled her. It always does, when it's not part of one's culture. But it didn't take her long to accept it. She was very open-minded."

That didn't surprise me at all. "And you think Alex's case stacks up?"

Stephenson didn't hesitate. "I do. And it's a really interesting case for me. It's a more or less immediate rebirth—a soul finding a new home shortly after losing its old host. He was born, what, just under a year after McKinnon was killed? It doesn't happen that often. There's usually a gap—weeks, months, years even—which opens up a whole other question."

"About where the soul goes during that gap?"

He nodded. "Exactly. We call it the interlife. And that's another whole can of worms." He was now standing by the door, staring at it. Then he turned to me. "Do you think we're ever going to get out of here alive?"

"I don't know." I was being charitable.

He seemed to read it, and his face sank. He sucked in a deep breath to calm himself and ran his hands through his hair, pulling back tightly against his scalp. "What is this drug this psychopath is after? Why is he so determined to get his hands on it?"

I heard some shuffling outside the door, then a key rattled in the lock and the door creaked open.

"Maybe we're about to find out."

64

The two hard-faced goons nylon-cuffed my hands behind my back before leading me and Stephenson out of our cell.

We walked down a humid, centuries-old barrel-vaulted corridor that had a series of doors on either side. They had similar hinges and locks to the door of the cell we'd been kept in, and I suspected that's where Navarro had been keeping the scientists he kidnapped over the months and years. I didn't see any of them, though. The place was quiet and had an ancient solemnity to it, which, given what it was being used for, felt pretty perverse.

We were led up a stairwell at the far end of the hall and emerged aboveground, in another long and narrow corridor. This one, however, had a flat roof raised over a row of clerestory windows. Sunlight flooded the beige stucco walls, and the heat and the smell of the air immediately reinforced my suspicions. It sure felt like we were on Navarro's home turf. Not far from the ocean was my guess. But that was about it. Which didn't narrow it down to anything useful, not that I knew what I could have done with that information anyway.

We passed a room that had some antique exposed machinery in it, like mills or something from the last century. I guessed we were in some old factory or maybe what used to be an agricultural or industrial estate, which meant that wherever we were, Navarro was possibly living in plain sight among people who didn't have a clue as to who he really was.

We were led through a steel-edged door and into a large room with a double-height ceiling. It had small windows about fifteen feet off the ground and its walls were lined with empty, faded bookcases that gave it the air of an old library. Sitting in the lone armchair in the middle of the room was the man I'd glimpsed in the darkness and upside down back at the safe house.

Raoul Navarro, undoubtedly.

El Brujo.

I was finally getting a good look at the soulless barbarian who had caused all this, and I made sure I committed every feature in his face to memory. Who knows, even if I didn't manage to get him in this life, maybe—if all they were telling me was true—I'd get another crack at him one day. He was casually, but expensively, dressed and looked fresh and showered, the polar opposite to my current status. He was reading something before he looked up to watch us come in, and as he closed it carefully, I saw that it was the journal I'd first seen with McKinnon in his lab five years ago.

He noticed me looking at it and said, "You remember this, eh?"

I remembered that we brought it back with us that night. I also remembered how he got it back from Corliss. But I had something far more pressing on my mind.

"Where are Alex and Tess?" I asked, charging at him.

One of the goons held me back and gave my shoulder a deep pinch that sent a burning spasm searing through it and stopped me in my tracks.

"They're fine," Navarro replied coolly. "Why wouldn't they be? They're what I was after. You should be more worried about yourself, my friend. You're the expendable one here."

He studied us, then glanced at the journal again. "Funny how things never really change, even after all these years." He held it up, waving it slightly. "This Jesuit priest, Eusebio de Salvatierra . . . he wanted to bring his discovery back to Europe and share it with the world. He wanted to let people know death wasn't the end. But they wouldn't let him." He fixed me with a curious stare and asked,

"Why do people always assume they have the right to dictate what others can or can't try out for themselves?"

I kept an intentional vacant stare on my face for a moment, then I feigned a sudden awareness. "I'm sorry, was that rhetorical, or are you expecting an answer?"

He didn't seem amused.

"Eusebio ran, and he hid, and he never did spread his great discovery. All he did was keep writing in this journal until the end of his days." He smiled. "I intend to help finish what he started."

"So that's why you're doing it? To help the rest of the world lose their minds?"

He looked at me quizzically. "Lose their minds? Have you even read this?"

I shook my head, and a tremor of unease rumbled somewhere deep inside me. "No. DEA had it. They said it was useless."

Navarro smiled. "Useless? Maybe. But interesting . . . very. The one thing it doesn't say, though, is how to make the damn thing."

"What thing?" Stephenson asked. "What does this drug do anyway?"

"Oh, I think you, more than anyone, will appreciate this, doctor. You see, this drug, this miraculous concoction that Eusebio and McKinnon stumbled upon . . . it lets you relive your past lives."

65

Navarro's words just hung there, freeze-framed in midair like bullets in a *Matrix* movie.

Neither I nor Stephenson said anything.

Navarro was more than happy to step in. "You see that? Your reaction, *amigos*, is exactly why this is going to be a huge hit, why everyone's going to want to try it, even those who aren't into drugs. 'Cause that's what it does. It's the ultimate mind trip. It takes you back years, decades, centuries even—back to moments from lives you never knew you lived. It's like time-traveling in your head, to real places and real memories and real feelings and real people . . . it's like dreaming, only much clearer and more vivid—and it's not fantasy. What you experience really happened."

"How do you know?" I asked. "How do you know it's not just your imagination?"

"Oh, I know all about cryptoamnesia," he countered before turning to Stephenson for corroboration. "I know all the arguments against past-life regression . . . that what we remember under hypnosis is nothing more than random things we read or saw on TV or heard about and forgot, long-lost memories that regression therapy are bringing up from the deepest folds of our minds. But these aren't fantasies. Trust me. I've taken it. I've experienced it, more than once. And I know fantasy from reality. The things this drug brings up, the things you experience . . . the emotion, the richness of the experience, the level of detail, right down to the smells. It's beyond imagination. It's like you're there. And it's tangible. It's clear enough to give you something to research. Specific memories, names, and places. And that's what I did. I looked into them."

"You researched the past lives you experienced while you were under the drug?" Stephenson asked.

Navarro's face beamed with palpable pride. "Of course."

He just looked at Stephenson, as if teasing him to ask. Which he quickly did. "And?"

"I discovered who I'd been. Where and when I'd lived. And what I found was . . . amazing. The days of the revolution, fighting against the Rurales. And before that, right here, in this place." He spread his arms wide, gesturing at the walls around him. "This hacienda. Why do you think I bought it? Why do you think I chose this place?" He smiled. "I was here. In this very place, over a hundred years ago. I worked like a slave in the fields out there, harvesting the *henequén* cactus for the *hacendado*, Don Francisco Mendoza. I can tell you how that shredding machine you passed on your way here worked. I can even tell you what it sounded like. And I can assure you that I knew nothing about this place or about *henequén* or Mendoza before I tried McKinnon's magic potion. Nothing at all. You want to explain to me how else it could have happened?"

I felt light-headed listening to him. If this were true, it would be a game-changer in so many ways. But we weren't there yet. The guy was a psycho, and it wouldn't exactly be out of character for him to lie. For a true skeptic like me, it would take a lot more than the words of a crazed narco to convince me that this was all true.

But if it were . . . the implications would be unimaginable.

I looked across at Stephenson. His face was locked in concentration, visibly awed by what he'd just heard. I felt an unwelcome tinge of unease. Navarro had just dangled him the prize he'd been waiting for all his life. Proof of reincarnation. Vindication of his life's whole work.

I found myself wondering if my fellow captive was about to join the dark side.

"Real or not," I put in, "it'll be hard to prove it."

Navarro shrugged. "When thousands of people start taking it, they'll start asking questions about what they've seen, they'll do their research and I'll bet they'll find a lot of evidence that what they saw really happened. Which will be a lot of fun to watch. And even if there was no way to prove it, even if some people will stubbornly insist that it's only our imagination . . . it won't matter. It's still one hell of a trip. Better than anything any other pill can give you."

I saw the logic in what he was saying. Regardless of whether or not it gave its users a look at their actual previous lives—assuming there was such a thing—it would still be a hard drug to resist.

Then Stephenson surprised me. He didn't look as excited as I thought he would be.

"And it's basically, what, some kind of psychoactive alkaloid?"

Navarro nodded. "Yes. But the exact composition is still a mystery."

Stephenson frowned.

"What?" Navarro asked.

"If that's what it does," Stephenson replied, "you can't just unleash it like that. It has to be properly tested. A drug that can open doorways like that in the mind . . . it could be very dangerous. If it can really open up pathways to past life experiences, it could bring up suppressed memories from those lives that might be best left suppressed. Past-life memories usually come out because of some trauma, and bringing up these . . . these psycho-spiritual epiphanies could unhinge you and send your spirit spiraling into, I don't know, some kind of primordial chaos. You could turn into someone you don't really want to be and end up with a lifetime of hell."

That didn't seem to alarm Navarro at all. "There are good trips and bad trips. A lot of people prefer that to no trip at all."

Stephenson looked stunned. "Yes, but this is a trip that could turn them into mental wrecks."

Navarro shrugged. "Life's about choices, isn't it?"

"So all this," Stephenson shot back, "Alex . . . Bringing me here. You really think he can help you recover the formula for this drug?"

"Why not? He remembers everything else." Navarro held up the old journal. "Eusebio's writings are very illuminating about the whole experience, but the one thing he didn't write in this was how to make the damn thing."

"But McKinnon found it," I chimed in. "He tracked down the tribe Eusebio wrote about."

"Yes. He was obsessed with it. He spent years following Eusebio's trail. And he did it." Navarro's gaze hardened into an icy glare. "And then you came down here and killed him and took it away from me."

I wasn't moved. "So you came after Alex."

"I didn't have years to waste, and McKinnon's tribe didn't want to be found. I knew Eusebio's mission was in Wixáritari territory—that was in his journal, and that's where McKinnon started following his trail. The tribe originated in the mountains around San Luis Potosí, and to escape the conquistadors, they spread west. That's where Eusebio founded his mission, in Durango. Then the Jesuits got pulled out by the king of Spain, and the natives found themselves at the mercy of the miners who wanted to use them as slave labor. So they scattered again, ending up all over the place. There are a few of them still around. We call them Huichol now.

"I hired some anthropologists to try and follow McKinnon's trail," he continued. "We went down south and talked to Huichol and Lacandon tribes in the rainforests around Chiapas, which is where McKinnon said he came across the formula. We found some tribesmen who remembered meeting him, who remembered him and his old journal and his questions. And then the trail went cold. We couldn't find the tribe he'd ended up with or the shaman who'd shown him how to make it. Who knows? Maybe he'd lied about where he'd found it. Maybe he found it somewhere else completely. And all I had left was this," he said, picking up a small stainless steel vial with a sealed lid, about the size of a cigar tube. "The leftovers of what McKinnon gave me."

"So you started kidnapping scientists to get them to recreate it for you," I speculated.

"They couldn't do it," he told me. "They couldn't identify all the ingredients or the chemical reactions that produced it. I was losing patience. And then I heard about Alex and his sessions with you, doctor." He swung his gaze back to me. "And when I discovered he was your son," he said, his face lighting up, "the stars had aligned. It was perfect karma."

"How?" Stephenson asked. "How did you know I was treating Alex? My work isn't public."

"You're the West's top authority on reincarnation, doctor," Navarro said. "And I probably know more about your own work than you do." He gave him a smug, cold smile. "College computers aren't as safe as you think. It wasn't hard for a hacker to get me into your hard drive. I read everything you were working on, all your emails to your inner circle of researchers."

I was still working through what he was telling us about the drug. It lets you relive past lives. And he was going to get hold of it through the past-life experience of someone—of my son—who was the reincarnation of the guy who'd brought it to him.

My temples were pounding.

Navarro stepped up to Stephenson and put his arm around him. "I need you to get me this formula from Alex, doctor. I need you to make sure all of this hasn't been a waste of my time. I can be very generous. Or I can be unpleasant." He moved closer to him and cupped Stephenson's chin in one hand, squeezing it hard. "And to make sure you understand what I mean, I want you to pay careful attention."

He turned to me. "Sadly, for you all this will be nothing but talk, as your soul is about to take its final journey. A journey from which there is no way back."

Navarro opened an intricately carved wooden chest and took out a length of silicone tubing, a terracotta bowl, a carved wooden stick, and five clay vials. He crouched down and began to pour liquids from the vials into the dish. As he did so he muttered under his breath. The mixture took on a sickly mustardy color and had the consistency of sludge.

His men positioned themselves on either side of me and began to steer me toward a heavy wooden chair. I decided to at least not make it too easy for them. I barged into one of them with my right shoulder, linebacker style, catching him off guard. My momentum carried us forward till I had him against the wall, and I kept pushing, forcing the air from his chest.

Then a searing pain erupted in my back, where the lower spine is right up against the tissue. I spun around to see that the other goon had hit me full force with a length of metal pipe. He swung the pipe back and hit the same spot again. I tried to turn all the way, to take the next blow to my front, but the guy I had pushed against the wall grabbed my arms and was holding me firm. The goon with the pipe swung it at me one more time for good measure, and I screamed out in pain before crumpling to the floor, groaning.

The goons lifted me up, one under each shoulder, and dragged me over to the chair, beside which Navarro was now standing. They strapped me into the chair. The fact that my now swelling back felt tender against the hardwood of the chair's upright wasn't helping.

One of the goons grabbed my chin with one hand and squeezed my nose shut with the other, forcing me to open my mouth. Navarro then expertly inserted the tube down my throat. I fought the urge to gag, but I couldn't breathe. My throat tried unsuccessfully to eject the foreign body that was being forced into it, but to no avail. Navarro held the end of the tube in my throat till I had no other choice but to swallow. Then he continued to push the tube down into my stomach.

The goon let go of my nose and I took a few deep breaths. Both goons moved away from the chair and Navarro stepped around to face me.

"You've been a pain to me in this life, and the last thing I want is for your soul to cause me more trouble in the future. Because after you die, your soul will move from this body of yours to a new body. From one life to another. But the soul can also be annihilated completely, if it leaves the body and can't find a path back. If it is in so much pain that its only option is to blink out, like someone has extinguished a flame."

He held up the bowl.

"This will force your soul from your body. Then it will attack your soul with such brutal force that the only way to put a stop to the torment will be its own end. If your soul dies before your body, then the connection between the world of souls and the world of matter is broken forever. Your chain of birth and death will end with you. It will end now. Soon even the blackest darkness will be lost to you."

He began to stir the mixture inside.

"I know you probably don't believe a word of it. I have no way of knowing if it's true or not myself, or if it's just the naïve belief of the shaman who taught it to me. But all that really matters is that, either way . . . you'll be dead. And that's good enough for me."

66

I could feel the tube pressing against my esophagus. I desperately wanted to gag, but I tried to slow my breathing, to ignore what the back of my throat was shouting at me. Navarro finished stirring the mustard-colored mixture and nodded to himself, obviously satisfied that his creation was ready. Stephenson was watching him, too, his face white and glistening with fear.

In three words, we were screwed. There was no way out of this. Tess and Alex would die—and not quickly—and even then it probably wouldn't be the end. The monster would probably go after Kim, too. What goes around really was coming around. With interest.

I closed my eyes briefly and, for some reason, I had this thought that I wanted a priest. It gave me a small measure of peace. Navarro must have seen my expression shift somehow, even though half of it was incapacitated by the tube. A quizzical expression animated his face. For a moment he must have wondered why I wasn't pissing myself and begging for my life. He needn't have worried; after seeing what he did to Wook and Torres, I was pretty sure I'd become a gibbering wreck given half the chance.

What hurt most was I couldn't even say good-bye to Tess.

"Ready?" he asked, as if my saying no would change anything.

He raised the end of the tube and began to pour the gloopy liquid into the other end. I could see it dripping down the inside of the tube. It would be inside me in seconds and, I imagined, in my bloodstream in minutes. There was absolutely nothing I could do, no fanciful ninja move that would whip my arms free and slaughter my tormentors in seconds, so I fought with myself to accept that. An odd thought sailed into my mind. For the first time in my life, I wished I'd let my hair down a bit more in college. Maybe tried hallucinogens once, so I had some idea of what was about to happen. Would have maybe helped dampen the fear I was feeling right now. And, apparently, I wasn't going to get a do-over either.

My eyes were locked on the sludge oozing its way down the tube when a deafening noise cracked the air, accompanied by a sodium-white flare.

Flashbang.

The whole place shook.

Navarro dropped the bowl and spun his head away in total surprise—

Then another explosion, almost on top of the first. I summoned every iota of strength left in my bruised body and threw my entire weight to my left. The chair topped and flew, just as something flew into the room as another stun grenade filled it with blinding light.

The noise of the third flashbang was immediately replaced by the sound of machine gun fire from outside the building.

From my limited point of view on my side and pressed down against the floor, I spotted frantic movement around the room. Navarro may have been nuts, but he'd already well demonstrated that he was also a pragmatist when it came to self-preservation, and by the time the air cleared, he and his henchmen had already left the room through another door at its other end.

I craned my neck to try to get a better view, but I was facing the wall and couldn't see anything. Then a familiar voice barked, "Get him up. The target's heading back to the main house. Follow him."

A couple of soldiers in full black Special Ops gear were all over me, and I felt the straps loosening and the tube being slowly pulled from my throat. I retched and threw up the bit of goop that had made it into me. My head was pounding. After giving me a couple of seconds, they dragged me to my feet, and I turned round to find myself facing Munro.

"You good to go?" he asked.

My head felt like it had been tossed through a giant pinball machine.

"How'd you find us?"

He dismissed it with a grimace. "Long story."

"Alex, Tess—where are they?"

"In the main house."

I snapped with surprise. "They're not with you?"

"They're in the main house," he repeated, stern and a bit slower, like I was having trouble understanding the language.

I was furious. "Why didn't you go for them first?"

"You were about to fucking die here, *amigo*," he fired back. "You sure you want to second-guess my choices?"

I just glared at him in disbelief, then asked, "So where's the damn house?"

"Follow me," he said, pointing.

"I need a weapon."

Munro swung his MP4 submachine gun off to one side, pulled his Glock from its holster, and handed it to me.

He moved to head out, then I remembered something.

"Wait," I hollered. I scoured the room looking for the stainless steel vial that Navarro had shown us, but I was still dazed and couldn't see it. I had no choice but to mention it.

"The drug. There's a sample of it somewhere."

I looked around urgently—then I spotted it, lying innocuously on the floor.

By Munro's feet.

He read my reaction, followed my gaze to it, and picked it up. Then, with a smug grin, he pocketed it.

"Come on," he barked, then he set off toward the house.

I followed, hot on his heels.

We followed a narrow passage that led to an old stairwell, then we were outside again, and we sprinted in a slight crouch along a tree-lined path that led across a football-field-size landscaped quadrangle and back to the hacienda. Off to the right, I spotted several men from Munro's unit who were locked in a manic firefight with Navarro's guards, the latter firing away from behind a pickup truck while three of Munro's guys had taken cover behind a stone water trough.

Munro didn't even cast a look at them as he ran toward the house.

We were still more than a hundred yards from the house's main entrance when I saw Tess run out of there. I could see blood on the side of her face, but she was moving smoothly and didn't seem badly hurt. I didn't need any more information to know that Navarro had taken Alex and that she'd been helpless to stop him. I gestured with my arm and shouted out, "Stay down," and as I pushed myself to move even faster, the sound of an engine straining to its limit rose above the gunfire. It was coming from the other side of what looked like some derelict stables off to the left of the house, and through an arcaded walkway, I glimpsed a Jeep tearing off away from us.

Navarro. And Alex.

Munro turned to me and pointed at the other side of the main house.

"I saw a couple of quad bikes over by the cemetery."

Without waiting for an acknowledgement from me, he banked away and was running full tilt toward the handful of broken grave markers that were visible at the left-hand end of the house. Every muscle in my body wanted to run directly toward the engine noise. If we lost sight of Navarro and Alex, I was worried we'd never find them again, but Munro had made the right move. We'd certainly never catch the Jeep on foot. I also couldn't take the time to go to Tess, much as I wanted to. Agonizingly, it would have to wait. So I ignored the thudding pain in my back and the torment in my head and forced myself into a run.

I caught up to Munro at the far end of the cemetery. He had already started one bike and yelled out to me, "Come on."

I hopped onto the second four-wheeler and churned its engine to life, then twisted hard on the gas handle and powered off after the Jeep, with Munro no more than ten yards behind me.

We drew level with a big dilapidated stone building at the opposite end of the quadrangle, and it was clear that Munro's unit was gaining the upper hand in the firefight with Navarro's hired guns. Two of them were slumped dead behind the truck, which was riddled with bullets and not going anywhere anytime soon.

I gunned the quad and sped toward what looked like some stables, Munro now riding level with me.

As we rounded the stable block, we could see the dust cloud thrown up by Navarro's Jeep as it was swallowed up by the dense tree line that marked the edge of the main compound.

We aimed our bikes at the jungle and charged after the Jeep.

The road was cut through the thick foliage that barely let any light through. In virtual darkness, we wound our way through some undulating ridges, then a couple of minutes later, we hit a sun-blasted clearing and slid to a halt.

Three different roads wound away from us in three entirely different directions.

And we had no way of knowing which one of them Navarro had taken.

67

I killed my engine and gestured for Munro to do the same—maybe we could hear the Jeep and get a direction that way—but Munro kept his engine running. I was about to ask him what the hell he was doing when he removed an oversize PDA from his black BDU pants' thigh pocket, flipped open the plastic cover, and looked intently at the screen. I thought back to how Munro had managed to find us, and Munro could obviously hear the wheels spinning inside my head.

He just pointed skyward and said, "Predator," then swung his attention back at his screen.

I looked up to the sky, which was *Fantasy Island* blue. I couldn't see any drone.

"Ours?" I asked.

Without taking his eyes off his screen, he said, "Well it ain't *federale*, that's for sure."

"You've been tracking us? For how long? Why didn't you pick us up before we left U.S. soil?"

He gave me a look that reeked of disdain. "We didn't know if Navarro was there or not. We had to follow you to get to him. What's your problem? You're all in one piece, aren't you?"

"Hey, Navarro has Alex, asshole."

He shrugged and shoved the device into his pocket.

"This way." He pointed to a road to the left that seemed to head off the plateau and dip down toward lower ground.

I charged my quad forward and blocked his way. I scowled at him and yelled, "Alex comes first, no matter what."

He raised his hands in feigned surrender. "Absolutely."

I'm sure my expression betrayed the fact that I didn't fully believe him on that.

"No. Matter. What," I repeated, firmly.

"You got it, buddy," he protested.

I still wasn't buying it, but I had no choice.

I hit the gas and stormed ahead. He followed close behind as I wondered how Alex was feeling right now and hating Navarro even more for it.

The road started to slope down and turned into a dirt trail that was so narrow we had to ride single file. There was barely enough room for a Jeep to make it through, but the cluster of birds that had just burst into the air maybe half a mile ahead seemed to confirm that Navarro wasn't too far.

We followed the trail until the tree cover fell away and we emerged into the open again. I got a clearer view of the geography and realized the track we'd been following ran along the top of one side of a wide ravine. Up ahead, the trail switched back in front of a wall of solid rock that closed the ravine at the near end.

We maneuvered the quad bikes around the 180-degree bend and were rewarded with a view down the length of the valley, which was completely open at the other end, although the ravine narrowed before it got there. This was clearly Navarro's target. The perfect place for an escape chopper to get him out of any unexpected jam—like maybe his ex-narco buddies finding out he was still alive. It was isolated and completely out of sight while the bird was on the ground, the ravine cushioned the rotor noise, and it had good cover from the air due to the surrounding jungle.

Hence the chopper with its rotors spinning up in a flat clearing down at the far end of the ravine, with the Jeep thundering toward it, out of reach.

Rage tore through me and I choked the handle as far as it would go. The quad's engine roared in protest as I hurtled down the trail, pushing the four-wheeler as fast as I could, sliding around the bends at the edge of adhesion with my body slung out as far as it reached as a counterweight, my heart flailing against my throat—

I burst into the clearing and beelined for the chopper as, up ahead, Navarro and his two men were hustling out of the Jeep, with Alex in the madman's grip. They all saw me. Navarro kept herding Alex to the chopper while the *pistoleros* turned around and whipped their guns out toward me.

I bent down and kept going.

Bullets whizzed by me, but within seconds I'd reeled them in, aiming straight at the gunmen, and I plowed straight through one of them, hitting him with a jarring thud. He bounced off the front of the bike and disappeared behind me, and I hit the brakes while spinning the handlebars as far as they would go. I leapt off the quad before it had even slid to a stop and, with my gun already out, just charged at the other gunman. He fired off a couple of rounds at me, then I saw him flinch sideways as Munro cut him down from his bike.

I rushed up to the chopper, with Navarro and Alex almost at its door, the rotor wash beating the air into us and kicking up an infernal dust cloud.

"Stop," I yelled.

Navarro turned and glared at me—

Then he pulled Alex right up against him, a four-year-old human shield—not a very effective one, given that Alex only reached his waist, leaving his entire torso exposed. I had a shot, clear and true— but Navarro had a blade pressed against Alex's neck, and visions of what happened to Corliss's daughter froze my trigger finger.

"Whoa, whoa, whoa. Everyone calm down here, all right," Munro shouted as he sauntered up close to me, his gun arm also held straight out at Navarro, his other hand making a staying gesture. "Let's all take a breath here, guys."

"Put your guns down or the kid dies," Navarro yelled back, edging backward, closer to the chopper's cabin.

I felt my limbs go rigid with dread, but from the corner of my eye, I caught Munro's impassive look and something was very wrong about it.

"No one's going anywhere," he told Navarro. "Just put the fucking knife down and get your ass over here or I'll take the kid out myself."

He lowered his aim.

His gun was now leveled at Alex.

68

I couldn't believe what I was hearing and swung my gun over at Munro. "What?"

He turned, his face cracking with that grin I couldn't stand. "Sorry, buddy. He's worth a hell of a lot more to me alive."

He seemed to be getting a real kick out of my utter confusion. My mind bounced through a maze of permutations, and since we didn't have a reward out on him—until a couple of days ago, he was assumed to be dead—and since this was Munro we were talking about, the sleaziest option leapt out almost instantly.

Navarro had run off with three hundred million dollars of cartel money.

"How much are they paying you?"

He smiled. "Five percent."

Fifteen million dollars.

He kept silent as if to let it sink in, like he was really getting a kick out of this, then added, "What, you think I went through all this bullshit just so some cranky old man could get his revenge?"

And then it all went very fast.

I saw Munro grin at me, like he really didn't need me around anymore, and his gun panned slowly away from Navarro, heading my way—

I glimpsed Navarro's face broaden in a smug grimace and noticed his hand relax and move away from Alex's neck—

And despite some disturbing visions of Corliss's daughter falling to the ground with a fountain of blood coming out of her neck, I whipped my gun back at Navarro and took a shot—

I saw his right shoulder flinch back like it had been pounded by a sledgehammer—

And my eyes zeroed in on Alex's terrified gaze and I shouted to him, "Run, Alex!" while launching myself at Munro.

My arm grabbed his MP4's muzzle just as he pulled the trigger, and I just managed to push it off target as it erupted, my body weight bulldozing into Munro full-on.

We fell to the ground, kicking and punching as we rolled together across the scrub. Munro caught me with a vicious right hook to the jaw then threw a lightning-fast combination at my kidneys. It was enough to make me release the grip I had on his jacket. He pushed himself to his feet, and had already pulled back his right foot, ready to kick the toe of his boot into my head, when I rolled to my right, his boot slicing through the air where my head had just been.

I clambered to my feet and took a couple of labored breaths, and got a quick glimpse of Alex. He hadn't run. He was kicking and punching as though he'd gone completely feral, but Navarro had a firm hold on him and was shoving him into the chopper. Then Munro got my attention back by sending a roundhouse at my chest. I stepped inside the arc of his boot and hammered my right elbow up into his chin, absorbing the force of his kick with my already battered back.

I took an uppercut to my own chin for my troubles, but he put too much force behind the punch and lost his footing for a moment.

Stepping forward, I stamped my left boot into Munro's right knee. As he tipped forward I threw a piledriver into the back of his neck, which sent him sprawling to the ground.

I leapt onto him, straddling his torso, pummeling his head with punches from both sides, but the bastard wouldn't stay down. He lashed out with his knee and caught me full in the back. Right where Navarro's man had caught me with the metal pipe. I grunted loudly with agony. Munro clearly liked the sound of that, and channeled all his remaining energy into driving his knee into the same spot, again and again, seemingly oblivious to the punches I was landing on his face, even though his nose was split right open and blood was gushing down his face.

I felt a spasm rip through my lower back. For a second I thought I was going to black out from the pain. One more knee directly on that bruise and I would have to throw myself off him, and at this point that was going to give the fight to Munro, with no chance of a rematch.

He swung out his right leg as far as it would go, in preparation to land the killer blow to my back, but before he could drive his knee back in again, I grabbed his head with both hands, wrenched it up, and crashed it back against the ground.

I slammed Munro's head against the soil, and again, battering him to submission—

Then I heard the chopper's turbine grind up deafeningly before it lurched off the ground.

And in that instant, all I could think was, *I'm not about to lose my son forever.*

Not a chance.

And like in all of life's most important decisions, my brain had already relayed its decision to my central nervous system before deigning to let me in on which way it had voted. By the time I realized what I was doing, I had scooped up my Glock and stuffed it in my pants, and I was sprinting at the rising bird and launching myself into the air and onto one of its runners.

My left hand hit the metal tube and slipped right off again, but my right hand held firm. With the chopper banking away and air rushing against me, I swung my right leg up over the runner and hooked it around.

My mind was leaping from *I can't believe I fucking made it* to *What now?* when a hail of bullets slammed into the helicopter. I spun around to see Munro, standing again, blood all over his face, MP4 in hand. He'd obviously decided that dead was better than not at all.

Another volley strafed the chopper, punching a streak of ominous holes through its fuselage and sending the engine into a high-pitched wail. I hoisted myself up around the runner, hooked my left leg over my right, pulled my Glock, and emptied the entire clip at the rapidly diminishing figure who was intent on bringing us down.

Somewhere before the clip ran out, Munro jerked backward, staggered, then toppled to the ground, saving whichever cartel he was working for the trouble of severing his limbs one by one with a machete.

Navarro and his pilot were now well aware they had a stowaway, but they didn't seem too keen to credit me with saving their asses. And in that brief instant of calm, Alex peered through the window, and his face lit up with surprise when he saw me. Our eyes met, and I saw them flare up with an elation that recharged me to no end.

The pilot began to execute a series of side-to-side rolls in a concerted attempt to dislodge me—then after a handful of those, the engine gave a piercing squeal, cut out for a heart-stopping second, then coughed back to life.

I knew we weren't going to be aloft for long.

I pulled myself up and peered into the cockpit, wondering why the pilot wasn't attempting to land. Navarro had leaned right forward and was clearly shouting instructions at him, obviously telling him that landing was not an option. At least they'd stopped trying to shake me from the runner. Then Navarro spotted me, pulled his gun, swung it around to me, and fired through the chopper's window.

I ducked away from his sight line, squeezing myself as far under the fuselage as I could, hoping Navarro wasn't suicidal enough to try to fire at me through the chopper's floor.

We sped across the jungle, low over the tree cover, gathering speed, the engine seemingly having decided that we were all going to live. Less than a minute later, the ocean came into view. Even from my precarious vantage point, it was stunningly beautiful, the kind of shot I always assumed was airbrushed to perfection, only it was right there in real, living color. If it was the last thing I saw, it would certainly be miles better than looking at the business end of a force-feeding tube.

The ocean had heard me. As we sped toward it, the engine emitted a series of whining sputters, then cut out completely.

We were going down.

69

I squeezed out from my cover and caught sight of Alex again, and I was thankful to have another moment with him. And with death getting closer by the yard as we plummeted toward the sea, I could see the appeal of reincarnation—although I wasn't ready to give up on this life just yet.

My thoughts were cut short as the water rose to meet us and we belly-flopped into the ocean. I hung on as, almost immediately, the big chopper started to sink. The mere fact that I could tell we were sinking also told me that I was still alive, and that meant Alex may be alive, too.

He had to be.

I kept my legs wrapped tightly around the runner as we went under, the chopper listing to its side from the momentum in its blades. After a few seconds, I glimpsed the ocean floor, white and sandy, through the swarm of air bubbles. It wasn't deep. I let go of the runner with my legs, but held on with both hands as we hit the bottom.

The chopper landed in a billowing cloud of sand and an eerie groan from the runner that took most of the impact.

I pulled myself close to the window and looked in.

The pilot was already dead, his side of the cockpit having taken the full brunt of the collision between machine and ocean. Dark ribbons of blood spiraled upward from his head and chest before thinning out into crimson clouds.

I looked in the rear cabin, looking for Alex, and I saw him, his arms stretched out to beckon me, but he seemed trapped—then I understood why as Navarro's face lurched into view from behind him. I flinched back, ready to pull away from any gunfire, only he didn't seem to have his gun anymore. He was pinned in place by a piece of cabin frame that had bent in under the impact and seemed to have his right foot trapped against the frame of his seat, and he was holding firmly onto Alex while trying to wrest his leg loose.

Alex was thrashing, desperately looking for a way to wriggle free, his little features imploring me to save him.

I needed to reassure him quickly and gestured to him that I was on my way, then I slithered around the craft and made my way to the smashed cockpit window. I wedged my boot up against it and started pulling at it with everything I had. Pain lit up in the small of my back, but I kept going, and after what seemed like an eternity, it bent out and pulled free.

I pulled myself inside and snaked through as fast as I could, past the empty co-pilot seat, until I was face to face with Alex. He thrust his hand out to me and I took it, pulling myself closer until I had my right hand clamped around his wrist and the big Omnitrix wristband he never seemed to take off.

Navarro still had both arms wrapped around Alex's legs, and I had only a few seconds left before I involuntarily gulped a lungful of sea water.

I grabbed Navarro's arm with one hand and stabbed him in his shoulder wound with the other. His grip instantly loosened, and he released Alex's legs. Then I pulled Alex out of the cabin the way I'd come in and started kicking us upward.

As we ascended to the surface, my eyes drifted back down to Navarro.

He was still in the deep end of the cabin, pushing against the seat, desperately trying to work himself free. And right then, before I turned away, I was treated to a glimpse of a sudden, large cloud of air bubbles that blew out of his mouth. He couldn't hold his breath anymore, and I knew he was gone.

I kept kicking my way to the surface, pulling Alex up with me, heading for the sunlight with my lungs shrunken inside my chest and every molecule of oxygen squeezed out and devoured—but as I opened my mouth and braced myself for the breath that would mean death, not life, I finally broke through with Alex right beside me.

He shook the water from his eyes as we both gulped down big, grateful lungfuls of air.

I looked toward the shore. We were only a couple of hundred yards away from land, and I knew we'd make it. Even better, I knew it was over, what with Navarro literally sleeping with the fishes underneath us.

Alex and I bobbed up and down in the deceptively peaceful turquoise water, looking at each other, his arms clasped tight around my neck. His eyes were calmer now, and seemed to me to be back to those of a four-year-old boy. Not only that, but they were holding my gaze without any trace of fear in them. And that was a first.

"How did you do that?" he asked, his face all alight with wonder.

I broke out in a big, deeply contented smile.

"I'm your dad, Alex. That's all. And it's what any dad would do."

He thought about this for a moment, and for the first time since I'd met him, he smiled back. Not a huge, big toothy grin. But a smile. And right now, that was plenty.

But I couldn't enjoy it fully.

A rush of malignant thoughts was poisoning the moment and swooping in and out of my head, echoes of things I'd heard or felt that were now falling into place, and I knew I didn't yet have all the answers.

70

Tess, Alex, and I hadn't been back in San Diego more than a few hours, but this couldn't wait.

Tess was fine. She'd done like I told her and ducked into a safe corner and waited until the firefight had died down. The Special Ops guys had then escorted her out of there and cleaned her wound. Once Alex and I had broken the surface, I'd been worried sick about her, and the smile she gave me when I finally got her back is definitely up there in the top five memories of my life.

After the dust had settled in Merida, I'd been relieved to hear that Jules and the new guy were also okay. I'd been extremely saddened, though, by the news that Villaverde had been found dead at the rented beach house Navarro had used. It was a terrible loss, and I felt gutted. He was a decent, down-to-earth, capable guy who'd really proved himself to be a solid ally when I needed him. I guessed that he and Navarro had had some face time together, which was probably how Navarro's men got to us at the safe house. And the bastard wasn't in the business of leaving behind any witnesses.

The hacienda itself had kicked in some decent news. The scientists who'd been kidnapped from Santa Barbara were found in the basement lab complex, along with two others who'd been grabbed previously. They were in as good shape as could be expected for people who'd been held captive like that for months.

Closer to home, Stephenson had offered to work with me and Tess on helping Alex work through everything that had happened.

But I didn't think the book was yet closed on that front.

A few things were bothering me, starting with the drone.

I knew drones. We'd had one circling over us the night we hit McKinnon's lab, but more relevantly, I'd made use of a Predator much more recently, in Turkey, in broad daylight, while chasing the sadistic Iranian agent Zahed. I knew what they looked like. And in that perfect azure dome that towered over us down in Merida that morning, I didn't see a thing. Not a glint, not a spot, nothing. Admittedly, I hadn't had all the time in the world to sit and stargaze to look for it. But I knew I should have seen it and it really bugged me. It bugged me enough to look into it with the guys over at the 9th Reconnaissance Wing at Beale Air Force Base in California, from where the drones were controlled. I knew it wasn't easy for the DEA to run a drone over Mexico. They'd done so a couple of times over the last year or so, and it had caused a big stink with the *federales*. But the guys at Beale confirmed to me that they didn't have any drones over California or Mexico that day.

Which meant Munro was lying.

Which meant that if Munro didn't track us that way, he had to have used something else. And the only other way to track us would have been to track something we had on us—specifically, something either Navarro or Alex had on them, given that the tracker on Munro's screen was showing their live position. It didn't seem possible he had a tracker on Navarro. If Munro had managed that, he'd have hauled El Brujo's ass in and sold him out to the narcos before pocketing the cash and retiring into a mojito-fueled, perma-tanned sunset.

Which meant the tracker had to be on Alex.

Which meant Munro somehow knew that Navarro would come after Alex.

Which is where my pesky little rule about coincidences starts doing its thing and turns into a real nag.

Which is why I was now getting out of my car and walking up to a mountain cabin at the edge of the Sequoia National Forest.

Hank Corliss's cabin.

71

The cabin was a steeply raked oak A-frame that was dwarfed by trees that were more than a hundred feet tall. I found Corliss sitting on the back deck of the split-level cabin, looking out over a fast-flowing creek and mile after mile of dense forest. The loud calls of warblers and swallows filled the air.

Corliss had clearly heard me drive in and pull up to the house, but he hadn't made any effort to get up and see who it was. I suspected he knew it was me, just as I suspected he'd been expecting me to show up at some point.

He didn't even look over as I stepped out to join him.

It had just fit too perfectly. Alex happens to be the reincarnation of McKinnon. Munro happens to get wind of that somehow. He then decides to use that to bait Navarro out of hiding—the one thing he knew Navarro couldn't possibly resist going after.

Like I said, it was a coincidence too far, and although my horizons had broadened about the so-called nonphysical world in the last few days, that was one coincidence I wasn't prepared to believe. Not when it fit that perfectly.

I'm not into perfect fits.

Life doesn't work that way.

And if it wasn't a rare alignment of stars, if it wasn't serendipity spreading its wings and giving Jesse Munro the gift of a lifetime, then it had to be something else. Something more human. Which then got me wondering about how much Munro could pull off by himself. And that got me wondering about Corliss.

Whoever did this had to know Navarro was obsessed with reincarnation. He also had to know what McKinnon's drug was all about. And he needed to be, in my eyes anyway, insanely desperate to get Navarro.

Which brought me back to Corliss and to something Munro had said, out in Merida, by the chopper. *You think I went through all this bullshit just so some cranky old man could get his revenge?*

His words had been rattling inside me ever since he said them.

I thought I knew what they'd done. What I didn't know was, how long had it been going on?

That, and the how, was what I was here for.

There was no point in getting into any pleasantries.

"Did you know Munro was running his own game?" I asked him.

That got his attention.

He turned to face me, and he looked even more tired than I remembered. The lines across his forehead were like furrows, and he had dark pouches under eyes that already looked like they'd had all life drained out of them.

"He wasn't going to bring him back to you, you know," I added. "He was going to sell him on to the cartel for fifteen million dollars. And you know what the worst part is? You probably never would have known. He'd have come up with some story about Navarro being killed out there, and you'd be sitting here thinking you pulled off your plan perfectly."

He shrugged, impassive. "I doubt they would have kept him alive too long," he replied.

If I still had a smidgen of doubt about Corliss's involvement, his reaction killed it there and then. "True, but that's not what this was about, was it? This was about revenge. You, getting your revenge. And I can't imagine it would have been anywhere near as satisfying for you not to have him right there in front of you and be able to stare into his eyes when you did whatever you were planning to do with him."

He didn't reply. He just kept his tenebrous gaze on me while he breathed out slowly through a half-open mouth.

"It would have all worked out, too. If Michelle hadn't fought them off at the house. That was the plan, right? He'd grab them. And Alex would lead you right back to him."

I reached into my pocket and pulled out Alex's Omnitrix wristband and chucked it onto the side table by his side.

I'd had it checked.

It's where the tracker was.

"You knew Navarro believed in reincarnation," I told him. "You had the journal. You knew Eusebio's story. And you knew Navarro didn't just believe in it. He was obsessed with it, and he was obsessed with getting McKinnon's formula back. So you decided to use that to flush him out. And what better way to flush him out than to have him think McKinnon had been reincarnated."

I saw a reaction flicker in his eyes.

"Then you decided to load the dice," I continued. "You decided it couldn't be just any kid. You wanted to be sure he'd believe it, you wanted him so motivated that he'd definitely come after this kid. And who better for the job than the son of the guy who shot McKinnon? Which you knew, because Munro knew that Michelle was pregnant with my son."

The reaction calmed, and I saw that he was already wondering about the consequences.

"Are you here to kill me?" he asked

"I should. And maybe I will. I mean, you got Michelle killed. And Villaverde. And Fugate. And Michelle's boyfriend. And all the rest of them." I couldn't control my temper and my tone blew. "And you put my son at risk. You screwed with his mind and you dangled him out as bait for one of the biggest psychos on this planet."

"None of this should have happened," Corliss said. "The plan wasn't for anyone to get hurt. But then . . . the best laid plans, right?"

"That's horseshit," I replied. "You were dealing with Navarro here. What did you think would happen?"

Corliss sucked in a deep breath through thin, tight lips, and his eyes narrowed defiantly. "You, of all people, should understand why I did this. You know what happened. What he did to my family." He paused, as if looking to see if any of his words were striking home.

For a second, I put myself in his shoes, and I wondered about that. I wondered about what I would have done had I seen my daughter butchered in front of my eyes and had my wife end her life because of it. But I also felt like strangling him for what he did.

"And he was going to keep looking," he added. "He was going to keep looking until he found that drug. Where would we be then, huh? How many parents would be standing there saying, 'Why didn't you do everything you could to stop him?'"

I'd wrestled with the same arguments after shooting McKinnon, so his words weren't falling on deaf ears. But I still had a few burning questions for him.

"How'd you do it?" I asked, thinking about Alex and trying to keep the rage out of my voice. "How'd you get Alex to say the things he did, to do those drawings . . . how's you get him to be so convincing that he'd fool someone like Stephenson?"

Corliss looked away, and for a moment, I thought I saw some regret there, some pain, something human that told me maybe this hadn't been as cold and heartless for him as I thought.

"We brought in a spook. A guy who'd been in on MK-ULTRA back in the day." He was referring to the CIA's now widely known mind-control experiments, back in the sixties.

The sick bastards had brainwashed my four-year-old boy.

"Name?"

"Corrigan," he said grudgingly. "Reed Corrigan."

It wasn't a name I was ever going to forget. Corrigan would be hearing from me. Real soon.

"How'd he do it?"

Corliss looked away, wearily. "We drugged Michelle's water. She went to bed every night and for a week or so, she didn't have a clue about what was really going on in Alex's bedroom."

I was really having a hard time stopping myself from reaching down his throat and ripping his heart out.

"He fed him key bits of information about McKinnon's life. About his background, his travels, his work. He showed him photographs. He also showed him the video from the night you killed him. From the cameras on your helmets." He winced as he said it, and I couldn't imagine what kind of monster would show a four-year-old something like that. "But we had to be very careful," he added, as if sensing my anger about that last reveal and wanting to move on. "We had to seed only the information that would be sure to mean something to Navarro, but wouldn't alert Michelle as to who Alex was really talking about. And you played a part in that, even though it wasn't intentional. You didn't tell her what really happened that night."

I'd been wondering about that, and it was another dagger through my heart. It was my turn to want to move on. "So Alex couldn't know the name McKinnon?"

"No. That would have told Michelle who he was claiming to be. But he could talk about McKinnon's past, about his life and his family and big moments in his career. He could talk about Mexico. About the journal. About Eusebio de Salvatierra. And about the tribe."

"And Stephenson was part of the plan all along?"

"He's the expert. The world authority. And he's right here in California. If he gave it his stamp of approval, Navarro would believe it. We just made sure the local shrink Michelle first took Alex to see pointed her in his direction."

"How?"

He shrugged again. "Homeland security and the threat of being branded an enemy combatant go a long way these days. No one wants to end up in an orange jumpsuit."

I nodded. "But how'd you know Navarro would hear about it?"

"I knew what he was after. I'd read the full transcript of Eusebio's journal. The one I asked the analyst to keep to himself. Navarro . . . he wasn't just obsessed with reincarnation. He was beyond obsessed.

It's all he lived for. You didn't see him that night at my house. You didn't see the look in his eyes. I knew he had to be following Stephenson's work. And Alex would have been a big story for Stephenson. A kid, here in the United States, reliving a past life that was so recent. He'd be talking about it with his peers, writing about it. And the odds were that sooner or later, Navarro would hear about it and come after him. We just had to make sure we had enough trackers in place to find him."

He had said *trackers* with an *s*. "So there were more of them?"

"A few. One in each of his sneakers. Some of his toys. His favorite stuffed animal." He waved it off with disinterest. "They're small and they're a dime a dozen."

"And all along, all this time, you knew Navarro was still alive?"

"Come on." He sneered. "I didn't buy that car bomb horseshit for a minute. Then when he started grabbing these scientists . . . they were all working on psychoactives. One of the guys he took over in Santa Barbara was synthesizing *iboga* to turn it into a pill for heroin addicts. They fit too closely to what I knew he was after."

I felt a fresh surge of anger. "You could have asked Stephenson to just create a fake report. Or made him do it using your charms."

His mouth bent downward at its edges, and he shook his head. "No. There was a high risk that Navarro would have had him grabbed by some hired guns, like he did with the others. Some bikers or what not. And Stephenson would have broken under questioning in a heartbeat. It was pointless to even try that. No, Stephenson also had to believe in our story." He paused, then his expression softened. "How is he, anyway? Alex?"

I didn't think I owed him an answer, but I still said, "He'll be fine. Now that we know what you did to him, we can start to undo it."

He just nodded vacantly. "Good."

He didn't say he was sorry. I guess he wasn't.

"So what happens now? Is this where you pull out your gun as I'm 'resisting arrest'?"

My expression soured, and I just shrugged. "No. I'm just going to go back." I paused, then added, "And write my report about what happened."

He looked at me, like he was sussing out what I meant. I guess my face said all I had to say.

I turned to go, and he called out after me. "For what it's worth . . . it wasn't easy. It wasn't an easy call. But I couldn't see any other way."

It wasn't worth much to me.

I walked out of his front door, and as I opened the door to my car, I heard the bullet.

I didn't go in to check.

I just strapped on my seat belt, swung out of his gates, and set off to spend the rest of the day with Tess and my son while trying not to think too hard about what Navarro had said about the past lives of his that he'd researched nor about what I would do with the stainless steel vial I'd taken off Munro's dead body.

ABOUT THE AUTHOR

RAYMOND KHOURY is the author of four consecutive *New York Times* bestsellers: his debut, *The Last Templar*, *The Sanctuary*, *The Sign*; and *The Templar Salvation*. His books have been translated into more than forty languages. To find out more about his work, visit his website at www.raymondkhoury.com, or join him on his official Facebook fan page.